Harvest of Eyes

Clifton Wilcox

Fredericksburg, Virginia

Published by Windward Publishing LLC, Fredericksburg, Virginia.

The characters and events in this book are fictitious. Any similarity to real persons, living or dead, is coincidental and not intended by the author.

Library of Congress Cataloging in Publication Data

Wilcox, Clifton

Harvest of Eyes by Clifton Wilcox

Windward Publishing, LLC. 2025

Contents

Books by Clifton Wilcox

Non-Fiction

Scape Goat: Targeted for Blame

Groupthink: An Impediment to Success

Bias: The Unconscious Deceiver

Witch-hunt: The Assignment of Blame

The Fall of the Kingdom of Northumbria

Witch-hunt: The Class of Cultures

Road to War: The Quest for a New World Order

Envy: A Deeper Shade of Green

The Rise of the Nazi SS

The Horrible Void Between the Trenches

Fiction

Cool's Last Stand

Where Despair Comes To Play

The Monuments Must Bleed

Keeper of the Fallen Ages

I, Monster

The Case Against Jasper

Prologue

They say the scarecrow watches. That its button eyes don't just shine in the moonlight—they drink it in, sip by sip, until the whole field feels restless. No one talks about it when the sun's up. Daylight is for pretending. For lies. For saying the old stories are nothing more than that. But when the stalks start whispering at night and the wind drags a low groan across the rows, the children of Dry Creek know better than to glance back. Especially the ones who've stolen from it.

It all began with a dare—the way most bad ideas do. A group of teens, grinning through crooked teeth and shaky bravado, crept onto the Withers Field the night before the harvest moon. The air hung heavy with the smell of dying crops, and beneath it something darker, as if the soil itself was sour. At the heart of the field stood the scarecrow, arms stretched wide on its weathered post, burlap face stitched into a half-smile. Its button eyes, once dull black, glinted with a reddish hue that no one noticed until they were already too close.

Mark was the first to pluck an eye. It popped free with a soft snap, and he laughed, holding it high like a prize. "One for the collection," he said. The others followed, yanking free the second button, then bits of straw hat, even the twine that held its fingers together. By the time they left, the scarecrow was slumped and faceless. They thought that was the end of it. But corn doesn't forget. And neither does what lies beneath it.

The first body turned up three nights later. Propped upright at the field's edge, eyes gone. Not torn, not gouged—just…absent. Smooth skin stretched where sockets should be. No blood, no struggle. Only a single black button resting neat as a coin on the chest. Sheriff DuCard tried to fold it into reason, but a town can only swallow so many coincidences before the taste turns to rot.

Dry Creek was never the same. Locks doubled, curtains sealed tight. Parents pulled their children in close while the nights stretched longer. The school hallways buzzed with whispers—about buttons, about the sound in the corn, about a figure that didn't sway with the wind like the rest. And always about the eyes. Eyes stolen. Eyes missing. Eyes returned where no one wanted them.

The survivors tried to undo what they had done. They crept back with their trophies, laying them at the scarecrow's feet under a blood-colored moon. They begged forgiveness from stitched lips that had never spoken. But forgiveness belongs to the living, and the scarecrow wasn't among them. It didn't need eyes to see. Its curse was in the looking itself. Those who crossed its gaze came back broken—or not at all.

And so, when the corn turns brittle and the sky burns red each autumn, Dry Creek weaves new stories. Tales about trespass and punishment, about young fools and hungry fields. But the truth isn't in the telling. It's in the ground—buried under husks and bones, under silence and shame. Stand at the edge of the Withers Field at dusk, if you dare, and listen. You'll hear it. Breathing.

Chapter 1

The Shadow of Withers Field

The dust motes danced in the oppressive shafts of sunlight that pierced the perpetually hazy sky above Dry Creek. They weren't cheerful, sunlit particles, but rather tired, weary specks, mirroring the general disposition of the town itself. Dry Creek was a place where dreams went to wither and die, a forgotten settlement clinging precariously to the edges of existence, its inhabitants as bleached and faded as the paint on the clapboard houses that lined its one main street. The air here was thick, not just with the summer heat that seemed to bake the very life out of the earth, but with an intangible malaise, an undercurrent of perpetual unease that clung to everything like the persistent scent of dry rot and unspoken sorrows. The sun, rather than a benevolent source of warmth and light, felt like a malevolent eye, scrutinizing and exposing the town's every failing, its relentless glare seeming to scorch not just the parched fields, but the very hope from the hearts of its people.

This pervasive atmosphere of desolation wasn't an accident of geography or climate. It was woven into the fabric of Dry Creek; a tapestry stitched with threads of ancient dread and whispered warnings. The town's very identity, its reason for being, was inextricably linked to the Withers Field, a colossal, brooding expanse of land that seemed to swallow the horizon whole. The cornfield, a vast, undulating sea of green that ripened into a sea of gold, was the heart of this desolate kingdom, and within its shadowy depths, a darkness festered, a palpable sense of history, heavy and old, that clung to the very air like a shroud. It was a history that the older generation, their faces etched with the kind of weariness that comes from carrying too many burdens, spoke of only in hushed, reverent tones, their words like dry leaves skittering across forgotten graves. They knew, with a certainty born of generations of experience, that in Dry Creek, the mundane could so easily bleed into the macabre, and that the local legends weren't just fanciful tales spun to entertain or frighten children. They were grim warnings, etched into the collective consciousness, passed down from parent to child, a legacy of dread that permeated every aspect of life in this forgotten corner of the world.

The unease in Dry Creek was a tangible thing, a silent resident in every home, a shadow that stretched long and distorted even at midday. It wasn't the sudden, sharp fear of a jump scare, but a slow, insidious creep, a gnawing anxiety that settled deep in the bones. The silence here was never truly silent. It was filled with the buzz of unseen insects, the creak of ancient wood, the distant, mournful cry of a hawk, and underneath it all, a low, persistent hum of apprehension. This hum seemed to emanate from the very earth, from the dry, cracked soil that offered so little sustenance, and most of all, from the sprawling, relentless presence of the Withers land.

The Withers Field was more than just acres of cultivated land; it was a monument to something ancient and unsettling. The corn, rows upon rows of it, stood sentinel, its stalks a dense, whispering forest that seemed to mock the open sky. Even on the brightest days, shadows pooled within its depths, creating pockets of unnatural darkness. The air around the farm felt different, heavier, charged with a latent energy that prickled the skin and set teeth on edge. It was a place that drew the eye, a brooding presence that dominated the landscape and, by extension, the lives of everyone in Dry Creek. The town was tethered to it, its fortunes, its very existence, seemingly bound to the cycles of planting and harvest that occurred within its borders.

Old Man Hemlock, whose weathered face was a roadmap of Dry Creek's history, would often sit on his porch, a perpetual frown creasing his brow, and stare out at the Withers Fields. He wouldn't say much, his silence more eloquent than any pronouncement. But those who knew him understood. He saw more than just corn. He saw the stories, the whispers that the wind carried from that place, stories of things that preferred the shadows, things that demanded a price for the land's fertility. His family had been neighbors to the Withers for generations, their own small farm bordering the vast

6

expanse, and over the years, they had learned to respect its boundaries, to listen to its unspoken warnings. He remembered his grandmother's tales, hushed and fearful, of strange lights in the corn at night, of livestock that vanished without a trace near the property line, of the unsettling belief that the scarecrow, standing solitary and gaunt in the middle of the vast field, was more than just a guardian of crops. It was a sentinel of something far older, far more sinister.

The Withers themselves were a family shrouded in a similar mystery, their lineage as tangled and obscured as the roots of the ancient oaks that occasionally broke the monotony of the corn. They were the keepers of the land, and in Dry Creek, that meant they were also the keepers of its secrets, its burdens. The older generation spoke of them with a mixture of respect and fear, a deference born from a deep-seated understanding that the Withers connection to the land ran deeper, darker, than anyone else's. They were the conduits, the intermediaries, between the mundane world and whatever ancient force held sway over their small, forgotten town.

The perpetual unease wasn't just a feeling; it manifested in subtle ways. The crops, when they did manage to grow, often had a peculiar, almost unnatural resilience, thriving even in the harshest conditions, while other, more traditional farms struggled. The livestock, when they remained within their enclosures, often exhibited a nervous disposition, startled by shadows that weren't there, their eyes wide with an unnamed terror. Even the very weather seemed to conspire with the land, the sun beating down with unusual ferocity, the winds often carrying a mournful, sibilant sound that seemed to whisper secrets from the Withers Fields.

This sense of foreboding was amplified by the stories that circulated through Dry Creek like a contagion. They were fragmented tales, pieced together over years, of inexplicable disappearances, of travelers who had ventured too close to the Withers land and were never seen again, of a pervasive melancholic air that settled over the town whenever the corn grew particularly tall. These weren't ghost stories in the conventional sense, not tales of sheet-clad specters or rattling chains. They were deeper, more elemental fears, the primal terror of the unknown that lurked just beyond the edges of human understanding, a darkness that was as much a part of the land as the soil itself.

The history of Dry Creek was a story written in hushed tones and averted gazes, a narrative that acknowledged a powerful, ancient entity tied to the fertility of the Withers land, an entity that demanded a price for its bounty. This price, as the fragmented legends suggested, was a recurring offering, a ritualistic appeasement that ensured the land remained productive, and the town, by extension, continued to exist. The details of this offering were deliberately vague, obscured by time and fear, but the implication was clear: it was a sacrifice, and the cost was immeasurable. The older generation understood this implicitly. They lived with it, a quiet acceptance of a dark bargain struck long before they were born, a legacy they were bound to uphold, or at least, to acknowledge with a healthy dose of dread.

The Withers Field was the nexus of this power, the epicenter of the town's unease. The cornfield, a vast, brooding expanse, was more than just an agricultural enterprise; it was a sacred, or perhaps, a profane space, a place where the veil between worlds was thin, and where ancient forces held sway. The very air around it seemed to hum with a palpable energy, a silent testament to the sacrifices that had been made, the pacts that had been forged. It was a place where the natural order seemed to bend and warp, where the mundane was perpetually on the verge of surrendering to the macabre.

This undercurrent of unease wasn't something that the younger generation of Dry Creek fully grasped, not yet. They saw the Withers Field as a place of legend, a source of spooky stories for a boring summer. They didn't yet feel the true weight of the history, the deep ancestral dread that clung to the very air like the pervasive scent of dust and decay. They were on the cusp of understanding, of inheriting this legacy of unease, but for now, it remained a distant, abstract concept, a shadow on the periphery of their lives. Yet, the land itself, the Withers Field, the brooding corn, the solitary scarecrow, they all held their secrets close, patiently waiting for the moment when the mundane would once again bleed into the macabre, when the whispers of the past would become the screams of the present. The sun beat down, relentless and unforgiving, and

Dry Creek, bathed in its harsh, bleached light, hummed with a perpetual, unsettling unease, a town tethered to a history far darker than any of its inhabitants truly understood. The Withers Field was not just a farm; it was a reminder, a constant, looming presence that whispered of ancient pacts and the terrifying price of a bountiful harvest.

The figure in the cornfield was a monument to dread. Not a statue, not a mere effigy, but something that had taken root, that had become as much a part of Withers Field as the tenacious stalks of corn themselves. Its presence was a constant, a silent fulcrum around which the town's anxieties pivoted. The locals, when they spoke of it at all, did so with a reverence tinged with a profound, bone-deep fear. It was the scarecrow of Withers Field, and it was more than just a guardian of crops; it was a keeper of secrets, a silent witness to the unfolding history of Dry Creek.

Its form was simple, almost crude. A cross of rough-hewn wood, lashed together with coarse twine, supported a sackcloth head stuffed with dry, brittle straw. Empty burlap formed its face, a gaping absence where features should have been. Two mismatched buttons, one chipped and cloudy, the other a startlingly vibrant black, served as eyes. They were vacant, unseeing, yet in the periphery of vision, in the slivers of light that pierced the dense canopy of corn, they seemed to possess a disturbing animation. It was as if these inanimate objects held within them a spark of malevolent awareness, a sentience that observed, that judged, that *waited*. The tattered remnants of once-bright clothing, now faded to the color of dried blood and old earth, clung to its frame, flapping in the perpetual breeze that stirred the corn. These were not the garments of a farmer preparing for a season's toil, but something more. Whispers, carried on the wind that rustled through the field, spoke of clothes not bought, but *found*, remnants of those who had ventured too close, who had become entangled in the field's insatiable maw.

The legend, passed down through hushed tones and fearful glances, claimed that the scarecrow was not the work of human hands. It was said to be an entity born of the land itself, a physical manifestation of the ancient, primal force that permeated Withers

Field. It was woven from the very essence of the soil, its straw stuffing imbued with the dust of generations, its burlap skin tanned by suns that had witnessed unspeakable acts. It was an offering, a permanent fixture, a sentinel bound to the land by pacts forged in blood and desperation. Its purpose, they murmured, was tied to the fertility of the crops, to the unnatural bounty that Withers Field consistently yielded, a bounty that came at a terrible, unspoken price.

Old Man Hemlock, his voice raspy as a dry leaf scraping against stone, would often recount fragments of his grandmother's warnings. "She said it watched," he'd mutter, his gaze fixed on the distant, hazy line of the cornfield. "Always watching. Not with eyes like ours, mind you. But with a knowing. A hunger." He'd often trail off, lost in the labyrinth of his own memories, the words hanging in the air like the scent of impending rain. His grandmother, a woman of formidable spirit but fragile health, had spoken of the scarecrow not as a protector of grain, but as a collector. A silent, patient collector of… something. The details remained elusive, obscured by the passage of time and the collective desire to forget, but the implication was stark. The scarecrow was there to ensure the land's continued prosperity, and that prosperity demanded a perpetual tribute.

The villagers learned early to respect the invisible boundaries of Withers Field, to steer their carts and their conversations away from its brooding expanse. Children were warned in the sternest of tones not to stray too near, not to venture beyond the familiar dirt track that skirted its perimeter. The whispers about the scarecrow were potent deterrents, more effective than any locked gate or barbed wire. It was a psychological barrier, a silent guardian that instilled a primal fear, a respect for the unknown that dwelled within the rustling stalks. They learned to avert their eyes, to pretend it wasn't there, even as its desolate form dominated the horizon, a constant, unsettling reminder of the pact that sustained their town.

But the scarecrow was more than just a figure of folklore; it was a palpable entity that cast a long shadow over the lives of Dry Creek's inhabitants. Its presence was felt even in the quietest moments, in the stillness of the midday heat, in the hushed conversations that took place behind closed doors. It was the silent observer to the town's slow decay, the unblinking witness to its quiet despair. The button eyes, devoid of any discernible emotion, seemed to hold within them the accumulated sorrow of generations, the weight of unspoken fears. They were vacant, yet filled with a terrible knowing, reflecting the anxieties of those who dared to look upon them.

The younger generation, those who had not inherited the direct trauma of the old stories, often viewed the scarecrow with a mixture of morbid fascination and youthful bravado. They would dare each other to get closer, to wave at it, to shout taunts into the rustling corn. But even their bravado was a thin veneer, easily shattered by a sudden gust of wind that made the scarecrow's tattered clothes whip violently, or by the disconcerting way the button eyes seemed to fix upon them, even from a distance. They didn't understand the deep-seated dread, the primal aversion that clung to the older generation, but they felt it, a nascent awareness of something ancient and malevolent residing in the heart of the corn.

The scarecrow's immobility was itself a source of terror. It stood steadfast, unyielding, a fixed point in the ever-shifting landscape of the cornfield. Day after day, season after season, it remained in its solitary vigil, its gaze, if one could call it that, never wavering. It was as if it were rooted to the spot, a permanent fixture in a world of transient life. This unmoving presence amplified its unnerving quality. It wasn't merely a static object; it was a guardian that never slept, never faltered, its purpose unwavering. The straw within its body seemed to absorb the very essence of the land, the whispers of the wind, the sighs of the earth, transforming them into a silent, watchful aura.

The clothes it wore were a particular point of morbid fascination. They were a patchwork of faded denim, worn cotton shirts, and perhaps, a threadbare flannel. But the colors were muted, bleached by relentless sun and washed by infrequent, but heavy, rains. They were the anonymous clothes of no one in particular, yet they hinted at a history, a forgotten past. Some whispered that the clothes weren't simply discarded garments but remnants of those who had been claimed by the field, their very attire absorbed into the Scarecrow's being, a grim testament to its efficacy. The frayed edges, the rips and tears, seemed to mirror the unraveling sanity of those who had lived too long under the shadow of Withers Field.

The burlap sack that formed its head was coarse and weathered, the weave porous enough to allow the faint scent of dry straw and something else, something earthy and faintly metallic, to escape. This, too, was a source of speculation. Was it the scent of the earth itself, or something more sinister, a lingering aroma of what the scarecrow had claimed? The way the straw peeked out from torn seams, like dried blood from a wound, only added to the unsettling tableau. It was a figure designed to ward off birds, yet it seemed to attract a different kind of attention, a morbid curiosity that drew people in, even as it repelled them.

The button eyes were the most potent symbols of its unnerving sentience. They were dark, impassive voids that seemed to absorb light rather than reflect it. The chipped button, with its clouded surface, hinted at a deeper, older damage, a violence that had been inflicted upon it, or perhaps, that it had inflicted upon others. The stark black button, so unnervingly perfect against the faded burlap, offered a chilling contrast, a splash of defiant darkness. They were fixed, unblinking, yet it was easy to imagine them tracking movement, following the slow, deliberate progress of anyone who dared to trespass within the field's dominion. They were windows into an abyss, a silent testament to the unseen forces that held sway over Withers Field.

The wind, a constant companion in Dry Creek, played a crucial role in animating the scarecrow, giving it a semblance of life. When it gusted, the tattered clothes would billow and snap, the straw-stuffed limbs would sway, and the burlap head would seem to nod or turn, as if in acknowledgment of the whispers it carried. These were not just natural movements; they were gestures that seemed to carry meaning, a silent language understood by the very earth and its inhabitants. The rustling of the corn, always present, seemed to amplify these movements, creating a symphony of subtle, unsettling animation. The corn itself seemed to conspire with the scarecrow, its dense stalks rustling and whispering, obscuring and revealing the figure in a perpetual dance of concealment and exposure.

The very construction of the scarecrow was steeped in the lore of the land. It wasn't built with the care and precision of a farmer proud of his work. It was fashioned, it was assembled, from materials that seemed to possess a history of their own. The wood of the cross was dark and gnarled, as if it had been taken from a tree struck by lightning or blighted by some unseen disease. The twine used to lash it together was thick and rough, its fibers coarse and unyielding, reminiscent of the bindings used in ancient rituals. The straw, too, was not merely dried stalks; it was said to be harvested from the very fields it guarded, imbued with the essence of the land, with the sacrifices made upon it. The legend spoke of a time before the current iteration of the Withers family, a time when the land was first settled, and a dark bargain was struck. The fertility of the soil, the unnatural abundance that defied all reason, was not a gift, but a purchase. And the price was a guardian, a sentinel that would embody the land's dark power. The scarecrow was that guardian, its creation a ritualistic act, a binding of something ancient and untamed to the very purpose of the farm. It was not just a deterrent for crows; it was a deterrent for anything that sought to disrupt the delicate, unholy balance of Withers Field.

The children of Dry Creek, despite their youthful disregard for the elders' pronouncements, felt the weight of the scarecrow's gaze. They would play at the edge of the field, their laughter brittle and forced, their eyes constantly darting towards the solitary figure in the distance. A misplaced shadow, a sudden shift in the wind, could send them scattering, their bravado evaporating like dew in the morning sun. The Scarecrow was a tangible manifestation of the town's collective unease, a focal point for the anxieties that permeated the very air they breathed.

Even the farmers, those who worked the land and understood its fickle nature, treated the Withers Field with a grudging respect bordering on reverence. They knew that the Withers success was not solely due to hard work or favorable weather. There was something else at play, something tied to the land, and to the silent, watchful figure that stood at its heart. They spoke of the corn's unnatural resilience, its ability to withstand drought and pestilence when their own crops faltered. They attributed this to the "old ways," to the sacrifices made by the Withers ancestors, to the pact that bound the land and its guardian.

The scarecrow's purpose remained shrouded in mystery, a chilling enigma that fueled the town's imagination. It watched, it waited, and the unspoken fear was for what it was waiting for. Was it a harbinger of some future event? A silent participant in a ritual that was not yet complete? Or was its very existence a perpetual state of readiness, a constant vigilance against some unseen threat that only it could perceive? The ambiguity was more terrifying than any concrete explanation. It allowed the fear to fester, to grow, to take root in the fertile ground of the human psyche.

The story of the scarecrow was not a simple ghost story; it was a primal narrative, woven into the very fabric of Dry Creek's existence. It spoke of the dark side of nature, of the price of abundance, of the ancient powers that lay dormant beneath the surface of the mundane. It was a reminder that some things were not meant to be understood, only feared, and that the silence of a figure in a cornfield could be more eloquent, and more terrifying, than any spoken word. The button eyes, unseeing and yet all-seeing, held the secrets of Withers Field, and the town of Dry Creek was forever bound to its silent, watchful presence. The dust motes still danced in the oppressive shafts of sunlight, but now, they seemed to carry the faint, dry scent of straw and the lingering chill of a gaze that never faltered. The scarecrow stood, a dark sentinel, and the whispers of its purpose continued to echo through the rustling corn, a perpetual testament to the unholy bargain struck in the heart of Dry Creek.

The summer in Dry Creek settled over Kayla like a shroud. It wasn't just the suffocating heat, thick and cloying, that clung to her skin like a second, unwelcome epidermis. It was the weight of the town itself, a pervasive melancholy that seemed to seep from the very foundations of the clapboard houses and the cracked asphalt of Main Street. For Kayla, a girl teetering on the precipice of adulthood, this summer felt less like a transition and more like an extension of the perpetual, stagnant present. Her peers, a restless tide of budding hormones and fleeting enthusiasm, found solace in the flickering neon of the local diner or the predictable drone of shared gossip. But Kayla's gaze, more often than not, drifted towards the periphery, towards the places where the town's carefully constructed normalcy frayed at the edges.

Her attention, almost against her will, was perpetually snagged by the Withers Field. Not the manicured lawns or the sturdy, if slightly weathered, farmhouse that sat like a stoic sentinel at the end of a long gravel drive. No, it was the other part of the Withers domain that held her captive, the sprawling expanse that began where the cultivated fields gave way to something wilder, something ancient: Withers Field. Even from a distance, as she rode her bike along the dusty county road, the cornstalks seemed to thrum with a disquieting energy. They grew taller, denser, and greener than any corn in the surrounding farms, an unnerving vitality that felt less like a blessing and more like a symptom.

There was an unspoken understanding among the families of Dry Creek, a generational dread that clung to them like the summer humidity. Kayla felt it in the hushed tones her mother used when speaking of the Withers, in the way her father's jaw would tighten when the subject of Withers Field arose. It wasn't a spoken history, not a collection of clearly defined warnings, but a pervasive atmosphere, a silence that spoke volumes. It was the unspoken anxiety that settled in the pit of her stomach whenever her gaze strayed towards the dark, verdant mass that dominated the western horizon. She carried this dread not as a burden, but as an inherited truth, a secret knowledge that set her apart from the other teenagers who chased fireflies and fleeting romances.

She found herself drawn to the edges of the Withers property, not out of a reckless curiosity, but from a sense of morbid pilgrimage. It was as if an invisible tether pulled her, a gravitational force emanating from the heart of that unnaturally vibrant corn. She'd pedal her bike, the familiar ache in her legs a counterpoint to the growing unease in her chest, until the gravel road gave way to a narrow, overgrown track that skirted the vast field. Here, the air itself seemed to thicken, carrying the faint, earthy scent of churned soil mingled with something else, something dry and faintly medicinal, like desiccated herbs left too long in the sun.

The cornstalks loomed over her, a rustling, whispering wall of green. They were impossibly tall, their leaves broad and thick, forming a dense canopy that choked out the sunlight, casting the ground in perpetual twilight. The stalks themselves were unnervingly uniform, their rows as perfect as if drawn with a ruler, a geometric precision that felt almost unnatural in its stillness. Yet, within this stillness, there was movement. The wind, always present in Dry Creek, found its way through the dense foliage, creating a constant, sibilant murmur that sounded like hushed conversations, like secrets being shared just beyond the edge of comprehension.

Kayla would often dismount her bike, leaning it against a weathered fence post that sagged under the weight of years and neglect. She'd walk along the perimeter, her sneakers crunching on the dry earth, her eyes scanning the dense rows. She wasn't looking for anything in particular, not a specific sight or sound. It was more of an immersion, a voluntary exposure to the palpable aura of the place. She felt a strange kinship with the silence here, a recognition of the unspoken sorrow that seemed to permeate the very soil.

Her mother, bless her pragmatic heart, saw Kayla's fascination as a teenage phase, a misguided attempt to inject excitement into a predictable existence. "Why do you keep going out there, sweetie?" She'd ask, her brow furrowed with concern. "There's nothing out there but corn. And that… *thing*." The hesitation in her mother's voice, the way she avoided naming the Scarecrow, spoke volumes. It was the same way she'd avoided mentioning the hushed rumors that circulated whenever a stranger passed through town, the stories that always seemed to circle back to Withers Field.

Kayla couldn't articulate the pull. It wasn't about defying her parents or seeking thrills. It was a deeper resonance, a recognition of a shared melancholy. She felt the town's collective sorrow, the unspoken grief that seemed to have settled over Dry Creek like a persistent fog. Her family, like many others, had their own quiet burdens, their own hushed tragedies that were never fully processed, only buried deeper with each passing year. Her grandfather, a man of few words and fewer smiles, had been a farmhand at Withers decades ago, before a "workplace accident" had left him with a permanent limp and a haunted look in his eyes. He never spoke of his time there, but the hushed pronouncements of his wife, Kayla's grandmother, still echoed in the corners of her memory. "That place... it takes something," she'd whisper, her voice thin and reedy. "It always takes."

One sweltering afternoon, driven by an impulse she couldn't quite explain, Kayla ventured a few steps beyond the perimeter track, stepping onto the soft, yielding earth of the field itself. The cornstalks closed in around her immediately, their broad leaves brushing against her arms, their dry husks rustling with an unnerving intimacy. The air grew cooler, heavier, imbued with the scent of chlorophyll and damp earth. She could hear the buzzing of unseen insects, the occasional chirp of a bird, but these were muted sounds, as if swallowed by the sheer density of the vegetation.

She moved deeper, her heart thrumming a nervous rhythm against her ribs. The rows seemed endless, a labyrinth of green that offered no clear path, no discernible exit. She tried to retrace her steps, but the field seemed to shift and rearrange itself around her, the perfect rows blurring into an indistinguishable maze. Panic, cold and sharp, pricked at her. She was only a few dozen yards from the road, yet she felt utterly, terrifyingly lost. It was then, in the heart of the suffocating green, that she saw it.

It wasn't the scarecrow itself, not yet. It was the stillness. A pocket of absolute, unnatural silence within the rustling symphony of the corn. The wind, which had been a constant companion, seemed to die away in this particular spot, leaving behind an oppressive vacuum. And in the center of this silence, she saw a patch of ground that was different. The earth here was darker, richer, almost black, and it seemed to absorb the scant light that filtered through the canopy. There were no weeds, no errant stalks, just this perfectly cultivated, unnervingly bare patch of soil. It was as if something had been meticulously removed, or perhaps, meticulously planted.

A sudden, sharp rustle from her left sent a jolt of adrenaline through her. She spun around, her eyes wide, expecting to see a startled rabbit or a scurrying field mouse. Instead, she saw only more corn, swaying gently as if a phantom had just passed through. But the silence remained, an unsettling void that defied the natural order of the field. She felt a prickling sensation on the back of her neck, a distinct impression of being watched. It wasn't the casual observation of a bird or an insect; it was a heavy, sustained regard, a focus that seemed to pierce through the dense foliage.

She knew, with the certainty that chilled her to the bone, that she was not alone. The earlier bravado, the teenage defiance, had evaporated, replaced by a primal, gut-wrenching fear. The whispers of the corn suddenly took on a new meaning, no longer just the sound of wind, but the hushed utterances of something ancient and malevolent. She imagined eyes, unseen, fixed upon her from within the verdant depths, button eyes, perhaps, vacant yet all-seeing. The button eyes of the scarecrow.

Her instinct screamed at her to run, to break free from this suffocating embrace. But her feet felt rooted to the spot, caught in the invisible currents that flowed through Withers Field. She remembered her grandfather's limp, her grandmother's hushed warnings. She understood, on a visceral level, the unspoken anxieties of her family, the generational dread that had seeped into their very bones. It wasn't just a story; it was a legacy.

With a supreme effort, she wrenched herself free from the trance-like stillness. She turned and ran, not with the grace of a fleeing animal, but with the clumsy, desperate scramble of someone pushing through an unseen barrier. The cornstalks clawed at her, their dry leaves whipping against her face and arms, drawing thin, stinging lines. The rustling around her intensified, no longer a murmur but a chorus of indignant whispers, as if the field itself was protesting her intrusion.

She burst out of the corn, gasping for breath, her lungs burning in the humid air. Her bike was still where she'd left it, a reassuringly solid anchor to the world she knew. She fumbled with the handlebars, her hands trembling, and swung herself onto the seat. She pedaled away, not daring to look back, the image of the unnaturally bare patch of earth seared into her mind. The oppressive silence, the feeling of being watched, lingered long after the last rustle of corn faded behind her.

As she rode, the oppressive heat of the summer day seemed to press in on her more than ever. The monotonous cycle of stifling heat and the town's pervasive melancholy had never felt so suffocating. But now, there was a new layer to her unease, a creeping certainty that the melancholy wasn't just a mood, but a symptom. A symptom of something vast and ancient, something that resided in the heart of Withers Field, and which, she now understood with terrifying clarity, had taken notice of her. Her summer, she knew, was about to become very different indeed. The edges of her world, once clearly defined, had begun to blur, and the shadow of Withers Field had begun to stretch, long and dark, across her own young life.

The oppressive heat of the Dry Creek summer had begun its slow, reluctant retreat. A subtle shift in the air, a crispness that hinted at approaching change, stirred through the town. For most, it was a welcome reprieve, a promise of relief from the stifling, cloying humidity that had clung to them like a second skin. But for Kayla, it was a signal of something far more significant, a harbinger of a season steeped in shadow and whispered anxieties. Halloween beckoned.

The approaching festivities were a thin veneer of forced cheer draped over the town's perpetual melancholic hum. For the teenagers of Dry Creek, however, this was not merely a holiday; it was an opportunity. An escape hatch from the crushing monotony, a chance to inject a jolt of adrenaline into the stagnant pool of their existence. The allure of the forbidden, the thrill of defying the unspoken rules that governed their lives, was a potent intoxicant. And no forbidden prospect loomed larger, no dare more whispered, than that associated with the Withers Field, and specifically, the enigma that was its solitary, sentinel Scarecrow.

The legend of the Withers scarecrow was more than just a campfire tale; it was a rite of passage, a whispered challenge passed down through generations. It was the ultimate test of courage, a physical manifestation of the town's deep-seated fear. The sheer audacity of approaching it, of daring to step onto the hallowed, unnerving ground of Withers Field, was a benchmark against which bravery was measured. For the boys especially, it was a chance to prove their mettle, to shed the lingering vestiges of childhood and step into the uncertain territory of young manhood. For the girls, it was a shared daring, a collective nervous giggle and a tightened grip on each other's arms as they contemplated the unthinkable.

Kayla found herself observing this burgeoning excitement with a mixture of detachment and a peculiar sense of recognition. She saw the nervous energy crackling in the air around her peers, the hushed conversations held in the shadowed corners of the diner, the furtive glances cast towards the western horizon where Withers Field lay like a dark secret. They spoke of it in hushed, excited tones, their voices laced with a bravado that barely masked the tremor of fear. They planned, they boasted, they dared each other. The idea of a midnight excursion into Withers Field, of getting close enough to the Scarecrow to touch it, to perhaps even... dislodge it, was the ultimate prize.

Her own recent, unnerving experience in the field had imprinted itself upon her, a raw, visceral memory that refused to fade. The unnatural silence, the feeling of being watched by unseen eyes, the unnerving emptiness of that particular patch of earth – it all coalesced into a chilling certainty. The Withers scarecrow was not merely a figure of straw and burlap, a deterrent for crows. It was something else. Something ancient, something watchful, something that held a dominion over that patch of land. Yet, even with this chilling knowledge, a part of her, a part that felt irrevocably tied to the unspoken history of Dry Creek, was drawn to the unfolding drama.

The first whispers of the dare began, as they always did, with the boys. It was Mark Jenkins, with his swagger and his carefully cultivated air of recklessness, who first proposed the idea in earnest. He stood on the steps of the general store, the late afternoon sun glinting off his perpetually slicked-back hair, his voice carrying to the small cluster of friends gathered below. "Anyone got the guts?" he'd said, a smirk playing on his lips. "Anyone actually going to do it? Or is it all just talk?"

His challenge hung in the air, a tangible invitation to transgression. A chorus of nervous laughter and bravado-filled retorts followed, but Kayla saw the flicker of genuine apprehension in their eyes. They were all talk, all bluster, but the prospect of actually venturing into Withers Field, especially as the days grew shorter and the nights longer, was a different matter entirely.

Sandy Miller, a girl whose usual demeanor was a whirlwind of bright colors and easy laughter, surprised Kayla with her unexpected boldness. She'd always seemed to exist on the periphery of Kayla's own introspective world, a creature of sunshine and superficiality. But as the Halloween season began to cast its longer shadows, Sandy's conversations began to subtly shift. She'd started talking about the Scarecrow, not with the dismissive cynicism of some, but with a strange, almost morbid fascination.

"My older brother, Kevin, he went out there a few years ago," Sandy confided in Kayla one afternoon as they sat on the worn bleachers behind the school, the scent of dry leaves beginning to mix with the lingering dust of summer. "He said he didn't get close, not really. But he said he saw it. From the road. And he said... he said it looked like it was watching him." Sandy shivered, a genuine tremor that belied her attempt at a casual tone. "He swore he heard it whisper his name."

Kayla listened, her own unease prickling at the edges of her awareness. She knew the stories of Kevin Miller. He'd been one of the more popular, more reckless boys in his graduating class, the kind who chased every thrill, courted every danger. His death a year later, officially attributed to a car accident on a deserted stretch of highway, had sent a ripple of unspoken relief through the town, as if a volatile element had finally been removed. But Kayla remembered the hushed conversations, the way people avoided looking too closely at the accident report.

The approaching Halloween provided a fertile ground for such whispers and dares to fester and grow. It was a time when the veil between worlds was believed to be thinnest, when the spirits of the departed were said to walk among the living. In Dry Creek, this ancient belief felt less like folklore and more like a tangible presence, a shadow that had long settled over the community. The

Withers Field, and its silent guardian, seemed to embody this spectral essence.

The teenagers, caught between the fading light of childhood and the daunting reality of adulthood, latched onto this spirit of the season. Halloween was their collective rebellion, their annual opportunity to push against the boundaries of the mundane, to flirt with the darkness that seemed to permeate their town. The dare concerning the scarecrow was the ultimate expression of this rebellion. It was a way to confront the very fear that haunted their parents, their grandparents, the generations before them. It was a way to prove that they were not like them that they could stare into the abyss and not flinch.

Kayla watched as the dare evolved, growing in audacity with each passing day. It started with simple proposals: cycling past the field at midnight, honking horns in unison, shining powerful flashlights into the dense rows of corn. But these were quickly dismissed as too tame, too easily dismissed as childish pranks. The true dare, the one that held the real frisson of fear and excitement, was to actually enter the field. To walk amongst the unnaturally tall stalks, to approach the Scarecrow, to defy the unspoken prohibition that had held sway for so long.

She overheard snippets of conversations; fragments of plans being hatched. "We'll go on the Friday before Halloween," she heard one of them say, their voice a low murmur. "Less chance of anyone seeing us. We'll take bikes. We can meet at the old quarry." The quarry, a desolate, weed-choked pit on the outskirts of town, had always been a gathering place for those seeking a bit of clandestine adventure.

The idea of forming groups, of pooling their courage, became the prevailing strategy. The solitary approach was too daunting, too exposed. It was the collective bravery, the shared experience of fear and adrenaline, that would make the dare palatable, even exhilarating. They spoke of numbers, of allies, of how many of them would actually go through with it. The final tally was a fluid thing, constantly shifting as nerves frayed and resolve wavered. But the core group, the ones who craved the ultimate thrill, remained steadfast.

Kayla found herself drawn to the periphery of these discussions, not as a participant, but as an observer. She felt a strange sort of kinship with their youthful recklessness, a recognition of the desperate need to feel alive, to break free from the suffocating grip of Dry Creek's pervasive gloom. She understood the allure of the danger, the siren song of the unknown that called to them. It was the same call that had drawn her to the edge of Withers Field herself, that insistent whisper of something more, something beyond the predictable cycles of their small town.

Her own grandfather's stories, though rarely spoken, echoed in her mind. The faint scent of dried herbs, the subtle medicinal undertone she'd detected on the edge of the field – these were not figments of her imagination. They were echoes of a past she was only beginning to understand, a past inextricably linked to the Withers land and its silent, watchful guardian. The approaching Halloween, with its macabre traditions and its embrace of the spectral, felt less like a celebration and more like a prelude, a gathering of shadows that had been lurking in the periphery of Dry Creek for far too long.

The air grew colder, the nights longer, and the whispers about the dare intensified. The legend of the Withers scarecrow, already firmly entrenched in the folklore of Dry Creek, was about to be tested, rewritten, and perhaps, for some, utterly destroyed. The allure of the danger, the intoxicating promise of confronting the town's deepest fear, was a powerful, irresistible force. And as the last tendrils of summer surrendered to the encroaching autumn, Kayla knew, with a chilling certainty, that the coming Halloween would be unlike any other. The silence of Withers Field was about to be broken, not by laughter or merriment, but by the desperate thrum of young hearts, daring to trespass on ground that had long been claimed by something ancient and unforgiving.

The air, once thick with the humid breath of summer, now carried the sharp, clean scent of decay. Autumn had arrived in Dry

Creek not with a gentle sigh, but with a bracing, almost brutal efficiency. The fields, once a vibrant tapestry of green and gold, were succumbing to the season's relentless march. The corn, the town's lifeblood, was no longer a promise of abundance. Instead, its dry stalks, brittle and rust-colored, stood like a skeletal forest, whispering secrets to the wind as it whipped through their desiccated leaves. This was the harvest season, but in Dry Creek, the term felt hollow, imbued with an ancient, unspoken dread that clung to the land like a persistent fog.

The change wasn't just in the landscape; it was in the very atmosphere of the town. The usual melancholy that accompanied the end of summer felt amplified, curdled into something more sinister. It was a deepening of shadows, a subtle shift in the perceived weight of the world. The vibrant energy of the preceding weeks, fueled by the burgeoning dare surrounding Withers Field, seemed to have receded, replaced by a hushed expectancy. A collective holding of breath. The town, accustomed to its quiet rhythms, felt a new, unsettling cadence, a dark undertone that resonated beneath the surface of everyday life.

Kayla felt it most acutely. It was a prickling on her skin, a cold knot in her stomach that tightened with each passing day. The vivid memory of her brief, terrifying encounter at the edge of Withers Field continued to haunt her waking hours and seep into her dreams. The silence there, an unnatural absence of sound, had been more terrifying than any scream. It was a void, a vacuum that seemed to absorb all life, all warmth. And the scarecrow… she couldn't shake the image of it. Not as a crude effigy of straw and burlap, but as something else. Something that watched. Something that *was*.

The corn itself seemed to have undergone a transformation. Once a source of comfort, a tangible representation of sustenance and the cycle of life, it now appeared to writhe with an unseen life of its own. As the wind stirred, the dry stalks swayed and rustled, creating a sound that was less like the whisper of nature and more like the hushed murmurs of an unseen multitude. It was as if the very plants were alive with a shared, malevolent sentience, a collective consciousness born of the land's dark history. The rows, once orderly and predictable, seemed to twist and turn in the periphery of vision, creating disorienting patterns that played tricks on the eyes.

And then there was the scarecrow. Its silhouette, stark against the bruised twilight sky, had become a focal point of dread. The harvest moon, fat and pale, cast long, distorted shadows that stretched and writhed across the field. In its ethereal glow, the figure on its solitary post seemed to grow, to expand beyond its physical confines. The tattered clothes, the crudely fashioned limbs, the vacant stare of its button eyes – all these elements, bathed in the spectral light, took on a new, terrifying significance. It was no longer merely an object; it was an entity. A sentinel. A dark omen that seemed to presage a horror yet to be fully revealed.

Kayla found herself drawn to the edge of town, to the dusty roads that led towards Withers Field, not out of morbid curiosity, but out of a growing sense of inevitability. The dare, initially a flicker of bravado amongst the town's teenagers, had ignited into a wildfire of anticipation. The talk, once confined to hushed whispers in the diner or furtive conversations behind the school, now seemed to permeate the very air. The bravado was still there, a thin veneer over the pervasive fear, but it was laced with a desperate, almost feverish energy. They were preparing for something, a communal pilgrimage to the heart of their town's deepest anxieties.

She saw them gathering, the boys and girls who had been so eager to boast. They spoke in low, urgent tones, their faces illuminated by the weak glow of their phones. Plans were being finalized, routes scouted, supplies gathered – flashlights, rope, anything that might offer a semblance of control in the face of the unknown. The quarry, the old, abandoned pit on the outskirts, had become their clandestine staging ground. The air around these gatherings crackled with a nervous energy, a potent mix of fear and exhilaration. They were teenagers, on the cusp of adulthood, and the allure of the forbidden, the irresistible pull of confronting the town's most potent legend, was a force they could no longer resist.

Kayla understood this urge. She felt it too, a deep, resonant hum within her own being. It was the call of the unknown, the primal need to understand what lay beyond the veil of the ordinary. Her grandfather's cryptic words, the faint scent of something ancient and wild that she had detected near the field – these fragments of memory tugged at her, hinting at a connection she couldn't yet comprehend. The Withers land, she suspected, held secrets far older and more profound than the mere legend of a scarecrow. It was a place where the veil between worlds had thinned, where the echoes of the past refused to remain buried.

The corn stalks, reaching their skeletal fingers towards the sky, seemed to vibrate with an unseen energy. They were not just plants; they were witnesses. They had stood guard over Withers Field for generations, silent observers of whatever transpired within its boundaries. Now, under the watchful eye of the harvest moon, they seemed to lean in, their rustling whispers coalescing into a chorus of unease. The wind, a constant, mournful presence, carried their dry lamentations, weaving them into the fabric of the approaching night. Each gust seemed to carry a warning, a subtle plea to turn back, to leave the field to its solitary occupant.

Kayla remembered the specific silence she had encountered. It wasn't just an absence of sound; it was a palpable void, a crushing weight that pressed in on her from all sides. The usual chirping of insects, the distant calls of nocturnal birds, even the rustling of leaves underfoot – all had been swallowed by that unnerving stillness. It was the silence of a place that was fundamentally apart, a place that did not belong to the world of the living. And at its heart, standing sentinel over this desolate expanse, was the Scarecrow.

Its form, even from a distance, was unsettling. The burlap head, weathered and stained, seemed to tilt at an unnatural angle, as if observing something with a sinister intensity. The button eyes, crudely sewn into the fabric, gleamed with a dull, vacant malevolence. Its limbs, stuffed with straw and bound with twine, were rigid, unyielding. Yet, in the shifting moonlight, they seemed to possess a subtle animation, a fluidity that belied their static appearance. It was the kind of stillness that suggested immense power held in check, a coiled tension that spoke of an ancient, patient watchfulness.

The fear that permeated Dry Creek was not a new phenomenon. It was a part of the town's history, a shadow that had long been cast by the Withers land. But this year, the approaching Halloween had amplified it, sharpened it into a tangible, almost physical presence. The dare was a catalyst, a reckless attempt to confront and conquer that fear, to prove that they, the new generation, were stronger, braver, less susceptible to the old superstitions. But as Kayla watched the preparations, a chilling premonition settled upon her. They were not confronting the fear; they were walking directly into its embrace.

She thought of the stories, the hushed tales passed down through generations. Tales of livestock found dead, of inexplicable disappearances, of a pervasive sense of unease that clung to the Withers property like a shroud. Her grandfather, a man of few words and even fewer explanations, had always spoken of the land with a quiet reverence, a respectful distance. He had never explicitly forbidden anyone from going near it, but his silence, his averted gaze when the subject arose, had spoken volumes. It was the silence of someone who knew, who understood, who carried the weight of a knowledge too terrible to share.

The corn, as it swayed in the wind, created an illusion of movement within the field. Shadows danced, shapes shifted, and for a fleeting moment, it was easy to believe that figures were moving among the stalks, just beyond the reach of sight. The rustling grew louder, more insistent, like a thousand tiny whispers urging them forward, or perhaps, urging them to retreat. Kayla found herself listening intently, trying to decipher the language of the wind and the corn, trying to understand the message that the land itself seemed to be trying to convey.

The dare had coalesced into a specific plan. A group of about ten teenagers, a mix of boys and girls, were scheduled to make their attempt on the night before Halloween. They would meet at the old quarry at midnight, then cycle to the edge of Withers Field, leaving their bikes hidden in the dense brush before making their approach on foot. The objective: to reach the scarecrow, touch it, and return, proving their mettle. The air of bravado was thick, but Kayla saw the underlying tremor of genuine fear in their eyes. This was not a game; it was a challenge to the very fabric of their reality, a defiance of the unspoken forces that governed their small town.

The closer the night loomed, the more the atmosphere around Withers Field seemed to thicken. The corn, stripped of its life-giving moisture, had become brittle, its leaves crackling like dry bones with every gust of wind. The silence that had so unnerved Kayla was now a constant, oppressive presence, a blanket of dread that muffled the sounds of the world. It was as if the land itself was holding its breath, anticipating the arrival of those who dared to trespass.

And the scarecrow. Bathed in the unearthly glow of the harvest moon, it was no longer just a figure of straw and rags. It was a monument to dread, a silent, unblinking guardian of secrets best left undisturbed. Its tattered arms seemed to reach out, not in a gesture of warding, but in an invitation. An invitation to a darkness that lay coiled at the heart of Dry Creek, a darkness that was about to be awakened by the reckless courage of youth. The season of harvest had arrived, but it was a harvest of shadows, a reaping of fear, and the sinister presence of the Withers scarecrow was a dark omen, a harbinger of the horrors that were about to unfold in the heart of Dry Creek. The whispers of the corn, the chill in the air, the unnerving stillness – all pointed to a night of reckoning, a night when the veil would be lifted, and the true nature of Withers Field would be revealed.

Chapter 2

The Dare and the Taking

The sky above Withers Field that night was a bruised canvas, a deep, velvety indigo pricked by a million pinpricks of cold, distant light. The stars, indifferent to the anxieties brewing below, seemed to burn with an ancient, unfeeling brilliance. Kayla stood at the edge of the old quarry, the biting autumn air raising goosebumps on her arms, the phantom scent of damp earth and something else, something acrid and earthy, still clinging to the edges of her memory. Around her, the figures of her friends coalesced from the shadows, their faces pale and drawn in the weak beam of a single flashlight. There was Tommy, his usual swagger a little muted, his knuckles white where he gripped a worn flashlight. Beside him stood Helen, her eyes wide and darting, a tremor running through her as she pulled her jacket tighter. Mark was there too, his bravado a brittle shield, his gaze fixed on the dark silhouette of Withers Field. And then there was Sam, quieter than the others, his silence more unnerving than any boisterous declaration.

"So, we're really doing this?" Helen's voice was a thin thread against the encroaching night, barely audible above the rustling of dry leaves underfoot.

Tommy scoffed, though the sound lacked its usual conviction. "What else are we gonna do, Helen? Spend another Friday night watching reruns? This is it. The big one." He gestured vaguely towards the looming darkness of the field, his flashlight beam cutting a shaky arc through the air.

Kayla felt a familiar tightening in her chest. The dare, born from a restless boredom and a desperate need to inject some semblance of excitement into their stagnant lives, had taken on a life of its own. It had started as a whisper, a dare to simply *approach* the scarecrow, to stand before it for a count of ten. But the whispers had grown louder, bolder, morphing into something more daring, more transgressive. Now, the objective was to steal its eyes. The eyes, the vacant, plastic circles that seemed to hold an unnerving sentience, were the key. To take them, to possess a piece of that chilling stillness, felt like a victory, a tangible conquest over the intangible fear that clung to Withers Field like a shroud.

"Stealing its eyes," Sam murmured, his voice low and resonant. He was always the one to articulate the unspoken dread. "That's… that's different, Tommy. That's not just looking."

Mark nudged him. "That's the point, isn't it? Prove it's just a dummy. Prove it's nothing but straw and old clothes. And if we grab its eyes, well, then we've *really* got something. Something to show everyone." The idea, he believed, was simple in its audacity. Rip out the eyes, carry them back as proof, and forever be the ones who had dared to defy the heart of Dry Creek's deepest fear.

Kayla looked at the faces around her, illuminated by the dancing beam of Tommy's flashlight. Each one held a flicker of the same desperate hope, the same gnawing unease. They were young, on the precipice of something they couldn't quite articulate, a yearning to break free from the suffocating familiarity of their small town, to taste something wild and forbidden. Withers Field, with its silent sentinel and its whispered legends, represented the ultimate transgression, a forbidden fruit ripe for the taking.

"It's just a scarecrow," Kayla said, her voice surprisingly steady, though her heart hammered against her ribs like a trapped bird. She tried to convince herself as much as them. It was a construct, a prop in the town's collective nightmare. Yet, the memory of that unnatural silence, the suffocating void she'd felt at its periphery, was a ghost that clung to her. "Just some old button circles sewn onto burlap. We can do this." She forced a smile, a performance of courage she didn't entirely feel.

Tommy grinned, relief flooding his features. "That's the spirit, Kayla! See? We're not kids anymore. We can handle this. We'll go in, Kayla's got the light. Mark, you're with me for the… retrieval. Sam, help Billy and Sandy keep watch. Helen, you stick with Sam.

Billy and Sandy you keep watch on the bikes and signal Sam if anyone comes up the road." He clapped her on the shoulder, a gesture meant to be reassuring, but it felt heavy, laden with the weight of their shared undertaking.

The plan, hatched in hushed tones over lukewarm sodas at the diner, had seemed almost ludicrously simple. They would approach the field from the north, using the dense cluster of oak trees as cover. The scarecrow stood in the center, a solitary figure visible from miles around under the moon's glow. Tommy, the most agile and daring amongst them, would be the one to climb the rough-hewn post and pluck the eyes. Mark would be his backup, ready to steady the pole or provide a distraction if needed. Sam and Helen, stationed just inside the corn field would signal Tommy if Billy and Sandy saw any approaching headlights or, worse, any other disturbances. Kayla's role was to keep the flashlight steady, her nerves anchored, and to be the first to break the silence with a triumphant shout upon their return.

But as they moved from the relative safety of the quarry towards the desolate expanse of Withers Field, the bravado began to chip away, revealing the raw fear beneath. The corn stalks, dry and brittle, scraped against each other with a sound like a thousand whispering tongues. The wind, a mournful sigh, carried the rustle through the ranks of desiccated plants, a symphony of decay. Each gust seemed to carry a warning; a soft, sibilant murmur that spoke of things best left undisturbed.

"Are you sure about this, Tommy?" Helen whispered again, her voice trembling. She clutched Sam's arm, her fingers digging into his sleeve.

Sam squeezed her hand. "We're here now," he said, his gaze fixed on the distant, imposing silhouette of the scarecrow. It loomed against the star-dusted sky, a figure of stark, unsettling stillness. Even from this distance, Kayla could feel its presence, a silent, watchful weight that pressed down on the landscape. The painted eyes, even from afar, seemed to gleam with a malevolent awareness.

"It's just a scarecrow," Tommy repeated, his voice a little too loud, a little too strained. "Made of straw. Anyone could put it there.

Anyone could put anything in it." He swung the flashlight beam across the field, the light catching on the skeletal stalks, making them dance like phantoms.

Kayla felt a cold dread begin to creep into her own resolve. Her grandfather's words, fragments of warnings he'd never fully articulated, echoed in her mind. He'd spoken of the land's "temper," of respecting what you didn't understand. He'd never mentioned the scarecrow directly, but his stories of the Withers family, their strange ways and their isolation, had always been tinged with an unspoken reverence for the land they worked. He'd said the fields held memories, and some memories, he'd implied, were best left undisturbed.

As they drew closer, the silence deepened. The usual nocturnal chorus of crickets and frogs was absent. The wind, too, seemed to hold its breath as they passed the threshold of the field. It was a deliberate silence, an oppressive void that seemed to swallow sound. Kayla felt it in her teeth, a low-grade thrumming, a pressure that made her temples ache. The air grew colder, not the crisp chill of autumn, but a damp, bone-deep cold that seemed to emanate from the very earth.

Tommy led the way, his small flashlight beam bouncing ahead, illuminating the narrow, dry path winding through the corn. The stalks towered over them, their dry leaves brushing against their faces like skeletal fingers. Kayla kept her eyes fixed on the scarecrow, its silhouette growing larger, more defined, more menacing. The tattered clothes, hanging loosely on its frame, seemed to stir even in the absence of wind. The burlap head, tilted at an unnerving angle, appeared to follow their progress.

"Almost there," Tommy whispered, his voice strained. He stopped a few yards from the post; the flashlight beam now focused directly on the figure.

The scarecrow was more unsettling up close than Tommy had imagined. Its frame was crudely constructed, a thick wooden post with crossbeams forming a rudimentary body. Straw spilled from tears in its burlap clothing, clinging to the rough fabric like dried blood. But it was the eyes that truly held him captive. Two large, black buttons, crudely sewn onto the burlap face, seemed to stare out with an unnerving intensity. They were flat, lifeless, yet they held a depth, a darkness that seemed to absorb the flashlight's beam.

Tommy nudged Mark. "You gotta climb up, man. Just… rip 'em out."

"Hey man!" Mark protested. "I thought it was you going up?" Mark swallowed, his Adam's apple bobbing. Tommy looked up at the awaiting prize, the buttons. "Change of plans. You're nimbler and a better climber." Tommy paused, thinking. "Plus, your lighter than I am. We don't want to pull the damned thing down…do we?" He looked at Mark waiting for an objection. There was none.

Mark shrugged his shoulders reached out a tentative hand, his fingers trembling as they neared the burlap face. He hesitated; his gaze locked with the button eyes. It was a standoff, a silent battle of wills between a teenage boy and a silent effigy.

"Go on," Sam called softly from the edge of the field. "We're right here."

With a surge of nervous energy, Mark grabbed the post, his worn sneakers finding purchase on the rough wood. He began to climb, the dry stalks crunching under his weight. Kayla held her breath, her flashlight beam unwavering, illuminating Mark's determined ascent. He reached the top, his hands fumbling for the button eyes.

"They're… really sewn in tight," he grunted, his voice muffled. He tugged, then pulled harder, his muscles straining. The scarecrow's head tilted precariously, and for a heart-stopping moment, Kayla thought it might fall.

Then, with a sharp tearing sound, one of the buttons came loose. Mark let out a whoop of triumph, holding it up in the flashlight beam. "One for the collection." Mark muttered. It was a simple black button, unremarkable in itself, yet in that moment, it felt like a trophy of immense significance.

"Got one!" He shouted, his voice ringing with adrenaline.

He reached for the second eye. This time, his movements were more confident, fueled by his success. He grasped the button, pulled with all his might, and with another rasping tear, it too came free.

He held them both aloft, two small pieces of darkness against the vast night sky.

"Yes!" Tommy cheered, a surge of relief and triumph in his voice. "Told you it was nothing!"

But as Mark began his descent, something shifted. It was subtle, almost imperceptible. The rustling of the corn seemed to intensify, morphing from a whisper to a low, guttural murmur. The air, already cold, seemed to drop several degrees, and Kayla felt a prickling sensation crawl up her spine.

Mark landed softly on the ground, a triumphant grin on his face. Upon return he thrust the two buttons into Kayla's hand. "Here. Proof. We did it."

Kayla clutched the rough buttons, their edges sharp against her palm. She looked at the scarecrow. It was still there, its head now bearing two vacant, threadbare circles where its eyes had been. But something was different. The stillness seemed... deeper. More profound. The absence of its eyes didn't make it less menacing; it made it more so. It was as if the theft had merely revealed a more ancient, more terrible gaze.

Suddenly, a dry, rasping sound, distinct from the rustling of the corn, cut through the night. It was a sound that seemed to emanate from the scarecrow itself. A dry, creaking groan.

"What was that?" Helen whispered, her voice laced with terror.

Tommy, his bravado momentarily forgotten, swung the flashlight beam back towards the scarecrow. The light caught on the burlap head. It seemed to be... moving. Not swaying in the wind, but a slow, deliberate turn.

"No way," Mark breathed, his eyes wide. "It's just the wind, man. It's gotta be." But there was no wind. The air was utterly still, the silence now absolute, broken only by their ragged breaths and the increasingly loud, dry rustling of the corn. The scarecrow's head continued its slow, deliberate rotation, the empty sockets where its eyes had been seeming to bore into them. A low, scraping sound began, as if something rough was being dragged across wood.

Kayla's blood ran cold. This was not just straw and burlap. This was something else. The dare, the act of transgression, had awakened something. The pact they had forged under the indifferent stars was not one of triumph, but of terror. The buttons in her hand felt impossibly heavy, relics of a foolish bravado that had led them to this precipice.

The silence of Withers Field was not an absence of sound, but a presence of something ancient and watchful, and they had just stolen its sight. The pact was sealed, not with a handshake, but with the chilling certainty that they had made a terrible mistake. The night, once a canvas for their adolescent rebellion, had become a trap. And the scarecrow, stripped of its eyes, was now looking at them with something far more terrifying: a hunger.

The hour was late, the kind of late that bled into the cusp of a new day, where the world held its breath, poised on the edge of something unknown. Midnight approached, a silent sentinel gathering the stars in its inky cloak. They stood at the perimeter of the Withers property, a collective breath held tight in their chests. The corn, a dense, rustling sea of desiccated stalks, stretched before them, its dry husks whispering a language of disquiet. It wasn't the gentle sigh of wind through leaves, but a more insistent, almost rhythmic rasping, like a thousand dry tongues lapping at the edges of the night. Each rustle seemed to carry a fragment of warning, a low, insistent murmur that burrowed under their skin, raising the fine hairs on their arms.

The silence that otherwise blanketed the landscape was profound, unnatural. The usual nocturnal symphony of crickets, the distant hoot of an owl, even the hum of insects that usually filled the air – all were absent. It was as if the very world had muffled its sounds, holding its breath in anticipation, or perhaps, in dread. Their own heartbeats seemed to boom in their ears, a frantic, irregular drumming that echoed the tremor running through their limbs. Kayla could feel the pulse in her throat; a frantic bird trapped within her.

Tommy's flashlight beam, usually a confident spear, now wavered, its circle of light nervously dancing across the oppressive darkness, catching on the skeletal forms of the corn stalks. Each shadow cast by the swaying stalks seemed to writhe, elongating and contorting with an unnerving life of its own. Familiar shapes twisted into monstrous caricatures in their peripheral vision, playing cruel tricks on their over-stimulated senses. A gnarled branch momentarily resembled a skeletal hand reaching out, a cluster of dried leaves a hunched, watching figure.

Helen whimpered; a soft sound almost lost in the overwhelming silence. She pressed closer to Sam, her small frame trembling against his. "It's… it's so quiet," she whispered, her voice a fragile thread. "Too quiet." Sandy nodding her nodded agreement.

Sam's arm tightened around her, a gesture of comfort that felt inadequate against the palpable fear that permeated the air. He nodded; his gaze fixed on the dense wall of corn. "Yeah," he murmured, his own voice barely audible. "It is." Even his typically stoic composure seemed frayed, his eyes scanning the darkness with an unease that mirrored Kayla's own.

Mark shifted his weight, the dry dirt crunching under his worn sneakers. He tried to project an air of nonchalance, a bravado he clearly didn't feel. "Just the wind," he said, his voice a little too loud, a little too forced. "Plays tricks, you know? Especially out here." But even as the words left his lips, he knew they were a lie. There was no wind. Not a breath. The air was stagnant, heavy, pressing down on them like a physical weight.

Kayla felt the weight of their impending action settle upon her like a shroud. The dare, once a flicker of youthful recklessness, had now grown into a monstrous, all-consuming dread. The thrill of transgression had been replaced by a gnawing apprehension, a chilling certainty that they had stepped onto a path from which there might be no easy return. The buttons in her hand, still cold from the night air, felt impossibly heavy, tangible proof of their folly. They were more than just buttons; they were stolen eyes, a violation of something ancient and unseen, and the cost of that violation was beginning to make itself terrifyingly clear.

She looked at the scarecrow, its dark, unmoving silhouette stark against the faintly luminous horizon. Even from this distance, it commanded a presence, a silent, watchful sentinel that seemed to absorb the very light around it. The crudely stitched burlap face, the emptiness where its eyes should have been, created a void that seemed to pull at her very core. It wasn't just an absence of sight; it was an invitation to something far more sinister. The memory of Mark's triumphant yell as he'd ripped the buttons free, the sharp tearing sound that had echoed across the field, now felt like a prelude to something far more terrible. That small victory, that fleeting moment of exhilaration, had been the catalyst, the spark that had ignited a dormant dread.

Tommy, ever the one to push forward, took a tentative step towards the edge of the corn. He raised the flashlight, its beam cutting a wavering path into the dense rows. The stalks seemed to part before him, a silent, reluctant offering.

"Come on," he urged, his voice a low, strained whisper. "We gotta get moving. It's almost midnight." The unspoken implication hung heavy in the air: if they were caught, if something happened, it would be under the cover of this encroaching darkness.

Kayla followed, her steps hesitant. The dry leaves crunched underfoot; each sound amplified in the oppressive quiet. The corn stalks brushed against her jacket, their brittle texture like dried skin. She could feel the rough fibers snagging on her sleeves, an unsettling intimacy with the dying plants. The air grew colder as they ventured deeper, a damp chill that seeped into her bones, unrelated to the autumn air. It was a cold that felt… wrong. Ancient.

Sam and Helen trailed behind with Billy and Sandy, their figures a little more distinct in the flashlight's beam. Helen's hand was still clenched on Sam's arm, her knuckles white. Sam's gaze remained fixed ahead, his expression unreadable, but Kayla sensed the tension radiating from him, the careful control he exerted over his own fear.

As they neared the center of the field, the rustling intensified. It was no longer just a whisper, but a more defined, almost conversational murmur. It sounded like hushed voices, plotting, deliberating. Kayla strained her ears, trying to decipher the sounds, but they remained maddeningly indistinct, a constant, unsettling undertone to the night. It was as if the corn itself had become a living entity, its dry husks a thousand tongues whispering secrets they weren't meant to hear.

"Did you hear that?" Helen whispered, her voice trembling. "It sounds like... talking."

Tommy stopped, holding up a hand. He turned the flashlight the beam slowly, sweeping it across the rustling stalks. The light caught on the scarecrow, its burlap head tilting slightly, as if observing their every move. It was still there, a silent effigy, but the absence of its eyes had changed it irrevocably. The two empty sockets, dark and vacant, seemed to draw the very shadows into themselves, creating an abyss that hinted at a gaze far more penetrating than mere buttons could ever convey.

A low, scraping sound echoed from the direction of the scarecrow, a dry, rasping noise like fingernails dragging across rough wood. Kayla's breath hitched. It wasn't the wind. It wasn't the corn. It was a distinct sound, deliberate and chilling.

"What was that?" Mark's bravado finally cracked; his voice laced with a genuine fear that resonated with Kayla's own.

Tommy swung the flashlight beam directly onto the scarecrow's head. The burlap seemed to swell, to shift, almost as if a breath had been drawn. The head, which had been tilted at its usual unnerving angle, seemed to straighten, the empty eye sockets now facing them directly. It was a subtle movement, almost imperceptible, but Kayla felt it in the marrow of her bones. The stillness of the scarecrow was gone, replaced by a subtle, terrifying animation.

"It's just... settling," Tommy stammered, his attempt at reassurance falling flat. His own voice was tight with apprehension. "The post, it's old. Might be leaning."

But the scraping sound came again, closer this time, and accompanied by a soft, dry creak. It sounded like the straining of old wood, like the slow articulation of joints long stiffened. Kayla's gaze was fixed on the scarecrow. The vacant sockets seemed to deepen, to widen, and for a horrifying moment, she thought she saw a flicker of movement within them, a shift in the darkness that was not caused by the flashlight.

"It's moving," Helen choked out, burying her face in Sam's shoulder. "Sam, it's moving!"

Sam's arm tightened around her, but his own eyes were wide with a dawning horror. He stared at the scarecrow, his jaw tight. "It's… it's not just a scarecrow," he breathed, the unspoken truth hanging heavy between them.

The realization hit Kayla with the force of a physical blow. The dare, the casual disregard for the local lore, the bravado – it had all been a monumental, terrifying mistake. They hadn't just stolen eyes from a scarecrow; they had stolen something from the field itself. They had disturbed something that had been dormant, something that the hushed warnings and the eerie silence had been meant to protect. The pact they had made, the unspoken agreement to face their fears and emerge victorious, had morphed into a descent into a nightmare they had no control over.

Tommy, his face pale in the flashlight's beam, took a shaky step backward. "We should… we should go," he said, his voice barely a whisper. "Now."

But as he spoke, the rustling of the corn seemed to surge, growing louder, more insistent. It was no longer a mere whisper, but a cacophony of dry, scraping sounds, a thousand tiny movements all converging on them. The air grew even colder, the chill now sharp, biting. A faint, earthy odor, once barely perceptible, now filled the air, a damp, cloying scent of decay and something else… something metallic, like old blood.

Kayla clutched the two buttons tighter, her knuckles white. They felt like hot coals in her hand, searing her palm. She looked at the scarecrow, its burlap head now undeniably turning towards them, its empty sockets like black holes sucking the light and hope from the night. The scraping sound was no longer just a scraping; it was a dragging, a slow, inexorable movement. And from within the depths of its hollow head, from the very place where its eyes had been, a new sound began to emerge. A low, guttural hum, a vibration

39

that resonated not just in the air, but deep within their bones. It was a sound that spoke of an ancient hunger, a patient, waiting malevolence that had finally been awakened. They had come to steal its eyes, but in doing so, they had offered themselves as prey. The midnight hour was no longer a deadline for their dare, but a countdown to their reckoning. The pact was sealed, not with a trophy, but with the chilling certainty that they had awakened something that should have remained buried, something that now looked upon them with a terrifying, sightless hunger.

The oppressive silence of the cornfield pressed in on them, a tangible entity that seemed to swallow all sound. Each rustle of the dry stalks, once a mere whisper of the wind, now felt like a sinister prelude, a thousand dry tongues murmuring incantations of dread. They moved forward, a tight knot of nervous energy, their steps hesitant on the desiccated earth. The figure of the scarecrow loomed ahead, a jagged silhouette against the bruised twilight sky. It was more than just a collection of straw and burlap; it was an icon of their fear, a physical manifestation of the whispers and warnings that clung to Dry Creek like a persistent fog.

Kayla felt her breath catch in her throat, each inhale a shallow, ragged affair. The flashlight beam, held by Tommy, danced erratically, illuminating the skeletal forms of the corn, casting long, distorted shadows that writhed like trapped spirits. The air, stagnant and unnaturally cold, seemed to coil around them, a chilling embrace that had nothing to do with the autumn night. It was a cold that emanated from the very heart of the field, a cold that seemed to seep from the straw-stuffed effigy that stood sentinel before them.

As they drew closer, the details of the scarecrow resolved themselves from the gloom. Its burlap face, a patchwork of rough, earth-toned fabric, was stretched taut over some unseen structure, giving it a perpetually grimacing expression. The stitching that formed its mouth was a jagged line, a cruel caricature of a smile. But it was the eyes that held them captive, the two missing buttons that Tommy had so triumphantly ripped free just moments ago. Or rather, the absence of them. Where eyes should have been, there were now only dark, vacant voids, like twin abysses that seemed to swallow the scant light, hinting at a profound, unnatural emptiness.

A palpable aura of malevolence radiated from the scarecrow, a chilling presence that prickled their skin and sent shivers coursing through their veins. It was a cold that bypassed the physical, a frigid touch that settled deep within their bones, making their hands tremble uncontrollably as they approached. Kayla could feel her own pulse hammering against her ribs, a frantic drumbeat that echoed the growing dread in her chest. The two buttons, clutched tightly in her palm, felt impossibly heavy, burning against her skin as if imbued with a sinister energy.

Tommy, his face a mask of forced bravado, took another step forward, his gaze fixed on the scarecrow. He raised the flashlight higher, its beam piercing the darkness, momentarily illuminating the crude, X-shaped stitches that marked the scarecrow's crude nose. "Just a dumb scarecrow," he muttered, his voice a strained whisper, an attempt to reassure not only his friends but himself. Yet, the tremor in his voice betrayed his true feelings. The casual dare had curdled into something far more menacing, and the jovial bravado of earlier had evaporated in the face of this unnerving reality.

Mark stood beside him, his arms crossed, a nervous tic working at the corner of his jaw. He tried to maintain an air of detached amusement, but his eyes kept darting towards the scarecrow, then to the surrounding corn, as if expecting something to burst forth from the dense rows. "Yeah, just a bunch of straw and old clothes," he echoed, his tone lacking conviction. "Probably falling apart."

Helen, however, could no longer maintain even a semblance of composure. She was pressed tightly against Sam's side, her small frame quivering. Her eyes were wide, staring unblinkingly at the scarecrow, and a silent tear traced a path down her pale cheek. "It looks angry," she whispered, her voice barely audible, a fragile thread lost in the oppressive silence. "It's watching us." Billy offered.

Sam's arm remained a steady presence around her; his own gaze fixed on the looming figure. He offered a reassuring squeeze, but the tension in his shoulders was evident. He knew Helen's sensitivity to the unspoken, her uncanny ability to sense the undercurrents of fear and unease that permeated the air. And right now, the air around the scarecrow was thick with a palpable, ancient dread.

41

Kayla felt a sudden, sharp pang of regret, a wave of nausea washing over her. The thrill of rebellion, the giddy excitement of breaking the rules, had long since vanished, replaced by a gnawing certainty that they had crossed a line, a boundary that should have remained undisturbed. The dare, hatched in the bravado of youth and fueled by a misguided sense of adventure, now felt like a fatal miscalculation. They had come to steal a prize, a trophy to prove their courage, but the prize was proving to be far more than they had bargained for.

The buttons in her hand felt hot, an alien presence against her skin. She flexed her fingers, trying to dislodge the oppressive sensation, but they remained stubbornly fixed, like tiny talons digging into her flesh. The moonlight, weak and diffused, glinted off their smooth surfaces, making them appear almost luminous, like captured stars. But these were not stars; they were stolen fragments, pieces of a violated wholeness, and the weight of that violation was beginning to press down on her, crushing her with its unspoken consequence.

As they took another tentative step, the dry corn stalks surrounding them seemed to lean inward, their brittle husks whispering a dry, rasping chorus. It was a sound that was both everywhere and nowhere, a disorienting symphony of decay. Kayla strained her ears, trying to decipher meaning in the rustling, but it offered no comfort, only a deepening sense of unease. It was as if the very field was breathing, exhaling a cold, dry breath that carried the scent of dust and decay.

Tommy, his flashlight beam now steady, though his hand still trembled slightly, took a step towards the scarecrow. He reached out, his fingers hesitant, as if unsure of what he would touch. The burlap skin of the scarecrow felt rough, coarse, and strangely cold beneath his fingertips. As he looked up, the stitching around its mouth seemed to mock him, a silent, cruel jest.

"See? Nothing," he said, his voice still a little too loud, a little too forced. He was trying to convince himself as much as them. He ran his hand over the scarecrow's arm, the rough burlap yielding slightly, the straw stuffing shifting within. He gave it a gentle push, and the entire effigy swayed slightly, the wooden post groaning in protest.

But as Tommy's hand lingered on the scarecrow's arm a subtle shift of its head occurred. It was almost imperceptible, a movement so slight that Kayla initially dismissed it as a trick of the light, a flicker of her own overactive imagination. The scarecrow's head, which had been tilted at its customary, slightly askew angle, seemed to straighten, its gaze, or rather, its vacant stare, now directed squarely at them. The two dark voids where the buttons had been seemed to deepen, to pull the surrounding darkness into their hollow depths.

A collective gasp rippled through the group. Helen whimpered again, burying her face deeper into Sam's side, her small body rigid with fear. Tommy snatched his hand back as if he had touched something burning. His face, illuminated by the wavering flashlight beam, was ashen.

"Did you see that?" Mark whispered, his voice strained. "It... it moved."

"Yeah, like it knows we are here." Billy exclaimed.

Tommy shook his head, his eyes wide. "No, it didn't. It's just... the post. It's old. It's probably leaning." His explanation was weak, unconvincing, and they all knew it. There was a stillness to the scarecrow's movement, a deliberate, controlled shift that spoke of something far more than a rickety post.

Kayla's gaze was locked on the scarecrow's head. The vacant sockets seemed to pulse with a subtle darkness, and for a terrifying instant, she thought she saw a flicker of movement within them, a fleeting disturbance of the shadows that was not caused by the flashlight. It was as if something was stirring within the hollow shell, something ancient and malevolent that had been rudely awakened.

A low, dry scraping sound emanated from the scarecrow, like the dragging of rough, brittle material across a rough surface. It wasn't the rustling of corn; this was distinct, deliberate, and utterly chilling. It sounded like something being dragged, something heavy and unwilling, across the dry earth.

"What *was* that?" Mark's voice cracked, the last vestiges of his bravado dissolving into raw fear.

The scraping sound came again, closer this time, and it was accompanied by a faint, creaking groan, like old bones protesting movement. It was the sound of something old, something stiff, beginning to stir. Kayla's heart lurched into her throat. She felt a primal urge to run, to flee back into the relative safety of the darkness beyond the cornfield, but her feet felt rooted to the spot, ensnared by an invisible force.

Tommy swung the flashlight beam back to the scarecrow's head. The burlap seemed to swell, to stretch, as if the effigy were drawing a slow, ragged breath. The vacant eye sockets appeared to widen, the blackness within them seeming to deepen, to expand, drawing the very light into their depths. And then, from the heart of those empty sockets, a new sound began to emerge.

It was a low, guttural hum, a vibration that seemed to resonate not only in the air but deep within their very bones. It was a sound that spoke of an ancient hunger, a patient, waiting malevolence that had finally been stirred from its slumber. It was a sound that was utterly alien, a primal lament that carried the weight of centuries, a chilling melody of awakening.

Helen let out a strangled cry, pressing herself even closer to Sam. "It's... it's making more noises," she stammered, her voice trembling uncontrollably.

Sam's arm tightened around her, but his eyes were wide with a dawning horror. He stared at the scarecrow, his jaw clenched, his knuckles white where he gripped Helen's arm. "It's can't be...it's just... straw," he breathed, the unspoken truth hanging heavy between them, a terrifying revelation that confirmed their deepest fears.

Tommy, his face a pale mask in the erratic beam of the flashlight, took a shaky step backward. The desire to flee, to escape this unfolding horror, was overwhelming. "We... we need to really go," he stammered, his voice a mere whisper. "*Now.*"

But as the words left his lips, the rustling of the corn surged, growing louder, more insistent. It was no longer a mere whisper but a cacophony of dry, scraping sounds, a thousand tiny movements converging on them with unnerving unity. The air grew even colder, the chill now sharp, biting, carrying with it a faint, cloying odor of damp earth and something else... something metallic and faintly sweet, like old, dried blood.

Kayla's fingers tightened around the buttons, the smooth surfaces now feeling like hot coals against her palm. She looked at the scarecrow, its burlap head now undeniably turning towards them, its vacant sockets like black holes, sucking the light, the hope, the very air from the night. The scraping sound was no longer just a scraping; it was a dragging, a slow, inexorable movement that spoke of immense effort, of ancient limbs unfolding after a long stillness.

And from within the depths of its hollow head, from the very places where its eyes had once been, the low hum intensified, growing into a resonant thrum that vibrated through the soles of their feet, up their legs, and into the very core of their beings. It was a sound that spoke of a hunger that had endured for centuries, a patient, waiting malevolence that had finally been awakened. They had come to steal its eyes, but in doing so, they had offered themselves as tribute, as prey. The midnight hour was no longer a deadline for their dare, but a countdown to their reckoning. The pact was sealed, not with a trophy, but with the chilling certainty that they had awakened something that should have remained buried, something that now looked upon them with a terrifying, sightless hunger. The withered stalks of corn rustled around them, a whispering shroud that seemed to close in, trapping them in the malevolent gaze of the awakened sentinel. The dare was complete, but the taking had only just begun.

The air hung thick and heavy, a suffocating blanket woven from the dried husks of corn and the unspoken dread that had settled upon them like a shroud. Each breath felt borrowed, stolen from the suffocating stillness that pulsed around the looming effigy. Tommy's flashlight beam, though still held steady by a surprisingly determined hand, seemed to shrink in the face of the oppressive darkness, its narrow cone of light a fragile barrier against the encroaching night. Kayla clutched the two buttons in her palm, their smooth, cool surfaces a stark contrast to the feverish heat that seemed to emanate from the very ground beneath their feet. They were tangible proof, solid anchors in the swirling vortex of unease, yet they felt like a damning indictment.

Kayla felt a cold dread wash over her, a certainty that they had crossed a line from which there was no return. The dare had been accepted, but the price of admission was far greater than any of them had imagined. The buttons found their way back to her. Her hand felt searingly hot now, an alien presence that burned against her skin. She opened her palm, the two black discs lying starkly against her clammy skin, and a terrifying thought struck her: perhaps they weren't meant to be taken. Perhaps the act of removing them was not a victory, but an invitation. An invitation to something that had been waiting, patiently, in the heart of the cornfield.

The rustling of the corn reached a crescendo, a dry, rasping roar that seemed to engulf them. The stalks leaned inward, forming a suffocating canopy, and the shadows deepened, coalescing into indistinct, menacing shapes. The hum from the scarecrow's head grew louder, a deep, resonant thrum that seemed to penetrate their very beings, rattling their teeth and making their vision swim. It was a sound that promised a hunger centuries in the making, a primal need that had finally been awakened by their reckless act. The dare had been fulfilled, the buttons taken, but in that moment, under the oppressive gaze of the eyeless scarecrow, Kayla knew with a chilling certainty that the true taking had only just begun. The pact had been sealed, not with triumph, but with a terrifying understanding of the ancient forces they had so carelessly disturbed.

The sudden, piercing cold was the first tangible manifestation of their trespass. It wasn't the biting wind of an early autumn evening, but a deep, internal chill that seemed to seep into their very bones, bypassing the thin layers of their jackets. It felt as though the air itself had become rarefied, stretched thin, and in that sudden void, something ancient and impossibly hungry had taken root. The thrill that had propelled them into the cornfield, the heady rush of defiance and youthful bravado, had curdled into a thick, cloying dread. The two buttons, clutched tightly in Kayla's palm, no longer felt like trophies, but like cursed amulets, radiating a malevolence that prickled her skin. She could feel the rough texture of the burlap that accompanied the buttons. She could also see the faint, almost imperceptible tears where the buttons had been forcefully removed, and a sickening certainty began to bloom in her gut: they hadn't just stolen eyes from a scarecrow; they had pulled the lid off something that should have remained buried.

Kayla felt a sudden, overwhelming urge to flee, to run blindly out of the field and never look back. But her feet felt rooted to the spot, tethered by an invisible force, her gaze drawn inexorably to the scarecrow. The buttons in her hand felt impossibly heavy now, searing hot against her skin, as if they were burning holes through her hand. She opened her palm, the two black discs lying starkly against her clammy skin, and a terrifying thought took hold: what if these weren't just buttons? What if they were anchors, points of connection that had kept something at bay? And by removing them, had they not only unleashed it, but invited it in?

The air grew colder still, a biting, unnatural chill that seemed to steal the very breath from their lungs. It carried with it a faint, cloying scent, a mingling of damp earth, decaying vegetation, and something else, something subtly metallic and sickeningly sweet, like old, dried blood. Tommy coughed, a dry, hacking sound that seemed to crackle in the oppressive silence. He swung the flashlight beam around the perimeter of the field, his hand shaking so violently that the light danced erratically, illuminating nothing but the endless, undulating rows of corn. Yet, he felt watched, intensely watched, from the shadowed depths of the stalks.

"I don't like this," Helen whimpered, her voice barely audible. She buried her face against Sam's chest, her small body trembling. Sam held her tighter, his gaze still fixed on the scarecrow. He could feel her fear, a potent, visceral thing that mirrored his own burgeoning dread. The bravado that had brought them here, the collective desire to prove their courage, had utterly collapsed, leaving them exposed and vulnerable. They had sought a thrill, a fleeting moment of daring, but they had stumbled upon something far older and infinitely more terrifying. The scarecrow, a crude effigy of straw and burlap, had become something else entirely in the crucible of their fear. It was a focal point, a beacon for a darkness that had been waiting.

As they began to retreat, a unified, unspoken decision to flee, the rustling of the corn intensified. It was no longer a passive sound, but an active one, a dry, rasping roar that seemed to surround them, to close in. The stalks leaned inward, their brittle leaves brushing against each other with a sound like a thousand tiny claws scraping against bone. The shadows between the rows deepened, coalescing into indistinct, menacing shapes that seemed to writhe and shift with a life of their own. Tommy's flashlight beam, his only source of light and perceived safety, flickered violently, threatening to plunge them into absolute darkness. He batted at it with his free hand, a desperate, futile gesture.

Kayla stumbled, her ankle twisting on an uneven patch of earth. She cried out, a sharp, surprised sound that was immediately swallowed by the rising din of the corn. Sam reached out, his hand steadying her, his expression one of grim determination mixed with unfeigned fear. "Come on," he urged, his voice strained. He pulled her along, his pace quickening, but his eyes never left the scarecrow. It stood there, a silent, immobile sentinel, yet it felt like the source of all the malevolence, the conductor of this terrifying symphony of decay.

The hum from the scarecrow's head grew louder, a deep, resonant thrum that seemed to penetrate their very beings, rattling their teeth and making their vision swim. It was a sound that promised a hunger centuries in the making, a primal need that had finally been awakened by their reckless act. The dare had been fulfilled, the buttons taken, but in that moment, under the oppressive gaze of the eyeless scarecrow, Kayla knew with a chilling certainty that the true taking had only just begun. The pact had been sealed, not with triumph, but with a terrifying understanding of the ancient forces they had so carelessly disturbed.

As they broke free from the edge of the cornfield, the oppressive weight of the stalks seemed to lessen, but the unnatural chill persisted, clinging to them like a damp shroud. The hum, though fainter now, still echoed in their minds, a haunting reminder of what they had witnessed, what they had awakened. The familiar openness of the field beyond, bathed in the faint glow of distant farm lights, offered little solace. The world they had left behind, the world of ordinary nights and harmless superstitions, felt impossibly far away, separated by an invisible chasm of transgression. They had stepped across a boundary, and the consequences, as cold and sharp as the air that now clung to them, were just beginning to manifest. The thrill of the dare had been a fleeting illusion, a dangerous siren song that had lured them into a darkness far more profound than they could have ever conceived. The stolen buttons, symbols of their ill-fated courage, felt like embers burning in their hands, a constant reminder that the night was far from over, and the true horror had merely begun its slow, inexorable crawl from the heart of the corn. The silence that had fallen between them was not one of relief, but of a shared, profound terror, a silent acknowledgment that they had irrevocably altered the fabric of their reality with a simple, foolish act. The air itself seemed to press in on them, heavy with unspoken threat, each rustle of the wind through the distant trees sounding like the whispering of an unseen, ancient presence. They had dared to look into the void, and the void had looked back, its gaze as cold and unforgiving as the deepest winter night, even in the heart of autumn.

Tommy glanced at Mark, his face still etched with a fear that seemed to have etched itself permanently onto his features. The buttons, as if they were the proverbial hot potato, found their way back to Mark who clutched the buttons in his hand, his knuckles white, his gaze fixed on some point in the distance, as if he could still see the scarecrow, still hear its insidious hum. The bravado that had fueled him earlier was gone, replaced by a raw, animalistic terror. He had been the one to boast, the one to scoff, the one to instigate, and now he was the one most visibly shattered by the encounter. Kayla watched him, a mixture of pity and a chilling sense of shared culpability in her heart. They were all in this together, bound by the transgression, by the chilling knowledge of what they had awakened.

Sam, still holding Helen close, scanned the open field around them, his body tense, his eyes sharp and wary. He was trying to project a sense of calm for Helen, but Tommy could see the subtle tremor in his hands, the way his jaw was clenched tight. Even Sam, usually the most pragmatic and grounded of them, was visibly shaken. The ease with which their bravado had dissolved, the speed with which genuine terror had taken its place, was a testament to the sheer, palpable malevolence they had encountered. It wasn't just a story; it was a living, breathing entity, disturbed by their intrusion.

Mark felt a sudden, sharp cramp in his hand, where he still held the buttons. He opened his palm again, the two black discs seeming to glow faintly in the dim light. They were ordinary buttons, made of cheap plastic, yet they felt imbued with an unholy power. He imagined the stitched holes on the scarecrow's face, the dark, gaping voids, and a chilling thought struck him: what if those weren't just holes? What if they were eyes, and the buttons had been their lids, keeping something hidden within the burlap shell? The act of tearing them free had been more than just theft; it had been an act of violation, of unveiling.

The pervasive chill seemed to deepen, to coil around them like a serpent. It was more than just a drop in temperature; it was a presence, a tangible manifestation of the unseen forces they had disturbed. The air felt heavy, charged with an unspoken energy, and the silence that stretched between them was pregnant with the echo of that unsettling hum. It was a silence born of shared trauma, of a dawning, horrifying realization that their lives had irrevocably changed. The dare had been answered, the objective achieved, but the cost of their victory was a creeping dread that promised to haunt their every waking moment, and perhaps, their dreams as well. The cornfield, once a place of adolescent adventure, had become a tomb, a silent witness to their folly, and its shadow stretched long and cold across the landscape of their innocence. The night was still young, and the chill that had settled upon them felt like a harbinger of an even greater darkness to come, a darkness that had been patiently waiting, just beyond the rustling curtain of the corn.

Chapter 3

The Gaze Begins

The dawn broke not with the gentle blush of a new day, but with a stark, unforgiving clarity that illuminated the town of Dry Creek like an interrogation lamp. The mist that usually clung to the fields, softening the edges of the world, seemed to have retreated, revealing a landscape stripped bare, every detail stark and unforgiving. In the quiet hum of morning, as most residents stirred from their slumber, a different kind of awakening was unfolding, a rude, violent disruption that would shatter the fragile peace of their community.

It was Mrs. Jenkins, a woman known for her quiet, predictable routine, who shattered that peace. Her screams, sharp and piercing, rent the early morning air, a sound so alien to the placid suburban street that it jolted neighbors from their coffee cups and pulled them from the warmth of their beds. The screams were followed by a sickening silence, a void that was even more terrifying than the initial outcry, a silence that hinted at unspeakable horrors.

Sheriff DuCard was the first to arrive, his cruiser kicking up dust as he pulled into the Jenkins' driveway. He was a man carved from the very soil of Dry Creek, his face weathered, his eyes holding the quiet wisdom and the weary resignation of a man who had seen too much of the darkness that sometimes festered beneath the surface of ordinary life. But even DuCard, with his years of experience, was not prepared for the tableau that greeted him in the Jenkins' manicured backyard.

Young Billy Jenkins, a boy of thirteen, a classmate of Sam's younger sister, Helen, lay amidst the dew-kissed grass. At first glance, he might have appeared to be sleeping, his small body curled in a way that suggested an innocent slumber. But the stillness was too profound, the pallor of his skin too absolute. And then DuCard

51

saw it, the grotesque absence that stole his breath and turned his stomach. Billy's eyes were gone. Not just closed, or damaged, but entirely, horribly missing. The sockets were raw, empty cavities, a testament to a violence that was both brutal and disturbingly precise.

The scene was a nightmare rendered in agonizing detail. The grass around Billy was matted and stained, not with blood in the way DuCard was accustomed to seeing it – a spray or a pool – but with a dark, viscous ooze that seemed to have seeped from the very core of the boy. There were no signs of a struggle, no overturned garden furniture, no scattered objects. It was as if Billy had simply lain down and… something had reached in and plucked his sight away.

As other officers arrived, securing the perimeter and beginning the grim task of cataloging the scene, DuCard's gaze kept returning to the boy's face. He saw not just the horrific mutilation, but a chilling echo, a phantom memory that flickered at the edge of his awareness. The scarecrow. The dare. The missing buttons. It was a connection so outlandish, so deeply rooted in the realm of childhood superstition, that it felt like madness to even consider it. Yet, the emptiness where Billy's eyes had been… it mirrored, with a sickening fidelity, the vacant sockets of the scarecrow they had found in the deserted cornfield.

The horror of it spread through Dry Creek like a contagion. Whispers turned into frantic rumors, and the casual anxieties of everyday life were replaced by a pervasive, suffocating dread. Billy Jenkins, a boy who had laughed and played in these very streets just yesterday, was now a symbol of something ancient and terrifying that had been unleashed. The talk of the scarecrow, dismissed as a silly prank just hours before, now took on a terrifying significance.

The boys who had been part of the dare – Mark, Tommy, Sam – were among the first to be questioned. They sat in the stark interrogation room at the sheriff's station, the fluorescent lights casting long, accusatory shadows on their pale faces. Sheriff DuCard, his voice carefully devoid of accusation, asked simple questions, but the weight of their unspoken knowledge hung heavy in the air.

"Billy was with you last night, wasn't he?" DuCard's voice was soft, almost conversational, but it held the authority of a man who knew more than he was letting on.

Mark, his face a mask of utter devastation, could only nod mutely. Billy and Sandy stayed behind to guard the bikes that were parked on the edge of Withers Field. Mark's earlier bravado had evaporated entirely, replaced by a crippling guilt and a raw, animalistic fear. He had been the instigator, the one who had pushed them all, and now the consequences were too terrible to bear. He kept seeing Billy's laughing face, the boy's usual boisterous energy, and then the empty, gaping horror of what had been done to him. He felt as though he had personally ripped Billy's eyes out.

Tommy, his usual thoughtful demeanor replaced by a stunned, almost catatonic silence, struggled to process the enormity of what had happened. He remembered Billy's excited chatter about the dare, his eagerness to be part of the group, his wide-eyed anticipation. Tommy had seen the glint of mischief in Billy's eyes, the innocent excitement of a boy drawn into an adventure. Now, those eyes were gone. The shared transgression, the stolen buttons, the chilling cold – it all coalesced into a single, horrific truth: they had woken something up. And it had started with Billy.

Sam sat with his arm around Helen, who had been brought to the station as a witness to their outing, though her presence in the interrogation room was more for her own comfort than for any questioning. Helen, her face ashen, clung to her brother, her innocent eyes wide with a fear that was far too profound for her years. She hadn't understood the full implication of their actions, but she had felt the change, the suffocating dread that had settled over them in the cornfield. She remembered the rustling, the cold, the feeling of being watched, and now, she saw the same fear reflected in the faces of the older boys.

Kayla and Sandy were brought. Sandy sat there wide-eye and still in shock from Billy's discovery. Kayla, her hands still clammy, felt the phantom weight of the buttons in her palm. They were gone now, surrendered to the sheriff, but their absence felt like a brand. She remembered the chilling certainty that they weren't just buttons, but something more, something that had held a gaze at bay. And

Billy… Billy had been the most enthusiastic, the most eager. Had he been marked from the start? Had his participation in their foolish dare somehow made him a target? The thought was unbearable, a twist of the knife in her already fractured psyche.

Sheriff DuCard watched them, his expression unreadable. He knew this was not the work of any human being. The sheer brutality, the surgical precision of the mutilation, spoke of something far more ancient, far more malevolent. It was a violation of a primal order, a gruesome statement made in the language of blood and absence. He had seen the fear in their eyes, the genuine terror that went beyond the natural grief and shock of witnessing such a horrific event. They knew something. They had done something.

"Did you see anyone else out there last night?" DuCard asked, his gaze sweeping over the four teenagers. "Anyone near the cornfield?"

Mark shook his head, his eyes downcast. Tommy remained silent, his mind replaying the events of the previous evening, searching for any clue, any explanation that wasn't steeped in the supernatural horror that now gripped him. Sam, his voice steady despite the tremor beneath, answered for them. "No, Sheriff. Just us. The corn. And the scarecrow."

The word hung in the air, laden with unspoken dread. The scarecrow. It was the nexus of their terror, the silent witness to their transgression, and now, it seemed, the harbinger of unspeakable violence. DuCard knew he had to revisit the cornfield, to look at the scarecrow not as a discarded prop, but as a potential crime scene.

As the day wore on, the grim reality of Billy Jenkins' death seeped into every corner of Dry Creek. Parents clutched their children tighter, casting wary glances at shadows, at the rustling of leaves that now sounded like whispers of warning. The idyllic facade of the town had been ripped away, revealing the raw, exposed nerves of fear and primal terror.

The motive for such a monstrous act remained a terrifying blank. There was no robbery, no sexual assault, no apparent reason for such a gruesome display. The only clue, the only thread connecting this horrific event to the night before, was the desecration of the scarecrow. It was a chilling, undeniable link that suggested a retribution, a brutal and terrifying response to their trespass.

DuCard returned to the Jenkins' home late that afternoon, accompanied by a forensic team. The sun was beginning its descent, casting long, distorted shadows across the lawn. He stood in the backyard, the emptiness where Billy's eyes had been a constant, gnawing presence in his mind. He looked at the small, upturned face, the vacant sockets that seemed to stare into an unseen abyss.

"It's like something reached in and just… scooped them out," one of the forensic technicians murmured, his voice hushed with a mixture of professionalism and profound unease. "No sign of struggle. No defensive wounds. Whoever did this… it was quick. And it was deliberate."

DuCard knelt beside where the body had been, his gaze sweeping the surrounding grass. He noticed something then, something small and dark half-hidden beneath a fallen leaf. He carefully picked it up with a gloved hand. It was a button. A simple, black button, indistinguishable from any other. But it felt wrong. It felt… familiar. He remembered Kayla's description of the buttons from the scarecrow's eyes, the rough burlap they had been torn from. And a cold dread, colder than any he had ever known, began to seep into his very bones.

He looked up at the sky, the vibrant hues of sunset now seeming garish, offensive. The ordinary world, with its rules and its logic, felt impossibly distant. He knew, with a certainty that chilled him to the marrow, that they had not just taken buttons from a scarecrow. They had stolen something far more precious, something that had been jealously guarded. And in doing so, they had invited a darkness into Dry Creek that would not be easily banished. The gaze had begun, and its first victim was a child. The silence left behind was not the silence of peace, but the deafening roar of an ancient, unslakable hunger.

The desecration of the scarecrow was not an end, but a beginning. And the boy in the yard was just the first to pay the ultimate price for their youthful folly. The night of the dare was over, but the true nightmare had just begun to unfold. The town, once a peaceful sanctuary, now held its breath, waiting for the next chilling manifestation of the terror they had so carelessly awakened. The emptiness in Billy Jenkins' face was a void that seemed to expand, to swallow the very light from the sky, a stark and terrible testament to the fact that some doors, once opened, could never truly be closed again.

The innocence of Dry Creek had been irrevocably shattered, replaced by a primal fear that would haunt its inhabitants for a long, long time to come. The horror, he realized with a sickening certainty, was no longer confined to the cornfield; it had infiltrated their homes, their streets, their very lives, and its gaze was now fixed upon them all. The laughter that had once echoed through the neighborhood now felt like a distant, fragile memory, a ghost of a happier time before the darkness descended. The buttons, he thought, clutching the small, dark object in his hand, were not just stolen items; they were keys, and by removing them, the boys had unlocked a door to a realm of unspeakable terror, a realm from which there would be no easy return.

Billy Jenkins was the proof, the horrifying testament to the power of what lay dormant, and the terrible price of disturbing it. The weight of that realization settled upon Sheriff DuCard, a heavy, suffocating burden, as he stood in the fading light, the silence of the backyard punctuated only by the distant, mournful cry of a lone bird. The town of Dry Creek had just been introduced to a darkness far older and more terrible than any of them could have ever imagined, and its tendrils were already beginning to spread.

The oppressive stillness that followed Billy Jenkins' death wasn't a comforting silence; it was a pregnant, suffocating hush that seemed to press in on Kayla from all sides. Dry Creek, once a haven of predictable routines and familiar faces, had warped into a labyrinth of suspicion and fear. The sun, which had always seemed to bless their small town with a warm, inviting glow, now felt like an interrogator's spotlight, exposing every tremor of her unease, every flicker of her terror. She couldn't escape the feeling, a prickling sensation on the back of her neck, that she was never truly alone. It was a phantom presence, an invisible weight that settled upon her shoulders, making her breath catch in her throat. Every creak of her old house, every whisper of the wind through the eaves, was amplified, twisted into a potential harbinger of something unspeakable. The familiar comfort of her own bedroom had dissolved, replaced by an alien landscape where shadows clung to corners like predatory creatures and the moonlight painting eerie patterns on her floor seemed to hold a knowing, watchful quality.

She found herself perpetually scanning her surroundings, her eyes darting from window to window, her ears straining to decipher the myriad sounds of the night. The chirping of crickets, once a soothing lullaby, now sounded like a coded message, a series of sharp, insistent clicks that seemed to be directed at her. The rustling of leaves outside her window, a sound that had always signified the gentle movement of nature, now carried the unmistakable cadence of stealthy footsteps, of someone or something deliberately trying to conceal its approach. It was a relentless, suffocating paranoia, a constant hum of anxiety that vibrated just beneath her skin. She'd catch herself pausing mid-sentence, convinced she'd heard a sound that wasn't there, only to realize the silence was even more profound, more terrifying, because it implied the watcher was simply waiting, observing her reaction, her fear.

Tommy, too, was adrift in this same sea of unease. He'd always prided himself on his logic, on his ability to dissect problems and find rational solutions. But logic offered no solace here. The brutal finality of Billy's fate, the sheer, unfathomable wrongness of it, had shattered his ordered world. He moved through his days like a ghost, his gaze unfocused, his mind a chaotic storm of unanswered questions and chilling possibilities. He avoided the cornfield, as if the very soil held a residue of the horror they had unleashed. But the avoidance was futile. The feeling of being watched followed him, an intrusive phantom that mirrored the hollowness in Billy's eyes. He'd find himself stopping dead in his tracks on the street, convinced a pair of unseen eyes were fixed on him, a cold, assessing gaze that promised no mercy. The houses he passed, the familiar faces of his neighbors, all seemed to hold a hidden judgment, a silent accusation that echoed the terrifying truth of their trespass.

Mark, who had once been the boldest, the most reckless of them all, was now a shadow of his former self. His bravado had curdled into a deep-seated terror, a gnawing guilt that manifested as a constant twitch in his jaw, a perpetual scanning of the periphery of his vision. He'd taken to staying indoors, drawing the blinds tight, as if physical barriers could shield him from the unseen. But the feeling of being observed seeped through the cracks, an intangible invasion that left him feeling exposed and vulnerable, even within the supposed sanctuary of his home. He confessed to Kayla one evening, his voice barely a whisper, how he'd woken in the dead of night, convinced someone was standing at the foot of his bed, the darkness coalescing into a shape that was both terrifyingly familiar and utterly alien. He hadn't seen it, not truly, but the *feeling* of its presence, of eyes boring into his soul, had been so potent that he'd pulled the covers over his head, shaking uncontrollably until dawn.

Sam, ever the protective one, found himself wrestling with a new kind of fear, a fear for Helen. His younger sister, usually so full of life and unburdened by the anxieties of the adult world, now carried the weight of that night like a shroud. She flinched at sudden noises, her eyes wide and questioning, her small hand constantly reaching for his. The innocence had been stripped from her gaze, replaced by a nascent awareness of a darkness that lurked just beyond the veil of everyday life. Sam felt the same pervasive sense of being watched, but his amplified when he looked at Helen. It was as if the unseen entity's attention had been drawn not just to their transgression, but to its potential consequences, to the vulnerability of the youngest among them. He found himself constantly positioning himself between Helen and any perceived threat, his innocent brotherly protectiveness hardening into a fierce, primal instinct to shield her from a danger he couldn't comprehend.

The stolen buttons, that had been clutched in the sweaty palms of the teenagers, had become more than just physical objects; they were talismans of their folly, burning reminders of the irreversible act, they had committed. The button she surrendered to Sheriff DuCard was one from her mother's sewing kit. Kayla had kept the original and kept hers in a small velvet pouch, hidden deep within her jewelry box, yet their presence felt palpable, a constant, prickling awareness that they were there. She'd find herself reaching for the pouch, her fingers tracing the rough, familiar texture of the burlap it had been torn from, a phantom chill running up her arm. Each touch sent a fresh wave of dread through her, a visceral connection to the vacant sockets of the scarecrow, and now, to the vacant sockets of Billy Jenkins. It was as if the buttons held a memory, a trapped essence that was now actively seeking retribution.

The paranoia wasn't confined to the immediate group. It began to spread like a miasma through Dry Creek. Neighbors eyed each other with a new suspicion, the easy camaraderie of their small-town fraying at the edges. Whispers about Billy's death, initially hushed and filled with grief, began to morph into something more sinister, tinged with a dark curiosity and a growing unease. People spoke of strange occurrences, of unexplained phenomena: livestock found inexplicably drained of blood, pets vanishing without a trace, disembodied whispers heard on the wind. These were not isolated incidents, but a tapestry of unease woven from a shared, unspoken fear. The town, once a picture of idyllic suburban life, was now a breeding ground for anxieties, where every averted glance and every hushed conversation seemed to confirm the terrifying truth: something had taken notice, and it was watching them all.

Kayla found herself replaying the events of that night in the cornfield over and over, searching for any detail, any subtle shift in the atmosphere, that might have signaled the impending horror. The dare, the foolish bravado, the stolen buttons – it all seemed so trivial then, a childish prank with no real consequences. But the chill, the profound sense of being an intruder, had been undeniable. She remembered the stillness of the air, a stillness that felt heavy, expectant. She recalled the feeling of the scarecrow's gaze, a malevolent presence emanating from those crude button eyes, a gaze that seemed to penetrate her very soul. It was this feeling, more than

59

anything, that had spurred her to snatch the buttons, a foolish, impulsive act driven by a primal urge to disrupt that suffocating scrutiny. Now, the very act of remembering was a torment, each recollection a fresh surge of the paranoia that had taken root so deeply within her. The feeling of being watched was no longer a vague apprehension; it was a tangible, suffocating reality, a constant companion that whispered insidious doubts and stoked the fires of her fear.

The incident at the sheriff's station had done little to assuage her fears. Sheriff DuCard, a man who usually exuded an air of calm competence, now seemed haunted, his eyes holding a flicker of something akin to disbelief, as if the very nature of the crime defied his understanding of the world. When he had shown them the button, dark and nondescript, Kayla's heart had plummeted. It was one of them, one of the stolen eyes. The confirmation was both a relief and a fresh wave of terror. It meant the connection was real, undeniable, and the retribution was already in motion. She remembered DuCard's curt nod, the grim set of his jaw as he had spoken about the need for further investigation, and the chilling implication that this was far from over.

She started seeing things. Or perhaps, she was simply becoming more attuned to the subtle shifts in reality that others dismissed as trickery of the light or overactive imaginations. A flicker of movement in her peripheral vision, a shadow that seemed to detach itself from the wall and melt back into the darkness. The reflection in her bedroom mirror would sometimes seem to hold a second face, a faint, distorted impression superimposed over her own, as if something were peering out from behind her eyes. These were not fleeting illusions; they were persistent, unnerving intrusions that chipped away at her sanity. She would rub her eyes, shake her head, trying to dispel the images, but they always returned, more insistent, more malevolent, than before.

The paranoia had infected her dreams, transforming them into fragmented, terrifying nightmares. She would find herself back in the cornfield, the stalks towering over her like skeletal fingers, reaching out to ensnare her. The scarecrow, its ragged form silhouetted against a bruised, twilight sky, would turn its head, those crude button eyes fixing on her with an unwavering intensity. In her dreams, Billy Jenkins was there too, his face a mask of silent accusation, his empty eye sockets seeming to bore into her, a silent testament to the price of her folly. She would wake up with a scream trapped in her throat, her heart pounding against her ribs, the feeling of being watched so potent that she would lie frozen in her bed, too terrified to move, too terrified to breathe, convinced that whatever had claimed Billy was now lurking just outside her door, waiting for its moment.

The stolen buttons were a constant, tangible reminder. Kayla kept them hidden, yet their weight seemed to press down on her, a physical manifestation of her guilt and fear. She would take them out in secret, turning them over in her hands, the rough texture a chilling echo of the burlap from which they'd been torn. She remembered the desperate, almost panicked scramble to get them, the thrill of transgression quickly overshadowed by a creeping dread. And now, that dread had blossomed into full-blown terror. She felt as though she carried a brand, a mark of their transgression that made her a target. The feeling of being observed was more than just psychological; it was a physical sensation, like a thousand tiny needles pricking her skin, a constant, invasive awareness that she was not alone, that something ancient and malevolent had taken notice, and its gaze was now fixed upon her. The stolen eyes were not merely objects; they were conduits, and through them, something had entered their world, something that saw everything, felt everything, and now, it seemed, it was hungry.

Tommy, too, found himself trapped in a cycle of heightened vigilance. He would walk with his head held high, feigning a confidence he didn't feel, while his eyes constantly scanned the rooftops, the darkened windows, the tree lines. He felt the weight of unseen eyes upon him during the day, but it was the nights that were truly unbearable. Every creak of the floorboards in his house, every rustle of leaves outside his window, sent a jolt of adrenaline through him. He started sleeping with a light on, the familiar glow of his bedside lamp offering little comfort against the encroaching darkness and the gnawing certainty that something was out there, watching, waiting. He imagined the scarecrow, its crude features twisted into a silent sneer, its vacant sockets now filled with a burning, unholy light, its gaze following him relentlessly, a constant, terrifying reminder of the pact they had unknowingly entered into. The once comforting familiarity of Dry Creek had been replaced by a pervasive sense of unease, a chilling awareness that the mundane world they knew was merely a thin veneer, and beneath it lurked a darkness that was now fully awake, and it was watching.

The casualness of their childhood games, the innocent thrill of exploring forbidden places, had been irrevocably tainted. The cornfield, once a place of adventure, was now a haunted ground, a scar on the landscape that mirrored the wounds inflicted on their innocence. The boys who had dared each other that night were now bound by a shared terror, a silent understanding that they had crossed a line, had disturbed something that should have remained buried. Each of them felt the invisible tendrils of the gaze, a suffocating pressure that made every breath a conscious effort, every moment a test of their fraying nerves. They were no longer children playing games; they were prey, and the hunter was patient, observant, and utterly terrifying. The feeling of being watched was not just a sensation; it was a tangible presence, an invisible entity that had imprinted itself upon their very souls, forever altering their perception of reality and plunging them into a darkness from which there seemed to be no escape. The theft of the buttons had been a physical act, but its consequences were far more profound, a spiritual violation that had opened the door to a horror that was now meticulously, and chillingly, observing their every move.

The air in the Withers Field was thick and cloying, a tangible presence that seemed to press in on Kayla and Tommy, muffling the sound of their own ragged breaths. They moved with a hesitant, almost reverent dread, each rustle of the dry stalks a potential betrayal, each shadow a lurking phantom. The path they had so carelessly taken that fateful night now felt like a passage into a deeper, more ancient darkness. The moon, a sliver of bone-white in the bruised velvet sky, offered scant illumination, casting long, distorted shadows that writhed and shifted with a life of their own. It was a landscape stripped of its familiar comfort, transformed into a stage set for their escalating terror.

As they pushed through the final barrier of corn, the clearing where the scarecrow stood came into view. It was a tableau they both dreaded and desperately needed to see, a pilgrimage to the heart of their burgeoning nightmare. The scarecrow, Ragmouth, as Mark had picked up on the morbidly christened name, was still there, a gaunt sentinel against the indifferent night. But the Ragmouth they remembered, the clumsy, pathetic effigy of straw and tattered cloth, was no longer entirely accurate. A profound, sickening change had taken root.

The absence of the buttons, those stolen pieces of their transgression, was stark. Where the crude, dark circles had once been, there was now something else, something that defied easy description. A faint, unsettling luminescence emanated from the hollows of the scarecrow's head, a sickly, phosphorescent glow that pulsed with a slow, deliberate rhythm. It was the color of stagnant water in a forgotten well, a nauseating hue that seemed to absorb the moonlight rather than reflect it. This wasn't the warm light of life, but the cold, predatory gleam of something awakened, something ancient and hungry. The glow seemed to throb in time with the pounding in Kayla's chest, a macabre heartbeat syncing with her own mounting terror.

Tommy reached out, his hand trembling, as if drawn by an invisible, magnetic force. He stopped inches from the scarecrow's arm, his fingers hovering just above the eerie light. "It's... it's looking at us," he whispered, his voice cracking with a fear that had long since usurped his usual stoicism. Kayla felt it too, an unyielding pressure against her very being, a palpable weight of malevolence emanating from the inanimate object. The gaze, once an imagined torment born of their guilt, now felt undeniably, terrifyingly real, a focused intensity that pinned them in its unblinking stare.

But the change was not confined to the vacant sockets. A dark, viscous fluid, thicker than blood, seemed to weep from the seams of the scarecrow's burlap skin. It trickled down its straw-stuffed limbs, pooling on the dry earth at its feet, creating an unnatural, glistening stain that seemed to absorb the very essence of the surrounding darkness. The fluid had a peculiar sheen, catching the meager light and reflecting it back with a disturbing, oily iridescence. It smelled faintly of damp earth and something else... something metallic and foul, a scent that clawed at the back of Kayla's throat and threatened to send her spiriting.

The tattered fabric, too, appeared to be undergoing a subtle, horrifying transformation. The rough, weather-beaten burlap seemed to stretch and reform, the ragged edges pulling taut as if some unseen force was meticulously reshaping it. It was as if the straw within was coalescing, tightening, the very material of the scarecrow beginning to adapt, to solidify. The frayed threads looked less like decay and more like the sinews of a creature preparing to move, to unfurl. The stuffing, once loose and shapeless, appeared to be compacting, giving the scarecrow a more defined, more menacing silhouette. It was no longer a simple effigy; it was a vessel, and the emptiness was being filled.

A low, guttural sound, like the scraping of dry leaves against stone, emanated from the scarecrow's form. It was a sound that seemed to vibrate not just in the air, but deep within their bones, a resonant frequency of dread. The tattered straw protruding from its arms and legs seemed to twitch, to stir as if imbued with a nascent life. The once clumsy, dangling limbs now possessed a strange, coiled tension, a readiness that sent a fresh wave of primal fear through Kayla. This was not the random movement of wind; this was something else, something intentional, something that was awakening from a long, dark slumber.

"Kayla," Tommy breathed, his voice barely audible above the pounding of his own heart, "It's... it's changing."

Kayla could only nod, her gaze fixed on the horrifying spectacle. The innocence of the act, the childish dare, had been irrevocably shattered. The buttons had been a gateway, a catalyst, and now, the entity they had inadvertently awakened was making itself known, not through spectral whispers or phantom touches, but through a terrifying, physical manifestation. The scarecrow was becoming more than just a scarecrow; it was becoming itself, whatever 'itself' truly was. The locus of malevolent energy was undeniable, a tangible, suffocating presence that radiated from the figure in the corn. It felt as if the very air around Ragmouth crackled with a dark, unleashed power, and they were standing at its epicenter.

The transformation was subtle yet profoundly disturbing. It was the kind of horror that burrowed deep, the kind that whispered in the quiet corners of the mind, fueling the paranoia that had already taken root. The faint glow in its eye sockets seemed to follow their movements, tracking them with an unnerving persistence. The oozing fluid glistened like a dark promise, a viscous herald of whatever was to come. And the stretching, reforming fabric... it spoke of an entity adapting, preparing, its hunger beginning to manifest in physical ways. The scarecrow was no longer just a reminder of their transgression; it was a living, breathing testament to it, a terrifying embodiment of the darkness they had disturbed.

Kayla remembered the feel of the buttons in her hand, the rough texture of the burlap they had been torn from. Now, the burlap itself seemed to writhe, to absorb the darkness around it. It was as if the very material of Ragmouth was being remade, rewoven by an unseen hand, for a purpose far more sinister than mere warding off crows. The straw that spilled from its seams was no longer just decaying plant matter; it seemed to pulse with a faint, unnatural warmth, and the dark fluid that oozed from its form was a stark, undeniable sign that something fundamental had shifted. The scarecrow was no longer a silent observer; it was an active participant, and its transformation was a terrifying prelude to something far worse. The air grew colder, despite the late summer night, and the silence that had fallen was more profound than any they had ever known, a silence that felt heavy with anticipation, pregnant with an impending horror. They had stumbled upon something that was not meant to be found, and now, it was revealing itself, slowly, deliberately, and with a terrifying hunger that was etched into every stitch of its being. The night was no longer just dark; it was alive with a dreadful, burgeoning sentience, and the scarecrow was its terrifying, evolving heart.

The oppressive silence of the Withers Field continued to cling to Kayla and Tommy, a suffocating blanket woven from fear and the undeniable wrongness of the transformed Ragmouth. The phosphorescent glow in the scarecrow's hollow eyes seemed to deepen, to burn brighter, a malevolent beacon in the encroaching darkness. Kayla's gaze, however, was no longer fixed solely on the horrifying spectacle before them. A gnawing unease, a desperate need for comprehension, was beginning to override her immediate terror. The sheer unnaturalness of the scarecrow's metamorphosis was too profound, too deeply unsettling, to be dismissed as a mere hallucination or the product of their overactive imaginations. This felt ancient, something that predated their own reckless trespass. It was a chilling intuition, a cold dread that whispered of forgotten practices and slumbering powers. She needed answers, and the only place she could think of finding them was buried within the hushed histories of their small, isolated town.

Back in the hushed quiet of her bedroom, the scent of old paper and dust a familiar comfort against the lingering, metallic tang that seemed to have seeped into her very pores, Kayla poured over the contents of a battered leather-bound journal. It was her grandmother's, a repository of local lore, folk remedies, and the occasional, unsettling anecdote that had always felt more like a veiled warning than a simple story. Kayla had always dismissed some of her grandmother's more outlandish tales as the ramblings of an old woman steeped in superstition, but now, with the image of Ragmouth's pulsing, empty gaze seared into her mind, those tales felt disturbingly prescient. Her fingers, still faintly trembling, traced the faded ink of a handwritten entry, the script elegant yet archaic. The entry spoke of the land itself, of its peculiar abundance, of seasons that always seemed to yield a richer harvest than neighboring farms, and of a price that was never explicitly named, but always, implicitly, understood.

Her grandmother's writings were a tapestry of the mundane and the mystical, threads of everyday life woven with whispers of the uncanny. She wrote of the Withers family, the original owners of the land, a lineage that had seemingly vanished into the mists of time, leaving behind only the overgrown fields and the weathered, silent farmhouse. There were cryptic references to *old ways*, to appeasing the spirits of the earth, to a pact forged in a time before the town was even a name on a map. Kayla found herself drawn to a particular passage, tucked away in a section titled, "Of the Harvest and the Gaze." The words seemed to shimmer with a hidden meaning, a dark current flowing beneath the surface of the prose.

"The earth demands its due," the journal read, the ink bleeding slightly as if written with a damp quill. "And the Gaze, ever watchful, requires its tribute. For the land to flourish, for the cycle to remain unbroken, a portion must be surrendered. Not of the grain, nor of the beasts, but of the sight itself. A sacrifice of vision, a voluntary blindness, lest the land wither and the bounty cease." Kayla's breath hitched. Sacrifice of vision? It sounded like poetic metaphor, but the chill that snaked down her spine was far from metaphorical. She continued to read, her heart pounding a frantic rhythm against her ribs.

Further on, she discovered fragments of what appeared to be transcribed oral histories, collected by her grandmother from the oldest residents of the town, their names now lost to time, their voices echoing through the brittle pages. These fragments hinted at a ritual, an ancient folk rite practiced generations ago, shrouded in secrecy and fear. It was called "The Gaze Offering." The details were sparse, deliberately so, as if the very act of writing them down was dangerous. But the core of it was terrifyingly clear: the offering was not merely symbolic. It was a cyclical appeasement, a ritual demanding a sacrifice of eyes, meant to imbue the land with dark power and ensure its prosperity, but at a horrifying cost. The texts spoke of a primal entity, an ancient, hungry force tied to the very soil of the Withers property, an entity that craved the essence of sight, the perception of the world, as its sustenance.

The descriptions were fragmented, disjointed, like pieces of a shattered mirror reflecting a terrible truth. One passage described the ritual taking place during the harvest moon, a time when the veil between worlds was said to be thinnest. Another spoke of a chosen few individuals who would voluntarily offer their sight to the land, their eyes plucked out and presented as a sacred tribute. The purpose, according to these hushed accounts, was not merely to prevent the land from turning barren, but to channel a potent, raw energy into the earth, an energy that amplified growth, ripened the crops with unnatural speed, and ensured a bountiful harvest year after year. It was a Faustian bargain, a dark symbiosis where prosperity was bought with the ultimate sensory sacrifice.

Kayla's mind reeled. The buttons. The stolen buttons from the scarecrow. They had been black, smooth, and round, eerily reminiscent of eyes. She remembered the almost magnetic pull she had felt towards them, the unsettling sensation that they were somehow watching her, even before they were removed. Had they been more than just buttons? Had they been imbued with some residual energy, some echo of the sacrifices made in this very field? The idea was preposterous, yet the chilling connection was undeniable. The ritual, the eyes, the Withers land, Ragmouth... it was all coalescing into a nightmarish pattern.

She found herself poring over more esoteric texts, books on local superstitions and forgotten pagan practices that her grandmother had collected with a mixture of scholarly interest and genuine fear. There were mentions of "eye-cults" in agrarian societies, of rituals designed to appease chthonic deities by offering them the "windows to the soul." One obscure volume, bound in what felt disturbingly like human skin, detailed the specific properties of certain natural materials that could act as conduits for spiritual energy. It described how smooth, dark spheres, particularly those found in nature, could be imbued with symbolic significance, acting as focal points for ritualistic offerings. The description of these spheres, their shape and color, sent a fresh wave of dread through Kayla. They sounded exactly like the buttons she had torn from Ragmouth.

The journal entries became increasingly frantic as her grandmother delved deeper into the history of the Withers land. She spoke of a growing unease in the town, of hushed whispers and averted glances whenever the Withers Field was mentioned. There were rumors of strange lights emanating from the fields at night, of animals found disoriented and terrified, and of a recurring, unnerving phenomenon: a collective blindness that seemed to afflict a small number of townsfolk every few generations, a sudden, inexplicable loss of sight that was never medically explained. These instances, her grandmother wrote with a shaky hand, were often preceded by an unusually bountiful harvest.

Kayla's thoughts kept returning to Tommy, to his primal fear, to the way he had described the scarecrow's gaze as being undeniably real. Had Ragmouth, in his crude, straw-filled existence, become more than just a scarecrow? Had he become a vessel, a focal point for the ancient power that lay dormant in the Withers Field? The folk rite, the Gaze Offering, spoke of appeasing an entity through the sacrifice of eyes. And the scarecrow, the sentinel of that very land, had had its "eyes" – the buttons – stolen. Was this the catalyst? Had their act of petty vandalism, their youthful defiance, not just disturbed something, but awakened it?

She stumbled upon a faded photograph tucked between the pages of the journal, a sepia-toned image of a group of stern-faced men and women standing in a field of ripe corn. Their faces were weathered, their eyes shadowed, but what struck Kayla most was the unnerving uniformity of their gaze. It was as if they were all looking at something beyond the frame, something unseen. And in the center of the photograph, partially obscured by a stalk of corn, stood a figure that bore an uncanny resemblance to Ragmouth, its form crudely made, its head perhaps adorned with something dark and round. A caption scrawled in her grandmother's hand read: "The Harvest Assembly, 1923. The Gaze is pleased."

The implication was staggering. This wasn't just a local legend; it was a practice, a tradition, however abhorrent, that had persisted for generations. The Withers Field was not just a patch of farmland; it was a sacred site, a place where a pact had been made, a pact that demanded a gruesome tribute to sustain itself. And Ragmouth, the scarecrow, was intrinsically linked to this ritual, a silent guardian or perhaps even a living embodiment of the entity that resided there. The missing buttons weren't just missing; they were taken, and their absence was a desecration of a sacred pact.

Kayla's mind raced, piecing together the fragmented clues. The primal entity, the land's unnatural fertility, the cyclical nature of the

Gaze Offering, the sacrifice of eyes, and the chilling presence of Ragmouth, now seemingly imbued with a terrifying sentience. It all pointed to a horrifying conclusion: they hadn't just stumbled upon an abandoned field; they had trespassed into a place of ancient, potent power, and their actions had triggered a response. The scarecrow's transformation, the oozing fluid, the pulsing light in its empty sockets – it was the awakening of something that had been slumbering, a creature or force bound to the land and sustained by a horrific ritual.

The weight of this newfound knowledge pressed down on her, heavier than any physical burden. The innocent dare, the childish game of stealing buttons, had inadvertently reawakened a long-dormant horror. She looked at the journal, at the warnings veiled in folklore, and a profound sense of dread washed over her. Her grandmother had known. She had documented it, had tried to preserve the memory of this dark tradition, perhaps as a way to warn future generations, or perhaps out of a morbid fascination that mirrored Kayla's own burgeoning terror. The folk rite's shadow had fallen upon the Withers Field, and in their youthful ignorance, Kayla and Tommy had stepped directly into its chilling embrace. The cyclical nature of the offering, the demand for eyes, and the scarecrow's disturbing evolution, were not mere coincidences; they were interconnected threads in a tapestry of ancient horror, and Kayla was beginning to understand that they had just pulled a very significant thread. The land demanded its due, and Ragmouth, the altered Ragmouth, was the terrifying herald of that demand.

The next morning, the creeping dread that had settled in Kayla's stomach overnight had solidified into a cold, hard knot of fear. Tommy was waiting for her by the ancient oak at the edge of the woods, his face etched with a weariness that went beyond mere lack of sleep. His eyes, usually so full of a restless energy, were dull, shadowed. He hadn't slept either. They had a plan, a desperate, fragile plan hatched in the hushed hours of the night: they would go

70

back to the field, armed with a newfound understanding, and try to undo what they had done. But first, they had to meet Sandy.

Sandy arrived late; her usual vibrant energy noticeably subdued. She walked with a slight stoop, her hand pressed to her temple. Her usually bright, intelligent eyes were clouded, unfocused. As she drew closer, Kayla noticed something else – a subtle hesitation in Sandy's movements, a way she seemed to be navigating their familiar path as if it were suddenly alien.

"Hey," Tommy said, his voice raspy. "You okay?"

Sandy forced a weak smile. "Yeah. Just… a killer headache. Felt like someone was drilling into my skull all night." She winced, her hand tightening its grip. "And… things are getting weird."

Kayla's heart gave a sickening lurch. "Weird how?" she asked, her voice barely a whisper.

"It's like… the world is going dim," Sandy confessed, her voice trembling. "The colors are fading. Everything looks… grey. And I keep feeling this… this pressure. Like something's watching me. Watching me *very* closely." She shuddered, rubbing her eyes. "It feels like it's staring right into me. Burning."

The words hit Kayla with the force of a physical blow. Burning. Watching. The descriptions mirrored Tommy's terrified account of Ragmouth's gaze, the unsettling sensation she herself had felt when she had seen the scarecrow's eyes glowing. The journal entries flashed through her mind, the cryptic passages about the Gaze demanding tribute, a sacrifice of sight. It wasn't just a folktale. It was real. And it was happening.

"What do you mean, Sandy?" Tommy pressed, his own fear finally breaking through his attempt at composure. "What's going on?"

Sandy's gaze drifted past them, her eyes wide and unfocused, as if seeing something far beyond the familiar landscape. "I don't know," she breathed, her voice thin and reedy. "But it feels… like a punishment. Like we did something wrong, and now… now it's taking something from us." She gestured vaguely towards her eyes. "It feels like it's trying to take… this."

71

The chilling realization washed over Kayla in a cold wave. They hadn't just disturbed Ragmouth; they had incurred the wrath of the ancient entity that resided in the Withers Field. The ritual, the Gaze Offering, wasn't just a historical curiosity; it was an active, malevolent force that had been slumbering, waiting. And their foolish act of vandalism, their casual disrespect for something they didn't understand, had awakened it. The entity didn't just kill; it consumed. It fed on perception, on the very essence of sight. The dimming vision, the searing headaches – these were not random ailments. They were the initial stages of the sacrifice. They were being blinded, one by one, their vision being siphoned away to fuel the land, to maintain the unnatural bounty of the Withers Field.

"Kayla," Tommy said, his voice tight with dread. "The journal... what did it say about the eyes? About the offering?"

Kayla could only nod, the words catching in her throat. The journal had spoken of a voluntary blindness, a sacrifice of vision. It had hinted at a collective blindness that afflicted townsfolk every few generations, often preceded by an unusually bountiful harvest. The Withers Field had always been known for its unnatural fertility, its crops always yielding more than any other farm in the county. It was a prosperity bought with a price, a price they had now inadvertently agreed to pay.

"It's the scarecrow, Ragmouth, isn't it?" Sandy whispered, as if the words themselves were dangerous. "That thing... it felt wrong. When we were there... it felt like it was *looking* at us. Not just with those creepy buttons, but... with something else." She hugged herself, a desperate tremor running through her. "It's like it's stolen our sight. It's taking it, bit by bit."

The sheer terror of Sandy's confession, the confirmation of Kayla's worst fears, was almost too much to bear. The dimming vision, the headaches, the feeling of being watched – it was a terrifying echo of what they had already witnessed, a grim harbinger of what was to come. They had invoked something ancient and hungry, and it was now claiming its tribute. The missing buttons, those smooth, dark spheres that had so eerily resembled eyes, were no longer just stolen trinkets; they were the keys that had unlocked this ancient horror, the symbols of their transgression.

"We have to go back," Kayla said, her voice firm despite the tremor running through her limbs. "We have to try and fix this. If the journal is right, maybe... maybe if we return what we took, if we show some kind of... appeasement..."

Tommy met her gaze, his own filled with a desperate resolve. "You think it will work?"

"I don't know," Kayla admitted, the uncertainty a cold blade in her gut. "But we can't just sit here and let it happen to all of us. Sandy, are you okay to come with us?"

Sandy nodded, though her expression was still one of deep distress. "I... I think so. I can still see, just... not as well. And I want to understand what's happening." She looked at Kayla with pleading eyes. "Is this... is this because of the buttons?"

Kayla swallowed, the metallic taste of fear thick in her mouth. "I think so," she said, the admission heavy with consequence. "I think we stole something that wasn't ours to take. Something that belonged to... to whatever is in that field. And now, it's demanding its payment."

The weight of their actions pressed down on them, a tangible force. They had stumbled into a darkness far older than they could comprehend, a darkness that fed on the very essence of life. The Withers Field wasn't just a place of agricultural abundance; it was a place of sacrifice, a nexus of ancient power where humanity had struck a terrible bargain with something primal and insatiable. And Ragmouth, the scarecrow, was its guardian, its instrument, a grotesque effigy imbued with the very essence of the entity's hunger. The theft of the buttons had been more than just a prank; it had been an act of desecration, a violation of an ancient pact that had slumbered for generations.

As they walked towards the edge of the woods, the morning sun seemed to offer little warmth. The world felt muted, the vibrant greens and blues of the familiar landscape tinged with a subtle desaturation. Sandy stumbled slightly, her hand flying to her eyes again. "It's getting worse," she murmured, her voice laced with panic. "The light... it's hurting my eyes."

Kayla felt a pang of guilt so sharp it was almost physical. They had brought Sandy into this, a friend who had been uninvolved until their recklessness had dragged her into its orbit. The thought of her own sight fading, of the world slowly dissolving into a hazy, indistinct blur, was a terrifying prospect. But the thought of Sandy suffering the same fate, of witnessing her vibrant spirit dimmed by this creeping, unseen predator, was even worse.

"We'll protect you, Sandy," Tommy said, his voice rough but earnest. He reached out, his hand finding hers, a small gesture of solidarity against the encroaching terror. "We're in this together."

Kayla nodded; her gaze fixed on the distant, dark silhouette of the Withers farmhouse. The journal had offered a glimmer of hope, a cryptic suggestion that understanding and perhaps even appeasement could avert further disaster. But the reality of the situation was far more terrifying than any tale. They were up against something ancient, something that fed on the very fabric of perception. The Gaze, as her grandmother had called it, was no longer a metaphor. It was a palpable, predatory force, and it had already begun its harvest. The fear that had begun as a prickle in the back of Kayla's neck had now blossomed into a full-blown terror, a primal, instinctual dread that whispered of an ancient hunger and a sacrifice that was only just beginning. The Withers Field was a monument to a pact, and they had just been marked as the next installment.

Chapter 4

The Harvest of Fear

The bravado that had fueled Mark's dare to steal the scarecrow's buttons had evaporated like morning mist under a scorching sun. The swagger, the defiant glint in his eye, the casual dismissal of any lingering unease – all of it had been scoured away by the relentless, invisible tide of dread that now consumed him. He was, after all, the instigator, the one who had pushed them, who had dared Tommy and Kayla to trespass, who had ultimately been the one to wrench the crude, obsidian spheres from Ragmouth's burlap face. And for that transgression, he was now the primary focus of an unseen, malevolent attention.

His days, once filled with the easy confidence of a boy who believed himself immune to the darker currents of their small town, had warped into a ceaseless, suffocating vigil. Sleep offered no sanctuary, his dreams a terrifying loop of Ragmouth's vacant stare, now burning with an infernal light. He'd wake with a gasp, drenched in sweat, the phantom sensation of being watched clinging to him like a shroud. It wasn't just a feeling anymore; it was a certainty, a gnawing, corrosive knowledge that something ancient and hungry had taken notice of him.

The hallucinations started subtly, insidious whispers at the edge of his perception. He'd see them in the intricate grain of his bedroom desk, the swirling dust motes dancing in the slivers of sunlight that pierced his curtains. Each dark speck, each knot in the wood, seemed to morph, to coalesce into the smooth, round, all-too-familiar shape of Ragmouth's missing eyes. He'd blink, shake his head, try to dismiss it as fatigue, as nerves, but the images would persist, mocking his attempts to regain control. They were everywhere, an omnipresent reminder of his folly, a constant, terrifying echo of his trespass.

His own vision began to betray him. At first, it was a faint dimming, a subtle loss of clarity, as if a fine layer of dust had settled over the world. Colors seemed less vibrant, the sharp edges of reality softening into a hazy, indistinct blur. He'd rub his eyes, convinced it was a trick of the light, a symptom of his sleepless nights. But the dimming persisted, growing more pronounced with each passing hour. When he looked in the mirror, his own eyes, once a clear, bright blue, now appeared clouded, filmed over with a strange, opalescent sheen. It was as if something was siphoning away the very light that allowed him to see, replacing it with a dull, encroaching grayness.

He started to avoid looking at anything too closely, afraid of what he might see, or rather, what he might *not* see. The simple act of reading became an exercise in frustration. The words on the page swam before his eyes, blurring into meaningless shapes. He found himself squinting, straining to decipher even the largest print, a growing panic tightening its icy grip around his chest. The world, once so clearly defined, was slowly dissolving into an indistinguishable muddle.

"It's just your imagination, man," Tommy had said, his voice tinged with a forced reassurance, though his own eyes held a haunted weariness that betrayed his words. "You're freaking yourself out."

"It's not in my head, Tommy," Mark had retorted, his voice raspy, desperate. "My eyes… they feel wrong. Like they're… going out." He tried to convey the chilling certainty that gripped him, the profound, visceral fear that his very ability to perceive the world was being systematically dismantled. But Tommy, caught in his own spiraling dread, could only offer hollow comfort.

Kayla, however, had looked at him with a dawning horror, a recognition in her eyes that mirrored his own burgeoning terror. She had seen it in Sandy, heard the same hushed whispers of fading sight and encroaching darkness. The shared experience, the undeniable evidence of their collective descent, only amplified Mark's own fear. He wasn't alone in this nightmare, but the realization offered no solace. Instead, it cemented the horrifying truth: their actions had awakened something ancient, something that fed on sight, and it was now claiming its due.

He remembered their dare, the thrill of it, the sheer recklessness that had seemed so exhilarating just days before. He'd been the one to suggest it, the one to mock Ragmouth, the one to boast about his courage. Now, that courage felt like a cruel joke. He was a coward, a fool who had invited a monster into his life, and it was systematically dismantling him. The psychological assault was relentless. Every shadow seemed to hold the lurking form of Ragmouth, every gust of wind carried the rustle of straw and the whisper of unseen movement. He'd jump at the slightest sound; his nerves frayed to a breaking point. He'd find himself staring blankly at walls, his mind lost in a labyrinth of fear, desperately trying to grasp onto the fading vestiges of his sanity.

He began to withdraw, isolating himself, unable to bear the pity or the confusion in the eyes of others. Even the familiar comfort of his home felt alien, the shadows in his room deepening, twisting into sinister shapes. He would sit for hours, staring out the window, watching the world go by in a blur, a world he was slowly losing the ability to truly see. He saw the shapes of trees, the vague forms of houses, but the details, the vibrant life, were all starting to recede, replaced by a uniform, dull gray.

The fear wasn't just about losing his sight; it was about losing himself. His identity was intrinsically linked to his perception of the world, to his ability to navigate it, to understand it. Without that, who was he? He was Mark, the boy who had been so full of life, so eager to push boundaries. Now, he was Mark, the boy who was slowly going blind, haunted by the eyes of a scarecrow, a victim of a darkness he had so carelessly invited.

He tried to recall the exact moment of the theft, the feel of the buttons in his hand, the rough texture of the burlap. He'd thought they were just simple, crudely made fasteners, but now, he understood. They were more than that. They were symbols, focal points, conduits for an ancient, hungry power. And in tearing them away, he had severed a connection, a pact that had been maintained for generations, and in doing so, had drawn the full, terrifying attention of whatever resided in the Withers Field.

The constant sense of being watched was the worst. It was an oppressive weight on his very soul, a palpable presence that seemed to bore into him, dissecting him, consuming him from the inside out. He would catch himself talking to himself, muttering pleas for it to stop, for it to leave him alone. His parents, worried sick, had tried to get him to talk, to explain what was happening, but the words felt inadequate, the truth too monstrous to articulate. How could he explain that he was being punished for stealing buttons from a scarecrow, that his sight was fading because an ancient entity was feeding on it? They would think he had lost his mind entirely.

And perhaps he had. The lines between reality and hallucination were blurring, his grip on the world loosening with alarming speed. He saw Ragmouth's eyes everywhere. In the patterned wallpaper of his room, in the swirling condensation on a glass of water, even in the fleeting reflection of his own increasingly clouded eyes in a dark windowpane. They were his constant tormentors, silent witnesses to his unraveling. He was trapped in a waking nightmare, a prisoner of his own fear and the consequences of a dare gone horribly, irrevocably wrong. The bounty of the Withers Field, the unnatural abundance that had always been a source of local pride, was now revealed to be a terrifying harvest, and Mark was its first, unwilling crop.

Sheriff DuCard, a man whose boots had trod the same dusty paths of Dry Creek for thirty years, listened with a practiced, weary patience. His office, a utilitarian space smelling faintly of stale coffee and worn leather, offered little solace to the three trembling figures huddled before his desk. Tommy, his face pale and drawn, recounted the events with a desperate earnestness that DuCard found... unconvincing. Kayla, usually so composed, kept glancing towards the window, her eyes wide with a fear that seemed to bloom even in the bright, sterile light of day. And Mark, well, Mark was a wreck. DuCard had known the boy since he was a toddler, a lanky kid with a mischievous grin. Now, that grin was gone, replaced by a perpetual, wide-eyed terror, and his vision, DuCard noted with a professional eye, was indeed impaired. He looked like a kid who'd seen a ghost, or rather, one who was convinced he was being hunted by one.

"A scarecrow, you say?" DuCard leaned back in his creaking chair, the springs groaning in protest. He steepled his fingers, his gaze sweeping over them, assessing. He'd seen it all in his time. Crop blights that farmers swore were curses, livestock deaths attributed to witchcraft, even the occasional vanishing act that usually turned out to be a runaway spouse or a poorly planned prank. But spectral entities feeding on eyesight? That was a new one, even for Dry Creek. "And this scarecrow… it's alive?"

Tommy nodded vigorously, his hands clenching and unclenching on his knees. "Not alive, exactly, Sheriff. Not like us. But it's… aware. It's Ragmouth. The one old Mr. Withers used to have. The buttons, Sheriff, Mark took the buttons off Ragmouth. And now… now Ragmouth is after us."

DuCard let out a slow breath. Ragmouth. The name resonated, a whisper from a bygone era of local folklore. Withers Field had been a staple of Dry Creek's agricultural history, its unnaturally bountiful harvests a constant topic of hushed, almost reverent, conversation. Old Man Withers, a reclusive man, had been known for his unique farming methods, and his scarecrow, Ragmouth, was as much a fixture of the landscape as the ancient oak at the edge of town. Locals spoke of Ragmouth in hushed tones, a sentinel against blight, a silent guardian of the Withers uncanny prosperity. DuCard, like most of the townsfolk, had always considered Ragmouth a folk tale, a story spun to explain the farm's unusual success. A scarecrow made of straw and burlap, a few buttons for eyes – it was hardly the stuff of nightmares.

"And you three," DuCard continued, his voice carefully neutral, "trespassed onto the Withers property, took something from this… Ragmouth, and now you believe it's hunting you, causing you to… lose your sight?" He glanced at Mark's clouded eyes again. He'd already had the local doctor, Dr. Peterson, take a preliminary look at Mark. Peterson, a pragmatic man himself, had initially suspected severe photophobia, perhaps brought on by stress or an unknown viral infection. But the progression, the peculiar way Mark described the dimming, was... unusual.

Kayla found her voice, a thin, reedy sound. "It's not just Mark, Sheriff. Tommy, Sandy, and I... we can see it too. The dimming. And it's getting worse. We see... shapes. In the shadows. And we hear things. Like... like whispers, right beside us."

DuCard, a man of logic and order, saw a simpler explanation. Adolescence, he'd learned, was a fertile ground for dramatic anxieties. The recent unsettling atmosphere in town, the unnaturally early frost that had nipped at the edges of the cornfields, the general sense of unease that had settled over Dry Creek like a persistent fog – it was enough to drive sensitive young minds to overactive imaginations. He'd seen it before. A spate of minor vandalism a few years back, attributed by some to a vengeful spirit, had turned out to be a group of bored teenagers.

"Look," DuCard said, his tone softening slightly, trying to anchor them in reality. "I understand you're scared. Trespassing is a serious, but I can't have you making up stories to cover it up. This business with your eyes... it's likely stress-induced. You've been through a lot, and Mark and Sandy's condition is concerning, but I can assure you, no scarecrow is out to get you. It's an inanimate object." He paused, letting his words sink in. "The deaths... the livestock missing from old Mr. Abernathy's farm last week? That was coyotes. We found tracks. And the... the incident down by the old mill? That was likely a drifter. A drifter passing through. Dry Creek isn't a place for monsters, kids. It's a quiet town."

Tommy's shoulders slumped. "But Sheriff, you haven't seen it. You don't understand. It's not just coyotes or a drifter. This is something else. Something... wrong."

DuCard's jaw tightened almost imperceptibly. He respected these kids, or at least, he respected their parents. But their insistence on this fantastical narrative was frustrating. He had real crimes like Billy's to solve, real threats to address. He couldn't afford to chase shadows conjured by overactive imaginations.

"I understand that you *believe* that," DuCard said, his voice firming. "And I'm not dismissing your feelings of fear. But I deal in facts. What I have are three, no, four teenagers who broke the law, and two of them who appears to be suffering from a genuine medical condition that we're addressing. The rest... the whispers, the living scarecrow, the supernatural vengeance... that's not something I can act on. Not without concrete evidence. And frankly, what you're describing defies any rational explanation."

He stood up, signaling the end of the interview. "Mark, I've spoken to Dr. Peterson. He wants to run some more tests. He'll be in touch with your parents. Tommy, Kayla, you both need to stay clear of the Withers property. Consider this a warning. Don't do anything like this again."

The teenagers rose, their faces a mixture of disbelief and despair. DuCard's skepticism, though perhaps born of a need for order and a lifetime of practical experience, felt like a betrayal. It was a wall of impenetrable disbelief, leaving them exposed and alone with a terror that was all too real. As they shuffled out of his office, the stark reality of their situation settled upon them like a suffocating blanket. Their cries for help had fallen on deaf ears, their chilling account dismissed as childish fantasy. They were facing a horror that transcended the mundane, a primal fear that their sheriff, their protector, couldn't or wouldn't acknowledge. They were on their own.

DuCard watched them go, a flicker of unease stirring beneath his professional detachment. He knew the Withers land. He'd patrolled its perimeter countless times, a vast expanse of fields that seemed to swallow the horizon. There was a stillness about it, a peculiar silence that even the wind seemed to respect. He'd never felt anything sinister there, but then again, he'd never been looking for it. He dismissed the thought. It was just the harvest season, a time of change, and the kids were spooked. That was all. He had more pressing matters to attend to. The unusually high number of missing livestock reports, the unsettling stillness in the air, the way even the most seasoned farmers seemed to carry a new, indefinable dread – it was all part of the season. Or so he told himself.

But as he turned back to his desk, the faint scent of coffee doing little to dispel the lingering sense of unease, DuCard couldn't shake the image of Mark's clouded eyes. He was a man of reason, a man who believed in evidence, in tangible proof. Yet, the sheer, unadulterated terror in the eyes of those three teenagers was a kind of evidence in itself. And the silence that descended upon Dry Creek with the approaching autumn felt deeper, more profound, than any he'd ever known. A silence that whispered of things unseen, of fears unnamed, and of a darkness that was beginning to harvest more than just crops. He'd brushed them off, labeled their fears as superstition, as adolescent drama. But a small, persistent voice in the back of his mind, a voice he'd spent thirty years trying to silence, wondered if he'd just made the biggest mistake of his career. He was the sheriff, the one who was supposed to protect the town. But what if the threat wasn't something he could arrest, something he could reason with, something that could be stopped with a badge and a firearm? What if it was something far, far older, and far, far hungrier?

He picked up the phone to call Dr. Peterson again, a knot of apprehension tightening in his gut. The harvest of fear, it seemed, had begun, and he, the town's supposed guardian, was caught utterly unprepared. He wished he could believe it was just coyotes and a drifter. He truly did. But the image of Mark's eyes, those vacant, clouded orbs, refused to leave him. They were a chilling testament to a reality that was rapidly eclipsing his carefully constructed world of logic and order.

The fear in the town wasn't just a feeling; it was a tangible, creeping presence, and his dismissal of the children's pleas felt like a dereliction of duty, a blind step into a darkness he was entirely unequipped to face. He had underestimated the unsettling undercurrent of dread that had permeated Dry Creek for weeks, a subtle unease that had now erupted into outright terror for the children. He'd always prided himself on his ability to separate fact from fiction, to remain grounded in the harsh realities of rural life. But the sheer, unvarnished terror in the children's voices, particularly Mark's fragmented whispers about the loss of his sight, chipped away at his resolve. He couldn't simply dismiss it as a collective delusion. The physical manifestation in Mark's eyes was undeniable. He owed them more than a cursory dismissal. He owed them an investigation, even if it led him down paths, he never believed existed.

He looked out his office window, at the darkening fields that stretched towards the horizon, the very fields that had always promised bounty, and now seemed to hold an unspoken threat. The air itself felt heavy, charged with an unseen energy, a prelude to a storm that no weather report could predict. He realized, with a chilling certainty, that his skepticism had not protected him; it had blinded him. And in Dry Creek, in the face of whatever it was that stalked the Withers Fields, blindness was a death sentence. He had to do something, anything, to push back against this encroaching dread, even if it meant confronting the possibility that his entire understanding of the world was fundamentally flawed.

He reached for his patrol car keys, a grim determination settling over him. He would drive out to Withers Field, perhaps not to find a mythical scarecrow, but to find the truth, whatever form it took. And for the first time in a long time, Sheriff DuCard felt a prickle of genuine fear, a fear that had nothing to do with coyotes or drifters, and everything to do with the silence of the fields and the desperate plea in the eyes of the children. The pragmatic sheriff, the man of law and order, was about to be confronted with a force that operated outside his jurisdiction, outside his understanding, and outside the comforting boundaries of his rational world. The harvest of fear was well underway, and he was no longer an impartial observer. He was, however reluctantly, being drawn into its terrifying yield.

The air in the Withers Field had always held a certain stillness, a hushed reverence that even the most boisterous summer winds seemed to respect. But now, in the encroaching chill of autumn, that stillness had curdled into something far more sinister. It was a palpable presence, a heavy shroud that pressed down on the very air, making each breath a conscious effort. The corn, once a proud, golden sentinel of the harvest, had mutated into something monstrous. It grew with an unnatural, almost furious vitality, its

83

stalks thickening, their emerald husks darkening to a sickly, bruised green. The rows, usually so predictable, had twisted into a bewildering, impenetrable labyrinth. It was no longer a field for harvesting; it was a trap, a vast, suffocating maze designed to disorient and consume. To venture into its depths was to invite a slow, suffocating embrace, a gradual surrender to the oppressive density that seemed to swallow light and sound alike.

Mark, his vision now so clouded that the world was a perpetual twilight, felt the oppressive change most acutely. Each step he took into the field, a clandestine, desperate attempt to retrieve what they had so foolishly taken, was met with a suffocating resistance. The corn stalks, thick as a man's arm, brushed against him with a dry, rasping sound, like skeletal fingers seeking purchase. They no longer swayed gently; they rustled with an almost predatory eagerness, whispering secrets he couldn't quite decipher, but which resonated with a primal dread deep within his bones. The darkness within the rows was absolute, a suffocating blanket that pressed in on his dwindling sight, exacerbating the terrifying dimming that was slowly stealing his world. He clung to the memory of sunlight, of the sharp, clear lines of the world as it once was, but these memories felt like fading embers against the encroaching, impenetrable gloom.

And then there was Ragmouth. The scarecrow, once a crude assemblage of burlap, straw, and weathered wood, had undergone a disturbing metamorphosis. Its burlap skin seemed to have thickened, the rough weave taking on a more solid, almost leathery quality. The stitches that held its form together appeared to have tightened, drawing its crude features into a mask of perpetual, silent malevolence. But the most chilling alteration was its movement. Subtle, almost imperceptible at first, it had begun to shift. No longer a static sentinel, Ragmouth now swayed with an unnerving fluidity, its straw-filled limbs articulating with a disturbingly organic grace. Mark found himself straining his eyes, trying to catch a glimpse of its form through the suffocating density of the corn, a primal urge to see confirming the horrifying truth that his eyes were failing him. He imagined it turning its head, its button eyes – the very buttons they had so carelessly plucked – now gleaming, somehow embedded within its burlap visage, radiating an unholy light. The stories whispered in the hushed corners of Dry Creek, the frantic tales

84

exchanged between Tommy, Kayla, and the terrified Mark, spoke of these stolen buttons, now returned to Ragmouth, pulsing with a stolen vitality, an unholy luminescence that was the very source of the entity's growing power. Each stolen glimpse, each rustle of corn that sounded too much like a footstep, amplified the terror, confirming that their transgression had not gone unnoticed, and that Ragmouth, the sentinel of the Withers Field, was far more than a mere effigy.

Kayla, her fear a cold, constant knot in her stomach, described it as a *presence*. "It's not just a scarecrow anymore, Tommy," she'd whispered, her voice barely audible over the wind's mournful cry, her own eyes darting nervously towards the shadowed edges of the field even in the relative safety of DuCard's office. "It's... awake. And it's getting stronger. I can feel it, even from here. It's like... like the whole field is breathing, and Ragmouth is its heart." She recounted how, during their desperate raid on the Withers property, Ragmouth had seemed to *watch* them. Not with the vacant stare of button eyes, but with a focused, unnerving intensity that had sent shivers down her spine. The stolen buttons, she claimed, had felt cold, dead, when they'd wrenched them from its face. Now, she could almost picture them, re-embedded, glowing like embers in the deepening twilight of the field, each flicker a testament to the stolen sight they had so carelessly pilfered. The very act of taking them, a reckless act of teenage bravado, had apparently been an act of appeasement, an unintended offering that had infused the inert effigy with a terrifying, burgeoning sentience.

The stories Tommy had pieced together from hushed conversations, from the fearful glances of older townsfolk who remembered tales of old Man Withers and his uncanny harvests, now took on a terrifying new dimension. They spoke of Ragmouth not just as a protector of crops, but as something... older. Something tied to the very soil of the Withers land, an ancient entity awakened by the ritualistic planting and harvesting that had occurred on that isolated parcel of earth for generations. The unnaturally bountiful harvests, the whispers of Withers secret methods, they were no longer simply rural anecdotes. They were fragments of a much darker truth, a truth that involved Ragmouth being more than just straw and burlap. It was a vessel, a conduit, for something that fed on the land's vitality, and now, it seemed, on the very essence of sight, on the vibrant perceptions of those who dared to disturb its slumber. The stolen buttons, Tommy now understood with a sickening certainty, were not mere adornments; they were focal points, anchors for an unseen power. Their removal had been a violation, a disruption of a delicate, terrifying balance. And Ragmouth, in its new, terrifyingly sentient form, was rectifying that imbalance with a chilling, systematic vengeance.

Sheriff DuCard, in his pragmatic dismissal, had underestimated the sheer, suffocating weight of the fear that had gripped Dry Creek. He saw it as adolescent drama, a manifestation of the unsettling harvest season, the encroaching autumn fog that blurred the edges of perception. But for Tommy, Kayla, Mark and Sandy, it was a visceral, terrifying reality. The dimming of their vision was not psychosomatic; it was a tangible loss, a slow erosion of their world. Mark's descriptions, fragmented and laced with terror, spoke of a creeping fog, a gradual fading of color and form, as if an invisible entity was systematically snuffing out the light within him. He'd spoken of seeing shapes move in the periphery of his vision, fleeting, indistinct forms that seemed to writhe just beyond the edge of perception, always accompanied by a faint, dry rustling, like wind through dead leaves, or the whisper of straw against burlap.

Tommy, driven by a desperate need to understand, to perhaps even undo what they had done, found himself drawn back to the perimeter of the Withers Field, even against DuCard's explicit warning. The air here was thick with a cloying, earthy scent, overlaid with something else, something metallic and faintly sweet, like decaying fruit. The corn stood sentinel, a wall of impenetrable green and gold, its rustling now a constant, unnerving murmur. He felt an invisible pull, a magnetic force emanating from the heart of the field, from the direction of Ragmouth. He imagined the scarecrow standing there, its newly acquired solidity a testament to their folly, its button eyes – those stolen buttons – now glowing with an inner fire, a malevolent beacon that pulsed in time with the unnatural thrumming that seemed to emanate from the very earth. He could almost feel the stolen luminescence, the stolen sight, radiating from it, a dark energy that fueled its transformation. The stolen buttons were no longer just buttons; they were eyes that had seen the world, now turned inwards, feeding a hunger that was insatiable.

The stolen buttons, the supposed trophies of their trespass, had become a source of potent, terrifying power for the entity. Tommy, haunted by the image of Mark's fading sight, had tried to rationalize the theft, to convince himself it was a harmless act of defiance. But now, he understood. They hadn't just stolen buttons; they had stolen fragments of Ragmouth's essence, and in doing so, had gifted it the means to grow, to manifest, to *become*. The whispers among the townsfolk, the hushed conversations about the Withers Field and its unnaturally prolonged prosperity, now seemed less like folklore and more like warnings. They spoke of a connection between the Withers family, their uncanny success, and the silent guardian that stood watch over their fields. Ragmouth wasn't just a scarecrow; it was an integral part of a dark pact, a symbiotic relationship that had been disturbed. The entity was feeding, not just on the land's bounty, but on something far more precious, something that could not be regrown: the very essence of perception, the ability to see and understand the world. The stolen buttons, now embedded within its burlap form, glowed with an unholy light, a beacon that drew the encroaching darkness closer, amplifying the entity's power and its insidious hunger. The field itself seemed to pulse with this newfound malevolence, the unnaturally tall corn forming a living, breathing labyrinth, designed to disorient and ensnare anyone who dared to venture too close. Ragmouth, no longer a static figure, moved with a subtly shifting presence, its straw limbs bending and twisting with a disturbing plasticity, its burlap skin tightening, taking on a more solid, almost hide-like texture. The stolen buttons, now the glowing eyes of this emerging horror, were the focal point of its burgeoning strength, a testament to the fear it was so expertly harvesting.

Kayla's investigation was a desperate plunge into the murky depths of Dry Creek's buried past, a search for answers fueled by a suffocating guilt and a fierce, protective instinct for Tommy and Mark. The air in the town's small, neglected historical society felt thick with dust and the ghosts of forgotten lives. It was a stark contrast to the suffocating, alien atmosphere of the Withers Field, but the unease it stirred within her was just as profound. She moved with a frantic energy, her fingers tracing the faded ink of brittle documents, her eyes scanning brittle pages filled with the mundane and the monstrous. The records of Withers Field, when she could find them, were eerily sparse, almost as if the land itself resisted documentation, or perhaps, as if those who had tried had been silenced.

She started with the town census records, tracing the Withers family lineage back to its origins in Dry Creek. The early entries were unremarkable – farmers, laborers, the steady backbone of a burgeoning community. But as the generations passed, a subtle shift began to emerge. The Withers men, always listed with a certain stoic regularity, became associated with an almost unnatural agricultural success, particularly during years when other farms in the region struggled. There were mentions of "unusual yields," "bountiful harvests," and "a touch of the old ways" in scattered newspaper clippings. These phrases, innocuous on their own, took on a chilling resonance when viewed through the lens of her current terror. They hinted at something more than diligent farming, a secret woven into the fabric of the Withers land.

Deeper still, Kayla unearthed fragmented accounts of disappearances. Not widespread tragedies, but isolated incidents, often dismissed as runaways or accidents. A young farmhand in the late 19th century, vanishing without a trace during harvest. A couple, new to town, who bought a neighboring plot of land and were never seen again, their belongings left as if they'd simply stepped out for a moment. Each disappearance was a dark footnote, a ripple in the otherwise placid surface of Dry Creek's history, and each time, the Withers Field was mentioned in proximity, often as the nearest established homestead. It was the kind of correlation that would have seemed outlandish a week ago, but now, it felt like a terrifyingly solid pattern.

Then she found it – a tattered journal, its leather cover cracked and peeling, tucked away in a box marked "Miscellaneous – Uncatalogued." The handwriting was spidery and archaic, belonging to a woman named Eleanor Young, who had lived in Dry Creek in the early 1900s. Eleanor's entries began with the common anxieties of rural life – weather, crops, the well-being of her family. But a recurring theme soon dominated her writings: Ragmouth. Not *a* Ragmouth, but *the* Ragmouth. Eleanor described it as "the effigy," "the watchful guardian," and, most disturbingly, "the silent collector." Her descriptions of the scarecrow were far more detailed and unsettling than anything Tommy had managed to glean from local lore. Eleanor wrote of Ragmouth's eyes – not buttons, but small, dark stones that seemed to hold a strange luminescence in the twilight. She spoke of its ability to shift, to turn its head, to *observe*.

"The harvest this year is... troubled," Eleanor wrote in one entry, dated October 14th, 1908. "Old Man Withers claims his Ragmouth is responsible for the bounty, that it draws prosperity from the very air. But I feel a disquiet in its presence. It stands too still, yet its gaze seems to follow me. My young Thomas – he went near the Withers Field yesterday, chasing a stray dog. He returned pale as death, speaking of eyes that burned and a whisper that chilled him to the bone. He says he saw the effigy's head turn. I scolded him, told him it was the wind, his imagination. But the boy... he has not been himself since. He stares blankly, his eyes like clouded glass. He no longer sees the world as he once did."

Kayla's breath hitched. Clouded glass. Blank stares. It was chillingly familiar, echoing Mark and Sandy's own terrified pronouncements. Eleanor's journal continued, detailing more unsettling events. A local man, known for his sharp wit and keen eyesight, began losing his vision shortly after a drunken dare led him to "taunt the scarecrow" on the Withers land. He ended up blind, babbling about a figure in the corn that watched him, its gaze like piercing needles. Eleanor meticulously documented these occurrences, her initial skepticism slowly giving way to a profound dread. She began to believe that Ragmouth was not merely a scarecrow, but something else entirely – an entity bound to the land, an ancient keeper of secrets that demanded a terrible price for its protection.

Eleanor's journal entries became increasingly fragmented and desperate. She wrote of a "Gaze Offering," a ritualistic act performed by the Withers family, passed down through generations. She didn't understand the specifics, only that it involved a sacrifice, a giving of something precious to Ragmouth, a way to appease its hunger and ensure the land's fertility. "The old stories speak of blood and light," she'd scrawled in a shaky hand. "But this... this is different. It takes the *seeing*. It feeds on the very essence of sight. The harvest is bountiful, yes, but the cost... the cost is the light in our children's eyes."

The climax of Eleanor's journal was a frantic, barely legible account of a night when the Withers Field was unusually active. Strange lights, chanting, and a palpable sense of dread emanating from the property. She wrote of seeing Ragmouth move, of its head turning towards her window, its dark, stone eyes seeming to bore into her soul. The final entry was abrupt, a single, chilling sentence: "It comes for me. It has seen me, and it is hungry." After that, nothing. Eleanor Young, like so many others, had vanished.

Kayla closed the journal, her hands trembling. The pieces were fitting together with horrifying clarity. The Gaze Offering. The Withers secret. Ragmouth, not just a scarecrow, but a sentient, predatory entity bound to the land, a collector of sight, an ancient hunger personified. The stolen buttons, Tommy's impulsive act of defiance, had not been a petty theft; it had been an unwitting offering, a disruption of a long-established, terrible equilibrium. Ragmouth, robbed of its focal points, had compensated, and in doing so, had awakened a deeper, more voracious hunger. It wasn't just Mark and Sandy's sight that was fading; it was their sight, their very ability to perceive the world, that Ragmouth was systematically siphoning.

She recalled the whispers of old Man Withers, the patriarch of the family, a man shrouded in an almost mythical aura of reclusiveness and uncanny success. He was rumored to have conducted rituals on his land, to have made pacts with forces beyond mortal understanding to ensure his farm thrived, even during the harshest winters. The Withers land had a history of being both incredibly fertile and strangely cursed. It was a place where crops

90

grew with an unnatural vigor, but where people also seemed to disappear, or to return irrevocably changed, their eyes vacant, their minds lost.

Kayla knew she couldn't simply present this fragmented, terrifying account to Sheriff DuCard. He would dismiss it as the ramblings of a frightened girl, a product of overwrought imaginations fueled by local superstitions. She needed more. She needed concrete proof, something undeniable that would force him to acknowledge the monstrous reality they faced. Her gaze fell upon a faded map of Dry Creek, pinned to a corkboard on the wall. The Withers property was marked with a small, almost insignificant label, but the surrounding land was dotted with notations – old property lines, forgotten homesteads, and at least two marked locations where previous, unexplained disappearances had been officially recorded.

Her investigation took on a new, more dangerous dimension. Armed with Eleanor Young's journal and a grim determination, Kayla began to physically retrace the steps of those who had vanished. She sought out the sites of these forgotten tragedies, venturing to the overgrown foundations of long-demolished houses, to the quiet, neglected cemeteries where unmarked graves were rumored to exist. Each location was a whisper of past horrors, a testament to the land's insatiable appetite.

One afternoon, she found herself at the edge of a dense, untamed patch of woods, the supposed location of the neighboring farm that had belonged to the couple who had disappeared. The air here was heavy, unnaturally still, and the trees seemed to press in, their branches gnarled and skeletal, even in the lingering autumn sunlight. She stumbled upon a rusted metal object half-buried in the decaying leaves – a child's toy, a small, intricately carved wooden horse, its paint long since faded. It was the kind of object that spoke of innocent lives abruptly extinguished, of a family's future stolen. As she brushed away the dirt, she felt a prickling sensation on her skin, a subtle shift in the atmosphere. Looking up, she saw it – a solitary scarecrow, its form weathered and indistinct in the encroaching shadows. It wasn't Ragmouth, not the one from the Withers Field, but it bore a chilling resemblance, its silhouette a dark mockery of humanity against the darkening sky. And then, as if sensing her gaze, it tilted its head, a slow, creaking movement that echoed through the oppressive silence. A primal, suffocating fear gripped Kayla, a chilling confirmation that this malevolent presence, this *thing*, was not confined to a single field, but had likely spread its influence, its tendrils of darkness, across the Withers cursed land.

She returned to the historical society, her mind a whirlwind of terrifying revelations. The Withers family's prosperity was built on a foundation of stolen sight, of a ritualistic exchange of human perception for agricultural bounty. Ragmouth, the silent guardian, was the instrument of this exchange, a vessel for an ancient, predatory force. The Gaze Offering wasn't just a historical curiosity; it was a living, breathing horror, and Sandy and Mark were its latest victims. The stolen buttons, she now understood with sickening clarity, were not merely trophies; they were the keys that had unlocked Ragmouth's true hunger, the catalysts that had transformed a mere effigy into a monstrous collector of sight. The land itself seemed to bear the scars of these past transgressions, a silent witness to generations of unspeakable acts. Kayla felt the weight of history pressing down on her, the collective despair of all those who had suffered, who had been consumed by the Withers grim harvest. She knew, with a certainty that chilled her to the bone, that her investigation had only just begun, and that the true nature of the darkness that plagued Dry Creek was far more profound, and far more terrifying, than she had ever imagined. The memory of Eleanor Young's last, desperate words haunted her. *It has seen me, and it is hungry.* And now, it had seen them.

The edges of Sandy's vision began to fray, not with the slow, predictable dimming of age or illness, but with a horrifying, invasive creep. The once-sharp lines of the world softened, blurring into indistinct smudges. The vibrant greens of the overgrown garden outside her window bled into a muddy brown, the sharp angles of the house opposite dissolving into a hazy, indistinct mass. Panic, cold and sharp, began to claw at her throat. It wasn't just a loss of acuity; it was an active erasure, as if a vast, invisible hand were systematically smearing the very fabric of reality before her eyes. She blinked, rubbed her eyes raw, but the distortion persisted, intensifying with each frantic attempt to clear it. The world was becoming a watercolor painting left out in the rain, colors running, forms dissolving, until only the faintest suggestions of what had once been remained. The sunlight, which had always felt like a warm caress, now felt like a blinding, indifferent glare, illuminating nothing but the encroaching darkness.

Night brought no respite, only a more visceral torment. Sleep became a treacherous landscape, a gateway to nightmares that clawed at her sanity. In these dreamscapes, the burlap sacks that had once adorned the effigy on the Withers land were no longer mere sacks. They were instruments of a horrifying violation. She felt herself being dragged, her body a dead weight, across fields that stretched into infinity, the dry stalks of corn rasping against her skin like a thousand tiny, insistent whispers. Unseen hands, rough and chillingly firm, dug into her arms, her legs, pulling her deeper into the suffocating darkness. And then, the burlap gloves. They were always the burlap gloves, stiff and coarse, their texture more terrifying than any smooth, cold steel. They fumbled at her face, a clumsy, brutal pursuit of her eyes. She felt a terrifying pressure, a sickening *pop* as if something within her were being forcibly dislodged, ripped from its socket. The sensation was one of violation, of being utterly consumed, her very essence being siphoned away. She would wake with a strangled cry, her heart hammering against her ribs, her eyes wide and useless in the suffocating blackness of her room, the phantom touch of those rough gloves still lingering on her eyelids. The terror wasn't just in the loss of sight, but in the visceral, deeply personal way it was being taken. It was a theft of self, a brutal excision of her connection to the world.

Her screams, when they came, were raw and uninhibited, torn from the deepest wellsprings of her fear. They weren't the polite, contained sounds of someone in mild distress; they were primal howls of agony and terror, echoes of the unspoken dread that had settled over Dry Creek like a shroud. They were the sounds of a soul being systematically dismantled, piece by agonizing piece. Sandy's pleas for help were no longer directed at the phantom figures in her dreams, but at the empty air of her room, at the silent walls that seemed to absorb her terror without offering any solace. She'd beg for someone to stop it, to make it end, her voice cracking with the sheer force of her desperation. But there was no one to hear, no one to intervene. Her suffering was a private, agonizing spectacle, witnessed only by the encroaching darkness that claimed her vision, and by the unseen entity that seemed to feed on her every tremor of fear. The town's own silent dread, the unspoken anxieties that permeated Dry Creek, found a voice in Sandy's torment. Her escalating cruelty was a chilling testament to the entity's growing hunger, a stark demonstration of its insatiable need for what it was so systematically stealing. It wasn't just taking sight; it was taking *them*, piece by piece, until nothing of their former selves remained but a hollowed-out shell.

The blurring continued, an insidious process that rendered familiar objects into abstract shapes. The worn quilt on her bed, once a comforting patchwork of familiar patterns, became a shifting, indistinct mass of color and texture. The grain of the wooden furniture, the subtle imperfections in the plaster of the walls – all dissolved into a featureless haze. Sandy found herself reaching out, her hands fumbling in the air, trying to orient herself, to reassert some semblance of control over her rapidly disintegrating reality. She would trace the contours of objects she could no longer truly see, her fingers seeking the comfort of familiar shapes, but finding only the frustrating, unyielding sameness of the encroaching blur. The world was becoming a place of pure sensation, of touch and sound, devoid of the visual cues that had always anchored her.

Her waking hours were now punctuated by moments of profound disorientation. She'd misjudge distances, walk into furniture, her hands instinctively reaching out to brace herself against unseen obstacles. The simple act of navigating her own home had become a perilous undertaking. The sunlight, no longer a source of warmth, became a painful reminder of what she was losing. Even the brightest daylight offered no clarity, only a harsh, undifferentiated brightness that intensified the disorienting blur. She started to fear the daylight, to retreat into the dim, shadowed corners of her room, as if by minimizing light, she could somehow slow the relentless assault on her vision. The world outside her window, once a vibrant tapestry, was now a muted, impressionistic canvas, its details lost to the ever-present fog.

The nightmares, however, were the true crucible of her terror. They were not merely dreams; they were terrifyingly vivid rehearsals of her impending doom. The burlap gloves felt more real than her own hands. The sensation of being dragged across the unforgiving earth was as palpable as any physical pain. And the moment of violation, the terrifying dislodging of her eyes, was a recurring horror that left her gasping, clawing at her own face, trying to ward off an attack that was already underway. The fear was not abstract; it was a visceral, physical agony that wracked her body. She felt the tearing, the pulling, the final, sickening detachment, and the subsequent plunge into an even deeper, more absolute darkness. It was a violation so profound, so intimate, that it threatened to shatter her very identity. She was no longer Sandy; she was merely a vessel being systematically emptied, her very essence being extracted by unseen forces.

The screams that escaped her were not mere vocalizations of pain; they were the desperate cries of a soul in extremis. They were the sound of a mind grappling with an incomprehensible horror, the raw, guttural expression of a terror that transcended the physical. They were the sound of sanity fraying at the edges, of a spirit being consumed by an encroaching darkness. Her pleas for help, uttered in the suffocating silence of her room, were addressed to a void, to an indifferent universe that offered no respite, no intervention. She was alone in her torment, a solitary victim of an unseen predator. The entity, whatever it was, seemed to relish her agony. It was a predator that fed not on flesh, but on fear, on the sheer, unadulterated terror of its victims. And Sandy was providing an unparalleled feast. The escalating cruelty wasn't random; it was deliberate, calculated to inflict the maximum psychological damage. The entity was not just stealing her sight; it was stealing her spirit, leaving behind only the raw, exposed nerve of her fear.

The psychological torment was as potent, if not more so, than the physical deterioration. The constant, gnawing fear of what was happening, of what *would* happen, wore her down, eroding her sense of self. She found herself becoming jumpy, startled by the slightest sound. The rustle of leaves outside her window, the creak of the house settling – each noise sent a fresh wave of dread through her. She began to anticipate the nightmares; to dread the moment she closed her eyes, knowing that sleep would usher in a fresh wave of torment. The cyclical nature of her suffering – the waking terror, the dream-induced agony, and the lingering dread that permeated every moment – began to wear her down, leaving her hollowed out and fragile. Her world, once vibrant and full of promise, had shrunk to the confines of her own pain, a desolate landscape of fear and encroaching darkness. The entity was not just an attacker; it was a tormentor, a psychological torturer who understood the depths of human despair and exploited it with chilling precision. Sandy was becoming a living embodiment of Dry Creek's own quiet, suffocating dread, her suffering a mirror of the town's unspoken anxieties.

She remembered Mark's words, his initial confusion and terror, his attempts to describe what was happening to him. Now, she understood. The vacant stare, the fumbling, the fear of shadows – it was all a prelude. The entity, Ragmouth, was systematically collecting, not just their ability to see, but their very capacity to perceive, to interact with the world, to *be*. It was a horrifying revelation, a confirmation that the idyllic facade of Dry Creek hid a darkness that was far more ancient and predatory than she could have ever imagined. The Withers land, the cursed farm, was the epicenter of this encroaching blight, and its tendrils were now reaching out, ensnaring innocent lives. Sandy's own deterioration was a chilling testament to the entity's unflagging hunger, its relentless pursuit of its dark harvest. She was a single thread in a tapestry of stolen sight, a victim of a ritual that spanned generations, a sacrifice offered to an ancient, insatiable need. The beauty of the world was being systematically leached away, replaced by a terrifying, formless void.

Chapter 5

The Withers Legacy

The hushed stillness of the archive was a stark contrast to the tempest raging within Kayla. Each brittle page she turned, each faded ink stroke she deciphered, felt like another thread pulled from a monstrous tapestry, revealing a pattern of horror woven over centuries. Her initial inquiries, fueled by a desperate desire to understand Sandy's escalating blindness and the unsettling events plaguing Dry Creek, had led her down a rabbit hole lined with hushed whispers and half-truths. Now, deep within the dusty confines of the town's historical society, the full, terrifying scope of the Withers legacy began to crystallize. The name "Withers" had been a constant, a looming shadow over Dry Creek's past, associated with a sprawling, isolated estate and hushed rumors of strange traditions. But the reality, Kayla discovered, was far more sinister than mere eccentricity.

The Withers, it seemed, were the original architects of Dry Creek's present-day suffering. Their prosperity, the very land they cultivated, was rooted in an ancient, unspeakable covenant. Kayla found herself poring over what appeared to be fragmented journals, their entries penned in a spidery, almost frantic hand. The earliest belonged to a Craig "Ragmouth" Withers, a man who suffered from hypersalivation and used a rag incessantly to wipe his mouth was now a name that felt like a brand seared into Kayla's mind, forever linked to the primal fear radiating from Sandy's affliction. Craig Withers accounts, though cryptic, spoke of a deep reverence for the land, a belief that its fertility was not a gift, but a debt owed. He described seasons of famine, of crops withering and livestock falling ill, a desolation that had gripped his ancestors for generations. Then, a turning point. A discovery, or perhaps a revelation, that promised salvation. He spoke of the "Gaze Offering," a ritual that would bind the land's prosperity to a terrible, recurring act of appeasement.

The initial sacrifices, as Craig Withers disjointed ramblings suggested, were not human. He alluded to offerings of the land's bounty, of its purest waters, its richest soils. But the entity, whatever primordial force the Withers had invoked, demanded more. It craved not just sustenance, but a connection, a mirroring of its own existence. And so, the "offering" evolved. Kayla's breath hitched as she read Craig Withers increasingly disturbing entries detailing the selection of "outsiders," those without deep roots in Dry Creek, those whose presence was fleeting, whose absence would go unnoticed. He wrote of their "sight" being taken, a gradual dimming, a severing of their connection to the world, mirroring the land's own barrenness when the entity was not appeased. It was a horrifyingly methodical process, a slow, insidious siphoning of life and perception. The journals painted a picture of a community that, while perhaps initially hesitant, had become complicit, trading the discomfort of their conscience for the surety of full granaries and healthy livestock.

The land itself, the Withers sprawling estate, was not merely the site of these rituals; it was the conduit. Kayla found references to ley lines, to convergences of natural energies, all focused on a central point – a place Craig Withers referred to only as the "Nexus," a name that resonated with an ancient, chilling power. The Withers, in their desperation, had unearthed something ancient, something that predated human memory, and had forged a pact. They had become custodians, not of a legacy, but of a curse. The land, once a source of life, had become a prison, a feeding ground for this entity, its power amplified by the very soil that sustained Dry Creek. The cycles of appeasement, the Gaze Offering, became the lifeblood of the Withers prosperity, a grim testament to their willingness to sacrifice the innocent for their own aggrandizement.

Kayla traced the lineage of the Withers, a chilling progression. Each generation, while inheriting the stewardship of the ritual, also bore the burden of its escalating demands. The "outsiders" were not enough. The entity grew bolder, its hunger more voracious. Craig Withers descendants, driven by a desperate need to maintain their ancestral pact, turned their gaze inward. The journals became more fragmented, more desperate, hinting at a descent into madness. There were entries that spoke of "necessary sacrifices," of the "blood ties" that bound them to the land. The Gaze Offering, once an externalized horror, began to claim its own. The whispers of madness that had always clung to the Withers family, once dismissed as the product of isolation, now took on a horrifying clarity.

One particular entry, penned by a woman named Evelyn Withers, sent a wave of nausea through Kayla. Evelyn's writing was more lyrical, yet laced with a profound, chilling resignation. She described the "weight of the pact," the "whispers from the soil." She spoke of her own son, a boy barely past his tenth summer, his eyes growing clouded, his laughter fading. She described the ritual performed under a gibbous moon, the burlap, the ritualistic blinding. Her words dripped with a sorrow that was almost palpable, yet beneath it lay a terrifying acceptance, a grim understanding that this was the price of the Withers continued existence. "The land demands its due," she had written, the ink smudged as if from tears or trembling hands. "And we are its willing instruments. To refuse is to invite ruin upon us all."

The entity, Kayla realized, was not merely a force of nature or a malevolent spirit; it was a parasitic consciousness, a being that fed on perception, on the very essence of sensory experience. It didn't kill; it consumed, leaving behind a hollow shell, a life devoid of the vibrant colors and sharp edges that defined existence. The Withers had become its willing hosts, its facilitators, perpetuating a cycle of suffering that had seeped into the very foundations of Dry Creek. The land was not just a farm; it was a meticulously crafted altar, a meticulously maintained prison for a being that thrived on the stolen light of others. The Withers legacy was not one of wealth or power, but of a generations-long act of horrific devotion, a blood pact sealed with the sight of the innocent.

Kayla's mind reeled, connecting the dots. Sandy's terrifying experiences, the burlap, the feeling of her eyes being taken – it wasn't a hallucination or a delusion. It was a horrifyingly accurate premonition, a psychic echo of rituals performed for generations. Mark's vacant stare, his fumbling fear – it was the terrifying aftermath, the slow, agonizing fade into the entity's grasp. The Withers land, the site of these unspeakable acts, was the epicenter, the source from which this blight spread, its tendrils reaching out, not just into the lives of those who stumbled upon its cursed ground, but into the very fabric of Dry Creek itself. The power of the entity wasn't constant; it waxed and waned, its strength directly proportional to the fervor of its appeasement. The Withers had ensured its continued existence, its perpetual hunger, by weaving the Gaze Offering into the very tapestry of their family and, by extension, the town.

The journals spoke of a growing resistance within the Withers family itself, of individuals who recoiled from the escalating barbarity, who sought to break the pact. These were the silenced voices, the individuals whose dissent had been brutally extinguished, their own sight offered as a testament to the entity's terrifying authority. Kayla found oblique references to *unfortunates* who had disappeared, their fates never recorded, their absence a silent testament to the Withers ruthlessness in maintaining their grim secret. It was a chilling realization: the Withers weren't just victims of the entity; they were its enforcers; their lineage steeped in the blood and tears of those they sacrificed.

The very air in the archive seemed to thicken, growing heavy with the weight of the past. Kayla felt a profound sense of dread, a cold certainty that her research had placed her in a precarious position. The Withers legacy was not a forgotten history; it was a living, breathing horror, an entity that had slumbered but never truly died, its power carefully cultivated over centuries. The ritual of the Gaze Offering, she now understood, was not a singular event, but a cyclical necessity, a grim bargain struck for continued prosperity, a bargain that had corrupted an entire family and cast a long, dark shadow over Dry Creek. The current manifestations of the entity's power, Sandy's agonizing deterioration, were not isolated incidents, but the inevitable resurgence of an ancient, insatiable hunger, awakened by the Withers continued, albeit perhaps forgotten, custodianship. The land pulsed with a malevolent energy, a testament to generations of stolen sight.

The brittle parchment felt impossibly fragile beneath Kayla's trembling fingers, as if the very act of touching it might cause centuries of dust and dread to disintegrate into nothingness. Yet, what it contained was far from nothing; it was everything. The earliest records, stark and brutal in their simplicity, spoke not of prosperity or bountiful harvests, but of a gnawing, existential fear. This was the genesis of the Withers legacy, the moment the shadow first fell upon Dry Creek, a shadow cast by the desperate act of a man named Craig "Ragmouth" Withers, the patriarch who had dared to bargain with the unseen. The entry, penned in a hand that was surprisingly steady, given the enormity of the confession, detailed the 'First Sacrifice,' a term that sent a shiver crawling down Kayla's spine, an unwelcome herald of what was to come.

Craig Withers words painted a vivid, agonizing picture of a land on the brink of death. He wrote of a spring that had refused to flow, of fields that lay fallow and barren, choked by an unnatural blight that defied all explanation and remedy. Livestock succumbed to a wasting sickness, their ribs protruding like skeletal accusations. The once-fertile soil, the very bedrock of their existence, had turned to dust, crumbling and lifeless beneath the relentless sun. Famine was not a threat; it was a suffocating reality, pressing in on the Withers family, on the nascent community they had established. The whispers of starvation were louder than any prayer, the gnawing hunger in their bellies a constant, tormenting reminder of their impending doom. Craig Withers described the desperation that had clawed at him, the sleepless nights spent watching his family grow weaker, their faces gaunt, their eyes hollow with a despair that mirrored the land's own desolation. He had exhausted every avenue, consulted every learned scholar, and sought aid from every known remedy, all to no avail. The land was dying, and with it, so were they.

It was in this crucible of despair, amidst the silent screams of a dying earth, that Craig Withers discovered it. Not a hidden spring, nor a forgotten seed, but something far older, far darker. His fragmented accounts hinted at ancient texts unearthed from the very earth, scrolls bound in withered hide, inscribed with symbols that seemed to writhe with a malevolent energy. These were not the words of men, but the pronouncements of something that existed beyond the veil of comprehension, something that resided in the primal heart of the world, a consciousness deeply attuned to the land's suffering, and more importantly, to its potential for growth. Craig perceived this entity not as a destroyer, but as a primordial force, a necessary sculptor of existence, one that demanded balance, a quid pro quo that was as absolute as the turning of seasons. The text spoke of a covenant, a binding agreement to be forged, a pact that would intertwine the Withers fate with this ancient power.

The entity, as Craig understood it, did not seek mere sustenance; it craved recognition, a reciprocal relationship where its dominion over the land was acknowledged and honored. It fed on the very essence of life, not to extinguish it, but to reshape it, to channel its energy. The blight that afflicted Dry Creek was, in Craig's warped interpretation, a manifestation of the entity's displeasure, a sign that the land was out of balance, that its vitality was being hoarded rather than shared. The solution offered by these unearthed texts was not a matter of appeasement through offerings of the earth's bounty, such as the grains or livestock that had failed to satisfy the deeper hunger. Instead, it demanded a more profound exchange, a sacrifice that resonated with the very core of existence: the obliteration of sight.

The concept of the 'Gaze Offering,' as Craig termed it, was not initially a ritual of violence against a human victim, but a symbolic act of surrender, a profound acknowledgment of the entity's power over perception. The initial offerings, as Craig meticulously detailed, involved not the blinding of a living soul, but a ritualistic effacement of vision through a symbolic representation. He described creating effigies, painstakingly crafted from the finest clay and woven with the straw of their last meager harvest, their faces featureless but for two empty sockets. These effigies were then subjected to a ceremonial blinding, their vacant eyes being either gouged out with obsidian shards or covered with the rough burlap, a stark visual metaphor for the wilting and deterioration of the land.

102

Craig believed that by offering this representation of sight, they were symbolically returning a portion of the land's stolen vision to the entity, thereby re-establishing the vital connection and appeasing its primordial hunger. This act, he reasoned, would unlock the land's dormant fertility, coaxing life back into the barren fields and ensuring their survival.

However, the entity's hunger, Craig soon discovered, was not so easily satisfied by mere symbolism. The texts, unearthed from a deeper, more ominous stratum of forgotten knowledge, revealed the entity's true nature. It was a parasitic consciousness, a being that fed not on physical matter, but on the very essence of sensory experience, on the vibrant tapestry of perception that made life meaningful. It thrived on the richness of sight, on the ability to perceive the world in all its glorious detail, and it craved this not as a passive consumption, but as an active siphoning, a parasitic draining of life's most profound attribute. The initial symbolic offerings, while a testament to the Withers desperate attempt to understand and appease this ancient power, proved insufficient. The blight, though slightly abated, persisted, a constant reminder of the pact's unfinished business.

The true turning point, the moment the Withers legacy irrevocably shifted from desperate survival to active perpetration, was marked by a desperate escalation. Craig's journal entries became more frantic, the ink smudged with what appeared to be sweat or perhaps tears. He described a profound, almost unbearable silence from the entity after the symbolic offerings, a chilling void that spoke of an unfulfilled demand. The land was still suffering; the whispers of starvation still echoed in the hollows of their homes. The texts, when deciphered further, revealed a more terrible truth: the entity craved a direct mirroring, a visceral connection that transcended mere effigy. It demanded a piece of the *living* world, a conduit through which its power could be directly channeled, and its hunger satiated. The 'Gaze Offering' was not meant to be a pantomime; it was meant to be a communion, albeit a horrifying one.

The crucial passage in Craig's journal, the one that Kayla read with a growing sense of horror and morbid fascination, detailed the reasoning behind the shift to a human sacrifice. He spoke of the land as a vessel, and the Withers as its caretakers, but also as the conduits through which the land's vitality was to be replenished. The entity, in its insatiable desire to manifest its power through the land, required a direct, potent link to the sensory world, and the purest form of that link was sight. By taking the vision of a living being, they were not just offering a sacrifice; they were performing a transfusion, injecting a vital component of life's sensory richness directly into the earth, thereby empowering the entity and, in turn, revitalizing the land. The obliteration of sight was the key, the act that would unlock the land's dormant potential, binding its fertility to the Withers willingness to pay the ultimate price.

Craig's rationale was chillingly logical, if utterly depraved. He believed that the entity's power was cyclical, its strength waxing and waning with the seasons and the purity of its offerings. To ensure a consistent and bountiful harvest, a perpetual state of prosperity for Dry Creek, a continuous appeasement was necessary. The initial symbolic acts had been a test, a preliminary negotiation. Now, the true cost of the pact was revealed. The entity demanded a portion of that which allowed them to perceive the world, to appreciate its beauty and bounty, to feel its warmth and life. By sacrificing sight, they were offering the very faculty that allowed them to *experience* the fruits of their labor, thereby demonstrating their ultimate surrender and devotion to the land and the power that now governed it.

The choice of victim was, therefore, paramount. Craig's writings reveal a chillingly pragmatic approach. The first human sacrifice was not to be an act of random cruelty, but a carefully considered offering. He reasoned that the entity would be most receptive to an offering from those who had not yet fully integrated into the fabric of Dry Creek, those whose roots were shallow, and whose presence was ephemeral. The 'outsiders,' as they were referred to, were deemed the most suitable. Their absence would create less disruption, their sacrifice less likely to rouse suspicion or incite widespread dissent within the fledgling community. It was a cold calculation, a horrifying equation of social expediency and spiritual necessity. Craig believed that by offering the sight of such individuals, he was not only appeasing the entity but also reinforcing the sanctity of Dry Creek's core inhabitants, creating a protective buffer of shared sacrifice that would bind them together, albeit through a shared secret and a shared sin.

The ritual itself, as described by Craig, was steeped in an ancient almost primal solemnity. It was performed under the stark, unblinking eye of a crescent moon, a celestial witness to their transgression. The chosen individual, described only as a 'wandering soul,' was led to a pre-selected clearing within the dense woods surrounding the Withers estate. The air was thick with the scent of damp earth and decaying leaves, a fittingly somber perfume for the impending act. Craig detailed the preparation: a rough burlap sack, coarse and abrasive, was to be drawn over the victim's head, plunging them into immediate darkness, a symbolic prelude to the permanent sensory void that awaited them. The intention was not to kill, but to blind, to extinguish the light in their eyes, to sever their connection to the world.

The act of blinding was to be performed with a sharpened shard of obsidian, a tool imbued with ancient ritualistic significance, believed to hold a keen edge capable of cleanly severing the optic nerve. Craig's prose, while clinical in its description of the procedure, betrayed a tremor of the immense psychological burden he carried. He spoke of the victim's initial confusion, their terror, and then, as the burlap descended, their desperate struggle against an unseen force. The descriptions were vague, fragmented, as if Craig himself could not bear to fully recall the raw horror of the moment. He mentioned sounds – muffled cries, the frantic scrabbling of hands against the rough burlap, the sickening thud of the obsidian shard. He wrote of a palpable shift in the atmosphere, a sudden, chilling stillness that descended upon the clearing once the act was complete, as if the very air had been held captive, then released, now imbued with a new, unspeakable energy.

Following the blinding, Craig described the ritualistic preparation of the land. The earth in the chosen clearing was to be turned, its virgin soil exposed to the night sky. Into this freshly turned earth, the Withers family, including Craig himself and his wife, were to press their hands, their palms sinking into the cool, damp soil. This was the moment of communion, the transference of energy. Craig believed that by physically connecting with the earth after the 'Gaze

105

Offering,' they were acting as conduits, channeling the residual energy released from the extinguished sight into the land itself. This, he wrote, was the critical juncture, the moment the pact was sealed, the entity's hunger temporarily sated, and the land's latent power awakened. He described a faint, almost imperceptible tremor that ran through the ground, a subtle thrumming that seemed to emanate from the very heart of the earth, a silent acknowledgment from the entity of the Withers devotion and the efficacy of their sacrifice.

The consequences were immediate and profound. Craig's journal entries spoke of a miraculous transformation that began to unfold in the days and weeks that followed. The spring, once choked and stagnant, began to flow with renewed vigor, its waters clear and pure. The blighted fields, touched by the Withers hands after the sacrifice, showed signs of life, tentative green shoots pushing their way through the earth. The livestock, previously wasting away, began to regain their strength, their coats growing glossy and healthy. The famine that had threatened to engulf them receded, replaced by an abundance that seemed almost miraculous. The Withers, once on the precipice of oblivion, found themselves not just surviving, but thriving. Their harvests were plentiful, their livestock robust, and their prosperity grew with each passing season, a direct testament to the power of the pact they had forged.

However, this newfound prosperity came at a terrible cost, a cost that Craig, in his desperation, had either downplayed or rationalized away. The *wandering souls* whose sight had been extinguished were never heard from again. Their fate was a silent, unacknowledged stain upon the Withers legacy. The act of blinding, though intended to be an obliteration of vision, was a violation that resonated deeply, a theft of a fundamental human experience. While the land flourished, a darkness had been irrevocably sown into the Withers own existence, a secret that would bind future generations to a cycle of horrifying necessity. The *First Sacrifice* was not an end, but a beginning, the terrifying genesis of a tradition that would ensure Dry Creek's survival, but at the expense of innocent lives and the very essence of human perception. The pact had been made, and its tendrils, as Kayla was now horrifyingly aware, had already begun to spread, weaving a tapestry of darkness that would ensnare them all.

The curse, Kayla understood with a sickening lurch of her stomach, wasn't a localized affliction. It was a blight that had seeped from the very earth Craig had so desperately sought to invigorate, a parasitic tendril that had wrapped itself around the entirety of Dry Creek. The Withers family were merely the first to feel its chilling embrace, the architects of a pact that had, in turn, enslaved them. The entity, once invoked, once fed, had become an insatiable parasite, its hunger for sensory experience, specifically sight, a voracious maw that would never truly be sated. This realization struck her with the force of a physical blow, explaining the pervasive undercurrent of melancholy that had always seemed to cling to Dry Creek, a quiet desolation that most dismissed as rural malaise. It wasn't just the Withers who bore the burden of the past; it was the entire town, whether they knew it or not.

She recalled the hushed conversations, the local folklore that spoke of "bad luck" befalling certain families, of unexplained disappearances, of a general air of weariness that settled over the community like a perpetual twilight. These weren't random occurrences. They were echoes, ripples spreading outward from the original transgression, a psychic residue left by the constant, unseen siphoning of vitality. The entity, dormant for periods, had clearly been reawakened, its dormant hunger stirred by some new provocation, some disturbance of the dark balance that Craig had so painstakingly, and horrifyingly, established. Kayla felt a profound, terrifying kinship with Craig, not in his act, but in his understanding of the deep, interconnected nature of their predicament. He had initiated a cycle, and that cycle, once set in motion, could not simply be stopped. It could only be perpetuated, or perhaps, eventually, broken.

The land itself seemed to bear witness to this enduring truth. The soil, while fertile, carried a subtle, almost imperceptible chill, even on the warmest days. The trees, though verdant, often bore a strangely gaunt appearance, their branches reaching out like skeletal fingers towards a sky that, to Kayla's newly awakened senses, seemed perpetually veiled in a thin, grey haze. The flora, too, seemed to possess a muted vibrancy, their colors less saturated, their scents less potent than they should have been. It was as if the very essence of their sensory appeal had been diluted, a part of their vitality siphoned off, never to be returned. She remembered how her grandmother, a woman of deep intuition and quiet observations, had always spoken of the woods with a certain reverence, but also a hint of apprehension. "There's a stillness in these woods," she'd say, her voice a low murmur, "a stillness that watches." Kayla had never understood the true weight of those words until now. The stillness wasn't peace; it was anticipation.

The entity's parasitic nature manifested in subtler, yet more insidious ways as well. The townsfolk, though generally healthy, possessed a certain lack of zest, a subdued vitality that was difficult to pinpoint. Their laughter, when it came, often felt fragile, as if easily broken. Their joys seemed tempered, their sorrows prolonged. It was as if a vital spark, the very effervescence of life, had been diminished. This was the curse extending beyond the physical, into the emotional and spiritual well-being of everyone who lived within Dry Creek's shadowed embrace. They were all, in a way, living on borrowed light, their own inner radiance subtly dimmed to feed an ancient, unseen hunger. The shared melancholy wasn't a demographic inevitability; it was a communal inheritance, a psychic inheritance passed down through generations, a silent acknowledgment of the sacrifice that had been made to ensure their very existence.

Kayla thought of the local artists, the few who had tried to capture the essence of Dry Creek, their paintings and sculptures often imbued with a haunting beauty, but also a pervasive sense of unease. Their work, while technically proficient, frequently lacked the vibrant spark that defined true artistic expression, as if the raw material of inspiration itself had been leached of its most potent colors. They were attempting to capture a world that was, in essence, muted, and their art reflected that muted reality. Even the local fauna seemed to exhibit a certain timidity, the birds' songs less jubilant, the deer more skittish, their senses heightened, perhaps, to perceive the unseen currents of dread that permeated the very air they breathed. It was a town perpetually holding its breath, waiting for the next quiet catastrophe.

The realization that the curse wasn't confined to the Withers bloodline was a heavy one, but it also brought a strange sense of clarity. It meant that the responsibility, the burden of understanding, perhaps even the potential for breaking the cycle, didn't solely rest on her shoulders as the last of the direct Withers line. It extended to every soul within Dry Creek, to every life that had unknowingly been touched by Craig "Ragmouth" Withers desperate bargain. The entity, a being of immense, ancient power, had woven itself into the very fabric of their lives, a dark thread running through the tapestry of their existence. And like any parasite, its influence grew, its demands insatiable, its reach ever widening.

She revisited Craig's journals, poring over his increasingly erratic entries, seeking any hint, any clue that might illuminate a path forward. He had written of the "symbiotic relationship," a term he used with disturbing frequency, as if attempting to rationalize the horror by cloaking it in the language of mutual benefit. But the benefit was one-sided, a grotesque imbalance. The land was replenished, yes, but at the cost of individual sensory experience, a cost paid by those who were most vulnerable, most easily overlooked. The Withers family had become, in Craig's own words, "custodians of the land's vitality," a title that now sounded chillingly like "keepers of the sacrifice."

The concept of the 'Gaze Offering' had been a terrible innovation, a perversion of a natural cycle. Craig had believed he was offering a symbolic representation, a mere effigy, but the entity, in its ancient wisdom and primal hunger, had understood the true meaning. It craved the genuine, the raw, the intensely felt. And what was more intensely felt than the act of seeing, of perceiving the world in all its breathtaking, terrifying detail? The entity didn't just want to be acknowledged; it wanted to *experience* through others, to siphon the richness of perception, to live vicariously through the eyes of those it consumed. This was the true horror of the curse: it wasn't just about blindness; it was about the theft of connection, the severing of a fundamental way in which humans interacted with and understood their world.

Kayla felt a surge of anger, hot and sharp, at Craig's justifications. He had convinced himself that he was acting for the greater good, for the survival of his family and his community. But in doing so, he had unleashed something far more terrible than starvation. He had unleashed a spiritual decay, a slow erosion of the very essence of what it meant to be alive. The *First Sacrifice* was not an isolated incident; it was the beginning of a lineage of terror, a tradition that had been meticulously maintained, its bloody origins carefully concealed beneath layers of prosperity and communal amnesia. The whispers of the land were not prayers of gratitude; they were the silent screams of the stolen senses, echoing through the generations.

The weight of this inheritance pressed down on Kayla, a palpable pressure in her chest. She was not merely a descendant of Craig; she was a potential link in the chain, a guardian of a secret that was both a curse and a responsibility. The dormant darkness of Dry Creek had been stirred, and its awakening was tied to the very survival of the town. The unexplained misfortunes, the pervasive melancholy, the subtle draining of vitality – these were not isolated incidents but symptoms of a deeper affliction, a chronic condition that had been managed, appeased, but never cured. The entity was a patient that demanded constant attention, and the Withers, by their very lineage, were the designated caregivers.

The history was not merely a narrative of the past; it was a prophecy, a roadmap to the present and the future. The entity's insatiable nature meant that the appeasement would never truly end. It would always demand more, always seek to expand its dominion, always push the boundaries of its parasitic consumption. Kayla understood now why the old stories, the fragmented tales of the Withers grim devotion to the land, had always held a sense of foreboding. They were not merely cautionary tales; they were acknowledgments of a truth that had been buried deep, a truth that was now surfacing, demanding to be confronted. The Withers legacy was not one of prosperity, but of perpetual, bloody stewardship. And the cost of that stewardship was the light in the eyes of the innocent. The cycle had begun with Craig, and Kayla, holding the brittle parchment, knew with chilling certainty that it was far from over. The darkness had merely been waiting for its moment to return.

The humid air, thick with the scent of drying hay and something else, something vaguely metallic and earthy, pressed against Kayla as she approached the dilapidated farmhouse. It sagged like an old man's weary shoulders, the paint peeling in long, mournful strips, revealing weathered wood beneath. This was the home of Old Man Hemlock, a name whispered with a mixture of pity and suspicion in Dry Creek. His family, the Hemlocks, had been peripheral figures in the Withers orbit for generations, their farms bordering the vast, shadowed expanse of the Withers estate, touching the fringes of its disquieting influence. They were the watchers from the periphery, the ones who saw the faint flickers of strangeness that the core townsfolk, blinded by comfort or ignorance, never registered.

Kayla's heart hammered a nervous rhythm against her ribs. She'd heard the stories about Hemlock – that he was a hermit, a madman, a repository of the town's forgotten fears. But he was also, according to the hushed conversations she'd overheard at the general store, the last one who might remember the *before* of the Withers, the time before the shadows grew so long, before the peculiar stillness settled over Dry Creek like a shroud. He was, if the whispers held any truth, a living archive of the land's deepest secrets, secrets passed down not in written word, but in the ingrained memory of those who lived closest to the precipice.

The front door, a warped slab of oak, creaked open before she even had a chance to knock. A figure, stooped and skeletal, stood framed in the gloom, his face a roadmap of wrinkles carved by sun and hardship. His eyes, sunken deep within their sockets, were the color of weak tea, but held a startling, sharp clarity, like chips of flint. He wore overalls patched with a dozen different shades of denim, and his hands, gnarled like ancient roots, clutched a worn walking stick fashioned from a branch of hawthorn.

"You're the Withers girl," he stated, his voice a dry rasp, like leaves skittering across a dusty road. It wasn't a question. He knew. How did he know? The Withers name, even now, carried a weight, a subtle recognition that transcended the generations.   Kayla nodded, a lump forming in her throat. "Yes. My name is Kayla. Kayla Withers. Although I must admit we are part of the Withers that they want to forget. More or less, the less fortunate ones."

He grunted, a sound that might have been agreement or dismissal. "Figured. Ain't nobody else comes out this way. Not no more." He stepped aside, gesturing her into the dim interior with a slow, deliberate movement of his head. The air inside was close, thick with the smell of dust, dried herbs, and something faintly animalistic. The single window was so coated in grime that it offered only a murky, diffused light. Cobwebs draped the corners like forgotten lace.

"Come in, then," he said, his eyes never leaving her face. "Don't stand there letting the good air out."

She stepped across the threshold, the floorboards groaning under her weight. The room was sparsely furnished: a rough-hewn table, two chairs, a sagging armchair by a cold hearth, and shelves crammed with jars filled with unidentifiable substances. It was a life pared down to its essentials, a testament to a man who had, perhaps, seen too much to cling to the fripperies of the world.

"I... I came to ask about the Withers family," Kayla began, her voice faltering slightly under his unwavering gaze. "And about... about the land."

Hemlock shuffled to one of the chairs and sank into it with a sigh that seemed to carry the weight of centuries. He reached for a chipped enamel mug on the table, filled it from a jug of murky water, and took a slow, deliberate sip. "The land," he repeated, his eyes distant. "Always comes back to the land, don't it? Especially this patch."

He set the mug down with a soft clink. "My people. They were here before your people got... interesting. We scratched a living from the edges, always keeping a respectful distance. We learned early on that some places... some places are best left undisturbed."

Kayla leaned forward, her entire being focused on his words. "Disturbed by what, Mr. Hemlock?"

He chuckled, a dry, brittle sound. "By the things that the land keeps. The things that sleep. The things that wake." He gestured with his walking stick, the hawthorn tip tapping a silent rhythm on the dusty floorboards. "You people, you always reached too far. Craig Ragmouth Withers, he was the worst. Reached so far, he broke somethin' that oughta stayed broke."

"Ragmouth the scarecrow?" Kayla prompted, her voice barely a whisper. Craig Ragmouth Withers, her ancestor, the one who had initiated the pact.

"He thought he was planting. Feeding. What he was really doing was… inviting." Hemlock's eyes narrowed, his gaze sharpening. "We saw things, back then. Things you wouldn't believe."

He paused, as if gathering his thoughts, or perhaps bracing himself against a memory too heavy to bear. "My grandfather, he'd tell stories. Late at night, when the wind was just right, moaning through the pines. He'd talk about the lights. Eerie lights, he called 'em. Not like fireflies, not like lightning. These lights… they pulsed. Greenish, bluish. Dancing in the cornfields, out towards the Withers place. Always in the Withers place."

Kayla felt a prickle of unease crawl up her spine. Lights in the cornfield. It echoed fragmented tales her own grandmother had alluded to; tales she'd dismissed as fanciful ramblings.

"He said they were not of this world," Hemlock continued, his voice dropping lower, a conspiratorial murmur. "Said they were the eyes of something that watched. And when those lights were brightest, people disappeared."

Disappearances. Dry Creek had a history of them, hushed up, chalked up to wanderlust or unfortunate accidents. But what if they weren't accidents? What if they were… offerings?

"Disappeared?" Kayla repeated, her voice catching. "Who disappeared?"

"Folks who strayed too close," Hemlock said, his gaze unfocused now, fixed on some distant, horrifying tableau. "Travelers who lost their way. Even some from Dry Creek, if they were foolish enough to go looking for trouble near the Withers woods. They'd go into the fields, chasing after those lights, or maybe just curious about the... the quiet. And they'd never come back."

He took another sip of water, his hand trembling slightly. "My grandfather, he swore he saw a man, a farmer from the next county over, walking towards the Withers property one evening, just as the sun was setting. He was a tall man, with a kind face. Never seen him again. Just... gone. Like he'd walked into a mist and vanished."

The image was chilling. A man simply ceasing to exist.

"He also spoke of the scarecrow," Hemlock added, his voice tightening. "The one that Craig Ragmouth... he had it made special, they say. Taller than any man, made from Craig Ragmouth's own clothes, stuffed with... well, no one knew for sure what it was stuffed with. But it stood sentinel. Right at the edge of the main field, closest to the house. It was a focal point, my grandfather always said. A guardian known as Ragmouth."

A guardian. The word resonated with a sinister undertone. What was it guarding? And from whom?

"He said the scarecrow... it wasn't just straw and rags," Hemlock continued, his eyes widening slightly as the memory resurfaced. "He said it was... watching. And that people sometimes saw it move. Not swaying in the wind, no. Moving with purpose. Turning its head. Its stitched-on smile... it wasn't a smile. It was a rictus. A hungry grin."

Kayla's breath hitched. The scarecrow Ragmouth. She remembered seeing a sketch of it in Craig's journal, a crudely drawn figure that had always unsettled her. She'd dismissed it as a product of his declining sanity. But now...

"My grandfather believed," Hemlock's voice was barely audible, "that the scarecrow was the anchor. The point where the land's... hunger... focused. He said if you disturbed it, if you took anything from it, if you even looked at it too long with ill intent, the land would claim you. Or worse."

"Worse?" Kayla's mind raced. What could be worse than disappearing?

"It would take something from you," Hemlock said, his gaze piercing. "Not your life, not at first. It would take… a piece of your sight. A sliver of your senses. You'd start to see things wrong. Colors would fade. Shadows would deepen. You'd lose the ability to truly see the beauty in things. It was the land's way of taking payment. A slow, creeping blindness. A blindness that wasn't just in the eyes, but in the soul."

The entity's hunger for sight. It was not a metaphor. It was literal. Craig Withers had tethered it, somehow, to this… this effigy.

"The Withers family," Hemlock said, his voice now laced with a grim understanding, "they were the keepers of that anchor, weren't they? Bound to it, whether they knew it or not. Craig Ragmouth Withers, he must have understood. He must have known what he was unleashing, or perhaps, what he was appeasing."

He coughed, a dry, rasping sound that wracked his frail body. "My father, he told me, 'Hemlock, stay away from the Withers land. Stay away from their fields. And whatever you do, never look too closely at the things that stand still when they ought to be moving.' He was talking about that scarecrow; I know it now."

Kayla's mind was a whirlwind of terror and dawning comprehension. The unsettling stillness of Dry Creek, the muted colors, the pervasive melancholy – it all began to make a horrifying kind of sense. It wasn't just a general malaise; it was a symptom of a localized, and yet widespread, sensory starvation. The Withers legacy was not one of prosperity, but of a desperate, horrifying pact. And Craig Ragmouth Withers, in his attempts to placate or control, had created a monstrous focal point.

"Did you ever… see the scarecrow yourself?" Kayla asked, her voice hoarse.

Hemlock closed his eyes for a long moment. When he opened them, there was a profound sadness etched into them. "Once. As a boy. My father was sick, and we needed to get some herbs from the woods that bordered the Withers land. I was curious, I admit it. I crept closer than I should have. The sun was low, casting long shadows. And I saw it. Standing at the edge of the field. It was... immense. Taller than my father ever was. And it seemed to... lean. Not with the wind. It seemed to lean towards me."

He swallowed, his Adam's apple bobbing. "I didn't see anything move, not exactly. But there was a... a presence. A coldness that had nothing to do with the evening air. And then, just for a second, I thought its head... just its head... it turned. Towards me. And the grin... oh, that grin. It was carved into the burlap, but it looked too real. Too wide. Too hungry."

He shivered, despite the stuffy warmth of the room. "I ran. Ran faster than I'd ever run in my life. And when I got home, my father was worse. And for weeks after, everything looked... dimmer. The sky wasn't as blue. The grass wasn't as green. It took a long time for the colors to come back. A very long time."

The admission hung in the air, heavy and suffocating. This was it. The physical manifestation of the curse, passed down through the generations, whispered in hushed tones around the firesides of Dry Creek. The Withers secret was a tapestry woven with fear, sacrifice, and the chilling reality of a hungry, unseen entity tethered to their land.

"And the lights, Mr. Hemlock?" Kayla pressed, needing to understand the full extent of this nightmare. "The lights in the cornfield?"

"My grandfather said they were not lights at all, not really," Hemlock explained, his voice weary. "He said they were the *absence* of sight. The places where something had been, and then... wasn't. Like afterimages burned into the world. And they were always strongest when the entity was... fed. When it was satisfied. Or when it was looking for more."

He looked directly at Kayla, his ancient eyes filled with a depth of sorrow that seemed to encompass all the unspoken tragedies of Dry Creek. "You Withers... you're tied to it. Always have been. Craig Ragmouth, he didn't start it, not really. But he sure as hell

116

amplified it. He gave it a focus. A point of entry. And that scarecrow..." He shook his head slowly. "That scarecrow, Ragmouth is the heart of it all. A dark heart beating in the soil."

Kayla felt a profound, chilling certainty settle over her. The Withers legacy wasn't just a history of eccentricities or misfortunes. It was a burden of immense, terrifying proportion. Craig Ragmouth's pact, his desperate attempt to secure his family's future, had instead damned them, and by extension, the entire town, to a slow, sensory decay, feeding an insatiable hunger that was rooted in the very soil of Dry Creek. The scarecrow, the eerie lights, the disappearances – they were all pieces of a single, horrific puzzle, a puzzle that pointed to a truth far more ancient and malignant than she had ever imagined. The farmer's secret wasn't just a secret; it was a curse, etched into the land, and now, it seemed, it had found its way back to a Withers door.

Hemlock's words, each one a carefully placed stone in a path leading to an abyss, solidified Kayla's dread. The entity's hunger wasn't for mere flesh or spirit; it was a more insidious, more fundamental craving. "It doesn't just take a life," he rasped, his voice rough as sandpaper, "it consumes the *sight*. It drinks it in, like a parched throat drinking cool water. And it uses it to make itself... whole. Or at least, more whole than it was before."

He leaned forward, his sunken eyes fixing on Kayla with an intensity that belied his frail frame. "Craig Ragmouth, in his ignorance, or maybe his desperation, he'd found a way to feed it. And the scarecrow... it wasn't just a marker. It was a conduit. A focal point for that hunger. Each life taken, each pair of eyes stolen, it wasn't just a sacrifice. It was a *repair*. It was like the entity was rebuilding itself, using the stolen senses to mend its own fractured existence."

Kayla swallowed, the dry air in the small cottage suddenly feeling suffocating. "Repair? What do you mean, 'repair'?"

"Think of it like this," Hemlock said, his gaze drifting, as if watching an unseen spectacle unfold before him. "The entity, it's... incomplete. It's a shadow, a void. But sight, the very act of seeing, of perceiving the world – that's a powerful force. It's what anchors

117

us to reality. When it took those eyes, it wasn't just taking them for its own consumption. It was grafting them onto itself, in a manner of speaking. Making the scarecrow more aware. Sharper. Able to perceive more, to *gaze* more intently."

He traced a gnarled finger along the rim of his mug. "My grandfather, he called it the 'Gaze Offering.' A gruesome name but fitting. It was an offering of sight, perpetually renewed. The scarecrow, being the anchor; it became the receiver. With every stolen glance, every stolen flicker of light caught in a victim's eye, the scarecrow grew. Its awareness expanded. It wasn't just a silent sentinel anymore. It was a predator, made more cunning, more potent, by the very essence of those it had consumed."

The image was horrific. A scarecrow, not just a construct of straw and burlap, but a living, growing thing, fed by the stolen visions of the lost. Each empty socket left behind was a source of power for this monstrous effigy. "So, the more people disappeared," Kayla murmured, the thought chilling her to the bone, "the more 'aware' the scarecrow became?"

"Precisely," Hemlock confirmed, his voice dropping to a near whisper. "It learned. It adapted. The entity, through the scarecrow, became a more refined hunter. It understood the patterns of the land, the habits of its prey. It wasn't just random chance that people wandered into its grasp. It was a calculated acquisition. The entity was refining its methods, using the stolen eyes to see the world through its victims' perspectives, learning their weaknesses, their fears."

He paused, a heavy silence settling between them, punctuated only by the ticking of a grandfather clock in the corner, each tick a slow, deliberate beat of a dead heart. "My grandfather told me that during times of great harvest, or when the Withers family experienced some significant change – a birth, a death, a significant undertaking – the entity would demand a more potent offering. And with each offering, the scarecrow would seem to… ripen. Its silhouette would grow more defined, its stitched-on smile more pronounced. People would talk of it looking less like a scarecrow and more like a *figure*. A figure that seemed to watch them, even from a distance."

Kayla felt a cold sweat prickle her skin. She'd always felt an unseen presence around the Withers property, a prickling sensation on her skin, the feeling of being watched. Now she understood why. It wasn't a vague, generalized unease; it was the amplified awareness of a meticulously crafted predator, its gaze sharpened by the stolen perceptions of countless souls. Craig Ragmouth had indeed sown the seeds of something unspeakable, a cycle of consumption that perpetuated itself, strengthening its hold with every life extinguished and every glimpse stolen.

"It's a cycle, you see," Hemlock continued, his voice gaining a somber cadence. "The entity hungers. It takes sight. It uses that sight to become more effective at taking more sight. The scarecrow is the embodiment of that cycle. It's the monument to its hunger. And the Withers family... they were its gardeners. Tending to this gruesome harvest."

He looked at Kayla, his gaze surprisingly steady. "You carry the Withers name, girl. That name is bound to this land, and to what resides within it. Craig Ragmouth didn't just dabble; he plunged headfirst into this. He wanted power, or protection, or whatever it was that drove him. But he created something that fed on more than just life. It fed on the very essence of perception. And that, that is a hunger that can never truly be sated. It just... grows."

Kayla felt a sickening lurch in her stomach. The thought of her ancestors, her lineage, being so intimately involved in such a horrifying perpetuation of suffering was almost unbearable. The story of the Withers wasn't a tale of success or even eccentricity. It was a narrative of a Faustian bargain, a pact sealed with stolen light, a legacy of predation masked by the placid surface of Dry Creek. Craig Ragmouth's journal, with its fragmented entries and cryptic warnings, now made a terrifying kind of sense. He hadn't been descending into madness; he had been grappling with a monstrous truth, a truth he'd tried to control, and in doing so, had amplified its reach. The "eyes" he'd written about were not metaphorical; they were literal, harvested and repurposed, fueling a parasitic existence rooted in the very soil of their ancestral lands. The scarecrow, that grotesque sentinel, was not merely a symbol, but the pulsating, living heart of this macabre cycle. The quiet of Dry Creek wasn't peace; it was the hushed awe of something ancient and hungry, a hunger amplified, refined, and made terrifyingly aware by the Gaze Offering, a perpetual consumption of sight, an unending demand that bound the Withers, and by extension, the entire town, in a web of chilling interdependence. The farmer's secret was no longer just a secret; it was a curse, woven into the fabric of existence, and now, it had come to reclaim its own.

Chapter 6

The Second Harvest

The world had ceased to be a place of tangible forms for Mark. It had dissolved, collapsing into a churning, suffocating vortex of pure, unadulterated darkness. The few fleeting moments of lucidity that still flickered within him were not glimpses of reality, but shards of a nightmare made manifest. Before his eyes, or rather, where his eyes used to truly see, he perceived only the grotesque silhouette of the scarecrow. It was no longer a static effigy in a distant field; it was everywhere. It loomed in the suffocating blackness, its straw-stuffed limbs seeming to writhe with an unseen life, its burlap face a rictus of vacant hunger. And within that vacant hunger, Mark saw them – a thousand, a million, a ceaseless cascade of eyes. They were not the eyes of the living, nor the dead, but something in between, shards of stolen light, each one a tiny, burning ember reflecting his own terror. They swirled and coalesced, forming the vacant sockets of the scarecrow, filling them with a borrowed, malevolent awareness.

He tried to scream, to push back against the encroaching void, but no sound emerged. His throat felt impossibly tight, choked with the dust of his own dissolving senses. His lips moved, forming guttural, incomprehensible sounds, a desperate attempt to articulate the horrors that clawed at the edges of his consciousness. "Eyes… so many eyes… they watch… they see…" he mumbled, the words a broken river of dread flowing from him. The darkness was not an absence of light; it was a presence, heavy and suffocating, a palpable entity that pressed in on him from all sides, stealing his breath, his thoughts, his very sense of self.

He felt a phantom touch, cold and dry, like withered hay caressing his skin. It was the scarecrow, he knew, its presence an invasive parasite, burrowing deeper into his mind, feeding on the dwindling remnants of his perception. He could feel it leaching the color from his thoughts, draining the warmth from his memories, leaving behind only the sterile, empty canvas of its own insatiable need. Each whispered word, each frantic gesture he tried to make, felt like a surrender, an offering. He was the next to be harvested, his sight, his essence, the final ingredient in the entity's grotesque recipe.

The sterile, impersonal white of the hospital room had become a backdrop against which his internal torment played out with agonizing clarity. The hushed efficiency of the medical staff, their concerned frowns and whispered consultations, only served to amplify his isolation. They moved around him, their voices distant, their touches gentle but ultimately useless. They were trying to mend a broken body, but the damage was far deeper, far more insidious. They poked and prodded, their instruments unable to find the source of his affliction. They spoke of neurological anomalies, of psychological trauma, of phantom sensory input, but none of it captured the truth. How could they understand a hunger that consumed sight itself? How could they comprehend an entity that fed on the very fabric of perception?

"Mark? Can you hear me?" A voice, smooth and concerned, cut through the fog. He recognized it as Dr. Albright, the physician who had been overseeing his case. Mark tried to focus, to grasp onto the anchor of that familiar voice, but it was like trying to catch smoke. The swirling darkness pulled at him, dragging him further into its depths. He could feel his own body weakening, the physical shell that housed his spiraling terror growing listless, unresponsive. His limbs felt heavy, disconnected, as if they belonged to someone else. His spirit, once a vibrant flame, was now a dying ember, its last warmth leached away by the insatiable hunger that had claimed him.

He felt a prick in his arm, the sting of a needle. It was meant to soothe, to sedate, but it only served to further blur the already fractured lines of his reality. The visions intensified, the scarecrow's form becoming more distinct, its stitched smile stretching wider, wider, until it seemed to consume the entire world. He could feel its gaze upon him, a thousandfold, piercing and relentless. It wasn't just

122

seeing him; it was *knowing* him, dissecting his fear, relishing his descent. The light in his eyes, the very spark that allowed him to perceive and interact with the world, felt like it was being physically siphoned away, drawn into the gaping void that the scarecrow represented.

He was losing himself, piece by agonizing piece. The entity, through its gruesome conduit, was systematically dismantling him, not by force, but by a perverse form of consumption. It was the ultimate violation, a stripping away of his very capacity to experience existence. He was becoming a vessel, emptied of his own light, ready to be filled with the darkness that fueled the scarecrow. His mind, once a refuge, was now a battlefield, and he was losing. The relentless terror had finally broken him, leaving him adrift in a sea of despair, his final hours a testament to a horror that defied understanding, a horror that had stolen his sight before it even took his life. He was a casualty of the second harvest, his awareness, his very perception of being, the final offering to the insatiable appetite of the ancient evil that resided in Dry Creek. The darkness wasn't just around him; it was within him, a chilling testament to the entity's victory. He was fading, not into death, but into a profound, eternal blindness, a living monument to the Gaze Offering. The sounds of the hospital room were now a distant hum, like the faint buzzing of flies around a carcass, a sound that only underscored the profound emptiness that had taken root within him. He was no longer Mark, the man who had stumbled upon a horrifying truth. He was just a receptacle, his consciousness a flickering flame about to be extinguished by an unseen, unfeeling force. His body lay still, but within the ruined landscape of his mind, the horror continued, an endless, silent scream lost in the overwhelming darkness.

Sheriff DuCard stood at the edge of the overgrown field, the same field where young Billy Jenkins had met his untimely, and frankly, grotesque end. The early morning mist clung to the damp earth, swirling around his worn boots like a spectral shroud. He'd dismissed the initial reports, chalking them up to farm accidents gone horribly wrong, the ramblings of panicked townsfolk in the wake of a tragedy. Sandy losing her sight day-by-day; and then there was Mark's sudden, violent descent into a catatonic state, coupled with the palpable shift in Dry Creek's atmosphere – a creeping dread that seemed to seep from the very soil – gnawed at him. It was a feeling that defied logic, a prickle of unease that had been growing into a full-blown anxiety attack. He wasn't one for superstition, DuCard wasn't. He believed in facts, in evidence, in the tangible. But the facts here were unsettling, and the evidence, if one could call it that, was as bizarre as it was disturbing.

He'd initially chalked up Billy's death to a freak accident involving farm machinery, a tragic but ultimately explainable event. The initial reports detailed a horrific mauling, the kind that left no room for imagination, but also no room for the supernatural. Yet, the sheer ferocity of it, the sheer *wrongness* of the scene, had left a lingering question mark in the back of his mind, a question he'd tried his best to ignore. Now, standing here again, the memory of the crime scene tape, the hushed, horrified whispers of his deputies, and the sickeningly sweet smell of decay that had permeated the air, returned with an unnerving clarity. He'd dismissed it then as the shock of a gruesome death, but what if it was something more? What if the sheer brutality was a symptom, not the cause?

DuCard knelt, his gloved fingers tracing the dew-kissed grass. He remembered the meticulous, almost ritualistic arrangement of the… *remains*. It wasn't just a mess; it was an arrangement. Almost like a sacrifice. The thought sent a shiver down his spine, a sensation he vehemently suppressed. He was a lawman. He dealt with the earthly, the tangible. The idea of some ancient, malevolent force at play was the stuff of campfire tales, not the reality of Dry Creek, a town built on pragmatism and hard work.

He walked slowly, his eyes scanning the ground, searching for anything, anything at all, that might have been missed in the initial chaos. The terror frozen in Billy's expression, as described by the first responders, had been described as something beyond fear, something that spoke of an utter loss of self, a soul-wrenching terror that had frozen him as his eyes were miraculously removed. DuCard had dismissed it as the ramblings of young officers faced with a particularly gruesome scene. But now, with Mark's vacant, staring eyes, the doctors unable to explain his condition, he started to wonder if those young officers had seen something more than just gore.

He recalled the odd, almost geometric pattern of the foreign substance spatter, something the forensics team had also noted as peculiar but ultimately explained away by the nature of the attack. Yet, the sheriff found himself drawn back to it, the unsettling symmetry of it all. It was as if the killer, or whatever had been responsible, had been... deliberate. Every splatter, every rupture, had its place. He was looking for an explanation, a rational one, for the irrationality that was beginning to infect his town.

The sun began to break through the mist, casting long, distorted shadows across the field. The scarecrow, a grotesque sentinel on its wooden cross, seemed to mock him, its burlap face a canvas of vacant malice. DuCard had always seen it as a harmless, if slightly unnerving, effigy. Now, its stillness felt like a coiled threat, its tattered clothes like dried blood, its straw stuffing like the innards of some unspeakable beast. He found himself staring at it, really *staring* at it, for the first time. He noticed the way the tattered cloth of its arms seemed to mimic outstretched, grasping hands, the way its empty eye sockets seemed to bore into him. It was just a scarecrow, he told himself, just straw and cloth and wood. But the feeling of being watched, of being judged, was undeniable.

He noticed something else, half-buried in the loose soil near where Billy's body had been found. It was a small, intricately carved wooden bird, weathered and worn, but undeniably crafted with skill. It wasn't the kind of trinket a farmer would leave lying around. It felt... old. And out of place. He carefully picked it up, turning it over in his hand. It was smooth to the touch, the wood dark and aged. Was this Billy's? Or something left behind? He'd seen no mention of such an item in the initial reports. Another detail overlooked, or perhaps, intentionally ignored?

The silence of the field was broken only by the chirping of unseen birds, a sound that, in another context, might have been comforting. Here, it felt like a mournful dirge. He thought of Billy's parents, their grief a raw, gaping wound. He thought of Mark's parents, their desperation as they watched their son fade before their eyes. He was supposed to protect them, to bring justice. But how could he bring justice for something he couldn't even begin to comprehend?

DuCard stood and brushed the dirt from his knees. He had to find answers, even if those answers led him down a path he didn't want to go. He had to consider the unthinkable. The raw, unbridled brutality of Billy's death, the chilling stillness of Mark's mind, the pervasive sense of dread that had settled over Dry Creek like a toxic fog – it all pointed to something beyond a simple explanation.

He looked towards the tree line, the dense, dark woods that bordered the field. He'd always warned his deputies to stay out of those woods, especially after dark. There were old stories, of course, whispers passed down through generations of Dry Creek's inhabitants, tales of things that lurked in the shadows, things that preyed on the unwary. He'd always dismissed them as folklore, the product of isolated rural communities and overactive imaginations. But now, standing at the edge of this cursed field, the woods seemed to hold a sinister promise, a silent invitation to delve deeper into the darkness.

He remembered the hushed conversations he'd overheard between some of the older residents, cryptic remarks about *the old ways*, about *offerings*, about *the harvest*. He'd always brushed them off, but the words now echoed in his mind with a disturbing resonance. What if the scarecrow wasn't just a scarecrow? What if it was a symbol, a focal point for something far older and far more sinister than he could imagine? He turned his gaze back to the Ragmouth the scarecrow. It stood against the rising sun, its silhouette stark and unnerving. He saw it not as a collection of inanimate objects, but as a focal point. A nexus. And he realized, with a chilling certainty, that his investigation into Billy Jenkins' death had only scratched the surface of a much deeper, much darker truth. The rational façade he had clung to so fiercely was beginning to crack, revealing a landscape of fear and uncertainty he had never anticipated. He was a sheriff, sworn to uphold the law, to protect his community. And the law, he was beginning to suspect, had no jurisdiction here.

He made his way back to his patrol car; the wooden bird clutched tightly in his hand. The mist was burning off, revealing the stark reality of the day, but the internal fog of doubt and dread that had enveloped him remained. He knew, with a sinking heart, that his investigation had just taken a turn he could never have predicted. He was no longer just investigating a death; he was investigating the soul of his town, and the darkness that threatened to consume it whole. He drove back towards the station, the silence in the car amplified by the turmoil in his mind. He needed to talk to someone, to go over the details again, to try and find a thread of logic in the encroaching madness. But who could he talk to? Who would believe him if he spoke of malevolent scarecrows and harvests of souls? He was alone in this, the sole guardian of a truth too terrifying to articulate. The weight of his badge felt heavier than ever, a burden of responsibility for a threat he was only just beginning to understand. The woods behind him seemed to watch his departure, a silent, patient witness to the seeds of dread he was now carrying with him.

Kayla knelt beside Sandy's makeshift bed, the air in the small room thick with the scent of antiseptic and a coppery tang that spoke of something more primal. Sandy's eyes, once the vibrant blue of a summer sky, were now milky cataracts, devoid of light, yet they seemed to focus on something beyond the peeling wallpaper, something Kayla couldn't see. The silence between them was heavy, punctuated only by Sandy's ragged breaths, each one a fragile victory against an unseen foe.

"It came for me," Sandy whispered, her voice a dry rasp, like dead leaves skittering across pavement. Her hands now trembling with a fear that transcended her physical infirmity, clawed at the worn quilt. "Like a shroud... no, heavier. It *pressed* down. Suffocating."

Kayla's own breath hitched. She remembered the stories, the hushed warnings from the older townsfolk, tales of a darkness that settled over Dry Creek during certain times of the year, a darkness that fed on more than just fear. She'd dismissed them, of course. Dry Creek was a town built on practicalities, on the turning of seasons and the yield of the earth. But Sandy's words, the raw terror that laced them, painted a picture far more visceral, far more horrifying, than any folklore.

"What did it feel like, Sandy?" Kayla asked, her voice gentle, a stark contrast to the turmoil raging within her. She reached out, her hand hovering just above Sandy's, not daring to touch, afraid of inflicting further pain.

Sandy's head lolled slightly; her sightless gaze fixed on some point in the middle distance. "Cold," she breathed, the word barely audible. "A deep, bone-chilling cold that wasn't of this world. It seeped into me, not just my skin, but my very core. And then... the whispers." Her voice grew tighter, a tremor running through her frail body. "Promises. Dark things. Promises of... release, of peace. But I knew. I *knew* they were lies. It wanted to take... it wanted to *consume*."

A sob caught in Kayla's throat. She imagined it, this intangible horror, slithering into the quiet room, a predator of the soul. It wasn't just about blindness, then. It was about a violation, a systematic dismantling of the self. The systematic nature of it; that was what truly chilled Kayla. It wasn't a random attack. It was deliberate. It was a harvesting.

"It... it tasted the light," Sandy continued, her words tumbling out in a rush of desperate confession. "It drank my vision. Like... like honey, sweet and thick. It tasted my memories, my hopes. It feasted on them. I felt it. Like tendrils, cold and sharp, reaching into my mind, plucking things away. It drank my future by showing me the color of the sky on my wedding day... the sound of my daughter's first laugh... all gone. Sucked away."

Kayla's eyes welled up. She thought of her own memories, her own hopes, the vibrant tapestry of her life. The idea of something so insidious, so utterly violating, stealing those things away, piece by

128

agonizing piece, was almost unbearable. It wasn't just the loss of sight; it was the obliteration of self.

"Did it… did it have a form, Sandy?" Kayla asked, her voice barely above a whisper. She needed to understand. She needed to grasp onto some tangible detail in this swirling vortex of dread.

Sandy shook her head slowly, her breath catching. "No. Not… not a form, not like you or me. It was more like… a presence. A void that filled the room. But I felt its hunger. Oh, God, its hunger. It was ancient, Kayla. And insatiable." Her hands, which had been clutching the quilt, now began to scrabble at her own face, her fingers brushing over her closed eyelids. "It felt like… being buried alive. In darkness. And the darkness was alive too. It writhed. It whispered my name. Mocked me."

A wave of nausea washed over Kayla. The predatory entity, feeding on Sandy's very essence, leaving her blind and broken. It wasn't just an attack; it was a methodical despoiling. The entity wasn't just taking something; it was consuming it, leaving nothing behind. And the whispers, the promises of darkness, were a cruel mockery of the terror it inflicted. It was a violation on the deepest, most profound level.

"I tried to fight," Sandy rasped, her voice cracking with a pain that was clearly not just physical. "I tried to hold on. But it was too strong. It was… everywhere. And it was so patient. It waited. It watched. It knew it would win. It told me so. It whispered that this was my turn. The Second Harvest."

The words hung in the air, heavy with an unspoken threat. The Second Harvest. It echoed the hushed rumors Sheriff DuCard had been hearing, the cryptic pronouncements of the older residents about the cyclical nature of this dread. It wasn't just a random event; it was part of a pattern, a deliberate, horrifying ritual.

"It said… it said others would come," Sandy continued, her voice growing weaker, the lucidity of her terror beginning to fade, replaced by a growing exhaustion. "It said it needed… the light. The memories. The *essence*. To keep… to keep the cycle going."

Kayla's heart hammered against her ribs. Others would come. It was systematic. Sandy was not an isolated victim. This was not a singular event. This was an orchestrated campaign of terror, and Sandy was just one casualty in a much larger, much more sinister plan. The responsibility settled on Kayla's shoulders like a physical weight, crushing her. She looked at Sandy, at the extinguished light in her eyes, and felt a surge of fierce, protective rage. She wouldn't let this happen to anyone else. She couldn't.

"It left me like this," Sandy murmured, her voice almost inaudible now. "Empty. Hollow. But I felt... I felt it *change* me. It didn't just take. It... it left a part of itself behind. A seed. A darkness inside. Waiting."

A seed. A darkness inside. The implication was chilling. Had the entity left a piece of itself within Sandy, a parasitic fragment that would continue to fester? Or was it a more metaphorical statement, a testament to the profound and lasting impact of such a violation? Kayla shuddered, the thought of such an intimate, internal corruption almost too much to bear.

Kayla stayed by Sandy's side, her own fear a cold knot in her stomach, but overlaid with a growing resolve. Sandy's testimony, fragmented and terrifying as it was, confirmed the encroaching darkness that Sheriff DuCard had begun to suspect. It was a darkness that fed on the very essence of its victims, a methodical, predatory force that operated with a chilling, ancient purpose. The Second Harvest was not a metaphor; it was a terrifying reality. And Kayla knew, with a certainty that chilled her to the bone, that her own fight had just begun. The responsibility to uncover the truth, to understand the nature of this entity, and to protect Dry Creek from its insatiable hunger, now rested squarely on her shoulders. Sandy's shattered vision was a beacon, a warning, and a call to arms. The darkness had revealed itself, and Kayla would not let it claim another soul. She would delve into the secrets of Dry Creek, no matter how terrifying, no matter how deeply buried. Sandy's fragmented whispers had ignited a fire within her, a desperate need to understand and to fight back against the encroaching night.

The sheer vulnerability of Sandy's state was a constant, agonizing reminder of the stakes. Her blindness was absolute, a total erasure of the visual world, and Kayla felt a profound pang of sympathy, mixed with a burgeoning dread for what such an experience must have entailed. Sandy's descriptions, though often delivered in hushed, broken phrases, painted a vivid, horrifying picture. The "shroud," the "pressing," the "suffocating" nature of the presence – these weren't merely metaphors for fear; they were sensory details of a terrifying, physical manifestation of something profoundly unnatural. It suggested a force that could manipulate its surroundings, creating an atmosphere of oppressive dread that was palpable and invasive.

"It whispered," Sandy repeated, her voice gaining a fraction of its former strength, a desperate attempt to articulate the inarticulable. "Not words, not really. More like… feelings. Intentions. Promises of oblivion. Of peace. But the peace felt… wrong. Cold. Empty. Like a promise from a grave. It wanted me to surrender. To give up the fight. To *want* to be consumed."

Kayla's own mind flashed back to the unnerving stillness of Mark who had fallen into a catatonic state after some inexplicable event. Was this the same fate? A willing surrender, a mental capitulation to the insidious whispers of the entity? Sandy's fragmented accounts were starting to weave a terrifying tapestry, a narrative of systematic psychological and sensory assault.

"It started with the edges," Sandy murmured, her sightless eyes darting, as if trying to track something unseen. "The periphery of my vision. A blurring. Then a darkness that… wouldn't go away. Like a smudge on a lens, but it was *in* my eyes. And it grew. Slowly, deliberately. It consumed the light. It drank it." She paused, a shudder wracking her frame. "I tried to wash it away. Rubbed my eyes until they burned. But it was inside. It was *part* of me, yet it wasn't. It was an invasion."

The image of something parasitic, something that burrowed its way into the very fibers of one's being, sent a fresh wave of revulsion through Kayla. This wasn't a simple illness; it was a violation, a systematic dismantling of the senses, a deliberate act of sabotage against Sandy's very perception of reality. And the "drinking" of light, the consumption of vision, was a grotesque, almost poetic description of the ultimate goal.

"Did you see anything, Sandy? Anything at all?" Kayla pressed, her voice laced with a desperate hope for a concrete detail, a clue that might unlock the mystery.

Sandy's head shook slowly, a weak, negative movement. "No... not a shape. Not a face. Just... the absence. The growing void. And the feeling of being... watched. Judged. Like an insect under a magnifying glass. It was observing my struggle, enjoying it." Her voice dropped to a whisper. "It fed on my terror. My despair. The more I fought, the stronger it seemed to become. It was a perverse kind of nourishment."

The systematic nature of the entity's attack was becoming chillingly clear. It wasn't just about taking sight; it was about orchestrating a symphony of terror, extracting every ounce of fear and despair from its victim. This was not the act of a simple predator; it was the methodical work of something far more ancient and calculating, something that understood the subtle art of psychological warfare. The "Second Harvest" wasn't just a morbid nickname; it was a description of a process, a deliberate reaping of human essence.

"It whispered about the 'season'," Sandy continued, her voice growing fainter, as if the sheer act of recalling the experience was draining her life force. "About the 'time of reaping.' It said... it said Dry Creek was fertile ground. That the fear here... it was like a rich soil. And that it was time to... to collect. To bring in the bounty."

The implications of her words sent a cold dread through Kayla. Fertile ground. Bounty. The "Second Harvest" wasn't a localized incident; it was tied to the very essence of Dry Creek, to its agricultural roots, its cyclical rhythm. The entity was intrinsically linked to the town itself, a parasitic force that drew sustenance from its inhabitants, its fear, its very lifeblood. The scarecrows, the fields, the encroaching darkness from the woods – it all began to coalesce into a single, terrifying narrative.

"It promised... it promised not to kill me," Sandy whispered, her voice barely audible now. "Not yet. It said... it said I was... preserved. For later. For... the culmination. It wanted me to be a vessel. To carry its... its purpose. Inside."

A vessel. The chilling implication sent a shiver down Kayla's spine. Had the entity left something of itself within Sandy, a parasitic fragment that would continue to grow, to fester, to await a future activation? The thought of this intimate, internal corruption was almost more terrifying than the initial violation. Sandy was not merely a victim; she was a repository for the entity's malevolent purpose, a living testament to its insidious nature.

Kayla squeezed Sandy's hand, a silent promise of support, of unwavering commitment. Sandy's fragmented, terrifying testimony had solidified the vague unease that had settled over Dry Creek into a concrete, horrifying reality. The darkness was not a figment of collective imagination; it was a tangible, predatory force, and its methods were as terrifying as they were systematic. The Second Harvest was not a distant threat; it was happening now, and Sandy was living proof. Kayla knew, with a chilling certainty, that she couldn't afford to doubt, to rationalize away the impossible. Sandy's blindness, her terror, her broken whispers – they were all threads in a much larger, much darker tapestry, and Kayla had to unravel it, no matter the cost. The weight of this knowledge was crushing, but beneath it, a flicker of defiance began to ignite. Sandy's sacrifice, her violation, would not be in vain. Dry Creek deserved to know the truth, and Kayla was determined to be the one to reveal it. The encroaching darkness had a name, and she was going to find it.

The rustle of dry stalks was a percussive symphony against the velvet silence of the night as Kayla, accompanied by a hushed, anxious contingent of Tommy and Helen, crept through the Withers vast cornfield. The air, still heavy with the day's oppressive heat, now held a preternatural chill, a palpable dread that clung to them like the morning mist. Each step was measured, each breath held, as they navigated the labyrinthine rows, guided by an unspoken, shared purpose. Sandy's whispered account of the "Second Harvest" had ignited a desperate need to see, to understand the unspeakable terror that had claimed her sight and so much more. The farm, which had always been a symbol of Dry Creek's enduring spirit, now felt like a tomb, the towering stalks their tombstone markers.

They moved with the practiced caution of those who knew this land intimately, yet tonight, its familiarity offered no comfort. The moon, a sliver of bone in the inky sky, cast long, distorted shadows that danced and writhed like specters. The familiar scent of ripening corn was now tinged with something acrid, something metallic and unpleasant, like old blood and decay. It was a scent that prickled the back of Kayla's throat, a silent herald of the horror that awaited them. Tommy, usually the stoic pragmatist, kept glancing over his shoulder, his hand instinctively tightening around the flashlight he'd insisted they bring, its beam cutting a trembling swathe through the darkness. Helen, ever the sensitive soul, clutched Kayla's arm, her knuckles white, her breathing shallow and ragged.

Their destination was the solitary scarecrow that stood sentinel at the heart of the field, a grotesque caricature of a farmer that had always unnerved Kayla, even in daylight. Sandy's words echoed in her mind: "It's not just a scarecrow, Kayla. It's... a vessel. It's watching." And now, as they drew closer, the sentinel seemed to warp in their vision, its presence growing, its silent vigil becoming something undeniably sinister. The familiar burlap sack head, stitched crudely onto a weathered frame, appeared to swell, to writhe, as if struggling against unseen bonds. The tattered clothes, usually limp and rain-soaked, seemed to billow with a life of their own, stirred by a wind that did not blow.

As they broke through the last line of cornstalks, the sight that greeted them stole the air from their lungs. The Withers scarecrow, Ragmouth, silhouetted against the pale moonlight, was no longer just a collection of straw and tattered cloth. It was... different. The vacant, impression of eyes, the crude, stitched smile – all of it seemed to pulse with an internal luminescence. But it wasn't the familiar, gentle glow of the moon reflecting off glass. This was a deep, pulsing light, an unholy radiance that seemed to emanate from within the very fabric of the effigy.

Tommy, his voice a rough whisper, pointed his flashlight beam directly at the scarecrow's face. The light caught the vacant sockets, and what they saw made Kayla's blood run cold. The familiar, dull buttons were gone. In their place, something far more disturbing had taken root. Two orbs, unnaturally round and unnervingly luminous, were set deep within the burlap. They weren't glass; they were fluid, shifting, like captured starlight held in a viscous medium. They pulsed with a slow, rhythmic beat, mirroring the phantom heartbeat Kayla felt hammering in her own chest.

"What the hell is that?" Tommy breathed, his voice laced with a disbelief that quickly morphed into terror.

Helen let out a choked gasp, burying her face in Kayla's shoulder. "It's... it's looking at us," she stammered, her words muffled.

And it was. The new "eyes" seemed to track their movements, shifting with a disconcerting, almost predatory awareness. They weren't reflecting light; they were *generating* it, a soft, phosphorescent glow that painted the surrounding corn stalks in an eerie, otherworldly hue. Kayla felt a primal scream building in her throat, a desperate urge to flee, to put as much distance as possible between herself and this abomination. But Sandy's words, her vacant, terror-filled eyes, anchored her to the spot. This was it. This was the manifestation of the darkness she had described, the consuming force that fed on light, on life.

Kayla slowly raised her own flashlight, her hand trembling, and directed its beam towards the scarecrow's figure. The details, previously obscured by the darkness, now came into horrifying focus. The scarecrow was adorned with more than just straw. Threaded through its ragged clothes, woven into its very being, were small, delicate objects. They glinted in the flashlight beam, catching the light and scattering it in a thousand tiny reflections. As Kayla's eyes adjusted, the sickening realization dawned. These were not decorative trinkets.

They were buttons. Countless buttons, of all shapes and sizes, sewn haphazardly onto the burlap and fabric. But these weren't the humble, utilitarian buttons of old clothes. These were the polished, iridescent buttons that adorned dresses, coats, and children's shirts. They were the very same kind of buttons that Sandy had described as being *taken*. They were the remnants, the discarded husks of the stolen essences.

And then, Kayla saw it. A single, familiar button, sewn precariously onto the scarecrow's tattered sleeve. It was a pearl button, with a faint, swirling pattern within its milky surface. It was the exact kind of button that had adorned Sandy's favorite cardigan, the one she'd worn on her grandmother's birthday, a memory Sandy had desperately clung to. Kayla's breath hitched. It was undeniable. This wasn't just a scarecrow; it was a gruesome mosaic of its victims.

Tommy swallowed hard; his gaze fixed on the scarecrow's unsettlingly alive eyes. "It's... it's wearing them," he whispered, his voice barely audible. "The eyes... they're real. And the buttons..." He trailed off, the unspoken horror of the implication hanging heavy in the air.

The sheer audacity of it was staggering. The entity wasn't just consuming its victims; it was *displaying* them, incorporating their stolen features into its monstrous form. The vacant sockets of the scarecrow were now filled with the stolen light, the very essence of its victims' sight, and the scattered buttons were the silent, damning evidence of their stolen identities. This was a harvest, indeed, but one that was far more personal, far more violating, than anyone had imagined. It was a trophy case of stolen souls.

Kayla took a hesitant step forward; drawn by a morbid fascination she couldn't suppress. The scarecrow seemed to lean towards her, its burlap head tilting as if in silent greeting, or perhaps, in anticipation. The stitched smile, usually fixed and inanimate, now seemed to possess a subtle, unsettling curve, as if acknowledging her presence. The darkness within its new eyes swirled, and for a terrifying moment, Kayla thought she saw a flicker of recognition, a ghost of a familiar shade of blue.

"Sandy said it wanted the light," Kayla murmured, her voice raw with a dawning understanding. "It wasn't just about blinding her. It was about *taking* the light. And it's... it's using it." She gestured towards the scarecrow's eyes, her hand shaking. "It's putting it to use."

The implications were terrifyingly clear. The entity wasn't merely a passive collector of stolen essences; it was an active participant, a craftsman of its own monstrous form. It was reassembling itself, piece by agonizing piece, using the very things it stole to enhance its own terrifying presence. The scarecrow, once a symbol of rural life and harvest, had been transformed into a grotesque effigy, a monument to its own predatory nature.

Tommy cautiously circled the scarecrow, his flashlight beam sweeping across its straw-stuffed body. "Look at this," he said, his voice strained. He pointed to the base of the scarecrow, where the rough-hewn wooden pole met the earth. Embedded in the churned soil around the base were more buttons, almost like offerings, or perhaps, markers of the entity's claim. Some were half-buried, their polished surfaces dulled by dirt, but their presence was unmistakable. They were a trail, leading from the field to this central, horrifying monument.

Helen, despite her terror, had edged closer, her curiosity battling her fear. She knelt down, her fingers brushing against one of the buttons near the base. "These... these are all different," she whispered, her voice filled with a mixture of awe and horror. "There are children's buttons, old-fashioned ones, some that look like they're made of bone."

The sheer variety of buttons was a chilling testament to the widespread nature of the entity's predation. It hadn't confined its harvest to a single demographic or age group. It had taken from anyone and everyone, indiscriminately plucking the threads of their lives and weaving them into its own terrifying tapestry. The scarecrow wasn't just a scarecrow anymore; it was a chilling embodiment of Dry Creek's collective fear, a repository of stolen memories and stolen light.

Kayla's gaze drifted up the scarecrow's body, tracing the path of the buttons. They were sewn with crude, thick thread, as if applied with a hasty, yet deliberate, hand. Some were clustered together, while others were scattered, like fallen leaves. Each button, each stolen eye, represented a life irrevocably altered, a soul diminished. And the scarecrow, at the center of it all, seemed to hum with a silent, malevolent energy, its unholy eyes fixed on them, as if relishing their terror.

"It's like… it's wearing them as trophies," Tommy said, his voice flat, the realization hitting him with full force. "It's showing off what it's taken. It's a… a declaration."

A declaration. Yes, that was it. This wasn't just a passive manifestation of the entity's hunger; it was an active statement. The scarecrow, imbued with the stolen essences, was the entity's visible presence, its terrifying banner planted firmly in the heart of Dry Creek. The Second Harvest was not a subtle invasion; it was a brutal, public display of power.

Kayla's mind raced, piecing together Sandy's fragmented warnings with the horrifying reality before them. The "seed" Sandy had spoken of the darkness left within her – could this be where it came from? Was this scarecrow the source, the focal point from which this parasitic force emanated? The idea was almost too vast, too terrifying to comprehend.

As they stood there, frozen in a tableau of fear and disbelief, a faint, almost imperceptible sound reached them. It was a low, guttural hum, emanating from the scarecrow itself. It wasn't a mechanical sound; it was more akin to a deep, resonant vibration, as if the very straw within it was alive, breathing. And with that hum, the lights in the scarecrow's eyes seemed to intensify, pulsing with a brighter, more urgent rhythm.

"Did you hear that?" Helen whispered, her eyes wide with renewed terror.

Kayla nodded, her gaze locked onto the scarecrow's unblinking, luminous orbs. The hum seemed to resonate not just in the air, but within her bones, a disquieting vibration that spoke of an immense, contained power. It felt like the prelude to something… inevitable.

Tommy raised his flashlight again, aiming it at the scarecrow's head. "Those eyes…" he muttered. "They're not just glowing. They're… moving. Like they're watching us. Really watching."

And they were. The unholy orbs, filled with the stolen light of Dry Creek's residents, seemed to follow their every move, their unnatural luminescence casting long, dancing shadows that distorted the familiar landscape of the cornfield. It was a silent, unnerving vigil, a constant reminder of the entity's pervasive presence. Kayla felt a chilling certainty settle over her: the scarecrow was not merely a display; it was an active participant, a sentinel that was very much alive. It was the embodiment of the Second Harvest, and it had just begun to truly awaken. The stolen light within its eyes wasn't just a visual phenomenon; it was a source of power, a beacon that drew the darkness, and the entity, closer to its ultimate goal. The air around them grew colder, and the hum from the scarecrow seemed to deepen, a promise of horrors yet to come. The second harvest had begun, and its first fruits were disturbingly, terrifyingly visible.

The whispers started that morning, insidious tendrils of dread weaving through the already strained silence of Dry Creek. Mark was gone. Not merely missing, not simply absent from his usual haunts. Gone. The news, delivered in hushed, urgent tones over backyards and through the thin walls of their homes, spread faster than any wildfire. It was a contagion of fear, and it infected every soul in the small town.

Kayla, Tommy, and Helen found themselves drawn together in the aftermath, a fragile alliance forged in the crucible of the cornfield. The spectral luminescence of the scarecrow, the horrifying tableau of stolen buttons and vacant, pulsing eyes, replayed endlessly in their minds, a waking nightmare that had shattered their innocence. They had seen the undeniable proof of the entity's predatory nature, its grotesque harvest. But Mark's death, confirmed by the grim faces of Sheriff DuCard and his deputy as they drove past Kayla's house, its windows already latched against an unseen threat, amplified their terror to an unbearable degree. Mark, their classmate, a familiar face in the crowded halls of Dry

Creek High, was now another victim claimed by the encroaching darkness.

"He was just... he was just walking home from the diner," Tommy recounted, his voice rough with a grief he struggled to articulate. They were huddled in Kayla's living room, the afternoon sun doing little to penetrate the gloom that had settled over the house. Helen sat with her knees drawn to her chest, her gaze fixed on the closed curtains, as if expecting something to peer through them. "Sheriff DuCard said... he said it looked like he'd just... evaporated."

Kayla felt a cold dread coil in her stomach. Evaporated. The word conjured images too horrific to fully grasp, yet it fit the chilling narrative they were slowly piecing together. The entity, this consuming force, didn't just take; it erased. It absorbed, leaving behind only the faintest echo, a void where a life had once been. Mark's disappearance, the manner of his 'departure,' was another brutal confirmation of Sandy's fragmented pronouncements. The Second Harvest was not confined to the shadows of the cornfields; it was now a palpable, deadly presence on their very streets.

"The buttons," Helen whispered, her voice barely audible. "The eyes... Mark loved that blue jacket he had. With the big, shiny buttons. Remember? He always wore it." Her words hung in the air, heavy with unspoken fear. The memory of the scarecrow, its body a horrifying collection of stolen adornments, flashed behind Kayla's eyes. Were Mark's buttons among them? Had his light, his very essence, been siphoned to fuel that grotesque effigy? The thought was a visceral punch to the gut.

Dry Creek, once a haven of quiet normalcy, had transformed overnight into a stage for their deepest anxieties. The familiar rhythm of daily life had faltered, replaced by an undercurrent of unease that permeated every interaction. Doors, which had always stood welcomingly ajar, were now firmly locked. Windows, usually thrown open to catch the summer breeze, were shuttered and secured as if against a siege. The friendly faces of neighbors were now tinged with suspicion, their smiles tight, their eyes darting nervously towards the periphery.

"Nobody's going out," Tommy stated, his voice heavy with the grim reality. "My dad said he saw Mrs. Henderson double-checking her locks at dusk. And the Myers, they're not even answering their door. It's like... everyone knows, but no one wants to say it out loud."

The fear was a suffocating blanket, muffling their voices, narrowing their world. It was a fear that went beyond the shock of a single, violent death. It was a creeping, insidious dread that whispered of an enemy unseen, an entity that preyed on the very light and life that sustained them. The scarecrow was a chilling, tangible manifestation of this horror, but the true horror lay in its invisible, pervasive reach. It had infiltrated their homes, their routines, their very sense of security.

Kayla remembered the way the townsfolk usually gathered, their lives interwoven in a tapestry of shared experiences. Now, that tapestry was fraying, threads being pulled loose by an unseen hand. The farmers who would gather at the market to discuss crops were now keeping their families close, their fields, once symbols of bounty, now perhaps harboring the very darkness that consumed their neighbors. The children, usually a boisterous presence on the streets, were confined indoors, their laughter replaced by the hushed tones of worried parents.

"It's not just us teenagers anymore, is it?" Helen murmured, her voice trembling. "It's everyone. It's like... it's feeding on all of us."

Her words struck a chord of cold, hard truth. The entity's hunger was not selective. It was indiscriminate, its harvest encompassing all who possessed the light it craved. Mark's death, the widespread panic, the palpable dread that had descended upon Dry Creek – it was all part of the Second Harvest, a chilling escalation of the entity's power. The scarecrow in the Withers Field was the focal point, the grotesque monument to its success, but the tendrils of its influence now stretched far beyond those shadowed rows of corn.

Tommy paced the room, his frustration a palpable force. "We saw it, Kayla. We saw what it did. We saw those eyes, those buttons. We know it's real. But how do we make everyone else believe us?

How do we fight something that no one even knows how to talk about?"

The dilemma was immense. How could they convey the sheer, unadulterated terror of what they had witnessed to a community paralyzed by a fear they couldn't yet name? Their experience was a nightmare made manifest, a surreal horror that defied rational explanation. To speak of luminous eyes and sentient scarecrows would likely invite disbelief, perhaps even ridicule, at a time when unity and clear-headedness were paramount.

Kayla looked at Tommy, at Helen. Their faces were pale, etched with exhaustion and a terror that mirrored her own. They had ventured into the darkness and had seen its horrifying truth. But that truth was a dangerous burden to carry in a town gripped by a fear that was rapidly spiraling into panic. The silence that had fallen over Dry Creek was not a silence of peace, but a silence of apprehension, a collective holding of breath as the community waited for the next blow to fall.

"We have to tell them," Kayla said, her voice firmer than she expected. "We can't let this continue. Sandy and Mark... they are just the beginning. If we don't do something, if we don't find a way to stop it, then... then the Second Harvest will claim us all." She thought of the scarecrow, its unholy eyes pulsing with stolen light, its form a gruesome testament to the entity's power. It was a silent, terrifying declaration of intent. And now, with Mark's death, that declaration had become a chillingly real threat to their entire town. The fear was no longer a distant rumor; it was a suffocating reality, and it was only just beginning.

Chapter 7

The Whispering Corn

The silence of Dry Creek was no longer the peaceful quiet of a sleepy town, but a taut, suffocating hush. It was the kind of silence that precedes a scream, the held breath before an inevitable fall. Kayla, Tommy, and Helen found themselves drawn, against their better judgment, to the perimeter of the Withers property, a place that had become a monument to their unraveling reality. The cornfield, once a familiar, comforting expanse of green that signaled the slow turn of seasons, now seemed to possess a malevolent sentience. Its stalks, impossibly tall, crowded together like a skeletal army, their hushed rustling an insidious undercurrent to the heavy air. Even in the absence of any discernible breeze, a ceaseless, unsettling murmur emanated from within its dense depths. It was the sound of a thousand hushed conversations, of secrets being shared, of promises whispered on the edge of annihilation.

Kayla strained her ears, trying to decipher the phantom symphony. The whispers weren't random sounds; they were directed, intimate, and utterly terrifying. They slithered into her mind, bypassing her eardrums and lodging directly into the most vulnerable corners of her consciousness. They spoke of things she'd tried to bury, of insecurities she'd nursed in the dark, of the gnawing fear that she wasn't enough, that she would be forgotten, that she would disappear like Mark had. The corn seemed to know her deepest anxieties, twisting them into cruel pronouncements, weaving them into its mournful song.

"Do you hear that?" Helen's voice was a fragile thread, barely audible above the disconcerting murmur. Her eyes, wide and unfocused, were fixed on the impenetrable wall of green. She clutched Tommy's arm, her knuckles white, as if seeking a grounding anchor in the shifting sands of their perception.

Tommy nodded; his jaw tight. He was usually the pragmatic one, the one who sought logical explanations, but even he seemed to be succumbing to the pervasive dread. "It's... it's like it's talking," he said, his voice strained. "Not with words, exactly. More like... like it's getting inside your head."

The whispers intensified, coalescing into distinct, chilling fragments. They weren't just echoes of their own fears; they were something else, something external and deeply sinister. Kayla heard a voice, low and sibilant, that seemed to whisper her name, promising an end to the pain, an escape from the suffocating fear, if only she would step inside, if only she would surrender. It was a siren's call, woven from desperation and laced with oblivion. She saw Tommy flinch, his head tilting as if trying to catch a specific phrase, his brow furrowed in a mixture of fascination and abject terror. Helen let out a choked gasp, her hand flying to her mouth.

"It said... it said my dad's name," she stammered, her voice trembling. "It said he was afraid. That he was going to be taken too."

The intimacy of the whispers was what made them so horrifying. They weren't general pronouncements of doom; they were personalized prophecies of despair, tailored to each of them. The entity wasn't just a force of destruction; it was a psychic predator, capable of exploiting their deepest emotional vulnerabilities. Kayla felt a cold dread seep into her bones, a dread far more profound than the fear of physical harm. This was an assault on their very sense of self, a violation of their innermost thoughts.

The cornstalks themselves seemed to lean in, the dense canopy above them darkening the already dim afternoon light. Each leaf, each rustling frond, felt like an eye, watching, judging, waiting. The sheer density of the field was suffocating; it was a living labyrinth designed to trap and consume. There was no discernible path, no break in the sea of green that offered even a hint of an exit. It was a solid, unbroken wall, and from within it, the whispers pulsed like a diseased heart.

"We should go," Kayla said, her voice betraying the tremor she was trying to control. "We shouldn't be here."

"But what *is* it?" Tommy demanded, his eyes still fixed on the shifting patterns of the stalks. "It's not just the wind. It's not just… sounds." He ran a hand through his hair, his usual composure shattered. "It feels like… like it's alive. Like the whole field is one thing."

His observation resonated deeply with Kayla. The cornfield wasn't just a collection of plants; it was an organism, a vast, interconnected entity with a singular, malevolent purpose. The whispers were its voice, the rustling its breath, the unnaturally tall stalks its sinewy limbs reaching out, seeking to ensnare. She remembered the feeling of being watched by the scarecrow, the unnerving stillness of its button eyes. Now, that feeling was amplified a thousandfold, emanating from every single stalk, from the very earth beneath their feet.

They took a tentative step back, a collective instinct for self-preservation kicking in. But as they retreated, the whispers seemed to follow, morphing into a mocking laughter that echoed through the eerie silence. It was a laughter devoid of mirth, a chilling sound that spoke of an ancient, insatiable hunger. Kayla felt a prickle of sweat on her brow, her heart hammering against her ribs. This was beyond anything they had ever imagined. The scarecrow was a harbinger, a crude effigy, but this… this was the true face of the darkness.

"It knows we're here," Helen whispered, her voice barely a breath. "It knows what we saw."

The implication was chilling. The entity was not merely a passive force waiting to be discovered; it was aware, it was observant, and it was actively engaging with them. The whispers weren't a byproduct of its existence; they were a deliberate tool, a weapon designed to sow discord and fear. Kayla imagined the roots of the corn, spreading deep into the earth, connecting every stalk, every whisper, every stolen light, into a vast, pulsing network of consciousness. It was a parasitic intelligence, feeding on their very sanity.

"We need to get back," Kayla said, her voice gaining a desperate urgency. "We need to tell someone."

"Tell them what?" Tommy countered, his frustration evident. "That the corn is whispering our fears? That it's trying to lure us in? They'll think we're crazy. Especially now, with Mark gone."

The truth of his words was a bitter pill. How could they articulate the surreal horror of their experience without sounding like they had lost their minds? The whispers were a form of psychological warfare, designed to isolate and discredit. The entity was not just harvesting bodies; it was harvesting minds, turning them against each other, against themselves. Kayla felt a wave of helplessness wash over her. They were trapped, not just by the physical barrier of the cornfield, but by the insidious nature of the entity itself, which operated on a plane of existence they were only beginning to comprehend.

They turned and began to walk, not running, but a quickened pace, as if the sheer act of moving away would sever the invisible threads that seemed to pull at them. Yet, the whispers persisted, a phantom chorus accompanying their every step. They morphed again, this time into a more insidious, intimate tone, each voice a familiar echo, distorted and cruel. Kayla heard her mother's voice, laced with disappointment, telling her she was a failure. Tommy heard his father's voice, echoing his own self-doubt, telling him he wasn't strong enough. Helen heard a distorted echo of her own deepest insecurities, amplified and weaponized against her.

It was a torment, a relentless barrage of psychological torment that chipped away at their resolve. The line between the external whispers and their own internal monologue blurred, making it impossible to distinguish what was real from what was being planted in their minds. Kayla felt a desperate urge to cover her ears, to block out the insidious voices, but she knew it would be futile. They weren't reaching her ears; they were burrowing into her soul.

As they reached the edge of the property line, the whispers seemed to recede, though not entirely. They lingered at the periphery of their hearing, a constant, unnerving reminder of what lay within the field. The sudden silence, relative as it was, was almost as jarring as the whispers themselves. It left a void, an emptiness that was quickly filled by the lingering dread.

"It… it knows," Helen repeated, her voice hoarse. "It knows everything about us."

Kayla nodded, the chilling realization settling deep within her. The scarecrow, with its stolen buttons and vacant eyes, was a crude, physical manifestation of the entity's power. But the whispers, the auditory hallucinations, were a far more insidious and dangerous weapon. They were the invisible tendrils that probed and exploited, the psychic assault that preceded the physical harvest.

The cornfield was not just a place; it was a living, breathing entity, a vast, interconnected consciousness that fed on their deepest fears, their most vulnerable emotions. And the Second Harvest was not just about taking bodies; it was about consuming souls. The sun, which had been a pale, diffused disc in the hazy sky, began to dip lower, casting long, distorted shadows that seemed to writhe and stretch towards the cornfield. The air grew colder, and a sense of profound unease settled over the three teenagers. They were no longer children playing in the summer sun; they were survivors of a glimpse into a horror that transcended the mundane, a darkness that whispered secrets and preyed on their very essence. The whispers from the cornfield were a promise, a threat, and a chilling testament to the unseen forces that now held Dry Creek in their suffocating grip.

Tommy looked back at the field, his face a mask of grim determination. "We can't just ignore this, Kayla. We saw what Mark's disappearance did to everyone. If this thing keeps going, no one is safe. We have to do something."

Kayla understood. The whispers were a testament to the entity's pervasive influence, a chilling indication that it was not confined to the Withers property. It had a reach that extended into their very minds, making every rustle of leaves, every creak of a floorboard, a potential harbinger of terror. The cornfield was a nexus, a focal point of the encroaching darkness, but the influence of the entity was far more widespread, far more insidious. The whispers were not just a sound; they were a symptom of a deeper infection, a disease of fear that was rapidly spreading through Dry Creek.

"I know," Kayla replied, her voice low but firm. The fear was still a tangible presence, a cold knot in her stomach, but a flicker of defiance had ignited within her. They had seen the horrifying truth, and to remain silent, to succumb to the fear, would be to betray Mark, to betray themselves. The whispers, as terrifying as they were, had also served as a confirmation, a terrifying validation of the horrors they had witnessed. They knew the stakes. They knew what was at risk. The battle for Dry Creek had begun, and it was a battle fought not only in the shadows of the cornfields but in the deepest recesses of their minds. The whispering corn was not just an omen; it was a declaration of war. And they, the unwilling witnesses, were now on the front lines. The rustling leaves seemed to conspire, weaving a narrative of their inevitable doom, but within that narrative, a fragile thread of rebellion was beginning to form. They would not be consumed silently. They would not be erased without a fight. The whispers had sown fear, but they had also sown a seed of resistance.

The edge of the Withers property offered no sanctuary. The silence that had descended felt like a prelude, a deliberate pause in the cacophony, amplifying the tension that coiled in Kayla's gut. It wasn't an absence of sound, but a perversion of it, as if the very air had been scoured clean of natural noise, leaving only the phantom echoes of the cornfield's insidious song. Tommy's hand, still clenched around Helen's arm, was a testament to their shared terror, a physical anchor in a world that seemed intent on dissolving into nightmare. The unnerving stillness of the surrounding trees, usually a comfort, now felt like a frozen tableau, as if they too were holding their breath, waiting for the next act of this unfolding horror.

"It's watching us," Helen whispered, her voice raspy, her gaze darting from the impenetrable wall of corn to the encroaching twilight that bled the color from the landscape. The familiar shapes of the distant farmhouse and the skeletal silhouette of the Withers barn seemed to warp and twist in the dying light, their solid forms appearing to shimmer and shift like heat haze on a summer road, though the air had taken on a distinct chill that had nothing to do with the setting sun. The entity, Kayla realized with a sickening lurch, wasn't confined to the cornfield. It was a pervasive presence, a miasma that seeped into every corner of their perception, twisting the familiar into the terrifying.

Tommy squeezed Helen's arm; his knuckles white. "It's trying to make us think it is." His voice was tight, a desperate attempt to inject logic into a situation that defied it. But even as he spoke, a subtle alteration in the wind seemed to carry the faintest rustle from the corn, a sound that was too deliberate, too rhythmic to be natural. It was as if the cornstalks were sighing, a collective exhalation of malevolence that prickled the hairs on Kayla's neck.

Kayla forced herself to look back at the field. The stalks, impossibly tall and dense, now seemed to writhe with a life of their own. The dying light played tricks, conjuring ephemeral shapes within the emerald depths. A flicker of movement, too quick to be real, too distinct to be dismissed as a trick of the eye. It was like watching a silent film, where every shadow held a hidden threat, every rustle hinted at a lurking predator. She could almost feel the unseen tendrils of the entity reaching out, not to touch, but to probe, to assess, to gauge their vulnerability.

"It's not just the whispers," Kayla said, her voice barely above a breath. "It's… everything. The way the light's changing, the way things look like they're moving…" She trailed off, the words feeling inadequate to describe the sheer wrongness of the atmosphere. It was a subtle orchestration, a deliberate manipulation of the environment designed to unravel their grip on reality.

Then, it began. Not with a roar, but with a whisper that was undeniably new, yet achingly familiar. It was Helen's mother's voice, laced with a profound disappointment that cut deeper than any accusation.

Oh, Helen, darling. I told you not to go near that place. You always were too curious for your own good. Now look at you.

Always getting yourself into trouble. The voice was a cruel parody, twisting a mother's concern into a weapon of guilt, dredging up every childhood transgression, every moment of perceived disobedience, and magnifying them into monstrous failures. Helen flinched as if struck, tears welling in her eyes.

Tommy visibly stiff, his head snapping towards a different part of the field. Kayla heard it too, a low, rumbling growl that morphed into her father's voice, the one she had strained to hear in the days after Mark's disappearance.

Kayla, why couldn't you have stopped him? Why weren't you watching? It's your responsibility. You let him down. You let us all down. The guilt she had buried deep, the unspoken accusation she had leveled against herself, was ripped from the earth and hurled back at her with the force of a physical blow. It was the voice of her own deepest insecurity, amplified and weaponized, echoing the very words she had screamed at herself in the dark.

Tommy, caught between them, let out a choked gasp. Kayla knew, without looking, what he was hearing. It would be his father, the man who had always pushed him, always demanded more, his voice a venomous blend of disappointment and scorn.

Tommy, you're a coward. Just like your uncle. You'll never amount to anything. You'll always be second best. It was the legacy of doubt, the inherited fear of failure that Tommy had fought so hard to overcome, now being twisted and used against him.

The whispers, once generalized echoes of their anxieties, had become surgical strikes, precisely targeting the softest parts of their psyches. They weren't just external sounds anymore; they were intrusions, violations of their most private thoughts, designed to shatter their fragile bonds and isolate them in a sea of their own despair. The entity was playing them like instruments of their own torment.

"No," Tommy choked out, shaking his head violently. "That's not true. That's not what he'd say." But his voice lacked conviction, his eyes wide with a terror that transcended mere fear of the supernatural. This was the fear of losing oneself, of having one's very identity dissected and corrupted.

The cornfield responded, the rustling intensifying, taking on a mocking, sibilant quality, like dry leaves skittering across a tombstone. The stalks seemed to lean closer, their shadows elongating, coalescing into shifting, indistinct forms that danced at the periphery of their vision. Kayla felt a dizzying sense of disorientation. The ground beneath her feet seemed to tilt, the familiar landscape blurring into a swirling vortex of green and shadow. Was she seeing things? Were these hallucinations, or was the entity bending the very fabric of reality to its will?

"It's trying to break us," Kayla said, her voice strained. She reached out, her hand finding Tommy's, her fingers interlocking with his, a desperate, silent pact of solidarity. Helen's small hand found Kayla's other side, their joined hands a fragile shield against the encroaching madness.

"It's showing us... regrets," Helen stammered, her voice trembling. "Things we can't change. Things we wish we could have done differently." She was staring at a specific patch of corn, her eyes wide with a horror that seemed to stem from within.

Kayla followed her gaze. For a fleeting moment, the green stalks seemed to part, revealing a scene bathed in an ethereal, sickly light. It was a distorted tableau, a fragmented memory playing out before them. She saw a younger Helen, her face streaked with tears, reaching out for her father as he left for work, a hurried goodbye that had become a permanent farewell. The phantom image was agonizingly real, the unspoken words of love and reassurance left hanging in the air, a testament to the moments lost, the opportunities squandered. It was a visual manifestation of Helen's deepest regret: the inability to say a proper goodbye.

Then, the scene shifted, the corn closing in again, only to reveal another flicker. This time, it was Tommy, younger, angrier, standing in the driveway, his fists clenched, his face contorted with a rage he had never fully unleashed. Kayla recognized the scene – it was the day his father had berated him for a minor mistake, the day Tommy had wanted to scream, to fight back, but had instead swallowed his pride and retreated, the resentment festering. The phantom Tommy in the cornfield was mouthing silent words, his posture radiating a frustration that mirrored Kayla's own unspoken anger at her father's perceived abandonment.

And then, Kayla's own personal hell. The corn parted again, revealing a desolate stretch of road, the headlights of a car receding into the distance. It was the night Mark had left, the night Kayla had been too caught up in her own teenage angst to fully register his goodbye, the casual "see ya later" that had become the last words she'd ever hear from him. The phantom Mark was turning, his face etched with a sorrow that Kayla had never seen, his eyes pleading, as if trying to impart a message she had failed to receive. The whispers intensified around this vision, coalescing into a chilling chorus:

If only… if only… if only…

The psychological assault was relentless, a systematic dismantling of their mental defenses. The entity wasn't just a force of nature; it was a meticulous manipulator, a predator that understood the art of psychological warfare. It didn't need brute force when it could shatter their minds from within. The cornfield was its canvas, their regrets its paint, and madness its masterpiece.

"Stop it!" Kayla cried out, her voice cracking. She squeezed Helen's and Tommy's hands tighter, as if their physical connection could somehow anchor them to reality. "It's not real! It's not us!"

The whispers seemed to laugh, a dry, rasping sound that echoed through the deepening twilight. The very air felt heavy, suffocating, as if the cornstalks were slowly closing in, their rustling a constant, unnerving counterpoint to the phantom voices. The shadows grew longer, more menacing, and Kayla could have sworn she saw the shapes within the corn shifting, morphing into something more solid, more defined. It was as if the entity was testing the boundaries of its power, pushing them further and further into the abyss.

Tommy pulled away slightly, his eyes fixed on the corn. His face was a mask of grim determination, the terror momentarily eclipsed by a flicker of defiance. "It's trying to make us hate each other, too," he said, his voice low and steady, a surprising anchor in the storm of sensory overload. "It's showing us our worst moments, our worst fears, trying to turn us against ourselves, against each other."

Kayla nodded; her own fear momentarily overshadowed by a surge of anger. This entity, this... *thing*... was actively trying to break them, to shatter the bonds that held them together. It was a testament to their strength, perhaps, that they had held on this long, but the assault was far from over. The cornfield was a breeding ground for despair, a place where hope withered and died.

The whispers shifted again, becoming more insidious, more personal. They no longer focused on past regrets, but on future fears, on the gnawing uncertainty of what lay ahead. Kayla heard the echo of her own dread, the fear of being alone, of being forgotten.

You'll end up just like Mark, a voice whispered, low and seductive, slithering into her ear. *Lost. Erased. No one will even remember you were here.*

Tommy heard the fear of failure, the dread of never living up to expectations.

They'll see you as weak, Tommy. Just like they saw your uncle. You'll never be good enough. You'll always be the one who broke.

Helen heard the terror of abandonment, the deepest fear of being left behind.

They'll leave you, Helen. Just like everyone else. You're too much to handle. They'll get tired of you and they'll go.

The whispers were a poison, seeping into their minds, corroding their resolve, planting seeds of doubt and suspicion. The entity was a master of psychological manipulation, its goal to drive them to the brink of madness before it claimed them entirely. The cornfield was its weapon, an extension of the scarecrow's malevolent will, an environment sculpted by its sinister intent. Every rustle, every shadow, every whispered word was a calculated move in its deadly game.

Kayla felt a wave of nausea wash over her. The sheer, suffocating weight of the entity's presence was becoming unbearable. It was more than just a visual or auditory hallucination; it was a palpable force, pressing down on them, seeking to crush

153

their spirits. The cornstalks seemed to pulse with an unseen energy, their unnatural height a testament to the unnatural life that thrived within them.

"We have to get out of here," Kayla said, her voice raspy with a fear that had now settled into a cold, hard knot of dread. "We can't stay here. It's going to… it's going to consume us."

Tommy nodded, his gaze still fixed on the field, but his stance was no longer one of defiance, but of grim resignation. He knew, as Kayla did, that they couldn't fight this with logic or reason. This was a battle of wills, and the entity had already demonstrated its terrifying capacity for psychological warfare. The personalized whispers, the phantom visions, the shifting shadows – it was all designed to shatter their minds, to leave them broken and vulnerable.

Helen whimpered, her eyes squeezed shut, as if trying to block out the barrage of torment. Her small hands were trembling, her knuckles white against Kayla's. Kayla could feel the tremor running through her, a chilling echo of the fear that had consumed the town.

The entity wasn't just playing with them; it was toying with them, a cat with a trio of trapped mice, savoring their terror, prolonging their agony. The whispers grew more frenzied, a chaotic symphony of their deepest fears, amplified and distorted, echoing the very essence of their individual nightmares. The cornfield, a seemingly passive landscape of agriculture, had transformed into a sentient weapon, an extension of the scarecrow's dark will, its tendrils of influence reaching deep into their minds, seeking to harvest not just their bodies, but their very souls. The Second Harvest was not merely about reaping the physical, but about consuming the psychological, leaving behind only hollowed-out husks, devoid of hope, stripped of sanity. Kayla felt a profound, icy dread, a certainty that this was only the beginning of their descent into the abyss. The whispers were a promise, and the cornfield was the altar upon which their sanity would be sacrificed.

The suffocating embrace of the cornfield had tightened its grip, not just on their senses, but on the very possibility of escape. Kayla's mind, a battlefield where the entity waged war with their deepest fears, latched onto a desperate, flickering hope: an external lifeline.

Dry Creek was a suffocating trap, but surely, beyond its cursed borders, there were people who could help, people who would believe them.

"The phone," Kayla gasped, her voice raw, her grip on Tommy and Helen's hands tightening as if to draw strength from their shared predicament. "We have to call someone. The police. Anyone."

Tommy's eyes, haunted by the spectral echoes of his father's disappointment, flickered towards the dilapidated farmhouse, a symbol of the town's isolation. "The lines were dead earlier," he rasped, the words catching in his throat. "When we first got here."

"Maybe they're working now," Kayla insisted, her voice a desperate plea against the rising tide of despair. She stumbled forward, pulling them with her, away from the malevolent whispers that seemed to cling to their very skin. The ground beneath their feet felt unsteady, as if the earth itself was a living, breathing thing that was slowly closing around them. The cornstalks, impossibly tall, seemed to lean in, their dry rustling a symphony of mockery.

They broke free from the immediate edge of the field, the oppressive stillness momentarily receding, replaced by the twilight chill that had settled over the Withers property. The skeletal silhouette of the barn loomed against the bruised, purple sky, a silent sentinel of their desolation. Kayla's heart hammered against her ribs, a frantic drumbeat against the encroaching silence. She spotted a tarnished, rotary phone mounted on the exterior wall of the barn, its cord dangling like a severed umbilical cord. It looked like a relic from another era, a forgotten artifact in a town that seemed frozen in time, or worse, perpetually trapped in a cycle of dread.

"There!" she cried, her voice cracking with a surge of adrenaline. She lunged towards it, her fingers fumbling with the cold, brittle plastic. Tommy and Helen stayed close, their eyes wide, scanning the perimeter, as if expecting the corn to rise up and swallow them whole. The air around them hummed with a subtle, disquieting energy, a low thrum that vibrated in Kayla's bones.

She lifted the receiver, the sound of the dial tone a hollow, mocking echo. "Come on," she whispered, her breath misting in the frigid air. She jammed her finger into the first dial, then the second, the metallic click unnervingly loud in the oppressive quiet. Nothing. No dial tone. No hum. Just dead air.

A wave of cold dread washed over her, far more chilling than the evening air. She tried again, her movements becoming more frantic, her hope dwindling with each failed attempt. "It's not working," she choked out, her voice laced with disbelief. "It's dead."

Tommy reached for the phone, his own face a mask of grim realization. He lifted the receiver, the dead weight of it in his hand a tangible symbol of their isolation. He shook his head, his gaze falling on the frayed cord that connected the phone to the wall. "It's cut," he said, his voice flat, devoid of emotion. "The wire's been cut, clean through."

Kayla's breath hitched. Cut. Not broken, not damaged by time, but deliberately severed. The implication was stark, chilling. Someone, or something, had ensured that this line of communication, this potential lifeline, was rendered useless. The entity wasn't just an abstract force of nature; it was a conscious entity, one that understood the importance of isolation, of keeping its horrors contained within the suffocating boundaries of Dry Creek.

Helen let out a small, heartbroken sob. "It doesn't want us to call for help," she whispered, her voice trembling. "It knows we're here."

Kayla's gaze swept over the sprawling, uncultivated fields that stretched out from the Withers property, a vast, unbroken expanse that seemed to swallow the last vestiges of daylight. The corn was everywhere, a relentless, suffocating sea of green that pulsed with a sinister life. Even here, away from the immediate edge of the whispering field, she could feel its presence, a subtle, pervasive influence that seeped into the very air. The shadows cast by the barn seemed to deepen unnaturally, elongating and twisting into grotesque shapes that writhed at the periphery of her vision. She could almost hear it, a faint, rustling murmur that seemed to emanate from the very earth itself, a constant reminder of its unyielding, predatory watch.

"We have to try somewhere else," Kayla said, forcing a resolve she didn't feel. Her mind raced, desperately sifting through the few remaining possibilities. The town's single payphone, near the shuttered general store? The Withers landline, if it even worked? But the thought of venturing back into the heart of town, with its empty streets and watchful, unseen eyes, sent a fresh wave of terror through her.

"There's no one else," Tommy said, his voice heavy with the grim finality of their situation. "We're alone here, Kayla. Completely alone." He looked at her, his eyes reflecting the growing darkness, a mirror to her own deepening dread. The realization that they were utterly cut off, that their pleas for help would likely go unanswered, was a crushing weight, heavier than any of the phantom whispers they had endured.

Kayla's gaze fell upon a small, weather-beaten shed nestled near the edge of the property, its paint peeling like sunburnt skin. "What about that?" she asked, pointing with a trembling finger. "Maybe there's another phone there. Or a radio. Something."

Tommy's brow furrowed, a flicker of something akin to memory passing over his face. "That's where Mr. Withers kept his old tools," he said slowly. "And... and some of his junk. I don't think there'd be anything like that in there."

But Kayla was already moving, driven by a primal instinct for survival. The shed offered a sliver of possibility, a dark, uninviting space that, for all she knew, could hold the key to their salvation. She pushed open the creaking door, a cloud of dust and the musty scent of decay assailing her senses. Inside, the gloom was thick, the only light filtering through a grimy, cobweb-laden window. Piles of rusted tools, discarded farming equipment, and forgotten remnants of a life lived on this desolate land lay scattered about.

Her eyes, accustomed to the encroaching darkness, scanned the cluttered interior. And then she saw it. Tucked away on a makeshift shelf, amidst a tangle of wires and defunct radio parts, was an old, transistor radio. It was an archaic piece of technology, its casing faded and scratched, but it was a radio nonetheless. A chance.

Her fingers, numb with cold and fear, fumbled with the dials, searching for a signal, any signal. Static hissed and crackled, a chaotic symphony of white noise that seemed to mock her efforts. She twisted the tuning knob, moving it painstakingly across the frequency band, her ears straining to catch any discernible sound amidst the cacophony. The whispers from the cornfield seemed to recede slightly, their malevolent influence momentarily diluted by the promise of connection.

"Anything?" Tommy asked, his voice barely audible above the static. He stood in the doorway, a silhouette against the fading light, his posture radiating a weary apprehension.

Kayla shook her head, her hope beginning to wane like the last embers of a dying fire. She tried different frequencies, desperately searching for a human voice, a news report, anything that would confirm the existence of a world beyond the suffocating embrace of Dry Creek and its insatiable corn. All she got was static, a relentless, unyielding wall of noise that seemed to absorb all other sounds, all other possibilities.

"It's no use," she whispered, her voice thick with despair. She slumped against the dusty shelves, the radio falling from her grasp and clattering to the dirt floor. The thud seemed to echo, amplified by the suffocating silence that rushed back in to fill the void. The realization that even this meager attempt at connection had failed was a devastating blow. The entity hadn't just cut the phone line; it had seemingly silenced all avenues of escape, all whispers of help from the outside world.

Helen, her face streaked with tears, clutched Kayla's arm, her small body trembling. "It's keeping us here," she whimpered, her voice barely a whisper. "It doesn't want anyone to know what's happening."

Kayla looked at her, at Tommy, their faces etched with a shared despair. The psychological torment of the cornfield had been a brutal assault on their minds, but this, this crushing isolation, was a slow, agonizing bleed. They were not just trapped physically; they were being systematically severed from the world, their cries for help destined to be swallowed by the vast, indifferent silence. The entity, with its insidious whispers and its manipulative visions, was not merely a threat to their sanity; it was a jailer, ensuring that its atrocities remained hidden, its victims forever bound to its terrifying dominion. The corn wasn't just growing; it was a sentient barrier, a living, breathing prison wall, meticulously constructed to contain the horrors within, ensuring that the Second Harvest would be a secret, a clandestine reaping of souls, unseen and unheard by a world that remained blissfully, terrifyingly unaware. The very isolation of Dry Creek, once a mere inconvenience, had become their most formidable enemy, a weapon wielded by an unseen hand, designed to break them before they could even cry for help.

The dust motes danced in the single shaft of moonlight piercing the gloom of the town archives, each a tiny, ephemeral ghost in the oppressive stillness. Kayla felt a phantom chill, not from the temperature, but from the weight of ages pressing down on her. Tommy had managed to find a loose floorboard behind a forgotten filing cabinet, a desperate hope born from the same gnawing instinct that had driven them to the derelict barn. It was a small, damp space, smelling of mildew and forgotten dreams, but it held a flicker of promise, a potential refuge from the suffocating presence of the corn. Helen huddled close, her small hand clinging to Kayla's, her breathing shallow and uneven.

"It's just… old papers, Kayla," Tommy murmured, his voice a low rumble, tinged with a weariness that mirrored her own. He sifted through stacks of yellowed documents, town council minutes from decades past, faded photographs of stern-faced men and women whose names were now lost to the dust. Each rustle of paper seemed amplified in the silence, a stark counterpoint to the unnerving quiet that had settled over Dry Creek since they'd last heard the whispers.

Kayla, however, was drawn to a different corner, to a heavy, oak chest that seemed to hum with a subtle, almost imperceptible energy. It wasn't locked, but the lid was swollen with age, resisting her initial efforts. With a grunt, Tommy joined her, and together they managed to heave it open. The smell of aged leather and something else, something metallic and coppery, like dried blood, wafted out. Inside, nestled amongst moth-eaten fabrics and brittle lace, was a single, leather-bound journal and a wrapped object.

It was larger than she'd expected, its cover worn smooth with countless touches, the gold tooling on its spine almost entirely faded. A thick, leather strap secured it, its buckle tarnished and green with verdigris. There was no title, no author's name, but as Kayla's fingers brushed against the supple, aged leather, a visceral tremor ran through her. This felt significant. This felt like the heart of the darkness that had consumed Dry Creek.

She carefully unbuckled the strap, the click of the metal against the leather echoing in the charged silence. Tommy pulled out the wrapped object. He unbundled it and noticed it was a shard of black glass shaped into a knife. Kayla was busy turning the pages within were a deep, creamy parchment, brittle with age but surprisingly intact. The script was elegant, precise, and chillingly familiar, flowing across the pages in neat, dark ink. It was Elias Withers hand, the patriarch of the family whose name was synonymous with Dry Creek, whose very legacy seemed to be interwoven with the cursed corn.

The initial entries were mundane enough – accounts of planting seasons, harvest yields, the daily comings and goings of a farming family. Kayla's hope, a fragile thing, flickered. Perhaps this was just a personal record, a historical curiosity, nothing more. But then, the tone began to shift. The entries grew shorter, more feverish. A sense of unease began to permeate the words, a creeping dread that mirrored the sensations she'd felt in the fields.

The Silence. It grows louder, one entry read, the ink bleeding slightly into the parchment. *The Eye watches. It hungers.*

Kayla's breath hitched. The Eye. It was the same word the whispers had used, the same chilling descriptor that had echoed in her mind during the harrowing experience in the corn. She flipped further, her heart pounding a frantic rhythm against her ribs. The journal spoke of a covenant, an ancient pact made by the Withers family generations ago, a desperate bargain struck in a time of devastating famine.

Our ancestors sought succor when the land yielded naught but dust and despair. They looked to the earth, and the earth offered a solution. A communion. A sacrifice. Not of blood, not of flesh, but of the very essence of perception. A Gaze Offering.

Tommy leaned closer, his gaze fixed on the page, his face a mask of horrified fascination. Helen, sensing the shift in atmosphere, burrowed deeper into Kayla's side, her small form trembling. Kayla's fingers traced the words, the ancient script burning themselves into her mind. The entity, it seemed, didn't feed on flesh or soul in the way they might have imagined. Its sustenance was far more insidious.

The entity demands not our lives, but our sight. Not our bodies, but our awareness. Each season, a tithe must be paid. A sacrifice of vision. The corn, a conduit, drinks the light from our eyes, leaving us blind to its true nature, but feeding it, appeasing it. Those who gaze upon the entity, those who witness its presence, offer the purest tribute.

The implications were staggering, a chilling confirmation of her deepest fears. The whispers weren't just auditory hallucinations; they were the entity's subtle manipulation, its way of drawing them in, of making them *see*. And the corn... the corn was its instrument, its sacred, blood-soaked field.

The ritual is precise. On the eve of the summer solstice, under the blood moon, the chosen must stand at the heart of the stalks. They must open their eyes, and witness. The entity will present itself, veiled in blinding light, a symphony of colors that no mortal eye was meant to behold. And in that moment, it will drink. It will consume the vision, the memory of sight, leaving behind only a hollow void. But the land will be fertile. The harvest will be bountiful. And Dry Creek will be safe, for another year.

Kayla swallowed, her throat dry and constricted. The Gaze Offering. The terrifying ritual that kept the entity sated, and the town alive, at a horrific cost. She looked at Tommy, his eyes wide with dawning horror. He'd spoken of his father's disappearance, of the

161

hushed whispers and the town's unspoken secrets. Now, the journal was beginning to unravel them, thread by horrifying thread.

My son, Jason, was the first to be chosen, the journal continued, the penmanship becoming more frantic, laced with a desperate, paternal grief. *He was a boy of great curiosity, his eyes too eager, too bright. He looked upon the entity for too long. He saw too much. Now, he walks in perpetual twilight, his mind a fractured mirror of what once was.*

Kayla's gaze snapped back to the worn photographs in the chest, to the stern faces of the Withers ancestors. Had Jason been among them? Had he been another victim, another soul claimed by this insatiable hunger? The journal detailed the cyclical nature of the appeasement, the dread that accompanied each solstice, the fear of who would be chosen next. It spoke of the town's complicity, of their silent consent to the sacrifice, a desperate measure to ensure their own survival.

The townsfolk understand. They offer their silence, their ignorance, in exchange for peace. They turn a blind eye, lest the entity turn its gaze upon them. They harvest the bounty, knowing its source, but daring not to question. For to question is to invite its attention. To acknowledge is to become its prey.

The chilling truth settled over Kayla like a shroud. Dry Creek wasn't just a town; it was a living sacrifice, its inhabitants bound by a terrifying pact, their collective denial a shield against an unimaginable horror. The corn wasn't just a crop; it was a monstrous altar, its stalks reaching towards the heavens like skeletal fingers, its rustling whispers the murmurs of a starving god.

My own sight dims, Elias Withers wrote, his final entries marked by a profound despair. *The entity calls to me. It is time. I have prepared the way. I have ensured the continuity of the pact. The corn will grow, and it will feed. The cycle will continue. May God have mercy on my soul, and on the souls of all who dwell in the shadow of the stalks.*

The journal ended abruptly, the last few pages smudged, as if Elias Withers had been unable to finish his confession. Kayla closed the book, her hands shaking, the weight of its contents pressing down on her, suffocating her. Tommy sat in stunned silence, his face pale, his eyes fixed on the journal as if it were a venomous snake. Helen, sensing the gravity of the situation, remained a silent, quivering presence beside them.

The narrative was clear, brutal, and horrifyingly definitive. The entity's hunger was not for blood, but for sight. It was a parasitic force, feeding on the very essence of perception, using the Withers family as its earthly stewards, its enforcers. The corn was its manifestation, its sacred, ever-growing temple, tended by the descendants of those who had made the original, desperate pact. The curse that plagued Dry Creek wasn't a random act of malevolence; it was a meticulously orchestrated ritual, a cyclical appeasement designed to keep a cosmic horror sated, ensuring the continued, albeit blighted, existence of the town.

The whispers weren't just in their heads anymore. They were the echoes of Elias Withers own tormented confession, the spectral residue of a family bound by an unspeakable duty. And the Gaze Offering... the thought of it sent a fresh wave of icy dread through Kayla. It wasn't a myth. It was a chilling reality, a terrifying ceremony that had been perpetuated for generations, claiming its victims, one pair of eyes at a time. The true extent of the curse wasn't just in the fear it instilled, but in the complicity it demanded, the quiet acceptance of a horrifying truth that bound every soul in Dry Creek to the insatiable hunger of the entity that resided within the whispering corn. They weren't just trapped; they were part of a horrifying, ancient tradition, a living sacrifice waiting to happen. The silence of the town wasn't ignorance; it was a conscious, terrified agreement. And the corn... the corn was not just growing; it was ripening, a morbid harvest of stolen visions.

The silence in the archives was no longer merely the absence of sound; it was a tangible pressure, a suffocating blanket woven from Elias Withers desperate words. Kayla reread the final, chilling entry, the smudge obscuring the last vestiges of his confession feeling like a deliberate, final act of concealment. The weight of generations, of a town built on a foundation of stolen sight and silent pacts, bore down on her. They had stumbled upon the truth, a truth more horrifying than any whispered fear, and now, they were inextricably bound to it. Tommy sat beside her, his face etched with a grim comprehension, the journal resting open between them like a forbidden artifact. Helen, sensing the shift from panicked searching to a profound, terrifying understanding, had finally stopped trembling and had become unnaturally still, her wide eyes reflecting the dim light, her small hand still clutched in Kayla's.

"The Harvest Moon," Kayla murmured, her voice raspy, barely audible in the echoing space. She ran a trembling finger over the worn parchment, tracing the faded ink that spoke of cyclical rituals and appeasement. "He mentions the Harvest Moon."

Tommy's gaze snapped to hers, his eyes darkening with a fresh wave of dread. "When?" he asked, his voice low and strained. "When is it?"

Kayla's mind raced, desperately sifting through the journal's fragmented accounts, searching for a specific date, a marker in Elias's descending spiral into despair. She found it, tucked away in a passage describing the town's annual Harvest Festival, an event usually marked by a veneer of forced gaiety that now, in the stark light of the Withers confession, felt like a macabre ritual in itself.

The Harvest Moon, the entry read, the script again growing more frantic, less controlled. *Its full bloom heralds the time of greatest power. The veil thins, and the Eye's hunger reaches its apex. We must ensure the tithe is paid before its light reaches its zenith, lest its reach extend beyond the fields, beyond our comprehension. The days are counted. The moon watches. And waits.*

Kayla looked up at Tommy, her heart a heavy, leaden weight in her chest. "Days, Tommy," she whispered, the word tasting like ash. "We have days. Not weeks. Days." The implications crashed down on her with the force of a physical blow. The Harvest Moon. It wasn't just a celestial event; it was the entity's apex, the moment its power surged, its influence reaching its absolute zenith. It was the culmination of the cyclical appeasement, the time when the Gaze Offering was most potent, and when the consequences of failing to appease it would be most dire. The journal, in its stark, unflinching narrative, painted a picture of a supernatural predator whose power ebbed and flowed, and the Harvest Moon was its peak.

Tommy's jaw tightened. He'd seen the signs, the subtle shifts in the town's atmosphere, the unnatural quiet that had descended, punctuated by the rustling whispers of the corn. He'd felt the oppressive presence, the chilling awareness of being watched. Now, he understood why. The entity wasn't a constant, unchanging force; it was a creature of cycles, of seasons, and the Harvest Moon was its time of greatest strength.

"The solstice... that was for the summer offering," Kayla murmured, piecing together the scattered fragments. "This is different. This is the Harvest Moon. It's about... consolidating power?"

"Or it's about the next sacrifice," Tommy said, his voice grim. "The journal talked about continuity. If the Gaze Offering is tied to the cycles of nature, then the Harvest Moon, being the peak of the harvest, would be a crucial point for the entity. A time to replenish, to exert its will before the lean months."

The thought of another sacrifice, another innocent blinded and broken to feed this insatiable hunger, sent a fresh wave of nausea through Kayla. She remembered the hushed stories, the whispers of Elias's son, Jason, a boy described as having had "too bright" eyes. Had he been taken during the Harvest Moon? Was this particular lunar phase a prelude to the most significant offering, the one that truly appeased the entity for the entire year?

"The journal mentioned 'the continuity of the pact'," Kayla recalled, her mind replaying Elias's despairing words. "He prepared the way. He ensured the cycle would continue. If the Harvest Moon is the period of highest power, then failing to meet the entity's demands now... it wouldn't just mean a bad harvest. It would mean its full attention, its unbridled wrath."

Tommy ran a hand through his hair, his movements agitated. "And we have no idea what the Gaze Offering actually entails for the Harvest Moon. The solstice description was specific – standing at the heart of the stalks, witnessing the blinding light. But this...

this is different. Is it another offering? Or is it something else entirely?"

The journal offered no further clues about the specific rituals surrounding the Harvest Moon. Elias Withers entries, after detailing the solstice ceremony, became more cryptic, filled with anxieties about the moon's approach, about a growing unease that permeated the very air of Dry Creek. He wrote of the townspeople becoming more withdrawn, more insular, their eyes averted, their conversations hushed, as if speaking too loudly would attract unwanted attention.

The moon waxes, and so does the dread, one passage read, the ink smudged as if his hand had trembled. *The whispers grow bolder, weaving themselves into the very fabric of our thoughts. The air thrums with an unnatural energy, a palpable expectancy. The corn sways in a wind that does not touch the leaves of the oaks. It knows. It waits.*

Kayla felt a prickle of unease crawl up her spine. She remembered the unnerving stillness that had fallen over the cornfields the last time they had ventured out, a silence that felt more menacing than any rustling sound. The corn itself seemed to be an extension of the entity, its stalks vibrating with an unseen power, its very growth dictated by the lunar cycles and the entity's inscrutable needs.

"What if the Harvest Moon isn't just about a sacrifice," Kayla mused aloud, her gaze drifting to the dusty shelves around them, as if the answer might be hidden amongst the forgotten histories. "What if it's about the entity *gaining* something? Something more than just sight?"

Tommy's brow furrowed. "What do you mean?"

"Elias wrote that the pact was made for 'succor' when the land yielded nothing. It was a bargain for survival. And the Gaze Offering was the price. But if the Harvest Moon is the time of its greatest power... maybe it's not just about appeasement. Maybe it's about influence. About extending its reach."   She flipped through more pages, her fingers brushing against the brittle parchment. She found a passage that seemed to confirm her growing dread.

166

The entity's hunger is not merely for sustenance, but for dominion. The cycles are a means to an end. Each offering strengthens its hold, weaving its consciousness into the land, into the very minds of those who dwell here. The Harvest Moon marks a crucial turning point, a moment when its influence can expand, when the boundary between its reality and ours becomes perilously thin. We are but conduits, and the corn, its sacred chalice.

The words resonated with a chilling accuracy. The town hadn't just been trying to survive; they had been actively facilitating the entity's expansion. The Withers family, as stewards of the pact, were not merely guardians of a sacrifice; they were its architects, its willing — or perhaps unwilling, at some point — collaborators in a slow, insidious takeover. The Harvest Moon was the time of greatest risk, the moment when the entity could solidify its dominion, when its whispers could become commands, its influence undeniable and absolute.

"So, it's not just about feeding it," Tommy said, his voice heavy with realization. "It's about it growing stronger, more pervasive. And we've just given it… what? A month of weakened defenses? We've been so focused on the solstice, on the immediate threat of the Gaze Offering, that we might have missed the bigger picture."

Kayla nodded, her mind racing ahead, picturing the vast expanse of the cornfields, the moon rising, a bloated, spectral orb in the night sky. The journal painted a picture of the entity's power waxing with the moon. If the solstice was a focused, intense burst of its energy, then the Harvest Moon was a slow, pervasive seep, a deepening of its roots into the fabric of their reality.

"The whispers," she said, recalling the first time she'd heard them, faint at first, then growing more insistent. "They weren't just random. Elias said they were the entity 'weaving itself into our thoughts.' It starts subtle, making us *see* what it wants us to see, making us *hear* what it wants us to hear. And the Harvest Moon… it amplifies that."

Helen stirred beside her, a soft whimper escaping her lips. Kayla looked down at her, her heart aching. The child had been through so much, her innocence already tarnished by the

167

encroaching darkness. The thought of the entity's influence extending to her, to her young mind, was unbearable.

"We have to find a way to break it," Kayla stated, her voice firm, a newfound resolve hardening within her. "Not just to survive the Harvest Moon, but to stop this cycle. Elias was trying to do something; to prepare the way... maybe he left clues about how to *unprepare* it."

Tommy picked up the journal, his gaze sweeping across the pages with renewed intensity. "He wrote about 'ensuring the continuity of the pact.' Maybe he was also looking for a way to break it. He was clearly tormented by what he had to do, by what happened to Jason."

They spent the next few hours immersed in the suffocating stillness of the archives, poring over Elias Withers increasingly desperate entries. The narrative of the Harvest Moon was one of heightened awareness for the entity, a period when its power was most palpable, its influence most potent. The journal spoke of the townspeople experiencing heightened anxiety, of a collective sense of unease that permeated every interaction. There were references to strange occurrences, to fleeting glimpses of movement in the periphery of vision, to an almost unbearable pressure building within the community.

The air is thick with anticipation, Elias wrote, his hand shaking. *The moon begins its ascent, and the corn trembles with a life of its own. It is a symphony of dread, a prelude to the inevitable. The entity's gaze is upon us all, and its hunger knows no season.*

Kayla noticed a recurring theme in Elias's later entries – his obsession with light. He wrote about seeking out the faintest glimmer, the smallest source of illumination, as if trying to push back against an encroaching darkness. There were passages describing his attempts to understand the nature of the entity's consumption, to discern if there was any weakness, any vulnerability that could be exploited.

The light is its bane, yet also its sustenance, he scrawled, the words almost illegible. *It consumes perception, but perhaps not illumination itself. The act of witnessing is what feeds it, but what if the witnessing is not of its own making? What if the light is external, a disruption to its manufactured reality?*

Tommy pointed to another passage; a cryptic note scribbled in the margin of a page detailing the town's annual festival preparations.

The old rituals. They speak of warding. Of protection. But the true ward is not of stone or symbol, but of perception. To see what is not there, and to deny what is. A paradox.

"'To see what is not there, and to deny what is'," Tommy repeated, his brow furrowed in concentration. "What does that even mean?"

"It means actively disrupting its control over perception," Kayla said, a flicker of understanding igniting within her. "The Gaze Offering makes people *see* the entity by taking their vision. But Elias is talking about something different. About using perception itself as a weapon. Maybe... maybe the Harvest Moon isn't about a sacrifice in the same way the solstice is. Maybe it's about *reinforcing* the entity's hold, and if we can disrupt that... if we can make people *see* what's really happening, or *not see* what the entity wants them to see..."

The approaching Harvest Moon was no longer just a deadline; it was a ticking clock, a countdown to a point of maximum vulnerability for Dry Creek, and perhaps, a point of ultimate power for the entity. The journal, a testament to generations of fear and desperate attempts at appeasement, had revealed the terrifying truth: the Harvest Moon was the entity's season of ascendance, its period of greatest influence. And the whispers, the unsettling atmosphere, the growing sense of dread – these were all symptoms of its impending resurgence. They had mere days to unravel the secrets of the Harvest Moon's curse and find a way to break the cycle, before the entity's power became absolute, its dominion over Dry Creek complete. The stakes had never been higher, and the encroaching moonlight seemed to mock their dwindling time.

Chapter 8

The Third Eye

Helen's small hand, still nestled in Kayla's, began to twitch. A low, guttural sound, not quite a whimper and not quite a gasp, escaped her lips. Her eyes, previously wide with a dawning, horrifying understanding, now flickered with something else entirely – a profound terror, raw and primal. It was the terror of a child of 12, who had glimpsed something that was never meant to be seen, a thing of shadows and impossible angles. Kayla's heart lurched. She tightened her grip on Helen's hand, a desperate anchor in the rising tide of fear. Tommy, his own face a mask of grim realization, looked from Helen to Kayla, his gaze sharp with concern.

"Helen?" Kayla whispered, her voice barely audible above the thumping of her own heart. "What is it, sweetie? What do you see?"

Helen didn't answer. Her head lolled back, her eyes rolling upwards, the irises wide and unseeing, yet simultaneously fixed on something beyond the dusty confines of the archives, beyond the mundane reality they thought they understood. A shiver wracked her small frame, a violent tremor that Kayla felt through their joined hands. It wasn't the subtle trembling of fear they had witnessed earlier; this was a deep, visceral convulsion, as if her very being was being subjected to an unseen, unbearable pressure.

"It's… it's there," Helen finally breathed, her voice a thin, reedy sound, laced with a terror that chilled Kayla to the bone. "It's watching."

The words hung in the air, heavy and suffocating. Kayla scanned the room, her eyes darting from the towering shelves of forgotten lore to the shadowed corners, half-expecting to see a pair of malevolent eyes staring back. But there was nothing. Only the

171

oppressive silence, the dust motes dancing in the weak light, and the suffocating weight of Elias Withers confession.

"What's watching, Helen?" Tommy asked, his voice pitched low, careful not to startle the child further. "Is it the scarecrow?"

Helen's head shook slowly, a jerky, unnatural movement. "No," she whispered, her voice growing weaker, more distant. "Not the scarecrow. It's… bigger. And it's… everywhere."

The description sent a fresh wave of dread through Kayla. The scarecrow, a tangible manifestation of the entity's influence, had been their focus, their immediate threat. But Helen's words suggested something far more insidious, something that transcended the physical form Elias Withers had described. A being that was not confined to a specific object, but was instead a pervasive presence, an atmospheric horror.

"Tell me what you see, Helen," Kayla urged, her own fear a cold knot in her stomach. She tried to project an aura of calm, of safety, but the words felt hollow even to her own ears. "Is it… is it like a shadow?"

Helen's breath hitched. Her lips parted, and a single, choked sob escaped her. "It's… like a tear," she whispered, her voice barely audible. "In the air. And… and things are looking out of it."

Kayla's blood ran cold. A tear in the air. A breach in reality. It was a terrifyingly accurate, if childish, description of what they were beginning to understand: the entity was not of their world, and its presence was a distortion, a tearing of the very fabric of existence. And Helen, with her heightened sensitivity, her innocent vulnerability, was seeing the raw, unvarnished truth of it. The fragmented glimpses were like shards of broken glass, reflecting a horrifying, alien reality.

Tommy moved closer, his hand resting on Helen's shoulder. "What kind of things, Helen? Can you describe them?"

Helen squeezed her eyes shut, her face contorted in an expression of pure agony. "Dark shapes," she murmured, her voice a frantic, breathless rush. "Twisting. And eyes. So many eyes. They don't have lids. They just... blink. Slowly. And they're all looking at us."

The image was almost too much to bear. Eyes without lids, blinking slowly, unceasingly. It conjured a vision of a detached, alien consciousness, an observer that perceived the world through a terrifyingly different lens. The entity wasn't just feeding on sight; it was an active participant in a cosmic voyeurism, its gaze a predatory act.

"Elias wrote about 'unblinking eyes'," Kayla recalled, her voice trembling. "He said the entity's awareness was constant, its gaze never wavering. It wasn't just watching; it was *consuming* what it saw."

Helen shuddered violently. "It feels... cold," she whispered, her voice fading. "So cold. And it's hungry. It's so, so hungry."

The hunger. It was the driving force, the insatiable need that had bound the Withers family, and now, Dry Creek, to this horrifying pact. But Helen's description went beyond mere physical sustenance. The cold, the pervasive sense of being watched, the chilling glimpse into a reality just beyond their own – it spoke of a deeper, more existential hunger, a yearning for dominion, for absorption.

Kayla felt a phantom sensation, a prickling on her skin, as if unseen eyes were indeed upon her. She fought the instinct to flinch, to avert her gaze. Elias Withers words echoed in her mind: "The act of witnessing is what feeds it, but what if the witnessing is not of its own making? What if the light is external, a disruption to its manufactured reality?"

Could Helen's visions be a disruption? A terrifying, unintentional exposure of the entity's true nature? The fragmented glimpses, the formless dread, the chilling cold – these weren't the carefully constructed illusions the entity might employ to lure or deceive. These were raw, unmediated perceptions of its alien existence.

Tommy, his face grim, pulled out his phone. "We need to document this," he said, his voice tight. "If she can see it, if she can describe it… it's vital."

Kayla nodded, pulling Helen closer. "What if it's not just seeing, Tommy? What if… what if the entity can't fully manifest in our reality, and it's using Helen to get a clearer picture, to get closer?"

The thought was horrifying. Helen, the innocent bystander, the unintended victim, was becoming a conduit, a window for this ancient, malevolent force. Her perception was being twisted, exploited, used to bridge the gap between dimensions.

Helen's breathing grew shallow. Her eyelids fluttered open again, and this time, there was a flicker of recognition, a terrifying clarity in her wide eyes. "It wants to… to show us," she whispered, her voice barely audible. "It wants us to see… what it is."

The implication was stark. The entity wasn't just observing; it was actively trying to communicate, to imprint its alien reality onto their minds. And Helen was the unwilling recipient of its terrifying message. The fragmented visions were not random hallucinations; they were deliberate exposures, meant to instill fear, to assert its presence, to solidify its claim.

"It's showing her its true form," Tommy said, his voice heavy with dread. "Or as much of it as she can comprehend. Elias's journal mentioned the entity's form was fluid, something that defied human description. He called it 'a tapestry of shadows woven with screams.'"

Helen whimpered, her body tensing again. "It's… it's changing," she gasped. "It's not just dark shapes. It's… made of memories. Of fear. And it's… it's reaching for us."

Kayla felt a phantom touch brush against her arm, a cold, insubstantial caress that raised gooseflesh on her skin. She wrenched her gaze away from Helen, her eyes darting around the archives, searching for the source of the hallucination, the trick of the light. But the sensation was too vivid, too real. It felt as if the very air around them was shifting, coalescing into a tangible, malevolent form.

"It's a perceptual assault," Kayla realized, her mind racing through Elias's cryptic notes. "It's not just about taking sight; it's about manipulating what we perceive, twisting our senses until we can see... it. It's breaking down the barriers of our reality."

Helen's small body went rigid. A sharp, piercing scream tore from her throat, a sound that seemed to echo with a distorted, unholy resonance. Kayla instinctively covered Helen's ears, pulling her close, a futile gesture against the invisible horror that was assaulting her.

"It's inside my head!" Helen shrieked, her voice a strangled cry of pure terror. "It's telling me things! Terrible things!"

The entity was no longer content with mere observation. It was actively invading, planting seeds of fear and madness into Helen's young mind. The fragmented glimpses were evolving into a direct assault, a terrifying telepathic intrusion.

"What is it telling you, Helen?" Tommy asked, his voice tight with urgency. He was trying to keep the conversation going, to keep Helen tethered to their reality, to pull her back from the precipice of madness.

Helen thrashed in Kayla's arms, her small fists beating against Kayla's chest. "It says... it says it's always been here," she sobbed, her words punctuated by ragged breaths. "Waiting. And that... that we woke it up. That we're going to pay."

The primal fear in Helen's voice was infectious. Kayla felt a cold dread creeping into her own mind, the insidious suggestion that their intrusion had unleashed something ancient and terrible, and that the consequences would be devastating. The entity's whispers were designed to sow despair, to break the will of its victims before it even touched them.

"It's a lie, Helen," Kayla said, her voice trembling but firm. "We're going to protect you. We're going to figure this out." She glanced at Tommy, a desperate plea in her eyes. They were out of their depth. The journal had provided clues, but it hadn't prepared them for the sheer, overwhelming terror of witnessing the entity's influence directly, especially through the eyes of a child.

Tommy knelt beside them; his gaze locked on Helen's contorted face. "Elias Withers... he tried to understand it," Tommy said, his voice a low rumble. "He was trying to find a way to counter it, to stop it. He wrote that the entity's power was amplified by fear, by the very act of *acknowledging* its presence. He was looking for a way to deny it, to make it powerless by its own rules."

Kayla focused on Tommy's words, desperately trying to latch onto any fragment of hope, any potential solution. "Deny it?" she echoed. "How do you deny something that's literally in your head, that's making you see things that aren't there?"

"That's the paradox he wrote about," Tommy replied, his eyes scanning the journal pages again, as if seeking a forgotten answer. "To see what is not there, and to deny what is. He believed that if they could perceive the entity as it truly was – not as a shadowy monster, but as something... less. Something that fed on their belief, their fear – then perhaps they could starve it."

Helen's sobs began to subside, replaced by shallow, ragged breaths. Her eyes, though still unfocused, seemed to lose some of their frantic terror, replaced by a deep, unsettling weariness. It was as if the entity, having made its terrifying point, had receded, leaving behind the wreckage of its intrusion.

"It showed me... it showed me the corn," Helen whispered, her voice barely a breath. "But it was... twisted. Like it was made of smoke, and it was always moving. And there were... faces in the stalks. *Watching.*"

Kayla felt a chill cascade down her spine. The corn, their supposed source of protection, was now a conduit for the entity's influence, a living manifestation of its perversion. The faces in the stalks – it was Elias's own description, a chilling testament to the entity's ability to weave itself into the very fabric of their lives, to corrupt even the most natural elements.

"It's trying to convince us that it *is* the corn, that it *is* the land," Kayla realized, the pieces clicking into place with terrifying clarity.

"It wants us to see it everywhere, so we can't escape it. It feeds on our perception of its omnipresence."

Tommy nodded grimly. "And if Helen can see its true form, even in fragments, then maybe... just maybe, we can too. Elias was looking for a way to disrupt its perceptual control. He was looking for a way to make people *see* the truth, not the lies the entity fed them."

He pointed to a passage in the journal, a scrawled note beside a description of the Harvest Moon rituals.

The ancients spoke of clarity in the face of deception. Not the clarity of vision, but the clarity of intent. To hold firm to what is real, even when the veil thins. The entity thrives on the confusion it sows. True power lies in the unwavering conviction of one's own reality.

"So," Kayla mused, her mind working furiously, "the Harvest Moon isn't just about its peak power. It's about its peak *influence*. It's about its ability to control what we perceive. And if we can maintain our own sense of reality, if we can reject the illusions it forces upon us..."

Helen, surprisingly, spoke again, her voice soft and distant, as if from a great remove. "It's lonely," she whispered. "It's so, so lonely. And it wants us to be lonely too."

The unexpected confession sent a ripple of unease through Kayla. The entity wasn't just a predator; it was a being driven by an unimaginable loneliness, a cosmic solitude that it sought to alleviate by drawing others into its own desolate existence. It wanted to strip away their connections, their relationships, their very sense of self, leaving them as isolated, empty vessels, mirroring its own state.

"It's trying to isolate us," Tommy said, his voice tight. "The whispers, the paranoia... it's all designed to break our bonds, to make us vulnerable."

Kayla looked at Helen, at Tommy, her heart aching with a fierce protectiveness. They were all they had. And the entity's ultimate goal was to shatter that. The Harvest Moon was the apex of this psychological warfare, the time when its influence would be strongest, its ability to sow discord and despair at its peak. They had to find a way to resist, not just with physical defenses, but with a strength of will, a clarity of perception that the entity could not overcome. The glimpses Helen had experienced, terrifying as they were, were also a key. They were a window into the entity's true nature, and perhaps, into its vulnerability. The challenge now was to learn to see past the illusions, to hold onto their own reality, and to deny the entity the very fuel it craved: their fear, their isolation, their stolen sight. The path ahead was shrouded in darkness, but in Helen's terrifying visions, a faint, chilling light of understanding had begun to dawn.

The air in the archives remained thick with the residue of Helen's terror, a palpable chill that seemed to seep from the very pages of Elias Withers journal. Kayla traced the faded script with a trembling finger, her eyes scanning the frantic, almost illegible scribblings that Elias had penned in his final days. Helen's fragmented visions had been a horrifying validation of their worst fears, a raw, unfiltered glimpse into the nature of the entity that stalked Dry Creek. But the journal, the tangible legacy of Elias's descent into madness and understanding, offered something more: a desperate, fragile hope.

"He writes about a counter-offering," Kayla murmured, her voice hoarse. "A way to… to push it back, even if only for a moment." Tommy leaned closer, his brow furrowed with concentration as he too pored over the delicate, yellowed pages. The weight of their discovery pressed down on them, a suffocating blanket woven from dread and the desperate need for answers. Helen, now quiet and curled against Kayla, still occasionally shuddered, her small breaths coming in shallow, uneven gasps, as if the echoes of the entity's intrusion lingered within her.

"What kind of offering?" Tommy asked, his gaze fixed on a particular passage marked with a series of agitated underlines.

"Light," Kayla replied, her voice barely above a whisper. "He calls it… 'the vanquisher of shadows.' But it's not just any light. He describes it as a 'purified luminescence,' something that can 'sever the unblinking gaze.'" Elias's words were a tapestry of metaphors, as if he struggled to articulate the true nature of the entity and the methods required to combat it. He spoke of its hunger not just for sustenance, but for connection, for the very act of being perceived. And in that perception, he believed, lay its strength.

"He mentions an artifact," Tommy said, pointing to a rough sketch that Elias had made. It depicted a jagged shard, seemingly carved from obsidian, with a faint crescent moon symbol etched onto its surface. Tommy picked up the shard of glass and looked at it more closely.

"A shard of obsidian, blessed by moonlight. He claims it can temporarily blind the entity, disrupt its connection to… to its victims." Kayla looked at the shard and felt a flicker of something akin to hope, a tiny ember in the vast darkness that threatened to consume them. This artifact. A tangible weapon against an intangible foe. It was a long shot, a desperate gamble based on the ravings of a man who had clearly succumbed to the very horror he sought to understand, but it was *something*.

"He theorizes that the entity's power is derived from its constant, pervasive observation," Kayla read aloud, her voice gaining a little strength. "That it exists and thrives in the act of *seeing*. If we can deny it that sight, even momentarily, we might create an opening. A chance to escape its influence, to break its hold."

Elias had spent years studying the cycles of the Harvest Moon, the times when the entity's power seemed to wax strongest. He believed that the moon, a celestial body of profound symbolic significance, played a crucial role in its manifestation, acting as a conduit or an amplifier for its spectral energies. His journal was filled with observations of the subtle shifts in atmospheric pressure, the unsettling stillness of the air, the unnerving silence that preceded each lunar peak. He had meticulously documented the growing unease in Dry Creek, the subtle changes in the behavior of both humans and animals, all coinciding with the waxing moon.

"He wrote that the entity itself is a 'perceptual parasite,'" Tommy added, his gaze intense. "It doesn't just observe; it *absorbs* the act of observation. It feeds on the energy of being seen. And the obsidian shard... he believed it could refract that stolen energy, sending it back in a way that overwhelmed the entity, blinding it to its prey."

The idea was almost mystical, steeped in folklore and ancient superstition, yet it resonated with the terrifying reality they had encountered. Helen's ability to see beyond the veil, Tommy's growing sensitivity to the unseen, Kayla's own unsettling premonitions – all pointed towards a world where perception was a far more potent force than they had ever imagined. Elias Withers, in his relentless pursuit of understanding, had stumbled upon a truth so profound and so terrifying that it had ultimately consumed him.

"But how do we use this shard?" Kayla asked, her gaze sweeping over the cluttered shelves of the archives, the dusty remnants of Elias's life. "He doesn't specify how, only that it's connected to his family's history, to the land itself."

Tommy flipped through the journal, his fingers brushing against a pressed wildflower, its petals brittle and faded. "He mentions that it came from a 'sacred grove'," Tommy read. "'Where the veil between worlds is thinnest, and the moonlight spills like liquid silver. He believed the shard was hidden there, protected by ancient rituals, intended to be used only in times of dire need."

A sacred grove. The words conjured images of ancient trees, dappled moonlight, and a sense of profound, almost sacred stillness. But in the context of their current predicament, such places also evoked a sense of unease, a feeling of stepping into territory that was not entirely their own, territory that might already be claimed.

"He also noted a specific lunar phase," Tommy continued, his voice hushed. "A 'Crimson Tide,' he called it. It occurs only once every seventy-three years, during the apex of the Harvest Moon. He believed that this specific alignment amplified the shard's power, making its blinding effect far more potent, far more permanent."

Kayla's breath hitched. Seventy-three years. They were living through that cycle. The Harvest Moon was upon them, its eerie glow already beginning to paint the darkened sky. The timing was both a blessing and a curse. It meant the shard that they now possessed should be used then, but it also meant the entity's power would be at its zenith.

"He suggests the shard was imbued with the moon's essence during this specific phase," Kayla elaborated, piecing together Elias's fragmented notes. "The moon's light, channeled through the obsidian, would create a temporary void in the entity's sensory perception. A moment of true darkness for a being that feeds on light, on being seen."

The concept was audacious. To weaponize darkness against a creature of shadow. It felt like a desperate gamble, a leap of faith into the unknown. But Elias had also detailed the ritualistic preparations required to harness the shard's full potential. It wasn't merely about possessing the artifact; it was about understanding its purpose and respecting its power.

"He wrote that the offering of light wasn't just about the shard itself," Kayla explained, her voice growing stronger with each word she deciphered. "It was about a symbolic act of defiance. A declaration that their own perception, their own reality, would not be subjugated by the entity's influence. The act of holding the shard, of focusing their intent through it, was meant to create a mental barrier, a shield against the entity's psychic intrusion."

Tommy nodded, his eyes wide with the implications. "So, it's not just about blinding the entity externally, but also about fortifying themselves internally. About reclaiming their own minds from its pervasive influence."

Helen stirred beside Kayla, her eyes fluttering open. She looked up at Kayla, her gaze still carrying a hint of the terror she had experienced, but also a nascent curiosity. "The moon…" she whispered, her voice fragile. "It looked… sad."

Kayla gently stroked Helen's hair. "It's just the light, sweetie," she murmured, trying to soothe her, though Elias's words about the moon's amplified power sent a shiver down her spine. Was the moon truly sad, or was it merely reflecting the oppressive weight of the entity's presence?

"He believed the entity's ultimate goal was not merely to feed, but to *become*," Elias had scrawled, his handwriting becoming almost illegible. "To merge with its victims, to consume their very essence, leaving behind hollow shells that would then serve as extensions of its own being. The 'Crimson Tide' phase, he theorized, was when this assimilation process was at its most potent. The harvested souls, the lingering fear... it all coalesces, feeding the entity's desire for dominion."

The horror of Elias's words washed over Kayla. It wasn't just about being watched or influenced; it was about utter annihilation, the complete erasure of self. Their fight was not just for survival, but for the preservation of their very identities.

"He talks about the ritual of 'severing the gaze'," Tommy said, pointing to another section of the journal. "It involves a specific incantation, a series of words meant to break the psychic link. He believed that if they could disrupt the entity's focus, even for a heartbeat, the obsidian's light could sever the tendrils of its influence."

Kayla's mind raced, piecing together the scattered clues. The sacred grove, the obsidian shard, the lunar alignment, the ritualistic incantation – it was a puzzle, a desperate quest for a weapon that might not even exist. But the alternative was unthinkable. To succumb to the entity, to become another forgotten soul woven into its tapestry of dread.

"He kept meticulous records of the grove's location," Tommy continued, his voice filled with a growing sense of urgency. "Descriptions of ancient oaks, a stream that flowed underground, a cluster of standing stones... it sounds like a place steeped in forgotten lore." He pointed to a crudely drawn map, a series of landmarks that Elias had painstakingly noted, interspersed with his own feverish annotations. "He marked a specific date in his calendar," Tommy added, his finger hovering over a circled day. "The night of the Crimson Tide. He wrote, 'The stone will reveal its secret. The gaze will be broken.'"

Kayla looked at Tommy, her heart pounding. The weight of Elias's final hopes rested upon them. They had to find the grove, armed with the shard, and perform the ritual. It was a race against time, against the encroaching darkness that threatened to engulf them all. The journal, once a testament to Elias Withers descent into madness, had now become their only beacon in the suffocating gloom.

"He believed the entity was not a singular being, but a collective consciousness, a parasitic entity that fed on fear and despair," Kayla read, her voice trembling slightly. "He theorized that its power was amplified by the shared anxieties of the community, by the collective dread that permeated Dry Creek. The Harvest Moon festivals, the very traditions meant to celebrate abundance and ward off evil, had inadvertently become conduits for its influence, allowing it to weave itself into the fabric of their lives."

Elias had spent years trying to unravel the entity's insidious network, attempting to identify its points of entry, its methods of manipulation. He had focused on the historical accounts of blight, of unexplained disappearances, of the lingering unease that had always seemed to haunt the edges of their community. He had drawn parallels between the cyclical nature of these events and the phases of the Harvest Moon, a chilling pattern that spoke of an ancient, predatory presence that had been dormant for generations, only to be reawakened by some unknown catalyst.

"He writes about the 'attunement,'" Tommy said, his brow furrowed. "The entity's ability to synchronize with the emotional state of its victims. He believed that by understanding the nature of this attunement, they could develop a method of 'dissonance,' a way to disrupt the psychic link and create a temporary rupture in the entity's control."

Kayla nodded, the pieces slowly falling into place. Helen's initial terror, her involuntary connection to the entity, was a prime example of this attunement. The entity had sensed her vulnerability, her openness, and had latched onto her, using her as a conduit to further its insidious agenda. The obsidian shard, with its moonlit blessing, was Elias's proposed method of disrupting this attunement, of introducing a foreign element that would shatter the entity's psychic harmony.

"He describes the shard as a 'key,'" Kayla whispered, her eyes glued to the journal. "'A key to unlock the prison of perception, a key to sever the chains of the unseen.' He believed that the ancient peoples of this land had understood the entity's nature, had developed rituals and artifacts to ward it off, but their knowledge had been lost to time, corrupted by fear and superstition."

The journal detailed Elias's frantic search for these lost traditions, his delving into local folklore, his attempts to decipher ancient symbols carved into forgotten standing stones. He had become obsessed with the idea that the answers lay not in fighting the entity directly, but in understanding its origins, its weaknesses, and the methods that had once kept it at bay.

"He mentions a particular glyph," Tommy said, pointing to a small, intricate symbol etched into the margin of a page. "He believed it represented the 'unblinking eye' of the entity, and that by drawing it in reverse, with a specific intent, it could serve as a form of psychic redirection, a way to blind the entity to its target."

Kayla's gaze fell upon the glyph. It was unnerving, a disturbing spiral that seemed to draw the eye inward, to twist and contort the very perception of form. The thought of replicating it, of using it as a weapon, sent a wave of nausea through her. Yet, Elias had poured his life into this research, his final days dedicated to uncovering these obscure methods of resistance.

"He writes that the shard itself was not merely a tool," Kayla continued, her voice gaining a desperate intensity. "It was a focal point for collective intent. The more people who could focus their will through the shard, the stronger its effect would be. He believed that the entity thrived on isolation, on breaking down individual resistance. And so, his counter-offering was also a call for unity, for shared purpose."

The idea of uniting the fragmented, fearful community of Dry Creek seemed almost impossible. Fear had become their constant companion, suspicion their default setting. But Elias's words resonated with a desperate truth: they could not face this entity alone. Their individual fears, amplified by the entity's influence, would only serve to strengthen it.

"He feared that without the shard, without this disruption, the entity would eventually achieve complete assimilation," Tommy said grimly, his voice barely audible. "That it would drain Dry Creek of its life force, leaving behind a hollow shell, a mere echo of what it once was. He saw it as an inevitable progression, a slow, inexorable march towards ultimate subjugation."

Kayla looked down at Helen, her small body still occasionally trembling. The child's innocent gaze had been the first to truly perceive the entity's horrific nature, and now, their hope for survival rested on them being able to shield her, and by extension, themselves, from its devastating influence. Elias's journal was more than just a record of his descent; it was a testament to the enduring human capacity for resilience, for the desperate, unyielding fight against the encroaching darkness. The shard, the grove, the ritual – they were fragments of a lost knowledge, a forgotten power that might just be their only salvation. The challenge now hold it, to understand it, and to wield it before the Crimson Tide of the Harvest Moon consumed them all.

The air crackled with an unseen energy, a prelude to the storm that was about to break. Kayla clutched Helen tighter, the child's small frame trembling against her own. Tommy stood beside them, his face a mask of grim determination, his eyes scanning the encroaching darkness beyond the skeletal remains of the cornfield. Elias Withers journal lay open between them, its cryptic words now a desperate roadmap in their fight against an enemy that defied understanding. They had found what Elias had called the "sacred grove," a place steeped in an ancient, unsettling stillness, where the trees stood sentinel, their gnarled branches reaching like skeletal fingers towards a bruised, moonlit sky. It was here, amidst the whispering silence, that Elias had believed the obsidian shard, their only hope, should be used here.

The journal's final entries had been a testament to Elias's unraveling sanity, a descent into the abyss he had so desperately sought to understand. He wrote of the entity not as a singular being but as a pervasive consciousness, a parasitic entity that fed on fear and despair. It thrived on isolation, on the breakdown of individual will. His meticulous notes detailed how the entity's power was amplified by the shared anxieties of Dry Creek, by the collective dread that permeated the very soil. He believed that the Harvest Moon festivals, the traditions meant to celebrate abundance, had inadvertently become conduits for its influence, allowing it to weave itself into the very fabric of their lives.

"He feared that without the shard, without this disruption," Tommy murmured, his voice barely audible, his gaze fixed on the shadowed depths of the grove, "the entity would eventually achieve complete assimilation. That it would drain Dry Creek of its life force, leaving behind a hollow shell, a mere echo of what it once was. He saw it as an inevitable progression, a slow, inexorable march towards ultimate subjugation."

Kayla's heart ached for Helen, her small body still occasionally shuddering. The child's innocent gaze had been the first to truly perceive the entity's horrific nature, and now, their hope for survival rested on their ability to shield her, and by extension, themselves, from its devastating influence. Elias's journal was more than just a record of his descent; it was a testament to the enduring human capacity for resilience, for the desperate, unyielding fight against the encroaching darkness. The shard, the grove, the ritual – they were fragments of a lost knowledge, a forgotten power that might just be their only salvation. The challenge now was to display it, to understand it, and to wield it before the Crimson Tide of the Harvest Moon consumed them all.

It was then, amidst the hushed reverence of the grove, that Helen stirred. Her eyes, wide and luminous in the dim light, fixed not on Kayla or Tommy, but on something beyond them, something that sent a primal chill down Kayla's spine. A faint, almost imperceptible shimmer pulsed in the air, a distortion of reality that only Helen seemed to truly perceive. The entity. It was here. Closer than they had dared to imagine.

"It's... it's looking," Helen whispered, her voice a mere breath of sound. "It's looking at us."

186

Kayla followed Helen's gaze, her own eyes straining to pierce the veil that Elias's journal had unveiled. She saw nothing, only the deepening shadows, the skeletal trees. Yet, Helen's fear was palpable, a tangible wave that washed over Kayla, a stark reminder of the horrors they faced. Tommy, ever vigilant, unsheathed the rusty shovel they had found in the archives, its weight a poor comfort against an immaterial foe.

Suddenly, the air grew heavy, suffocating. The faint shimmer Helen had seen intensified, coalescing into a swirling vortex of shadow and malice. It was an absence of light, a void that seemed to absorb the very moonlight around it. Kayla's breath hitched. She could feel it now, a prickling sensation on her skin, a disquieting pressure in her mind, as if unseen eyes were boring into her soul. Elias's words echoed in her mind: "It feeds on perception. It thrives in the act of being seen."

And then, Helen did something that made Kayla's blood run cold. With a strength that belied her small frame, she wrenched herself from Kayla's embrace. "Helen, no!" Kayla cried, but her voice was lost in the rising tide of unnatural silence.

Helen stood unmoving, a solitary figure against the encroaching darkness. Her gaze was fixed on the heart of the swirling void, her small face pale but resolute. She was drawing its attention. Deliberately. Intentionally. It was a sacrifice, a horrifying gamble born of Elias's desperate teachings. She was offering herself, her perception, as bait.

The entity, drawn by this unexpected beacon of defiance, shifted its focus. The vortex seemed to surge towards Helen, its form coalescing, solidifying into something that defied description. It was a formless horror, a shifting tapestry of darkness, punctuated by countless eyes that glittered with an ancient, malevolent hunger. Each eye seemed to bore into Helen, piercing her very essence.

Kayla watched, paralyzed by a terror so profound it stole her breath. Helen's small body convulsed, as if struck by an invisible force. A faint whimper escaped her lips, a sound of pure, unadulterated agony. But she didn't falter. She held her ground, her small hand reaching towards the very core of the entity's being.

"It's... it's so bright," Helen choked out, her voice raspy. "Even though it's dark."

Kayla's mind reeled. Bright? How could darkness be bright? Elias's words about the purified luminescence, the vanquisher of shadows, flashed through her mind. Helen wasn't seeing the entity's true form, not as they understood it. She was seeing something more, something that Elias had only hinted at. She was seeing the raw, untamed power that fueled its existence, a terrifying, paradoxical brilliance hidden within the absolute void.

Tommy, his face etched with horror, moved to intercept Helen, but a chilling force held him back, an invisible barrier that repelled him with suffocating pressure. He was trapped, a helpless observer to Helen's desperate act.

Helen's eyes darted to Kayla, a silent plea in their depths. Then, her gaze fell upon the shard, which Kayla had instinctively held up, her fingers closing around its cool, smooth surface. It was meant to be a weapon, a shield, but now it felt like a cursed talisman.

With a surge of desperate strength, Helen reached out, not towards Kayla, but towards the entity itself. As if guided by an unseen hand, she snatched the shard from Kayla's grasp. It was a swift, fluid motion, a testament to the terrifying clarity that sometimes accompanied moments of extreme peril.

Then, she did something truly unimaginable. She thrust the shard forward, directly into the swirling heart of the entity.

A blinding flash erupted, an explosion of pure, unadulterated light that seemed to consume the very air. It was the antithesis of the darkness, a searing radiance that pierced the veil, forcing reality itself to recoil. The entity shrieked, a sound that was not of this world, a cacophony of a thousand dying stars. Its form contorted, convulsed, its countless eyes flickering and dying like extinguished candles.

Helen, at the epicenter of this cataclysmic burst of energy, cried out, a single, piercing scream that was abruptly cut short. Her small body crumpled, falling forward as if struck by an invisible hammer.

The shard, still clutched in her hand, pulsed with a fading luminescence.

Kayla surged forward, the invisible barrier dissolving as the entity recoiled, its form dissipating like smoke in a gale. She reached Helen, her heart pounding a frantic, desperate rhythm against her ribs. The child lay still, her face serene in death, her eyes wide open, staring blankly at the sky. But there was something different about them now.

Where once there had been the innocent spark of life, there was now only an unnerving, vacant blackness. Her vision, the very thing that had allowed her to perceive the entity, had been consumed. In blinding the creature, Helen had, in turn, been blinded herself, her sight and life extinguished in the inferno of its unmaking.

Tommy knelt beside them, his hand reaching out to gently touch Helen's cheek. "She... she saved us," he whispered, his voice choked with emotion. "She bought us time."

Kayla stared at Helen's lifeless eyes, her own vision blurring with tears. The shard had done its work. It had severed the entity's gaze, disrupted its connection, and in doing so, it had exacted a terrible price. Helen's sacrifice was a brutal, visceral testament to the power Elias Withers had unearthed, a power that demanded everything in return.

The grove, moments before a place of terrifying confrontation, was now a tableau of profound sorrow. The moonlight, no longer distorted by the entity's presence, seemed to shine with a mournful glow, illuminating the tragedy that had unfolded. The air, though still heavy with the residue of conflict, carried a new stillness, a silent reverence for the life that had been so bravely given.

"Elias wrote about this," Kayla murmured, her voice raw with grief. "He called it... 'the final offering.' The severance of sight for the severing of the entity's hold. He believed that the entity's power was so intrinsically linked to perception that a complete denial of sight would shatter its very being, at least for a time."

Tommy picked up the obsidian shard, its surface now cool and inert. The crescent moon symbol seemed to mock their victory, a silent witness to the cost of their survival. "She used it perfectly," he said, his voice tinged with awe. "She understood. She knew what she had to do."

But understanding did not erase the pain. Kayla gently closed Helen's eyes, a futile gesture against the irreversible darkness that had claimed them. The entity was gone, at least for now. Its chilling presence had receded, leaving behind an echoing void. They had won a battle, but the war was far from over. And the cost of that victory was etched forever in the silent, sightless eyes of a child who had faced down the unimaginable.

The silence of the grove was broken only by the soft rustling of leaves, a mournful whisper that seemed to carry Helen's final breath. Kayla cradled the child's head, her own grief a suffocating weight. Helen, the innocent child who had seen too much, had ultimately paid the ultimate price for their survival. Her sacrifice was a stark reminder of the entity's terrifying power, and the brutal reality of their struggle.

They stood in the moonlit grove, the obsidian shard clutched in Tommy's hand, a chilling testament to Helen's courage. The immediate threat had passed, the entity's pervasive gaze temporarily blinded. But the victory was hollow, stained with the irreplaceable loss of a young life. They had been granted time, precious moments to regroup, to plan, to perhaps even find a way to truly banish the darkness that haunted Dry Creek. But the image of Helen's vacant, sightless eyes would forever be seared into Kayla's memory, a constant, agonizing reminder of the true cost of confronting the unknown. The path ahead was uncertain, shrouded in the same oppressive gloom that had consumed Helen's vision, but they would carry her sacrifice forward, a beacon of defiance against the encroaching shadow.

Sheriff DuCard, a man whose life had been a steadfast bulwark against the mundane chaos of Dry Creek, found his foundations crumbling around him. He had always believed in evidence, in logic, in the tangible world that could be measured, cataloged, and understood. The inexplicable had been relegated to the realm of rumor, of sensationalized headlines and the fanciful tales spun by those with too much time and too little sense. But the sight of Helen, her small form contorted in a silent scream, her eyes—once so full of life—now staring with a vacant, disturbing blackness, shattered that meticulously constructed reality. The blinding flash, the unearthly shriek that had ripped through the sacred grove, the palpable wave of malevolence that had momentarily convulsed the very air around them – these were not hallucinations, not tricks of the light, not the product of overwrought imaginations. This was something far older, far more terrifying, and far more real than any earthly threat he had ever encountered.

He had stood there, rooted to the spot, he had seen the whole thing transpire from the dirt road. His hand drawn his handgun which now felt absurdly inadequate against the encroaching tide of the unnatural. The invisible force that had held him captive, preventing him from reaching Helen, had been a chilling testament to the entity's power, a power that defied physics, defied reason, defied everything he thought he knew about the world. He had watched, helpless, as a child sacrificed herself to sever a connection he could only dimly perceive, a connection that had nevertheless held him in its terrifying grip. He had seen the shard, a fragment of something ancient and potent, plunged into a vortex of pure darkness, and witnessed the resulting explosion of light that had been both beautiful and utterly annihilating.

When the spectral presence finally receded, leaving behind the echoing silence of the grove and the heartbreaking stillness of Helen's small body, the invisible barrier around him had dissolved. He had stumbled forward, the world tilting precariously on its axis, his mind struggling to process the horrific tableau. Kayla was already there, cradling the child, her grief a raw, visceral wound laid bare. DuCard knelt beside them, the smell of ozone and something else, something ancient and foul, still clinging to the air. He looked at Helen's sightless eyes, and a profound, soul-deep terror, unlike anything he had ever known, washed over him. His faith, not in any particular deity, but in the inherent order of the universe, in the predictability of cause and effect, had been irrevocably broken.

"It… it was real," he breathed, the words catching in his throat. It was an admission that tasted like ash, a confession of years of willful ignorance. The rational man, the pragmatist, the lawman who dealt with tangible crimes and observable truths, had been forced to confront a truth so alien, so monstrous, that it threatened to unmake him. He had spent his career chasing shadows, but he had never truly believed they could bite back, not like this. He had seen things in his time, witnessed the darkest aspects of human nature, but this… this was a darkness that existed beyond humanity, a primal hunger that predated consciousness itself.

Kayla looked up, her face streaked with tears and grime, her eyes holding a depth of sorrow that mirrored his own dawning horror. "She saved us, DuCard," she whispered, her voice raspy with grief. "Helen saved us."

He nodded, unable to speak. He understood, with a clarity that was both agonizing and absolute, the terrible nature of Helen's sacrifice. She had seen the entity, truly seen it, and in doing so, had become its focal point. And then, in an act of unimaginable courage, she had used the obsidian shard, Elias Withers last desperate hope, to sever that connection, to blind the creature that had been feeding on their fear. Elias had written of such things, of the entity's reliance on perception, on being seen, and Helen, guided by some instinct or perhaps by the very essence of the shard itself, had weaponized that knowledge. Her sight had been the price for their temporary reprieve.

The weight of it all pressed down on him, a crushing burden of responsibility. He was the Sheriff. His duty was to protect the people of Dry Creek. But how could he protect them from something he couldn't even fully comprehend, something that defied the very laws of existence? His carefully cultivated skepticism, his reliance on the concrete, had left him woefully unprepared. He had dismissed Elias Withers as a madman, his journals as the ramblings of a disturbed mind. Now, he understood that Elias had been a prophet, a Cassandra whose warnings had gone unheeded.

He looked at Kayla, at her small frame trembling with exhaustion and grief, and a fierce, protective instinct, honed by years of service, surged through him. His personal crisis of faith was secondary to the immediate, overwhelming need to act. Skepticism had been his shield; now, it was a liability. He needed to believe, to embrace the horrifying reality, because the alternative was annihilation.

"We need to get Helen back," he said, his voice firmer now, imbued with a new, grim resolve. "We can't leave her here." His rational mind, though reeling, began to reassert itself, focusing on the practicalities of the immediate situation. This was his domain, the tangible, the actionable. He could secure the child, ensure her dignity in death, even if the circumstances of it were beyond his comprehension.

Kayla nodded, her gaze still fixed on Helen's serene, sightless face. "Elias wrote about the shard," she said, her voice gaining a measure of strength. "He believed it could disrupt the entity's hold. But he also warned that the price of such disruption would be severe. He didn't know exactly what, but he spoke of a profound cost." She gently stroked Helen's hair, her movements slow and deliberate. "This... this was the cost."

DuCard reached out, his hand hovering over the obsidian shard still clutched in Helen's small, lifeless fingers. It felt unnaturally cold, a dark mirror reflecting the horror they had just witnessed. The crescent moon symbol etched onto its surface seemed to pulse with a faint, residual energy. He understood, with chilling certainty, that this artifact was not merely a tool, but a conduit to powers beyond his understanding.

"We have to keep it safe," he stated, his voice low and steady. "And we have to figure out what Elias was trying to do. He clearly believed this was the only way to fight it." His mind was already racing, piecing together the fragmented clues from Elias's journal, which Kayla had somehow managed to preserve. The sacred grove, the entity's reliance on perception, the obsidian shard – they were pieces of a terrifying puzzle, and he was now inextricably a part of it.

He helped Kayla up and Tommy carefully lift Helen's small body. The child was lighter than expected, as if some essential part of her had been leached away in the violent confrontation. As they carried her from the grove, DuCard's gaze swept over the ancient trees, their gnarled branches now seeming like skeletal sentinels guarding a place of profound tragedy. The moonlight, which had seemed so ethereal moments before, now cast long, distorted shadows that played tricks on his eyes, conjuring fleeting glimpses of movement at the periphery of his vision. He resisted the urge to flinch, forcing himself to meet the darkness head-on.

Back at his patrol car, the silence was heavy, broken only by the mournful chirping of crickets and the soft, rhythmic sobs of Kayla. Tommy gently laid Helen's body in the back, covering her with a blanket, an act that felt both profoundly respectful and utterly inadequate. DuCard looked at Kayla, her face etched with a grief that transcended words and knew that his role had fundamentally changed. He was no longer just the Sheriff; he was a participant in this war against an unseen enemy.

"What do we do now?" Kayla asked, her voice barely a whisper.

DuCard met her gaze, his own eyes reflecting the grim reality they now faced. "We finish what Elias started," he said, the words resonating with a conviction that surprised even himself. "We find a way to stop this thing. For Helen. For Mark and for Dry Creek."

His crisis of faith had not led him to despair, but to a stark, unyielding determination. He had witnessed the impossible, and while it had shaken him to his core, it had also awakened a dormant resolve. He would not allow the entity to claim another victim, to plunge his town into an abyss of fear and despair. He would confront this darkness, not with skepticism, but with a fierce, desperate hope, armed with the knowledge that even the most terrifying of evils could be challenged, and perhaps, even overcome. The path ahead was shrouded in uncertainty, fraught with dangers he could only begin to imagine, but for the first time since the inexplicable events had begun, Sheriff DuCard felt a flicker of purpose, a clear and unwavering objective. He would not rest until the nightmare gripping Dry Creek was finally, irrevocably, banished. He would actively assist Kayla, pooling their strengths, his law enforcement experience now augmented by her understanding of Elias's research and the entity's nature. His skepticism was gone, replaced by the chilling certainty that they were in a fight for their very souls, a fight they could not afford to lose. The true horror had just begun, and he was ready to face it.

The obsidian shard, now cradled in Kayla's trembling hands, felt like a fragment of the deepest night. Its surface, smoother than any polished stone, seemed to absorb the scant light of the patrol car's interior, returning only a faint, frigid luminescence. It was cold, not with the biting chill of ice, but with a profound, ancient cold that spoke of places untouched by the sun, of depths where life dared not tread. Etched onto its dark face was the crescent moon, a symbol Elias Withers had painstakingly described in his journal, linking it to lunar cycles, to hidden knowledge, and to the very fabric of the entity's perceived reality. This was no mere souvenir of a horrific night; it was a weapon, a key, a desperate gambit snatched from the jaws of oblivion by a child's selfless act.

DuCard watched Kayla as she turned the shard over and over, her brow furrowed in concentration. The raw grief that had contorted her features moments before seemed to be momentarily eclipsed by a focused intensity, a nascent understanding blossoming in the desolate landscape of her sorrow. She was the conduit to Elias's arcane knowledge, the keeper of the fragments of his sanity that might just save them all. He felt a pang of guilt, a recognition that his own pragmatism, his reliance on the tangible, had nearly been their undoing. Elias, the town's resident eccentric, the man dismissed as a crackpot, had been right. And Helen, the innocent victim, had been the one to wield the truth.

"He called it the 'Eye of Nyx'," Kayla murmured, her voice a hushed reverence that underscored the artifact's significance. "Elias believed it was a sliver of something primordial, something that existed before the stars, before light itself. He thought it could… unmake the Gaze. Disrupt the Offering."

DuCard leaned closer, his earlier resolve hardening into a grim determination. The 'Gaze Offering'. The phrase echoed the disturbing passages in Elias's journal, the descriptions of the entity's process, its horrific method of consumption and control. Elias had theorized that the entity didn't merely possess; it *absorbed*, feeding on the very essence of its victims by forcing them to perceive it, to *see* it in its true, mind-shattering form. This act of forced perception, this 'offering' of sight, was the nexus of its power. And Helen, in her final moments, had blinded it, not just metaphorically, but perhaps, in some unfathomable way, literally.

"He thought this shard could break that connection?" DuCard pressed, his voice low, cutting through the somber quiet. He needed to understand the mechanics of this arcane warfare, the rules of this terrifying game they had been unwillingly drafted into.

Kayla nodded, her gaze never leaving the shard. "Yes. He believed that by presenting it with something that reflected its own primal nature – its darkness, its absence of light – it would recoil. That the shard, being forged from absolute void, would be anathema to its existence. He wrote that it would be like forcing a creature of shadow to stare into its own unmaking." She traced the etched moon with a fingertip. "He said the crescent was important. A symbol of the in-between, of the transition from darkness to a nascent form of light, or vice versa. It's meant to be a paradox, something the entity couldn't process."

The concept was dizzying, a leap of faith that required DuCard to discard every shred of his ingrained logic. He had spent his life dealing with laws, with evidence, with the predictable consequences of human action. Now, he was being asked to believe in weapons forged from mythology, in entities that fed on perception, in a child's sacrifice that had somehow disrupted a cosmic horror. But the memory of Helen's vacant, blank eyes, the chilling emptiness that had replaced her vibrant spirit, was a testament to a reality far more brutal and far stranger than he could have ever imagined.

"How does it work?" He asked, his tone devoid of his usual skepticism. There was no room for doubt now. Doubt was a luxury they could no longer afford.

"Elias's writings were… fragmented, after Helen's initial encounter with it," Kayla explained, a fresh wave of sorrow washing over her as she spoke of the child. "He believed the shard needed to be… presented. Not thrown, not wielded like a conventional weapon. It needed to be shown to the entity. And the Offering, the act of seeing it, had to be interrupted while the shard was actively radiating its… its essence." She looked at DuCard, her eyes pleading for understanding. "He thought that if someone could willingly offer their sight, their perception, to the entity, while simultaneously exposing it to the shard, it might cause a feedback loop. A kind of existential nausea that could break its hold."

DuCard's mind reeled. Willing to offer their sight? It was a terrifying prospect, echoing Helen's own sacrifice. But Helen didn't have a choice. She had been targeted, her innocence a beacon the entity had latched onto. This was different. This was about a deliberate, conscious act of defiance. He looked at the shard again, its cold glow seeming to intensify in the gloom. It was a physical manifestation of Elias's obsession, of his desperate search for a way to combat the encroaching darkness.

"He believed the shard itself was a catalyst," Kayla continued, her voice barely above a whisper. "That its presence alone could weaken the entity's grip, but that it needed to be activated by a conscious act of surrender, a willing 'offering' of perception, directed at the entity while the shard was at its most potent." She paused, taking a deep, shuddering breath. "Elias speculated that the ritualistic sacrifices he'd read about, the ones in the old texts, were perhaps not about appeasing the entity, but about providing the necessary 'offering' for something like the shard to function."

The implications were chilling. The entity didn't just want to be seen; it *required* it. And perhaps, in its ancient, alien way, it even craved the *willingness* of that perception. It was a parasitic relationship, a twisted symbiosis born of fear and cosmic hunger. DuCard's mind flashed back to the hollowed-out eyes of the few townspeople who had been found after the initial 'incidents' – the ones he had attributed to mass hysteria or environmental toxins. Now, he saw them for what they truly were: victims of the Gaze Offering, their very essence siphoned away, their sight extinguished by a horror they could not comprehend.

"So, we need someone to… look at it?" DuCard asked, the question sounding absurd even to his own ears.

"Not *at* it, Sheriff," Kayla corrected softly. "At the entity. And willingly. While holding the shard. Elias believed the shard would act as a… a focal point for the entity's attention. And in that moment of intense scrutiny, that moment of the 'offering,' if the shard was also presented, it would create the disruption he theorized." She looked at the shard in her hands, her gaze distant, as if seeing beyond the present moment, beyond the confines of the car, towards some unseen, terrifying horizon. "He didn't specify *how* the shard should be presented, only that it needed to be done in the direct vicinity of the entity, at the peak of the Offering."

The weight of Elias's cryptic pronouncements settled heavily upon DuCard. He was a man of action, of tangible solutions. But here, in the face of an enemy that defied all known laws, his usual methods were useless. They needed a plan, a strategy that involved esoteric artifacts and sacrifices of perception. He thought of Helen again, her small hand still clutching the shard before it had been passed to Kayla. She had seen the entity, and in doing so, had become its target. But she had also, in her own way, been an offering. An unwilling, innocent offering that had somehow broken its hold.

"Helen… she saw it, didn't she?" DuCard asked, the question a mere breath. "That's why it focused on her. That's why it attacked her."

Kayla nodded, tears welling in her eyes again. "Yes. Elias wrote that the entity's power is directly proportional to the clarity and willingness of the perceived 'offering.' Helen's sight was pure, innocent, and when it locked onto her, it was… overwhelming. The shard must have reacted to that intensity. It must have been drawn to the nexus of the Offering."

DuCard closed his eyes for a moment, trying to reconcile the disparate pieces of information. The shard, a weapon of void. The entity, a consumer of perception. The act of seeing, a fatal offering. Helen, a child who had paid the ultimate price for understanding. It was a tapestry of horror woven from ancient threads of myth and the brutal reality of their present nightmare. He opened his eyes, the resolve in them unwavering.

"So, we need to find it," he said, his voice firm. "And we need to get the shard close enough to… to do whatever it does. But someone has to be the one to *see* it."

Kayla looked at him, her expression a mixture of fear and a dawning, desperate hope. She knew what he was implying. Elias, in his later writings, had spoken of the 'Eyes of the Witness,' the necessary participants in the disruption. He had even, in his increasingly frantic scrawl, discussed the potential for self-sacrifice.

"Elias believed… he believed the act of witnessing, when combined with the shard, could sever the connection," Kayla whispered, her voice barely audible. "He wrote that the entity draws power from our fear of it, from our *resistance* to seeing. If someone were to willingly embrace that fear, to surrender their sight to it, while presenting the shard…" She trailed off, unable to voice the full, terrifying implication.

"Someone would have to willingly look at it?" DuCard finished, his gaze fixed on the obsidian shard. He could feel its cold energy resonating within him, a silent promise of terrible power. He understood now why Elias had been so obsessed with the shard, with its potential to disrupt the Gaze Offering. It was their only chance. Their only weapon against an enemy that existed in the unseen, in the intangible, in the very act of perception itself.

"He believed that the entity would try to overwhelm the witness, to force its true form upon them, to make them break," Kayla said, her voice trembling. "But if the witness held firm, if they maintained the Offering while presenting the shard, it would cause a catastrophic feedback. A rupture in the entity's very being. He called it the 'Shattering of the Gaze'."

DuCard's mind raced, piecing together the scant clues. The sacred grove, the site of Helen's sacrifice, had been a place of power, a nexus for the entity's influence. It was likely where they would find it again. And the shard… the shard was the key. It was the fragment of pure darkness, the antithesis of the entity's existence, capable of disrupting the very mechanism by which it fed.

"So, the plan is," DuCard began, his mind finally coalescing around a desperate, terrifying strategy, "we go back to the grove.

We find the entity. And then… someone has to look at it, knowing what it is, holding this." He gestured towards the obsidian shard.

Kayla nodded, her eyes wide with a fear that mirrored his own yet underscored by a newfound resolve. "And Elias believed that this act, this deliberate presentation of the shard, would sever the connection. It would blind the entity, at least temporarily. It would break the Gaze Offering."

The silence in the car stretched, heavy with the unspoken understanding of the immense risk involved. DuCard looked at Kayla, her face pale and drawn, her small hands still clutching the cold, dark shard. He knew what he had to do. He was the Sheriff, sworn to protect his town. And if this was the only way, then he would be the one to face the darkness, to offer his sight, to wield the obsidian shard against the encroaching horror. The pragmatic lawman was gone, replaced by something far more primal, something driven by a desperate need to save his town from a threat that defied comprehension.

"We'll go together," DuCard stated, his voice steady, a stark contrast to the turmoil raging within him. "You'll guide me. Tommy can be backup. And when the time comes… I'll be the one to offer my sight. For Helen. For Dry Creek."

Kayla looked at him, a flicker of disbelief and gratitude in her eyes. She knew the magnitude of the sacrifice he was willing to make. He was stepping into the abyss, armed with a shard of pure darkness and a desperate, fragile hope. It was a testament to the horror they faced, and to the man he had become in the crucible of their shared nightmare. The obsidian shard pulsed faintly in her hand, a silent promise of salvation, and a chilling harbinger of the terrible ordeal that lay ahead. It was their last hope, a fragment of the void, their only weapon against the Gaze Offering. And now, it was time to unleash it.

Chapter 9

The Scarecrow's Rage

The obsidian shard pulsed faintly in Kayla's palm, a shard of manufactured night that now felt less like a weapon and more like a dead weight. The silence that had descended after DuCard's pronouncement was a fragile thing, easily shattered by the hammering of their own terrified hearts. He was going to offer his sight. DuCard, the bedrock of their small community, the man who saw the world in black and white, in laws and evidence, was about to step into the heart of a nightmare and willingly offer the very sense that defined his reality. It was a sacrifice so profound, so terrifying, that Kayla found herself holding her breath, afraid to disturb the precarious balance of their grim resolve.

But the quiet was not destined to last. A low, guttural sound, like the scraping of stone against stone, vibrated through the patrol car. It was a sound that resonated not just in their ears, but deep within their bones, a primal tremor that spoke of something ancient and deeply wounded stirring from a disturbed slumber. The obsidian shard, which had felt inert moments before, now seemed to thrum with a faint, malevolent energy, an answering pulse to the growing dissonance outside.

"What was that?" DuCard's voice was taut, his hand instinctively moving to the sidearm holstered at his hip. His eyes, however, were fixed on the darkening fields beyond the shattered windshield.

Kayla's own gaze followed his. The familiar, comforting rows of corn, which had seemed so benign just hours ago, now appeared alien and menacing. The stalks, tall and dry, swayed with an unnatural ferocity, their rustling no longer a gentle whisper of the wind, but a frantic, agitated murmur. It was as if the entire field had collectively taken a sharp, terrified intake of breath.

Then, movement. Not the slow, shambling gait they had witnessed earlier, but something impossibly swift, impossibly violent. The scarecrow, or rather, the thing that wore its tattered remains, seemed to rip itself from its immobility. It didn't walk; it *moved*. A blur of frayed burlap and splintered wood, it tore through the cornfield with a speed that defied the very physics of the earthbound. The stalks, instead of bending before it, seemed to whip and snap, as if struck by invisible blows. It was a whirlwind of destruction, a manifestation of pure, unadulterated rage.

"It's angry," Tommy whispered, the words catching in his throat. The entity, wounded by Helen's sacrifice, by the unexpected severing of its connection, was now lashing out. The obsidian shard, by disrupting its feeding, by forcing it to confront a void within its own perceived existence, had not merely repelled it; it had *enraged* it. And its fury was now a tangible force, a palpable wave of malevolence radiating from the chaotic heart of the cornfield.

DuCard didn't respond, his focus absolute. He understood. Helen's selfless act hadn't been a death blow, but a wound. And a wounded predator, especially one of such unfathomable nature, was infinitely more dangerous. The entity's hunger for sight had been momentarily thwarted, but its hunger for vengeance, for retribution, had just begun. It had been denied its sustenance, and now, it craved blood. Or, more accurately, the cessation of sight.

The rustling of the corn intensified, rising to a diminishing crescendo. It was no longer just the sound of wind and stalks; it was the sound of a thousand unseen things moving with unnatural haste. Shadows detached themselves from the deeper gloom between the rows, coalescing into fleeting, distorted shapes that darted and flickered at the periphery of their vision. The entire field was a living, breathing entity of rage, a testament to the entity's unleashed fury.

"It's coming for us," DuCard stated, his voice a low growl that held no trace of his usual calm. He looked at Tommy and then Kayla, at the obsidian shard she still clutched, a grim understanding

202

dawning in his eyes. Helen had been the first offering; an innocent caught in the crossfire. Now, the entity's focus had narrowed, its predatory instincts honed in on the three remaining individuals who held the key to its disruption, and who, by extension, represented the ultimate insult to its being.

The scarecrow-like figure reappeared, closer this time, its silhouette a jagged tear against the twilight sky. It moved with a series of jerky, unnatural movements, like a marionette whose strings had been cut and then abruptly reattached by a maddened puppeteer. The tattered rags of its clothing flapped and writhed as if possessed by a life of their own, and the vacant sockets of its head seemed to stare directly at their vehicle, a silent accusation.

"It knows the shard is here," Kayla breathed, her fingers tightening around the cold stone. Elias had theorized that the shard acted as a beacon, an attractor of sorts, drawing the entity's attention not just to itself, but to whatever held it. It was a desperate gamble, but one they were committed to.

A sudden, violent lurch rocked the patrol car. Something heavy, impossibly heavy, slammed into the driver's side. The impact sent a jarring shockwave through DuCard, his knuckles white as he gripped the steering wheel. The glass of the driver's side window, already cracked from earlier encounters, spiderwebbed further, a network of fine lines spreading across the surface like a fractured memory.

"Get down!" DuCard yelled, shoving Kayla towards the passenger seat.

The entity was no longer confined to the cornfield. It was directly upon them, a manifestation of pure, unbridled aggression. The sound of tearing metal followed, a sickening shriek as something sharp and relentless gouged into the car's chassis. The scarecrow's form was visible through the widening cracks in the window, its wooden limbs twisted into impossible angles, its tattered clothes whipping around it like spectral banners.

The air itself seemed to thicken, to grow heavy and oppressive. It carried with it a scent that was both earthy and metallic, the smell of damp soil and something akin to rust, but deeper, more ancient. It was the scent of the entity, the scent of the Gaze Offering.

"It's trying to break in," Tommy said, his voice strained. DuCard fumbled for the ignition, the engine sputtering to life with a reluctant roar. But as he tried to shift into reverse, the vehicle lurched violently again, throwing them against their restraints. The front of the car dipped, then rose, as if being lifted by an unseen force.

Through the splintered windshield, Kayla saw it. The scarecrow's head, a burlap sack crudely stitched into a semblance of a face, was pressed against the glass. The vacant eyeholes were no longer empty. They were filled with a churning, inky blackness, a vortex of nothingness that seemed to pull at her very soul. It was the void Elias had spoken of, the primordial darkness that the obsidian shard was meant to counter.

And now, that void was looking back at her.

The entity's rage wasn't just a blind fury; it was a focused, intelligent malice. It understood that the obsidian shard was the key, and that Kayla, by holding it, was the keeper of that key. It wanted the shard, but more than that, it wanted to break Kayla, to shatter her resolve, to force her to drop the artifact, to reclaim its stolen power.

With a shriek that was more a tearing of fabric than a vocalization, the entity flung itself against the car again. This time, the impact was more violent, the sickening crunch of metal echoing through the small space. The patrol car tilted precariously, its tires losing purchase on the damp earth.

"It's trying to flip us!" DuCard grunted, fighting against the unseen forces attempting to upend them. His focus, however, was split. While he battled the physical onslaught, a deeper struggle was unfolding within him. He could feel the psychic pressure, the tendrils of the entity's influence attempting to worm their way into his mind, to sow doubt, to breed terror. He remembered Elias's writings, the warnings about the Gaze Offering, about the entity's ability to weaponize perception, to turn sight itself into a tool of destruction.

Kayla, her heart hammering against her ribs, felt the same oppressive force. It was a subtle invasion, a creeping dread that whispered of Helen's fate, of the emptiness that had consumed her. The entity was trying to replay that horror, to force Kayla to relive it, to make her believe that her own sight, her own perception, would lead to the same inevitable doom.

"No," Kayla whispered, clutching the shard tighter. She could feel its cold radiating through her glove, a subtle anchor against the encroaching mental chaos. "We won't let you."

The entity seemed to recoil slightly at her defiance, its movements becoming more erratic. The concentrated fury, the absolute focus, wavered for a fleeting moment, replaced by a surge of raw, uncontained power. The rustling of the corn grew louder, a swirling cacophony that seemed to vibrate with the entity's frustration.

Then, with a sudden, blinding burst of speed, the scarecrow figure vanished from the driver's side window. For a terrifying second, Kayla thought it had disappeared, that it had somehow slipped away. But the stillness was a deception. The entire field seemed to hold its breath.

Suddenly, the corn stalks on the passenger side, where Kayla sat, erupted. They didn't just bend or break; they seemed to *explode* outwards, as if propelled by some invisible force. The scarecrow's form burst through the wall of green, its burlap face mere inches from Kayla's.

A piercing shriek, like the grinding of countless sharp objects, tore through the air. It was a sound that promised not just pain, but annihilation. The entity wasn't just trying to break them; it was trying to *unmake* them.

DuCard reacted instantly. With a desperate surge of strength, he wrenched the steering wheel, forcing the patrol car to swerve violently. The sudden maneuver sent Kayla tumbling against the passenger door, the obsidian shard clattering from her grasp.

It landed on the floor mat with a soft thud, its dark luminescence momentarily flickering. The entity, its attention momentarily diverted by the shard's uncontrolled movement, seemed to hesitate.

"Get it!" DuCard roared, his voice raw with exertion.

Kayla scrambled, her hands blindly searching on the floor. Her fingers brushed against the smooth, cold surface of the obsidian shard. As she gripped it, a surge of power, raw and untamed, coursed through her. It was as if the shard itself was reacting to the entity's proximity, amplifying its inherent resistance to the encroaching darkness.

The scarecrow figure, its rage now a tangible force, lunged towards the shard, its jagged limbs reaching out. But before it could grasp the artifact, the obsidian shard pulsed with a blinding flash of pure, cold light. It wasn't the warm glow of dawn, but the sterile, absolute light of a star's final moments, a light that seemed to consume rather than illuminate.

The entity shrieked, a sound of pure agony this time, and recoiled violently. The blinding flash had struck true, disrupting its singular focus. The Gaze Offering, the very mechanism by which it consumed and controlled, had been momentarily overloaded by the shard's intrinsic connection to the void.

"Now!" DuCard yelled, flooring the accelerator. The patrol car lurched forward, tearing itself free from the entity's grasping tendrils. The cornfield became a blur of green and brown as they sped away. Tommy, from the back seat, offered the void his middle finger as the shrieking of the enraged entity fading into the oppressive rustling of the stalks.

They didn't stop for miles, the roar of the engine and the shuddering of the vehicle a constant reminder of their narrow escape. When they finally pulled over to the side of a desolate country road, the silence that descended was a stark contrast to the cacophony they had just endured.

206

Kayla, her hands still trembling, held the obsidian shard. It felt heavier now, imbued with the memory of the entity's unmaking, of the terrifying power they had managed to unleash. Helen's sacrifice had wounded it, but the shard, wielded in DuCard's desperate maneuver, had momentarily blinded it.

"It's not dead," DuCard said, his voice a low, rough whisper. He was breathing heavily, his face etched with a weariness that went beyond physical exhaustion. He had stared into the void, and it had stared back.

Kayla and Tommy nodded. Kayla's gaze fixed on the shard. "No. It's wounded. And it's furious."

"Yeah, like it is *super* pissed." Tommy offered. "And it knows we have the shard. It knows we can hurt it."

The rage they had witnessed, the unnatural speed and violence, was the direct result of Helen's intervention, and now, of their own desperate gambit. The entity, its power disrupted, its connection severed by the fragment of primordial darkness, was in a state of pure, unadulterated vengeance.

"It focused on you," DuCard stated, his eyes meeting Kayla's. "It knew you had the shard."

"And it knew you were the one who would try to use it," Kayla added, a fresh wave of fear washing over her. Elias had theorized that the entity was drawn to those who understood its nature, to those who possessed the means to disrupt it. Helen, in her innocence, had been a conduit for the shard. Now, Kayla was its keeper, and DuCard, the pragmatic sheriff, was willing to be its wielder.

The cornfield had become a battleground, a testament to the entity's wrath. The scarecrow's sudden, terrifying reappearance, its unnatural speed and the sheer destructive force it unleashed, had been a brutal escalation. It was no longer a harbinger of fear; it was an active agent of destruction, a physical manifestation of the entity's wounded pride and insatiable hunger.

The narrow escape had come at a cost. The patrol car was a wreck, its metal twisted and torn, its windows shattered. But more importantly, their understanding of the threat had deepened. The entity's rage was a potent force, and its focus had narrowed to them, the keepers of the Gaze Offering's undoing.

"We need to go back," DuCard said, his voice grim. "We need to figure out how to make this work. How to truly blind it, not just momentarily stun it."

Kayla looked at the obsidian shard, its surface seeming to absorb the meager light of the roadside. Elias's journal had spoken of the 'Shattering of the Gaze,' of a permanent disruption. But the path to that disruption was fraught with unimaginable peril. They had witnessed the raw fury of a wounded, ancient entity, and they knew, with chilling certainty, that its vengeance was just beginning. The scarecrow's rage was a terrifying awakening, a prelude to a storm that threatened to consume them all. They had touched the void, and the void, in its incandescent fury, was now hunting them.

Sheriff DuCard's hand tightened on the worn grip of his service pistol. The cold steel, a familiar weight in his palm, felt utterly inadequate against the encroaching darkness. Behind him, huddled within the skeletal remains of the patrol car, were the remnants of his responsibility – the teenagers, their faces pale masks of terror in the fading twilight. Kayla, the shard clutched tight, her eyes wide with a dawning, terrible understanding that their fear was a palpable entity in the vehicles confined space.

DuCard wasn't a man of faith, not in the traditional sense. His belief system was built on evidence, on procedure, on the tangible reality of the world. But the impossible had happened, shattering his carefully constructed reality like cheap glass. The rustling in the corn, a sound that had once signified the gentle breath of nature, now carried the weight of malevolence. It was the sound of a thousand unseen things, a prelude to the lumbering, ragged horror that had emerged from the earth itself.

The scarecrow. Or rather, the thing that wore its tattered skin. It moved with a disjointed grace, a mockery of life, its limbs jerking with an unnatural cadence. Its burlap face, a crude imitation of humanity, was now etched with a fury that bypassed mere animosity and plunged into the abyss of pure, unadulterated hatred. DuCard had seen it in the eyes of criminals, in the aftermath of violence, but this... this was something else. This was a primal rage, ancient and consuming.

"Stay near the car," DuCard commanded, his voice a low growl that he hoped conveyed more authority than the tremor he felt within. He wasn't sure if the entity could hear him, or if his words even registered in its alien consciousness. But the act itself, the positioning of himself between them and the advancing horror, was important. It was a statement. A defiance.

He knew, with a chilling certainty, that his weapon was useless. Bullets would pass through that ragged form, or perhaps be absorbed, becoming another insignificant detail in its monstrous tapestry. Fire might offer a brief respite, but what if it simply fed the flames, strengthening its unnatural hold? Elias's cryptic notes, his warnings about the 'Gaze Offering' and its vulnerability to the primordial darkness, echoed in his mind. The obsidian shard. Kayla. That was their hope. His role, then, was to buy her time.

He stepped around the relative safety of the patrol car, the damp earth yielding slightly beneath his boots. The corn stalks, tall and whispering, seemed to press in on him, their dry leaves brushing against his uniform like the skeletal fingers of the damned. He could feel it now, a palpable pressure in the air, a psychic weight that threatened to crush his very will. It was the entity's rage, its furious denial of the disruption Kayla represented.

The scarecrow figure, a grotesque silhouette against the bruised twilight sky, paused. It turned its vacant head, or where a head should be, towards him. The absence of eyes was more terrifying than any gaze. It was an invitation to project one's own fears into that void, to fill it with the horrors one carried within. DuCard held his ground, forcing himself to meet that emptiness with a steady, unwavering stare. He wouldn't give it the satisfaction of seeing him flinch.

"You want them?" DuCard's voice, surprisingly steady, carried across the field. "You'll have to go through me." It was a hollow threat, he knew, a desperate gambit. But the words needed to be spoken. They were a declaration of intent, a refusal to surrender the lives entrusted to his protection.

The entity responded not with a sound, but with a movement. A subtle shift in its posture, a tightening of its ragged form. It was as if it were weighing him, assessing the worth of his insignificant life against its monumental rage. The corn around it seemed to writhe, its stalks bending and snapping with an unnatural violence, as if the very earth was contributing to its fury.

DuCard raised his pistol, not with any expectation of success, but as a gesture. A last, futile stand. He could feel Kayla and Tommy's fear, a cold tendril reaching out from the patrol car, but he also felt a burgeoning resolve in them. Kayla was following Elias's plan, trusting in the shard's power. He had to believe in her. He had to give her the space to succeed.

The scarecrow began to advance, its gait a series of disjointed, lurching strides. It was faster than he had anticipated, its unnatural speed closing the distance between them with terrifying rapidity. The sound of its movement was a dry, rasping scrape, like bone grinding against wood, punctuated by the rustle of decaying fabric.

He fired. The shot echoed in the oppressive silence, a sharp crack that seemed to momentarily stun the surrounding night. The bullet struck the entity's chest, but instead of impacting, it seemed to pass through, as if he had shot at smoke. There was no visible damage, no reaction. Just a continuation of its relentless advance.

This was it. The moment of truth. He could feel the unseen tendrils of the entity's power attempting to invade his mind, to sow discord and fear. He saw flashes of distorted images, the faces of the lost, the screams of the terrified. It was trying to break him, to shatter his focus, to make him doubt his purpose.

DuCard gritted his teeth, forcing the intrusive thoughts away. He focused on the task at hand, on the immediate threat. He imagined the obsidian shard, a sliver of pure darkness, now held by

Kayla. He clung to the belief that this manufactured knife, this fragment of Elias's desperate research, was their only chance.

The entity was now mere yards away. He could discern the texture of its burlap skin, the frayed threads of its stitched-on mouth, the unsettling stillness of its vacant sockets. He could smell the earth, damp and decaying, mixed with something acrid and ancient, the scent of the entity itself.

He didn't aim for the head, or the chest, or any specific point. He simply leveled the pistol, a futile offering of lead against an impossible foe. He fired again, and again, emptying his clip in a rapid burst, the shots lost in the overwhelming symphony of the encroaching horror.

He saw Kayla then, through the shattered windshield. Her face was illuminated by a faint, internal glow emanating from the obsidian shard. Her lips moved, a silent incantation, a desperate plea. He knew, at that moment, that he had done all he could. His stand was not about victory; it was about defiance. It was about making a choice, in the face of overwhelming impossibility, to protect those who depended on him.

The scarecrow figure lunged. Its tattered arm, impossibly long and thin, shot out towards him. DuCard braced himself, not for impact, but for the inevitable void. He closed his eyes, a silent prayer for Kayla's success on his lips, ready to embrace whatever came next. This was his last stand, his testament to the oath he had taken, and the lives he had sworn to defend. Even if it meant facing the abyss, he would stand as a bulwark, a final, desperate shield against the unmaking. He was the Sheriff, and this was his town, and he would not yield it to the madness that had taken root in its fields. He could feel the essence of the entity begin to coalesce around him, the very air growing heavy with its predatory intent, its ancient hunger. His sacrifice, he hoped, would be enough.

Kayla's breath hitched, a ragged sound lost in the cacophony of rustling corn and Sheriff DuCard's increasingly desperate gunfire. The obsidian shard, cool and impossibly smooth against her clammy palm, pulsed with a faint, inner light. It was a shard of something ancient, something that resonated with the suffocating dread blanketing the field. Elias's fragmented notes, his ramblings about ley lines and 'primal resonance,' suddenly clicked into a terrifying, coherent whole. Old Man Hemlock's hushed warnings, the fear in his weathered eyes as he spoke of the 'heart of the harvest,' echoed in her mind. It wasn't just about facing the scarecrow; it was about severing its connection, its roots, to this blighted land.

The journal, its pages brittle and stained with what she now suspected was more than just ink, lay open on the patrol car's dashboard, illuminated by the dying headlights. Elias hadn't just documented the entity; he had sought to understand its power, its very essence. He'd spoken of the scarecrow as a nexus, a physical anchor for something far vaster and more insidious. The Gaze Offering, as he'd termed it, was a ritual of binding, a way to ensnare the land and its inhabitants in a cycle of fear and sustenance. And the scarecrow was the key.

DuCard's shots were like desperate prayers, each one met with an unnerving absorption by the shambling horror. It wasn't just a physical entity; it was a conduit, a manifestation of something the journal called 'primordial darkness,' a force that drew strength from despair and fear. The obsidian shard, Elias had theorized, possessed a unique property – it could disrupt these energies, acting as a counter-frequency, a dissonant note in the symphony of malevolence.

Kayla's plan was audacious, bordering on suicidal. She couldn't simply destroy the scarecrow; that would be like trying to kill a shadow by striking at its outline. She had to hit its core, its source of power. The shard wasn't merely a weapon; it was a key, a disruptor. She envisioned a ritual, not of appeasement, but of severance. She had to drive the shard into the scarecrow, not to kill it, but to unravel the energetic threads that tethered it to the field, to the very life force of Dry Creek.

A guttural cry, raw and inhuman, ripped through the air. DuCard stumbled, his movements becoming more erratic. The scarecrow was closer now, its tattered form a grotesque mockery of human shape, its burlap face fixed in an eternal, hate-filled grimace. The corn stalks around it seemed to writhe, the dry leaves whispering secrets only the damned could comprehend. Kayla could feel a psychic pressure building, a tangible weight pressing down on her mind, attempting to suffocate her nascent resolve.

It was the entity's consciousness, Elias had written, a vast, ancient awareness that fed on the fear of its victims.

"He's... he's not hurting it," Tommy whispered, his voice trembling.

"He's buying us time," Kayla replied, her own voice a low, determined murmur. She clutched the shard tighter, its coolness a stark contrast to the heat of her racing pulse. She had to trust DuCard. She had to trust Elias's research, even if it felt like the fevered dreams of a madman. The journal had detailed the Gaze Offering as a process of gradual ensnarement, a slow draining of vitality from the land and its people, culminating in a final harvest of souls. The scarecrow was the culmination of that ritual.

"We have to do something," Tommy stammered, his eyes darting between the advancing scarecrow and the back of DuCard's head.

"We are," Kayla said, her gaze fixed on the field. "We just have to do it right." She remembered Elias's words, scribbled frantically in the margins: *The focal point must be disrupted at its nexus. Not destruction, but severance. The shard, plunged into the heart of the offering, will sever the lines of sustenance, plunging the nexus into a chaotic void.* A chaotic void. The thought sent a shiver down her spine. What if she made it worse? What if her attempt to disrupt its power only amplified it, unleashing something even more terrifying?

The wind picked up, swirling dead leaves and dust around the scarecrow. It moved with a jerky, unnatural gait, its limbs appearing to operate independently of each other, like a poorly manipulated puppet. The burlap face seemed to twist, a silent scream frozen in time. DuCard reloaded and fired again, the shot echoing like a thunderclap. The bullet struck the entity's chest, disappearing into the tattered fabric without effect. Kayla saw DuCard's shoulders slump for a fraction of a second, a silent admission of his weapon's futility.

"Kayla, what's the plan?" Tommy asked, his voice a tight knot of fear.

She looked at him, huddled by the car, his face pale and etched with a terror that mirrored her own. "Elias wrote that the scarecrow isn't just a scarecrow. It's... it's like a focus point. For whatever this thing is. It's drawing power from the field, from... from everything." She hesitated, searching for the right words, the words that would convey the terrifying truth without completely shattering their already fragile hope. "The shard... it can break that connection. It can disrupt the energy."

"How?" Tommy whispered, his eyes wide.

"We have to get close," Kayla said, her voice gaining a strange, steadiness born of desperation. "We have to get the shard to the scarecrow." The thought of approaching the entity, of willingly entering its sphere of influence, made her stomach clench. But it was the only way. She was the one holding the shard. She was the one who had to do it.

She remembered another passage from the journal, a rough sketch of the field with lines radiating from a central point, labeled 'Nexus.' The scarecrow was at that nexus. The lines represented the *ley lines of sustenance*, channels through which the entity drew power. The Gaze Offering wasn't just a passive drain; it was an active siphoning, a parasitic relationship with the land. The shard, Elias had believed, could act as a 'resonance breaker,' shattering the established pattern.

"It's not about killing it," she explained, her gaze sweeping across the field, trying to map out a path. "It's about cutting its lifeline. If we can break its connection to the field, it... it should weaken. Maybe disappear."

"Should?" Tommy repeated, his voice laced with doubt.

"It's the only way," Kayla insisted, her heart pounding against her ribs. She looked at DuCard, still standing his ground, a lone figure against the encroaching horror. He was a shield, but a fragile one. He wouldn't be able to hold it off forever. She had to move.

She took a deep breath, the scent of dry earth and decay filling her lungs. The obsidian shard felt heavy in her hand, a promise of both salvation and annihilation. She would have to move through the corn, a maze of stalks that seemed to twist and writhe with a life of their own. The entity's awareness was a palpable force, a suffocating blanket that sought to smother any flicker of resistance.

"I have to go," she announced, her voice clear and firm.

Sheriff DuCard, in the midst of his futile stand, turned his head. His expression, even from this distance, conveyed a mixture of concern and grim understanding. He knew the plan. He'd seen Elias's notes. He knew the risk.

"Kayla, no," Tommy pleaded.

"I'm going," Kayla repeated, her eyes locked on the scarecrow, which had now turned its full, vacant attention towards DuCard. The entity seemed to be toying with him, a predator toying with its prey. The rustling of the corn intensified, a dry, sibilant whisper that seemed to mock the sheriff's bravery.

She slid around of the patrol car, the night air cool against her skin. The ground was damp, the earth clinging to her shoes. The corn stalks towered over her, their dry leaves brushing against her face like phantom caresses. She could feel the entity's awareness shift, a subtle but undeniable pull towards her. It sensed the shard. It sensed the threat.

She moved cautiously, sticking to the edges of the corn rows, trying to remain unseen. But invisibility was a futile hope. The entity was attuned to the very life force of the field, and she was a disruption, a foreign element. She could feel its gaze, not with her eyes, but with a deeper, more primal sense. It was an ancient, predatory awareness, a hunger that had been building for generations.

Elias's journal had spoken of the 'Gaze Offering' as a tapestry woven from fear, despair, and the very lifeblood of the land. The scarecrow was the loom, and the entity was the weaver. Kayla's plan was to unravel the tapestry, to tear at the threads of its power at the very point of creation. It was a delicate, dangerous dance. Too much force, too much disruption, and the entire structure could collapse, releasing an even greater force. But too little, and she would simply become another casualty, another offering to the hungry earth.

She reached the edge of the main cornfield, the dense stalks promising both concealment and entrapment. The scarecrow was now directly facing DuCard, its tattered arms hanging limply at its sides. DuCard stood his ground, his pistol still held at the ready, a futile gesture against the encroaching madness. The silence between gunshots was filled with the sibilant whisper of the corn, a chorus of dry leaves that seemed to applaud the entity's relentless advance.

Kayla took another deep breath, the scent of decay and something else, something metallic and acrid, filling her nostrils. It was the smell of the entity, the scent of ancient, corrupted life. She clutched the obsidian shard, its coolness a grounding force against the rising tide of panic. Elias's words echoed in her mind: *The shard must be driven into the heart of the nexus. The nexus is the scarecrow. Its essence is bound to the earth through the ley lines. Disrupt the lines, and the nexus withers.*

She began to move, weaving through the stalks, each step deliberate and measured. The corn closed in around her, the rustling leaves a constant, unnerving sound. She could feel the entity's awareness brush against her mind, a probing, insidious touch that sought to sow doubt and fear. Flashes of distorted images flickered at the edge of her vision: the faces of the lost, the terrified screams of those who had met their end in these fields, the gnawing emptiness of the void.

DuCard let out a roar, a sound of pure defiance, as the scarecrow lunged. Its movements were jerky, unnatural, but unnervingly fast. Its tattered arm, unnaturally long, shot out towards him. DuCard sidestepped, the burlap hand swiping through empty air. He stumbled, regaining his footing just as the entity recovered, its ragged form turning to face him again.

Kayla pressed on, her eyes fixed on the scarecrow. She had to get closer. She had to reach it. The obsidian shard pulsed in her hand, a silent promise of power. She could feel the energy radiating from the scarecrow, a low hum that vibrated through the very earth. It was a field of pure malevolence, a gravitational pull that sought to draw everything into its orbit of despair.

She stumbled, her foot catching on a hidden root. She fell to her knees, the corn stalks momentarily obscuring her from view. Panic flared, sharp and cold. Had it seen her? Had her misstep alerted it to her presence? She could feel the psychic pressure intensify, a deliberate effort to disorient and confuse. DuCard's shots continued, a desperate, rhythmic punctuation to the escalating horror.

Slowly, carefully, Kayla pushed herself back to her feet. She had to keep moving. She had to reach the scarecrow. She remembered the diagram in Elias's journal, the intricate web of lines converging on the scarecrow. The obsidian shard was meant to be the catalyst, the disrupting agent that would sever those lines.

She was getting closer. She could see the scarecrow more clearly now, its burlap face a grotesque mask of stitched-on features. The vacant sockets were more terrifying than any eyes, for they invited the projection of one's deepest fears. The ragged stuffing that spilled from its seams seemed to writhe with a life of its own.

Suddenly, the scarecrow stopped its advance on DuCard. It turned its head, or the place where a head should be, and its vacant gaze seemed to fix directly on Kayla. A chilling realization washed over her: it knew. It had sensed her intention. The psychic pressure intensified, no longer a general pressure but a focused, malevolent intent directed solely at her.

DuCard saw it too. He shouted her name, his voice strained. He fired again, aiming for the scarecrow's chest, a desperate attempt to draw its attention back to him. But the entity remained locked onto Kayla, its ragged form beginning to pivot, to orient itself towards her.

This was her chance. DuCard had bought her precious seconds. She broke into a run, her heart hammering against her ribs, the obsidian shard held out before her like a talisman. The corn seemed to conspire against her, its stalks reaching out, snagging at her clothes, impeding her progress. The whispers grew louder, more insistent, weaving a tapestry of doubt and fear in her mind.

You will fail. You are weak. You are just like the others.

She pushed through the final line of corn, emerging into a small clearing where the scarecrow stood, its tattered arms now raised slightly, as if in anticipation. DuCard was still some distance away, caught by the entity's initial focus on him. The scarecrow was now directly in front of her, its burlap face seeming to stare into her soul.

Kayla raised the obsidian shard, its faint glow intensifying in the oppressive darkness. This was it. The culmination of Elias's research, the desperate gamble. She had to trust that the shard's power was real, that it could indeed disrupt the Gaze Offering and sever the entity's connection to this blighted land. Her own fear was a potent fuel for the entity, but the shard, she hoped, was a weapon forged from a different kind of power, a power that could cut through the very fabric of the encroaching darkness. She took a shaky breath, her resolve hardening. She would not be another offering. She would fight back.

The very air thickened, not with the usual earthy scent of damp soil and decaying leaves, but with a palpable, suffocating pressure. It was as if the cornfield itself had exhaled, a slow, deliberate breath that choked the very will to move. Kayla found herself in a place that felt both familiar and terrifyingly alien. The towering stalks, once a uniform emerald sea, now seemed to shift and writhe with an unsettling fluidity. What had been clear pathways moments before were now choked with dense, impenetrable walls of green. Each rustle of the dry leaves was no longer a random whisper of the wind, but a directed, sibilant murmur, laced with a chilling cadence that seemed to coil around her mind.

This way... follow the sound... escape is near...

The whispers were insidious, weaving through the oppressive silence like spectral threads. They were not just sounds; they were suggestions, temptations aimed at her deepest anxieties. They promised escape but the direction they nudged her was always a dead end, a thickening of the stalks, a return to the very spot she had just left. The cornfield had become a labyrinth, meticulously crafted by an unseen, malevolent architect. It was a living maze, its walls shifting, its corridors rearranging themselves with a predatory intelligence.

She found herself circling, the same gnarled oak tree appearing with unnerving regularity, a silent sentinel in this unfolding nightmare. Each time she passed it, the whispers would intensify, a chorus of spectral voices urging her onward, deeper into the heart of the deception.

Don't trust your eyes... the path is not what it seems... listen to us... we know the way...

Tommy was somewhere to her left, his panicked calls muffled by the dense foliage. "Kayla! Where are you? I can't see anything!" His voice was a thin thread of desperation, easily lost in the rustling symphony of dread. She tried to call back, but the words caught in her throat, choked by the same oppressive force that had settled over the field.

Tommy was also lost in this green purgatory. The obsidian shard in Kayla's hand, once a source of cold comfort, now felt like a beacon, a target for the entity's undivided attention. She could feel its awareness, a vast, hungry presence that was now focused on her, on the shard. It wasn't just about scaring her; it was about *containing* her, about using the maze to isolate and consume her.

Elias's journal flashed in her mind. He had described the field as a "symbiotic prison," an extension of the entity's will. The corn wasn't just a crop; it was a manifestation, a physical representation of the entity's power to confuse and ensnare. He had written of ley lines not just as conduits of energy, but as pathways that the entity could manipulate, twist, and sever at will, creating pockets of temporal and spatial distortion. The maze was a physical manifestation of these distorted ley lines.

The whispers grew more insistent, more personal. They mimicked the voices of loved ones, of those she had lost, twisting their memories into instruments of torment. A child's laughter, innocent and sweet, echoed from a direction that seemed impossibly far, yet tantalizingly close.

Come play… it's safe here… no one will hurt you… Kayla's blood ran cold. She knew, with absolute certainty, that this was a trap, a siren song designed to lure her away from her purpose, to pull her into the suffocating embrace of the corn.

She forced herself to focus, to ignore the spectral seductions. She remembered Elias's final, frantic notes: *The nexus is the key. Disrupt the nexus, and the matrix collapses.* The nexus was the scarecrow. The maze was the matrix, the network of manipulated ley lines that sustained it. If she could reach the scarecrow, if she could plunge the shard into its heart, the maze should, theoretically, unravel.

But reaching it was the impossible part. Every turn seemed to lead her back to the same disorienting familiarity. The stalks pressed in, their dry leaves brushing against her skin like the touch of decaying fingers. The air was thick, heavy, making each breath a conscious effort. She felt a growing sense of despair, a creeping hopelessness that the whispers actively encouraged.

You are lost… forever… this is your grave…

A rustle directly behind her. She whirled around, her heart leaping into her throat. It was just a rabbit, darting through the undergrowth, its white tail a fleeting blur. But the entity's influence was so pervasive that even the natural world felt corrupted, imbued with its sinister intent. The rabbit's quick escape felt like a taunt, a reminder of the freedom she was denied.

She tried to find a landmark, anything to orient herself. A broken fence post, a patch of unusual moss, anything. But the cornfield seemed determined to deny her any such anchor. The landscape was a monotonous expanse of green and brown, a disorienting canvas upon which the entity painted its illusions.

She stumbled again, her foot catching on a thick root that seemed to have sprung from the earth specifically to trip her. She fell, the obsidian shard skittering from her grasp, its faint glow swallowed by the dense foliage. Panic, cold and sharp, pierced through her. Without the shard, she was truly lost.

"No!" she cried out, scrambling on her hands and knees, desperately searching for it. The whispers turned to mocking laughter.

Lost... truly lost... swallowed by the earth...

Her fingers brushed against something smooth, impossibly smooth, and cold. The shard. She snatched it up, relief washing over her in a powerful wave. It pulsed faintly in her palm, a small, defiant spark against the encroaching darkness. She took a deep, shuddering breath, trying to regain her composure.

She realized then that the entity wasn't just creating a maze; it was feeding on her fear, on her disorientation. The more lost she felt, the more it thrived. She had to push back against that fear, had to impose her own will, however fragile, onto this shifting landscape.

She remembered Elias's notes about resonance. The shard resonated with a different frequency, a frequency that could disrupt the entity's hold. She needed to project that resonance, not just physically carry the shard, but to *align* herself with it. She closed her eyes, focusing on the shard's cool energy, on the memory of Elias's conviction, on the desperate hope of Dry Creek.

I am not lost. I know where I am going. The thought was a defiance, a mental pushback against the entity's illusions.

When she opened her eyes, something had subtly shifted. The maze was still present, the stalks still unnervingly close, but the oppressive weight in the air seemed to have lessened, just slightly. The whispers were still there, but they seemed further away, less immediate.

She started to move again, not blindly, but with a new, albeit shaky, purpose. She didn't try to follow a path; she tried to *feel* it. She focused on the slight inclination of the land, on the direction of the subtle breeze that still managed to whisper through the stalks. She was searching for the nexus, for the heart of the disturbance.

The entity, sensing her renewed resolve, fought back. The whispers intensified, becoming a cacophony of terror. Images flashed before her eyes, fleeting and nightmarish: the vacant stare of the scarecrow, the faces of the missing townsfolk twisted in agony, the endless, suffocating darkness. The ground beneath her feet seemed to buckle, the stalks lurching and swaying as if in a violent storm.

She stumbled, falling to her knees again, the obsidian shard clutched tightly. This was it. The true test. She was in the heart of the labyrinth, the entity's domain. She could feel its full attention now, a crushing, omnipresent force.

You cannot hide from me, a voice, deep and resonant, seemed to emanate from the rustling leaves themselves. It was not the whisper of a single entity, but a chorus, a symphony of malevolence. *You cannot escape the harvest*.

Kayla gritted her teeth, forcing the fear down. "I'm not here to escape," she choked out, her voice raw. "I'm here to end this."

She pushed herself up, ignoring the searing pain in her knees. She looked around, desperately seeking a sign, a break in the oppressive green. Then she saw it. A subtle thinning in the stalks, a faint break in the seemingly endless expanse. It wasn't a clear path, but a suggestion, a hint of something beyond the immediate confusion.

She moved towards it, the entity's rage a palpable force pushing against her. The whispers became a roar, a deafening wave of psychic noise. The stalks whipped and flailed, lashing out at her like thorny vines. She ducked and weaved, her movements driven by a primal instinct for survival, and a desperate need to reach her objective.

The clearing was small, almost insignificant, yet it felt like a sanctuary. And in the center of that clearing stood the scarecrow. It was as Elias had described, a grotesquely crafted effigy, its burlap face stitched with crude, hateful features. But it was more than just straw and tattered cloth. It was alive, crackling with the dark energy of the Gaze Offering. Its vacant eyes seemed to follow her, and the tattered limbs twitched with an unnatural anticipation.

The labyrinth had served its purpose. It had disoriented her, weakened her, and now, it had delivered her directly to the nexus. The whispers ceased, replaced by a heavy, expectant silence. The entity had laid its trap, and she had walked right into it. But she had the shard. And she had a plan.

The scarecrow turned its head, a slow, creaking movement that sent a fresh wave of dread through Kayla. Its empty gaze fixed upon her, and she could feel the raw power radiating from it, a vortex of ancient hunger. The cornstalks surrounding the clearing seemed to lean in, drawn by the entity's focus, their dry leaves forming a living wall, trapping her with the source of Dry Creeks's torment.

She raised the obsidian shard, its faint glow a defiant spark in the oppressive gloom. The air around the scarecrow shimmered, distorting the surrounding corn, as if the very fabric of reality was being strained by its presence. She could feel the entity's immense power, a force that had been accumulating for generations, drawing sustenance from the fear and despair of Dry Creek.

This was it. The final confrontation. The maze had been a diversion, a test of her resolve. Now, she stood before the heart of the darkness, armed with a fragment of a forgotten power, ready to sever the ancient bonds that held Dry Creek captive. The fate of the town, and perhaps much more, rested on whether this shard, this seemingly insignificant piece of obsidian, could unravel the entity's terrifying tapestry.

The air in the heart of the field thrummed with an unspoken urgency, a dissonant hum that vibrated in Kayla's very bones. The harvest moon, a swollen, bruised orb hanging precariously in the ink-black sky, cast an eerie, sepia-toned light upon the endless rows of corn. It was close now, agonizingly close, to its zenith, and with its ascent, the entity's grip on Dry Creek tightened. Each passing minute was a victory for the malevolent force, a step closer to the complete consolidation of its power, a terrifying prelude to the inevitable cycle of sacrifice that would once again stain the soil of Dry Creek. Kayla felt it acutely – a primal, instinctual awareness that the window of opportunity was rapidly slamming shut.

The obsidian shard in her hand pulsed, a faint warmth against her chilled skin, a stark contrast to the creeping dread that threatened to paralyze her. It was a tangible connection to Elias's frantic research, to the desperate hope of disrupting the ancient ritual. But hope was a fragile thing, easily shattered in the face of such overwhelming, pervasive darkness. The entity was not merely an observer; it was an active participant, a predator that felt the shifting tides of power, that sensed the approaching climax. It was accelerating its own process, drawing strength from the encroaching moonlight, from the very fear that clung to Kayla like the suffocating humidity.

She looked back, her gaze sweeping across the disorienting expanse of stalks that had so recently ensnared her. Tommy – his panicked calls were now faint echoes, lost in the phantom whispers and the rustling symphony of the corn. She knew they he somewhere behind her, struggling against the maze's insidious influence, and the thought of their peril was a constant, gnawing ache. But her primary objective, the one Elias had drilled into her with his final, dying breaths, was clear: reach the scarecrow.

Disrupt the nexus. Break the cycle. The fate of the entire town, perhaps even more, hinged on her ability to succeed before the harvest moon reached its apex, before the entity's power became absolute, unassailable.

The whispers, which had momentarily receded, now returned with renewed venom, no longer seductive enticements but outright threats, laced with a chilling intimacy that spoke of deep, ancestral knowledge.

You are too late. The earth remembers. The blood will flow again. Your efforts are in vain. They were the chorus of the damned, the voices of generations sacrificed, amplified and weaponized by the entity. Kayla gritted her teeth, forcing herself to focus. Elias had warned her that the entity would try to break her spirit, to sow seeds of despair, to convince her of the futility of her actions.

She remembered the sketches in Elias's journal, the intricate diagrams of ley lines converging, focusing their energy onto a single point – the scarecrow. This field, this entire town, was a conduit, a carefully constructed network designed to funnel raw, primal energy towards that effigy. The scarecrow wasn't just a symbol; it was the anchor, the focal point of the Gaze Offering ritual, the physical manifestation of the entity's power. And as the harvest moon waxed, so too did its strength, drawing power from the land, from the fear, from the anticipation of the coming sacrifice.

The ground beneath her feet felt different now. It was no longer just soil and root; it seemed to hum with a low-frequency vibration, an unsettling resonance that spoke of immense, contained energy. The cornstalks, too, seemed to lean inwards, their dry leaves rustling with an almost predatory eagerness. They were not merely plants; they were extensions of the entity's will, its physical manifestation in this world, and they were closing in, attempting to herd her towards a final, inescapable confrontation.

Kayla broke into a run, her breath coming in ragged gasps. She couldn't afford to hesitate, couldn't allow the fear to take root. Every rustle, every whisper, was a deliberate attempt to slow her, to disorient her, to make her doubt. She pushed through the dense foliage, the rough leaves tearing at her clothes and skin, each step a defiance against the encroaching darkness. She visualized Elias's diagrams, his desperate calculations, the precise timing required for the counter-ritual. It had to be performed at the very peak of the harvest moon's power, a desperate gamble to sever the ritual's connection to the earth, to break the ancient pact.

The air grew colder, the moon's light now casting long, distorted shadows that danced and writhed like specters. She could feel the presence of the scarecrow growing stronger, a palpable vortex of malevolence pulling her forward. It was as if the very landscape was contorting itself, shaping a path for her, a path that led directly to her doom, or to salvation. The entity wanted her there, wanted her within its grasp, wanted to make an example of her, to solidify its reign of terror for another generation.

She recalled Elias's last, chilling words, scribbled in shaky handwriting: *The ritual is tied to the lunar cycle. Its power peaks at the zenith of the harvest moon. Disrupt the flow at that precise moment, or the nexus becomes unbreakable.* The words hammered at her, a constant reminder of the ticking clock. The moon was climbing higher, its pale light intensifying, bathing the field in an almost spectral glow. The entity was feeding, growing stronger, weaving its dark tapestry with every passing second.

A chilling realization dawned on her: the maze had not been designed to simply trap her, but to delay her. To keep her occupied, to drain her strength and her resolve, until the moment of the entity's absolute power was at hand. The whispers, the illusions, the disorienting pathways – they were all tactics to ensure she arrived at the nexus too late, too weakened to act. But she wouldn't let that happen. Not now. Not when she was so close.

She stumbled, her foot catching on an unseen root, sending her sprawling onto the damp earth. The obsidian shard flew from her grasp, skittering away into the dense undergrowth. Panic, cold and sharp, seized her. "No!" she cried out, scrambling on her hands and knees, her fingers desperately sifting through the thick mat of fallen leaves and corn husks. The whispers erupted into a triumphant chorus, a symphony of mocking laughter echoing through the stalks.

Lost. So easily lost. The harvest is assured.

Her heart pounded against her ribs like a trapped bird. She could feel the entity's attention sharpening, focusing on her vulnerability, on her desperation. It was reveling in her momentary defeat. Then, her fingers brushed against something smooth, unnaturally cold, and impossibly familiar. The obsidian shard. She snatched it up, a wave of desperate relief washing over her. It pulsed faintly in her palm, a small, steady light in the overwhelming darkness. She clung to it, a lifeline in the churning sea of fear.

Taking a deep, shuddering breath, Kayla forced herself to push past the panic. Elias had anticipated this. He had warned her that the entity would exploit every weakness, that it would prey on her fear and her desperation. She had to remain focused, to channel her resolve. She remembered his instructions about the shard's resonance, how it could disrupt the entity's hold if properly aligned. It wasn't enough to simply possess it; she had to become a conduit for its power, to project its disquieting frequency outwards.

She closed her eyes, focusing on the cool energy radiating from the shard. She envisioned the ley lines Elias had mapped, the converging points of power, and she pictured the shard's unique resonance cutting through them, severing the connections. She held onto the image of the scarecrow, not as a terrifying effigy, but as a knot in the fabric of reality, a knot that needed to be untied.

When she opened her eyes, the world seemed to have shifted, ever so subtly. The oppressive weight of the air hadn't lifted, but the whispers had lost some of their immediate, suffocating intensity. It was as if her renewed focus, her projection of the shard's resonance, had created a small pocket of resistance against the entity's pervasive influence. The maze was still there, a formidable barrier, but she no longer felt completely adrift. She had a sense of direction, a faint, almost imperceptible pull towards the epicenter of the entity's power.

She began to move again, not by sight, but by an inner compass, guided by the shard's subtle thrumming and her own burgeoning understanding of the field's warped energies. She felt a faint incline in the land, a subtle shift in the air currents, clues that Elias had taught her to decipher. She was moving towards the heart of the Withers Field, towards the nexus, towards the very source of Dry Creek's ancient curse.

The entity, sensing her renewed determination, its primal senses detecting her intent, unleashed its full fury. The whispers transformed into a deafening roar, a cacophony of spectral voices screaming in a primal, guttural rage. The cornstalks around her began to thrash violently, as if caught in a sudden, unnatural tempest, their dry leaves whipping and lashing out like venomous tendrils. The very ground seemed to buckle and heave, a violent tremor running through the earth.

Kayla stumbled, falling to her knees again, the obsidian shard clutched so tightly her knuckles were white. This was the true heart of the labyrinth, the entity's most sacred hunting ground. She could feel its immense, ancient power bearing down on her, a crushing, omnipresent force that threatened to obliterate her very will. The whispers coalesced into a single, resonant voice, deep and chilling, seeming to emanate from the rustling leaves themselves. *You cannot hide from me*, it boomed, the sound resonating through the very marrow of her bones. *You cannot escape the harvest.*

Gritting her teeth against the overwhelming onslaught, Kayla forced herself to rise, her knees protesting with a searing ache. She wouldn't succumb. She refused to. "I'm not here to escape," she managed to choke out, her voice raw and strained, yet laced with a newfound defiance. "I'm here to end this."

As the words left her lips, a subtle shift occurred in the chaotic symphony of terror. A faint thinning in the dense wall of stalks, a slight break in the oppressive green expanse, appeared before her. It wasn't a clear path, not an easy route, but a mere suggestion, a whisper of an opening that led beyond the immediate confusion. It was the nexus, or at least, the entrance to it.

She surged forward, pushing through the thrashing stalks, ignoring the sharp jabs and tears as they raked against her. The entity's rage was a palpable force, pushing against her, trying to force her back, to smother her resolve. The whispers became a deafening roar, the stalks writhed and lashed, but Kayla pressed on, her movements driven by a primal instinct for survival and an unwavering commitment to her objective. The clearing, when she finally broke into it, was small, almost insignificant, yet it felt like a sanctuary, a brief respite from the overwhelming chaos.

And there, in the very center of that clearing, stood the scarecrow. It was exactly as Elias had described, a grotesque, crudely fashioned effigy of straw and tattered burlap, its stitched-on features twisted into a permanent, hateful grimace. But it was more than just a farmers' deterrent; it was alive, crackling with the dark, potent energy of the Gaze Offering. Its vacant, button eyes seemed to fix upon her, and its tattered limbs twitched with an unnatural, predatory anticipation.

The scarecrow's head turned, a slow, creaking movement that sent a fresh wave of icy dread through Kayla. Its empty gaze locked onto her, and she could feel the raw, untamed power radiating from it, a vortex of ancient hunger that seemed to draw the very light from the clearing. The surrounding cornstalks, as if magnetized by the entity's focus, leaned inwards, their dry leaves rustling with a collective, sinister anticipation, forming an impenetrable, living wall that trapped her with the source of Dry Creek's enduring torment. The harvest moon, now at its zenith, cast a brilliant, baleful light,

228

intensifying the sinister aura of the scarecrow. She raised the obsidian shard, its faint glow a desperate, defiant spark in the oppressive gloom. The air around the scarecrow shimmered, distorting the surrounding corn, as if the very fabric of reality was being strained to its breaking point by its malevolent presence. She could feel the entity's immense, accumulated power, a force that had been gathering for generations, drawing sustenance from the fear, the despair, and the unyielding earth of Dry Creek. The clock was ticking down, the lunar cycle reaching its apex, and she had mere moments to act.

Chapter 10

The Heart of the Field

The labyrinth of corn seemed to breathe, a colossal, rustling entity that shifted and reformed around them with every step. Kayla's heart hammered a frantic rhythm against her ribs, each beat a desperate plea for clarity amidst the overwhelming sensory assault. The whispers, no longer a distant murmur but a pervasive, suffocating presence, slithered through the dry stalks, weaving insidious narratives of doubt and dread. They spoke of Elias, of his failed attempts, of the futility of her own desperate gamble. They coiled around her name, each utterance laced with a chilling intimacy, as if the entity itself had peered into her very soul and cataloged her deepest fears.

Sheriff DuCard, his face a mask of grim determination, walked beside her, his presence a fragile bulwark against the encroaching terror. His hand rested on the worn grip of his service weapon, a gesture of defiance against the unseen forces that held the field captive. Yet, even his stoic demeanor seemed to waver under the relentless psychological pressure. The air was thick with an unnatural stillness, broken only by the insidious whispers and the unnerving, rhythmic rustle of the corn, a sound that seemed to echo the very pulse of the malevolent entity.

"This way," DuCard rasped, his voice strained. He gestured towards a barely discernible parting in the towering stalks, a gap that seemed to promise passage but also to beckon them deeper into the suffocating embrace of the maze. His eyes, usually sharp and observant, darted nervously, scanning the oppressive green walls that seemed to lean in, their shadows elongating and twisting into grotesque, fleeting shapes. Kayla caught him glancing at the obsidian shard clutched in her hand, a silent question in his gaze.

She offered a curt nod, a silent affirmation that they were still on the right path, guided by Elias's cryptic notes and her own desperate intuition.

The Withers journal, clutched tightly in Kayla's other hand, felt like a fragile shield against the overwhelming darkness. Its pages, brittle and yellowed, were filled with Elias's frantic scrawls, his increasingly desperate attempts to decipher the ancient pact that bound Dry Creek to the entity. The crude map, sketched with shaky lines and punctuated by unsettling symbols, was their only guide through this organic nightmare. Each turn, each rustle, felt like a deliberate misdirection, a calculated attempt by the entity to lead them astray, to break their resolve before they reached the heart of the field, before the moon reached its zenith.

The whispers intensified, morphing into mocking laughter that seemed to emanate from the very stalks surrounding them.

Lost, a chorus of spectral voices hissed, their tones dripping with amusement. *So easily lost. The harvest is assured. You cannot escape the cycle.* Kayla flinched, squeezing her eyes shut for a brief moment, trying to shut out the invasive cacophony. The whispers were more than just sounds; they were insidious tendrils of psychic assault, designed to sow doubt and despair, to erode their will to fight. They preyed on their exhaustion, their fear, on the gnawing uncertainty of their mission.

DuCard gripped her arm, his touch firm, grounding. "Don't listen to them, Kayla," he said, his voice a low growl that cut through the spectral noise. "They feed on fear. Don't give them what they want." He pulled her forward, urging her into the narrow passage he had indicated. The cornstalks brushed against them, their dry, papery leaves rustling like a thousand brittle bones. The air grew colder, the moonlight that filtered through the dense canopy casting long, distorted shadows that writhed and danced like specters.

They moved deeper into the maze, the path twisting and turning with a disorienting regularity that defied logic. It was as if the field itself was a sentient being, deliberately contorting its pathways to ensnare them, to prolong their agony. The whispers continued their relentless assault, now focusing on DuCard, dredging up fragmented memories of past failures, of cases gone cold, of the lives he couldn't save.

A shepherd lost with his flock, the voices taunted him. *The darkness claims all. Even the strong ones fall.*

Kayla felt a prickle of unease at DuCard's sudden, sharp intake of breath. She risked a glance at him, her heart sinking as she saw the flicker of pain in his eyes. He shook his head, a barely perceptible movement, and squared his shoulders, his jaw set in a grim line. He was fighting it, just as she was, but the strain was evident. The entity was relentless, its methods honed over centuries of ritual and sacrifice. It was a master manipulator, adept at exploiting every weakness, every crack in their mental fortitude.

The Withers journal offered a sliver of hope, Elias's desperate attempts to provide a counter-measure. He had theorized that the obsidian shard, when properly attuned to the ley lines converging at the nexus, could disrupt the ritual. But the process was dangerous, requiring a precise alignment and a deep concentration that felt almost impossible to maintain in this environment of relentless psychic warfare. The journal described a specific incantation, a series of guttural, resonant words that were meant to channel the shard's disruptive energy. Kayla murmured them under her breath, the strange syllables feeling alien on her tongue, yet resonating with a faint, forgotten power.

As they navigated another seemingly identical row of corn, a chilling realization dawned on Kayla. The maze wasn't merely a physical obstacle; it was a carefully constructed psychological battlefield. The whispers, the illusions, the disorienting pathways – they were all designed to erode their mental defenses, to drain their resolve, to make them question their purpose, their sanity. Elias had warned her that the entity would try to break her spirit, to convince her of the futility of her actions. And it was succeeding, subtly, insidiously, with every rustle, every whisper, every fleeting shadow.

They reached a small, overgrown clearing, the air here thick with an almost tangible sense of dread. In the center stood a weathered, wooden effigy, its tattered clothes ripped and faded, its straw-stuffed limbs hanging at unnatural angles. It was a crude, unsettling figure, a silent sentinel that seemed to radiate an ancient, palpable malevolence. This was not the scarecrow from Elias's sketches, the nexus point, but something else, something that felt like a marker, a warning. The whispers grew louder here, coalescing around this disturbing effigy, as if it were a focal point for their torment.

He tried, a voice whispered, low and sibilant, seeming to emanate from the effigy itself. *He thought he could defy the natural order. He was wrong.* Kayla's blood ran cold. The voice was eerily familiar, a distorted echo of Elias's own. It was a cruel mockery, a spectral mimicry designed to plant seeds of despair, to remind her of his ultimate failure.

DuCard raised his revolver, his gaze fixed on the effigy, a flicker of primal fear crossing his face before he masked it with renewed determination. "It's a trick," he stated, his voice tight. "Just straw and rags. Don't let it get to you." He took a step towards the effigy, his hand steady, but Kayla grabbed his arm.

"Wait," she cautioned, her own voice trembling slightly. "Elias said the entity uses... echoes. Manifestations of our fears, of our past. This isn't the nexus. It's a distraction." She consulted the journal again, her fingers tracing the intricate lines of Elias's map. "The nexus... it's deeper. Further in."

She pointed to a symbol on the map, a crude depiction of a coiled serpent, nestled deep within the maze's seemingly endless expanse. "He marked this as a 'deception point'. A place where the entity would try to lead us astray, to lure us into a false sense of victory, or a dead end." The effigy, she realized with a chilling certainty, was designed to evoke a sense of closure, of accomplishment, a subtle trick to lull them into a false sense of security before the true danger presented itself.

As if in response to her words, the effigy's head slowly creaked, turning to face her. A faint, guttural sound, like the rasp of dry leaves, emanated from its burlap mouth. The whispers intensified, swirling around them like a vortex, their mocking tones growing louder, more insistent.

You are already lost, they hissed. *The path ends here. Surrender to the inevitable.*

DuCard fired a shot, the deafening roar of the revolver echoing through the clearing. The bullet struck the effigy, tearing through the tattered fabric, but it seemed to have no effect. The whispers merely laughed, a chilling symphony of spectral amusement. The effigy remained standing, its vacant gaze fixed upon them, an unnerving testament to the entity's power.

"Let's go," Kayla urged, pulling DuCard away from the unsettling tableau. "We're wasting time." She clutched the obsidian shard tighter, its faint warmth a small comfort against the encroaching dread. The journal indicated that the nexus was marked by a subtle shift in the land's energy, a convergence of the ley lines that Elias had painstakingly mapped. It was a subtle indicator, one that could easily be missed amidst the chaos and the relentless assault on their senses.

They pressed on, the maze seemingly endless, the cornstalks a suffocating green wall that pressed in on all sides. The whispers continued their relentless assault, each word a carefully crafted barb, designed to pierce their resolve. They spoke of doubt, of despair, of the futility of their mission.

Elias was a fool, a voice whispered, its tone a cruel imitation of DuCard's own. *He thought he could cheat death. He was wrong. And so are you.*

They met up with Tommy back at the car. Kayla saw DuCard flinch, his knuckles whitening as he gripped his sidearm. The psychological warfare was taking its toll. She knew she had to maintain her focus, to push past the invasive whispers and the disorienting shadows. She recalled Elias's final instructions, his desperate plea for her to remember the ritual, to stay true to his research. The obsidian shard was their key, their only hope of severing the ancient pact that bound Dry Creek to the darkness.

In front of them was another dense section of corn bordered by a slightly more open area, where the moonlight was less obscured. And then they saw it. In the center of the clearing, bathed in the stark, sepulchral light of the harvest moon, stood the scarecrow. It was exactly as Elias had described and sketched in his journal – a grotesque, crudely fashioned effigy of straw and tattered burlap, its stitched-on features twisted into a permanent, hateful grimace. Its vacant eyes seemed to bore into Kayla's soul, and its tattered limbs twitched with an unnatural, predatory anticipation.

The weight of generations, the echoes of past sacrifices, pressed down on her, a suffocating burden. Yet, within that crushing weight, a spark of defiance ignited, fueled by Elias's sacrifice and the desperate hope for Dry Creek's salvation. She would not falter. She could not.

The whispers coalesced, no longer individual taunts but a unified, deafening roar that seemed to vibrate through the very marrow of Kayla's bones. The cornstalks around the scarecrow contorted, not just leaning, but twisting, weaving, and rippling like a grotesque tapestry woven from living dread. It wasn't a physical entity, not in the way DuCard understood the world, but a manifestation of pure, primal terror, a shifting kaleidoscope of shadows and primal urges. It pulsed with an ancient hunger, its form fluid, amorphous, a nightmarish storm of grasping tendrils and unseen eyes. Kayla closed her eyes, the obsidian shard feeling impossibly small and fragile in her trembling hand. Tommy gasped.

Suddenly, a guttural shriek, a sound that tore through the very fabric of the night, erupted from the heart of the swirling darkness. It was a sound of immense pain, of raw, unadulterated fury, and it was directed squarely at Kayla. A massive, shadowy appendage, far thicker than any cornstalk, lashed out from the amorphous mass, aimed directly at her. She froze behind the car, mesmerized by the sheer, impossible violence of it, the obsidian shard forgotten for a fleeting, fatal second.

But Sheriff DuCard was not frozen and moved around the car and advanced towards the chaos. He saw the trajectory of the scarecrow; he saw the terror in Kayla and Tommy's wide eyes. In that split second, a decision, born of years of protecting this town, of a duty that ran deeper than any fear, flashed across his face. His grip tightened on his service revolver, not in anticipation of firing, but as an anchor, a tangible piece of his reality against the encroaching unreality.

"Kayla! Go!" DuCard's voice, though strained, cut through the infernal noise. He didn't shout; he roared, a primal sound of defiance that seemed to momentarily halt the entity's inexorable advance. He could see the entity, the scarecrow, and moved towards it squeezing off round by round. By doing so, DuCard had cleared Kayla a path for her to circle around. Kayla moved the obsidian shard clattered against her palm as she stumbled forward, her mind reeling from the unexpected shield DuCard was providing. She watched as DuCard emptied his clip and quickly reloaded. Although the rounds impacted the torso of the scarecrow; the scarecrow was seemingly impervious to their impact.

The entity, its attention momentarily diverted by DuCard's sudden and aggressive movement, shifted. The massive appendage that had been aimed at Kayla recoiled, then lashed out again, this time towards DuCard. It was a blindingly fast movement, a blur of shadow and malevolence. DuCard dodged and raised his service weapon, his face a mask of grim resolve, and fired.

The shot echoed through the clearing, a defiant, futile gesture against a force that defied comprehension. The bullet struck the shifting mass, a minuscule disruption in the overwhelming darkness. But the entity barely seemed to register it. It continued its assault, its tendrils coiling, wrapping, constricting around DuCard with terrifying speed. Kayla watched, paralyzed by horror, as the shadowy limbs enveloped him, his form disappearing within the swirling vortex of Dry Creek's ancient curse.

His screams, when they came, were choked, abruptly cut short, swallowed by the insatiable hunger of the field. A profound, chilling silence descended for a single, agonizing beat, a silence punctuated only by the frantic hammering of Kayla's own heart. Then, the whispers returned, no longer mocking, but triumphant, a victorious chorus that echoed the entity's victory.

Another offering, they hissed, their voices laced with a sickening satisfaction. *The shepherd falls. The flock is scattered.*

The loss of DuCard was a physical blow, a crushing weight that threatened to shatter Kayla's already frayed resolve. He had been her anchor in this descent into madness. His sacrifice, so sudden and

237

so absolute, was a testament to the true horror of their situation. This was not a game; it was a battle for survival, a battle where the stakes were measured in lives, in souls.

The entity, having dealt with DuCard, seemed to refocus its attention. The swirling mass around the scarecrow pulsed, expanding, its shadowy tendrils reaching out, not just towards Kayla, but towards the very edges of the clearing. It was claiming its territory, asserting its dominion over the land and all who dared to trespass. The cornstalks surrounding them began to vibrate, their dry leaves rustling with a collective, menacing hum, closing in, creating an impenetrable barrier.

Kayla felt a surge of primal fear, an urge to flee, to run blindly back into the labyrinth from which they had just emerged. But DuCard's sacrifice echoed in her mind. He had bought her time, precious seconds that she couldn't afford to waste. His life had been the price for her to reach this point, to stand before the nexus, to hold the obsidian shard. She couldn't let his death be in vain.

With a renewed, desperate strength, she pushed aside the encroaching tendrils of panic. Her fingers tightened around the obsidian shard, its rough surface a familiar, grounding sensation. She thought of Elias's journal; on the hastily scribbled incantation he had deemed essential. The words felt heavy on her tongue, ancient and charged with a power she could only begin to comprehend. The clearing seemed to expand and contract around her, the shifting nature of the entity making it impossible to gauge her surroundings, her distance from the scarecrow.

The entity, sensing her renewed focus, reacted. It didn't lash out with physical force this time. Instead, it unleashed a new wave of psychic assault, a torrent of images and sensations designed to break her spirit completely. She saw flashes of Elias's final moments, the terror in his eyes as he succumbed to the entity's influence. She saw the faces of the townsfolk, their eyes vacant, their souls already claimed by the harvest. She saw her own death, a gruesome end at the hands of the swirling darkness.

He chose this, a voice, distorted and chillingly familiar, whispered directly into her mind. It was DuCard's voice, twisted and corrupted by the entity's influence. *He sacrificed himself for nothing. You are next.*

Tears welled in Kayla's eyes, blurring her vision. The whispers, amplified by DuCard's corrupted voice, were almost unbearable. Doubt gnawed at her, whispering insidious truths about the futility of her mission, the impossibility of her task. Elias journal had warned her the entity would exploit her deepest fears, her most painful memories. It was a master of psychological warfare, and it was systematically dismantling her defenses.

She squeezed her eyes shut, forcing the intrusive images away. She focused on the warmth of the obsidian shard, on the faint, steady pulse of energy that emanated from it. She remembered Elias's words, his unwavering belief in the shard's power, his desperate hope that it could sever the ancient pact. He had died believing in this, and she would honor his belief, honor DuCard's sacrifice, by seeing it through.

She began to recite the incantation, her voice shaky at first, then growing stronger, more resonant. The guttural syllables felt foreign, yet strangely familiar, as if they were a forgotten language awakening within her. As she spoke the words, the obsidian shard began to glow, a faint, internal light that pushed back against the encroaching darkness. The surrounding cornstalks seemed to recoil slightly from the burgeoning light, their malevolent hum faltering for a moment.

The entity, sensing the shift in power, reacted with increased ferocity. The amorphous mass churned violently, and the whispers intensified, morphing into a cacophony of screams and wails. The very ground beneath Kayla's feet began to tremble, the earth cracking as if in agony. The scarecrow at the center of the nexus pulsed with an unholy light, its tattered form seeming to expand, to become one with the swirling darkness.

Kayla ignored it, her focus solely on the incantation, on channeling the shard's energy. She could feel the ley lines converging beneath her, a powerful network of ancient energy that Elias had so carefully mapped. The obsidian shard was meant to disrupt this flow, to sever the connection between the entity and the land, between the entity and Withers Field.

She raised the shard higher, its light now a steady, unwavering beacon. The whispers clawed at her mind, trying to pull her away from her focus, trying to drag her back into the abyss of despair. But with each word of the incantation, her resolve hardened, her connection to the shard strengthening. She could feel the ancient power of the earth flowing through her, guided by the shard, directed at the heart of the darkness.

The entity let out another ear-splitting shriek, a sound of pure, unadulterated rage. A wave of pure, raw energy slammed into Kayla, throwing her backward. She landed hard, the obsidian shard flying from her grasp, skittering across the churned earth. The light from the shard flickered, threatening to extinguish.

For a terrifying moment, despair washed over her. She had failed. DuCard's sacrifice, Elias's research, her own desperate courage – all for nothing. The entity's triumphant roar echoed through the clearing, the whispers reaching a fever pitch of victory. The shadowy tendrils began to advance, closing in on her, ready to claim their prize.

But then, she remembered Elias's journal, a detail he had almost dismissed as a minor anomaly. The obsidian shard wasn't just a conduit; it was also a key, designed to resonate with the ley lines themselves. Even displaced, it would still be attuned to the nexus. She needed to reach it, to make one final, desperate attempt.

Crawling, scraping her hands against the rough earth, Kayla fought her way towards the flickering light of the obsidian shard. The entity's tendrils whipped around her, narrowly missing their mark, its rage a tangible force that buffeted her. The whispers were a relentless barrage, promising oblivion, taunting her with her impending doom.

She could almost taste the darkness, the cold, suffocating embrace of the entity. But the shard was close now, its faint glow a beacon of hope in the encroaching night. With a final, desperate lunge, she snatched it up, its familiar warmth seeping into her chilled hand.

Ignoring the searing pain in her side, the exhaustion that threatened to pull her under, Kayla rose to her feet. The entity loomed before her, its form shifting, its rage palpable. She raised the obsidian shard, its light now blazing, fueled by the convergence of the ley lines, by her own desperate will. She spoke the final words of the incantation, her voice ringing with a newfound power, a power born of sacrifice and defiance.

The obsidian shard pulsed, sending a shockwave of pure energy through the nexus. The scarecrow, the focal point of the entity's power, began to disintegrate, its straw form unraveling, its eyes dissolving into nothingness. The cornstalks surrounding the clearing shrieked, their forms contorting as the ley lines were disrupted, the ancient pact torn asunder. The entity itself seemed to convulse, its shadowy form flickering, a piercing wail of agony echoing through the night. Kayla felt a profound sense of release, a connection to the earth that had been corrupted for so long, now cleansing, becoming pure. The darkness receded, not vanishing, but being forced back, its hold over Withers Field broken. The harvest moon, now beginning its descent, cast a gentler light, and for the first time since entering the field, Kayla could feel a fragile sense of peace settle over the land. But the victory came at a terrible cost, a cost etched in the silence left by Sheriff DuCard's absence, a silence that would forever haunt the heart of the field.

The air thrummed with an unnatural silence, a stark contrast to the cacophony of Elias's dying moments and DuCard's final, defiant roar. Kayla stood at the heart of the field, the obsidian shard clutched tight in her numb fingers. Before her, the epicenter pulsed, a wound in the fabric of reality. At its core stood the scarecrow, a grotesque mockery of its former self. It was no longer merely an effigy of burlap and straw. It had become a monstrous amalgamation, a shrine woven from the very essence of Dry Creek's dread.

The rough burlap was stretched taut over a skeletal frame that seemed too fluid, too *alive*. Straw spilled from rips and tears, not the dry, brittle straw of harvest, but something darker, richer, as if it had absorbed the very lifeblood of the earth. And the eyes. The eyes Elias had described were gone. In their place was a swirling vortex, a maelstrom of vacant, spectral gazes. Hundreds, perhaps thousands, of eyes, stolen and repurposed, swirled within the hollows of the scarecrow's head. They were not the eyes of the living, nor entirely the eyes of the dead. They were something in between, a reflection of souls trapped in a perpetual state of terror, their vacant stares boring into Kayla's very soul, promising a fate worse than death. This was the nexus, the physical manifestation of the Gaze Offering, the terrifying heart of the Withers curse.

The cornstalks that had once surrounded the clearing now seemed to bend and writhe in obeisance to this central, hideous monument. They formed a living, breathing throne for the abomination, their rustling leaves a chorus of whispers that sought to unravel Kayla's sanity. The ground beneath her feet was not soil, but a rich, dark loam that seemed to shimmer with an unholy luminescence, pulsing in time with the spectral eyes. It was as if the earth itself had been infected, its very essence corrupted by the presence of this malevolent construct.

Kayla felt the weight of those stolen gazes pressing down on her, each one a pinprick of psychic agony. They weren't just looking at her; they were *seeing* her, dissecting her fears, cataloging her vulnerabilities. She saw fragments of memories flicker within the swirling vortex – a child's terrified gasp, a farmer's desperate plea, a lover's mournful cry. These were the echoes of lives consumed, souls devoured, all gathered and amplified within this monstrous effigy.

This was the culmination of Elias's obsessive research, the physical anchor of the entity that had plagued Dry Creek for generations. The Gaze Offering. A ritual of sacrifice, a feeding of the land's insatiable hunger. The scarecrow, in its current form, was not merely a symbol; it was the conduit, the altar, the very embodiment of the curse. Its creation had been a slow, insidious process, a gradual absorption of the life force of those who had wandered too close, who had fallen prey to the whispers in the corn.

The obsidian shard in Kayla's hand felt like a tiny ember against the encroaching frost of the entity's power. Elias had been clear: the shard was the key, the means to sever the ancient pact, to shatter the nexus. But looking at the sheer, overwhelming malevolence radiating from the scarecrow, doubt gnawed at her. How could a single shard, a mere artifact, possibly contend with a force that had consumed so many?

She remembered DuCard's final moments, his sacrifice a raw wound in her memory. He had stood between her and that swirling darkness, a shield of flesh and blood against an immaterial horror. His final act of defiance had bought her this moment, this opportunity to face the heart of the blight. His absence was a gaping void, a silence that screamed louder than any noise. She couldn't let his death be in vain. She couldn't falter now.

Taking a deep, shuddering breath, Kayla focused on the incantation Elias had left her. The words felt alien on her tongue, ancient and potent, a forgotten language whispered by the wind through the dying corn. As she began to speak, the obsidian shard in her hand pulsed with a faint, internal light. It was a meager defiance against the oppressive darkness, but it was a start.

The swirling eyes of the scarecrow seemed to fix on her, their spectral intensity increasing tenfold. The whispers intensified, no longer merely a murmur, but a chorus of desperate, clawing voices, each trying to pry open the gates of her mind. They dredged up her deepest anxieties: the fear of being alone, the guilt over past mistakes, the gnawing dread of her own mortality.

You are weak, hissed a voice that was eerily like DuCard's, corrupted and twisted by the entity's influence. *He died for nothing. You will be forgotten. Just another pair of eyes for the harvest.*

Kayla gritted her teeth, the obsidian shard vibrating in her grip. The psychic assault was relentless, a barrage of insidious suggestions designed to shatter her will. She saw flashes of Elias's final moments, his eyes wide with terror, his body wracked by an unseen force. She saw the vacant stares of the townsfolk, their souls already claimed, their bodies hollow shells animated by the entity's will. She saw her own reflection in the swirling vortex of eyes, her face contorted in a silent scream, her own eyes becoming empty, spectral voids.

We are the land, the whispers coalesced, a single, ancient voice echoing from the scarecrow's hollow core. *We are the hunger that cannot be sated. We are the harvest that is eternal. You cannot escape us.*

The ground beneath her feet began to shift, the rich loam erupting in small, writhing mounds. The tendrils of cornstalks, previously held at bay by the shard's nascent light, now surged forward, their dry leaves scraping against each other like a thousand tiny fingernails. They reached for her, attempting to ensnare her, to pull her into the vortex of the scarecrow's throne.

Kayla stumbled back, her voice faltering as she recited the incantation. The entity was not just a physical manifestation; it was a parasitic consciousness, feeding on fear and despair. Elias had warned her that it would exploit her deepest vulnerabilities, and it was proving to be a master of psychological warfare. Every failed step, every moment of hesitation, only fueled its power.

She felt the oppressive presence of the entity, a crushing weight that threatened to suffocate her. It was not just around her; it was *within* her, probing her mind, seeking any weakness to exploit. The whispers were no longer just sounds; they were thoughts, invasive and vile, twisting her own deepest fears against her.

You are alone, the voices echoed, each syllable laced with the promise of eternal damnation. *No one can hear you. No one will save you. Elias is gone. DuCard is gone. Only the whispers remain.*

Tears streamed down Kayla's face, blurring her vision. The voices, so insidious, so personal, were a torment that threatened to break her. The memory of DuCard's sacrifice, of his selfless act of protection, warred with the entity's insidious whispers. He had faced this horror head-on, his duty a shield against the encroaching darkness. She had to honor that sacrifice. She had to find the strength within herself.

She closed her eyes, forcing the visions and the whispers away. She focused on the obsidian shard, its rough surface a grounding sensation in the chaos. She remembered Elias's meticulous notes, his conviction that the shard held the power to sever the connection, to break the cycle. He had poured his life's work into this, and his belief, though ultimately insufficient to save him, had to be her guide.

With a renewed surge of determination, Kayla reopened her eyes. She raised the obsidian shard, its faint light now a steady beacon against the encroaching gloom. She poured all her remaining strength, all her will, into the incantation. The guttural syllables felt like a physical exertion, a battle waged with her voice and her spirit.

The scarecrow's head, the vortex of spectral eyes, seemed to recoil slightly from the incantation. The whispers faltered, replaced by a low, guttural growl that emanated from the very earth. The cornstalks writhed more violently, their embrace tightening around Kayla, trying to pull her down into the pulsating loam.

She felt a surge of raw power surge through the obsidian shard, a response to her plea, to the ancient words. It was as if the shard itself was awakening, its purpose finally being realized. The nexus, the heart of the entity's power, pulsed in response, a violent counter-surge of malevolent energy. The ground trembled violently, cracks appearing as if the earth itself was tearing apart.

The scarecrow began to change. The burlap seemed to ripple, to stretch, to fray. The straw spilling from its form started to blacken, to crumble, as if the very essence of life was being leached from it. The vortex of eyes, however, remained, their spectral intensity growing more terrifying, their gazes now filled with a pure, unadulterated rage.

Kayla pushed harder, her voice growing stronger, more resonant. She could feel the ley lines converging beneath her, a powerful network of energy that Elias had so painstakingly mapped. The obsidian shard was meant to disrupt this flow, to tear apart the very foundation of the Withers curse. It was a delicate, yet brutal, operation, like severing a corrupted artery.

The entity shrieked, a sound of pure agony and fury that ripped through the clearing. It was the sound of something ancient and powerful being wounded, of a predator whose dominion was being challenged. A wave of pure, raw energy slammed into Kayla, throwing her violently backward. The obsidian shard was ripped from her grasp, skittering across the churned earth, its light flickering, threatening to extinguish entirely.

For a horrifying moment, Kayla lay stunned, the air knocked from her lungs. Despair washed over her. She had failed. DuCard's sacrifice, Elias's desperate gamble, her own terrifying journey – all for naught. The entity's triumphant roar echoed through the clearing, the whispers reaching a deafening crescendo of victory. The shadowy tendrils of cornstalks surged forward, their grasping limbs closing in, eager to claim their prize.

But as she lay there, gasping for breath, a flicker of hope ignited within her. Elias's journal. He had mentioned the shard's attunement to the ley lines, its ability to resonate with the very energy that sustained the entity. Even displaced, it would still be connected to this nexus. She had to reach it. One last, desperate attempt.

Crawling, her hands scraping against the rough, alien soil, Kayla fought her way towards the dim, flickering glow of the obsidian shard. The entity's tendrils whipped around her, narrowly missing their mark, its rage a palpable force that buffeted her, trying to push her back into oblivion. The whispers were a relentless barrage, promising annihilation, taunting her with her impending doom.

The obsidian shard pulsed, sending a shockwave of pure, untamed energy through the nexus. The scarecrow, the focal point of the entity's power, began to unravel. Its straw form disintegrated, its burlap skin tore apart, its eyes, the stolen gazes, dissolving into nothingness. The cornstalks surrounding the clearing shrieked, their forms contorting as the ley lines were violently disrupted, the ancient pact torn asunder. The entity itself seemed to convulse, its shadowy form flickering like a dying flame, a piercing, unearthly wail of agony echoing through the night. Kayla felt a profound sense of release, a connection to the earth that had been corrupted for so long, now cleansing, pure. The darkness receded, not vanishing entirely, but being forced back, its suffocating hold over Dry Creek broken. The harvest moon, now beginning its descent, cast a gentler light, and for the first time since entering the field, Kayla could feel a fragile sense of peace settle over the ravaged land. But the victory came at a terrible, soul-crushing cost, a cost etched in the profound silence left by Sheriff DuCard's absence, a silence that would forever haunt the heart of the field, a silent testament to the true horror of the Gaze Offering and the Scarecrow's Throne.

The obsidian shard in Kayla's hand was no longer just a tool; it was a conduit, a fragment of something ancient and deeply resonant. Its cold, smooth surface seemed to hum against her skin, a counter-frequency to the oppressive, pulsating dread that permeated the heart of the field. She felt the shard's energy, a stark, primal force, awaken in response to the concentrated malevolence surrounding her. It was a desperate echo of Elias's meticulous research, his final, frantic scribbles detailing not a weapon of destruction, but a disruption. The journal had described the shard as a key, capable of severing the flow of vital energy that sustained the entity, the unseen force that had woven itself into the very fabric of Dry Creek. It was not meant to annihilate, but to disrupt, to break the ancient, accursed cycle of sacrifice that had bled Dry Creek dry for generations. This was her only hope, a fragile sliver of possibility against the crushing weight of overwhelming darkness.

Elias had theorized that the entity was not a singular being, but a symbiotic manifestation, a parasitic consciousness that fed on the collective fear and despair of the town. The scarecrow, in its horrific, transformed state, was merely the anchor, the nexus point where this parasitic energy was most concentrated. The obsidian shard, Elias believed, possessed the unique property to interfere with the energetic currents that flowed through the ley lines, those invisible rivers of power that Elias had spent years mapping, converging at this very spot. By plunging the shard into the heart of the convergence, he theorized, the disruptive frequency it emitted would create a feedback loop, effectively strangling the entity's lifeline, forcing it to retreat, to loosen its grip on Dry Creek. The shard itself was said to be a fragment of a much larger, naturally occurring obsidian formation, a place where the earth's natural energies had been amplified to an extraordinary degree, and then, through some forgotten process, imbued with this specific disruptive property. Elias had found it buried deep within the old quarry, a place he believed had once been a site of ancient, pre-colonial rituals, long before the Withers curse had taken root. He had theorized that the quarry itself was a place of potent natural energy, and the obsidian found there was a natural amplifier of those energies. The shard, in its isolation, was dormant, but Elias had discovered through his experiments that it could be 'activated' by proximity to a strong source of psychic or spiritual energy, and that its purpose was intrinsically tied to severing connections.

The shard's resonance with the field felt like a silent conversation, a negotiation between two opposing forces. Kayla felt the obsidian drawing upon the ambient energy, amplifying her own desperate intent. It was a slow, painstaking process, this attunement. She could feel the subtle shifts in the air, the almost imperceptible tightening of the unseen bonds that held the field captive. The journal had warned her that the shard's effectiveness was directly proportional to the user's mental fortitude and their connection to the surrounding energy. It was not a simple act of insertion; it was an act of will, of channeling her own inner strength through the artifact. Elias had spent weeks experimenting with it, using various foci and locations, meticulously recording the subtle fluctuations in its output. He had described it as akin to tuning a complex instrument, where the wrong note, the wrong intention, could render it inert, or worse, amplify the very thing it was meant to disrupt. He had cautioned that the entity would fight back, not with physical force, but by attempting to corrupt the user's intent, to twist their fears and doubts into weapons against them, a psychological warfare waged on the very threshold of consciousness.

Kayla gripped the shard tighter, her knuckles white. The sheer scale of the entity's presence was a suffocating blanket, an almost tangible weight pressing down on her. It was more than just a malevolent force; it was a presence that had seeped into the very soil, the very air, the very memories of this place. The whispers, though muted now compared to their earlier crescendo, were still there, a low, insidious murmur at the edge of her hearing, probing, testing, seeking purchase. They spoke of Elias's failures, of DuCard's sacrifice, of her own inherent weakness.

He died in vain, a voice, chillingly familiar yet undeniably alien, slithered into her mind. *His bravery was a flicker, extinguished. Yours will be too. This field, this earth, it demands more. It always demands more.* The whispers were not just sounds;

they were invasive thoughts, insidious suggestions designed to erode her resolve.

She focused on Elias's words: *The shard does not destroy, Kayla. It disconnects. It severs the roots that feed the blight.* He had stressed that the entity was a network, a web of corrupted energy, and the obsidian was the tool to cut the primary strands. The Gaze Offering, as he had termed it, was not a single event, but a continuous process, a ritualistic feeding of the land's insatiable hunger for life force. The scarecrow was the altar, and the stolen gazes were the currency, each soul sacrificed a potent fuel. The obsidian shard's purpose was to interrupt this flow, to sever the connection between the altar and the source, to starve the parasitic entity at its very core. It was a delicate operation, like performing surgery on a diseased organ, requiring precision and an unwavering focus.

Kayla felt a subtle shift within the shard, a faint warmth radiating from its core, a sign that it was beginning to respond to the confluence of energies. It was as if the obsidian was awakening, its latent power stirring from a long slumber. The journal described this phase as the 'attunement,' where the shard aligned itself with the dominant energy signature of the location. This process, Elias had noted, could be uncomfortable, even painful, as the shard attempted to harmonize with or disrupt the surrounding forces. For Kayla, it felt like a dissonant chord being struck deep within her bones, a jarring vibration that threatened to dislodge her very sense of self.

The cornstalks, though seemingly static, pulsed with a hidden energy, their dry leaves rustling with a sound like dry, brittle whispers. They were not merely plants; they were conduits, channels for the entity's influence, extending its reach, its tendrils of power. Elias had described them as the 'veins' of the Withers curse, drawing sustenance from the corrupted soil and channeling it upwards, towards the nexus. The shard's purpose here was to disrupt this flow, to sever these vital connections, to stop the parasitic nourishment from reaching the core. It was a battle fought not with steel or fire, but with resonance and disruption, a war waged on the energetic battlefield.

She remembered Elias's diagrams, intricate webs of lines and symbols that depicted the flow of power across Dry Creek. He had marked this clearing as the epicenter, the point of convergence for the majority of the ley lines, the place where the entity's influence was strongest. The obsidian shard, when properly aligned, was supposed to create a disruptive ripple effect, a wave of discordant energy that would propagate outwards, breaking the established patterns, severing the parasitic connections. It was a desperate gamble, a Hail Mary pass into the heart of darkness, but it was all they had.

The obsidian shard pulsed again, a more definite thrum this time, its internal light growing steadier. Kayla felt a surge of raw, untamed energy coursing through her, channeled by the shard. It was a terrifying sensation, like holding lightning in her hand, potent and volatile. The entity, sensing this interference, reacted. The whispers intensified, coalescing into a single, guttural snarl that seemed to emanate from the very earth beneath her feet. The ground trembled, not violently, but with a deep, unsettling tremor, as if the field itself was recoiling from the shard's awakening power.

You cannot break what is eternal, the voice boomed, no longer a whisper but a resonant declaration of ancient, unwavering power. *This land remembers. It hungers. It always hungers.* The cornstalks seemed to lean in, their dry stalks rustling with a renewed intensity, their collective murmur a growing threat. They were the physical manifestation of the entity's hold, and the obsidian was meant to sever their connection to the corrupted earth, to starve them at their roots.

Kayla focused, pushing past the fear, past the invasive whispers. She visualized the energy flow Elias had described, the intricate network of ley lines converging beneath her. She saw the obsidian shard as a wedge, a disruptive force, designed to cleave through this network. Her task was to drive that wedge home, to create a tear in the fabric of the entity's power. The shard's purpose was not to destroy the energy, but to redirect it, to break its corrupted cycle, to starve the nexus by severing its primary lifelines. It was like cutting the main power cable to a monstrous machine.

She raised the shard, its light now a defiant beacon against the encroaching gloom. The obsidian pulsed with a powerful, steady rhythm, mirroring the frantic beat of her own heart. The entity's power, immense and ancient, was a tangible force, a pressure that sought to crush her, to extinguish the shard's light, and her own resolve. Elias had described this as the critical juncture, the moment when the shard's purpose was revealed in its entirety. It was a conduit for disruption, a key that unlocked the potential to break the cycle, but it required a vessel, a will strong enough to wield its power.

The obsidian shard's purpose was not to banish the darkness, but to sever the very roots that sustained it. It was a surgical strike, a disruption of the energetic currents that flowed through the corrupted ley lines, the invisible arteries that pumped life into the Withers curse. Elias had theorized that the entity was a manifestation of the land's own corrupted vitality, a parasite that fed on fear and despair, amplifying them into a self-sustaining cycle of dread. The scarecrow was the heart, the nexus, where these currents converged, and the obsidian, a fragment of pure, untamed earth energy, was the tool to disrupt that convergence. It was designed to create a discordant resonance, a feedback loop that would starve the nexus, effectively breaking the ancient pact that bound Dry Creek to its tormentor.

The obsidian vibrated in her hand, a cold, insistent thrum. It was beginning to resonate with the field's oppressive energy, a dissonant harmony that Elias had painstakingly documented. He had theorized that the shard possessed an innate ability to identify and disrupt corrupted energetic pathways. It was not a weapon of brute force, but a precision instrument, designed to sever the invisible ties that bound the entity to Dry Creek. The Gaze Offering was not just a ritual; it was a feeding, a constant draining of the town's life force, and the obsidian was the antidote, the means to cut off that supply.

The whispers grew more frantic, more insistent, like a thousand tiny claws scrabbling at the edges of her sanity. They spoke of futility, of the inescapable nature of the curse.

You are a fool, hissed a voice that had once been Elias's, now twisted into a grotesque parody. *You cannot undo what is woven into*

the earth itself. This land demands its due. It always claims its due.
But Kayla clung to Elias's conviction, to the detailed diagrams in
his journal, to the promise held within the cold, dark obsidian. The
shard was not meant to destroy, but to sever. To break the chain. To
starve the hunger.

The obsidian pulsed, a faint, internal luminescence flickering to
life. It was a tiny spark against the overwhelming darkness, but it
was a spark of hope, a testament to Elias's foresight. The shard's
purpose was to attune itself to the dominant energetic signature of
the nexus, to identify the primary conduits of the entity's power, and
then, through the user's intent, to disrupt that flow. It was a delicate
dance, a dangerous equilibrium, and the slightest waver in her focus,
the slightest flicker of doubt, could allow the entity to overwhelm
the shard, to corrupt its purpose, turning its disruptive power into a
weapon against her. The whispers were the entity's first line of
defense, an attempt to destabilize her, to break her will before the
physical act of disruption could even begin. She felt the chilling
tendrils of fear begin to coil in her gut, but she pushed them back,
focusing on the obsidian's steady pulse, on the cold, unyielding truth
of its purpose. It was a key, and she was the hand that would turn it
in the lock.

The scarecrow stood sentinel, a grotesque parody of agrarian
life. Its straw-stuffed limbs, contorted and unnaturally elongated,
seemed to writhe with a life not their own. The burlap sack that
served as its head was stretched taut, revealing two vacant sockets
that nevertheless felt as though they were drilling into Kayla's very
soul. This was the nexus, the focal point of the field's oppressive
malevolence, the anchor that held Dry Creek captive. The air around
it shimmered, a heat haze that had nothing to do with the sun, but
with the raw, concentrated power of the entity that had woven itself
into this accursed ground. It was a palpable presence, a suffocating
weight that pressed down on her, stealing her breath, her courage,
her very will to exist. This was the heart of the hunger, and she stood
directly before it.

A profound dread, cold and suffocating, washed over Kayla. It
was a primal fear, the kind that sent an ancient instinct screaming at
her to flee, to turn tail and run until the suffocating grip of the field

released her. But beneath the terror, something else stirred. A surge of desperate resolve, forged in the crucible of loss and fueled by Elias's sacrifice, ignited within her. She was here. She had come this far. DuCard's vacant stare, the chilling emptiness in his eyes, flashed before her mind's eye, a stark reminder of the price of inaction. Elias's meticulous notes, his unwavering belief in the obsidian shard's potential, echoed in her thoughts, a desperate, flickering beacon in the overwhelming darkness.

Her hand tightened around the obsidian shard. It was no longer just a shard; it was her last hope, the culmination of a journey steeped in terror and shadowed by loss. The cold, smooth surface was a stark contrast to the burning dread that clawed at her insides. It felt alive now, a conduit humming with a latent power that seemed to resonate with the very essence of the earth beneath her feet, an earth that was sick, corrupted, and ravenous. The entity's hunger was a tangible void, a gnawing emptiness that sought to consume everything it touched, to drain the life from the land, from its inhabitants, leaving behind only dust and despair.

The whispers, which had been a low, insidious murmur at the edge of her hearing, now coalesced into a single, terrifying voice. It was a voice that seemed to emanate from the very soil, from the rustling cornstalks that surrounded her like a suffocating shroud.

You are too late, it hissed, the sound like dry leaves skittering across barren ground. *The cycle cannot be broken. The hunger is eternal.* The words were not just sounds; they were probes, designed to burrow into her mind, to exploit her deepest fears and doubts, to twist her resolve into something brittle and easily shattered.

Kayla forced herself to breathe, each inhalation a painful effort against the crushing pressure. She remembered Elias's calm, measured words from his journal, his conviction that the entity was not a god, not an indestructible force, but a parasite, a corruption that could be starved, starved by severing its lifeline. The obsidian shard, he had written, was the key to that severing. It was a disruptor, a tool to break the energetic currents that fed the Withers curse, to disconnect the nexus from its corrupted source.

She raised the shard, its dark surface catching the faint, dying light. The obsidian pulsed with a steady, internal rhythm, a silent counterpoint to the frantic pounding of her heart. It felt as though the shard itself was awakening, its ancient power stirring in response to the concentrated malevolence surrounding it. This was the moment of truth, the confrontation with the ancient hunger that had claimed so many lives, so many sights, in this desolate corner of the world. This was Dry Creek's tormentor, and she was its challenger.

The scarecrow seemed to lean in, its tattered clothes rustling with an unseen breeze, its painted smile a rictus of ancient malice. The straw that spilled from its seams was not merely stuffing; it was a grim effigy of lives extinguished, of sacrifices offered at the altar of the land's insatiable appetite. The whispers intensified, becoming a cacophony of desperate pleas and chilling pronouncements.

He died for nothing, a voice, sickeningly like DuCard's, rasped. *His sacrifice was a whisper against the storm. Your own will be the same.*

Kayla squeezed her eyes shut for a fleeting moment, willing the spectral images to recede. She focused on the feel of the obsidian shard in her hand, on its cold, unyielding solidity. It was a physical anchor in a sea of spectral torment. Elias had described this phase as the 'crucible,' the point where the entity would launch its most potent attacks, not through brute force, but through the insidious manipulation of the user's psyche. He had warned that it would use their deepest fears, their most profound regrets, against them, attempting to break their will and corrupt the shard's purpose.

The cornstalks, which had seemed merely an unfortunate element of the landscape, now revealed themselves as extensions of the entity's reach. They were like living conduits, their dry, brittle stalks pulsing with a stolen vitality, channeling the corrupted energy from the soil upwards, towards the scarecrow, the nexus. Elias had theorized that these were the 'veins' of the curse, and the obsidian was meant to sever these vital connections, to starve the entity at its roots, to disrupt the flow of sustenance that allowed it to thrive.

She opened her eyes; her gaze fixed on the scarecrow. The sheer, overwhelming presence of the entity was like a physical weight, pressing down on her, threatening to extinguish the tiny spark of defiance that still flickered within her. The whispers were a constant barrage, a relentless assault on her sanity. They spoke of Elias's obsession, of his descent into madness, of the futility of her own quest.

He was a fool, the voice sneered, *and you are his foolish echo. This land remembers. It demands. It always demands.*

But Kayla held firm. She was not Elias, but she carried his legacy. She was not DuCard, but she carried the weight of his lost life. The obsidian shard pulsed again, a more distinct thrum this time, as if it were acknowledging her resolve. Elias had described this attunement as a delicate process, akin to tuning an impossibly complex instrument. The wrong note, the wrong intention, could render it inert, or worse, amplify the very forces it was meant to disrupt. Her intention was clear: to sever. To disconnect. To starve the ancient hunger.

The entity seemed to sense this shift, this nascent defiance. The ground beneath her feet began to vibrate, a low, unsettling tremor that seemed to originate from deep within the earth. The cornstalks rustled with a renewed fury, their dry leaves whispering a chorus of condemnation. They were not merely plants; they were the physical manifestation of the Withers curse, a suffocating embrace that tightened with every passing moment. The obsidian shard, Elias had explained, was designed to create a discordant resonance, a feedback loop that would disrupt the energetic flow, effectively strangling the entity's lifeline, forcing it to retreat, to loosen its suffocating grip on Dry Creek.

She raised the shard higher, its dark surface now imbued with a faint, internal luminescence. It was a defiant beacon against the encroaching gloom, a testament to Elias's meticulous research and his desperate hope. The Gaze Offering, the ritualistic feeding that sustained the entity, was a continuous process, a draining of the town's vitality, and the obsidian was the antidote, the means to cut off that parasitic supply. It was a surgical strike, designed to sever the very roots that sustained the blight, to break the ancient, accursed cycle of sacrifice that had bled Dry Creek dry for generations.

The whispers now took on a more venomous tone, laced with a chilling mockery. *You think this trinket can save you?* The voice scoffed, the sound a cruel parody of a human laugh. *It is a fragment of the very power you seek to defy. It will consume you, as it consumes all who dare to stand against the ancient hunger.* Kayla felt a tendril of Elias's own fear, his apprehension about the shard's untamed power, slithering into her mind. He had theorized that the quarry, where he found the shard, was a place of potent natural energy, and the obsidian was a natural amplifier, a conduit that could be harnessed but never truly controlled.

She pushed the thought away, focusing on the obsidian's steady pulse. Elias had described the shard as a key, capable of severing the flow of vital energy, of disrupting the symbiotic manifestation that had woven itself into the fabric of Dry Creek. The obsidian's purpose was to interfere with the energetic currents that flowed through the ley lines, those invisible rivers of power that Elias had spent years mapping, all converging at this very spot. By plunging the shard into the heart of the convergence, he theorized, the disruptive frequency it emitted would create a feedback loop, effectively strangling the entity's lifeline.

The scarecrow's vacant sockets seemed to glow with an inner malevolence, its straw-stuffed form rippling as if with an invisible tremor. This was not merely an effigy; it was a focal point, a gateway through which the land's ancient hunger manifested. The whispers continued their insidious assault, weaving tales of despair and futility, reminding her of every mistake, every failure, every moment of weakness.

He tried, the voice whispered, a silken caress of poison. *Elias tried. He failed. His knowledge was incomplete. His ambition, his undoing. Yours will be the same.*

Kayla gritted her teeth, her knuckles white where she gripped the obsidian. She could feel the shard drawing upon the ambient energy, amplifying her own desperate intent. It was a slow, painstaking process, this attunement, and she could feel the subtle shifts in the air, the almost imperceptible tightening of the unseen bonds that held the field captive. The journal had warned her that the shard's effectiveness was directly proportional to the user's mental fortitude and their connection to the surrounding energy. It was not a simple act of insertion; it was an act of will, of channeling her own inner strength through the artifact.

The cornstalks rustled like a thousand dry tongues, whispering secrets of decay and oblivion. They were the tentacles of the Withers curse, reaching, grasping, drawing sustenance from the corrupted soil, and channeling it upwards, towards the nexus. The obsidian's purpose was to sever these connections, to starve the nexus by cutting off its primary lifelines. It was like plunging a blade into the heart of a corrupted organism, a desperate attempt to stop the spread of a virulent disease.

The scarecrow, the effigy of malevolence, seemed to absorb the fear, to feed on it. Its burlap head, stretched impossibly taut, appeared to swell, the empty eye sockets darkening with an infernal light. The air grew heavy, thick with the scent of decay and something else, something acrid and ancient. Kayla felt a profound kinship with the obsidian shard, a shared defiance against the encroaching void. Elias's research had been her guide, his belief her shield, but now, it was her own will, her own burning desire to break this cycle, that would power the obsidian.

See, a voice whispered, a multitude of voices now, interwoven and discordant, like the rustling of a thousand dry leaves, *how it drinks your hope. How it savors your defiance. You are but another offering, another flicker in the long night.* The whispers were a venomous tide, seeking to erode the very foundations of her resolve. They spoke of DuCard's lost gaze, of Elias's frantic final moments, of the countless others who had fallen prey to the land's insatiable hunger.

Kayla tightened her grip, her breath coming in ragged gasps. She could feel the obsidian shard's energy surging, responding to the sheer force of her will. It was a volatile power, raw and untamed, a mirror to the entity's own consuming hunger. The shard was not a weapon of destruction, Elias had emphasized repeatedly, but of disruption. It was designed to sever, to disconnect, to starve the nexus by cutting off the corrupted ley lines that fed it. The Gaze Offering was not a singular event, but a continuous, parasitic feeding, and the obsidian was the precise surgical tool intended to interrupt that flow, to bleed the entity dry.

The scarecrow's straw-stuffed arms, once limp and lifeless, began to twitch, a subtle, unnerving movement that sent a fresh wave of terror through Kayla. They were like skeletal fingers, reaching out, beckoning her into the darkness, into the heart of the hunger. The cornstalks around her seemed to press closer, their dry rustling a suffocating symphony of despair. She could feel the earth beneath her boots vibrating, a low thrum that resonated deep within her bones, a chilling testament to the entity's ancient, enduring power.

This land, the voice boomed, a deep, guttural sound that seemed to shake the very foundations of the field, *remembers. It hungers. It always hungers. And it demands its due.* The words were a pronouncement, a declaration of an ancient, unyielding pact between the land and its unseen tormentor. Kayla's purpose was to break that pact, to sever the threads that bound Dry Creek to this primal, consuming hunger. The obsidian shard was the instrument of that severing, a fragment of pure, earthbound energy, imbued with the specific resonance to disrupt the corrupted flow.

She raised the shard, its dark surface catching the faint, dying light of the day. A faint, internal luminescence flickered to life within it, a tiny spark against the overwhelming darkness. It was a beacon of hope, a testament to Elias's meticulous research, his final, desperate scribbles that had led her here, to this terrifying confrontation. The shard was attuned to the nexus, to the heart of the entity's power, and it was ready to strike. The whispers intensified, seeking to break her focus, to sow seeds of doubt and fear.

He died in vain, they hissed, echoing the despair of so many who had walked this field before her. *His bravery was a flicker, extinguished. Yours will be too.*

But Kayla would not falter. She remembered Elias's unwavering conviction, his diagrams of intersecting ley lines, his theory that the scarecrow was the nexus, the anchor point where the land's corrupted energy converged. The obsidian shard, he believed, possessed the unique property to interfere with those energetic currents, to create a disruptive feedback loop that would starve the parasitic entity at its core. It was a battle fought not with brute force, but with resonance and disruption, a war waged on the energetic battlefield.

The obsidian shard pulsed, a cold, insistent thrum against her palm. It was a sign that it was beginning to resonate with the field's oppressive energy, a dissonant harmony that Elias had painstakingly documented in his journal. He had theorized that the shard possessed an innate ability to identify and disrupt corrupted energetic pathways, acting not as a weapon of destruction, but as a precision instrument designed to sever the invisible ties that bound the entity to Dry Creek. The Gaze Offering was not merely a ritual; it was a feeding, a constant draining of the town's life force, and the obsidian was the antidote, the means to cut off that supply, to starve the ancient hunger.

The scarecrow, a grotesque monument to the Withers curse, seemed to loom larger, its straw-filled form radiating a palpable aura of malevolence. The obsidian shard in Kayla's hand felt like a small, defiant spark against the overwhelming darkness, a fragile but potent tool for disruption. Elias's final words, etched into her memory, echoed in the oppressive silence: *It does not destroy, Kayla. It disconnects. It severs the roots that feed the blight.* The whispers, like a swarm of unseen insects, buzzed at the edges of her hearing, probing for weakness, for any crack in her resolve. *He was wrong,* they hissed, the voices a discordant choir of despair. *This land's hunger is absolute. It cannot be denied.*

Kayla ignored them, her gaze fixed on the scarecrow. The obsidian shard pulsed with a steady, internal rhythm, a silent testament to Elias's foresight and her own desperate courage. The entity, sensing the shard's awakening power, seemed to intensify its assault. The air grew colder, the oppressive weight of the field pressing down on her, trying to crush her spirit. The whispers coalesced into a single, guttural snarl that emanated from the very earth beneath her feet. The ground trembled, not violently, but with a deep, unsettling tremor, as if the field itself was recoiling from the shard's nascent power.

The scarecrow, the nexus of Dry Creek's torment, loomed before her, a grotesque sentinel carved from straw and despair. Its burlap face, stretched taut over unseen forms, offered no comfort, only the silent, watchful gaze of a predator. The obsidian shard in Kayla's hand pulsed with a steady, internal rhythm, a counterpoint to the frantic beat of her own heart. It was no longer merely a tool; it was a conduit, an extension of her will, a desperate plea for severance.

The whispers, once a low murmur, had swelled into a cacophony, a thousand insidious voices seeking to drown out her resolve. They spoke of futility, of the inescapable nature of the Withers curse, a blight woven into the very fabric of Dry Creek. Elias's research, his final testament, resonated in her mind: the obsidian was not meant to destroy, but to disconnect, to sever the roots that fed the land's insatiable hunger. This field, this cursed ground, demanded a Gaze Offering, a constant sacrifice of life force, and the scarecrow was the altar. The obsidian was the scalpel, designed to cut the parasitic lifeline. The entity's power, immense and ancient, was a tangible force, a pressure that sought to crush her, to extinguish the shard's light and her own resolve.

Chapter 11

The Ritual of Severance

Her voice, raw and trembling, began to weave the fragmented syllables, piecing together the forgotten language from Elias's cryptic notes. The words felt alien on her tongue, guttural and ancient, each utterance a deliberate unwinding of the entity's hold on Withers Field and Dry Creek. They were not meant to invoke, nor to appease, but to *unravel*. To pick apart the very threads that bound the Withers curse to the corrupted soil. The air around the scarecrow, the focal point of this suffocating malevolence, began to shimmer, distorting like heat haze under an unseen sun. It was a visual manifestation of the ritual's nascent power, a tremor in the fabric of reality as the ancient words began their work.

"Aeth-ra... 'n'gal..." she began, the sounds a struggle against the oppressive atmosphere, the very air resisting her pronunciation, pushing back like a physical force. The whispers of the entity, which had been a constant, insidious murmur, seemed to recoil, to swirl around her like agitated wasps, their tone shifting from taunting to a desperate, rasping anger. They were the echoes of those the land had consumed, a symphony of despair attempting to drown out her nascent chant. *You are breaking the ancient compact,* a thousand voices seemed to wail in unison. *The pact of blood and soil. You will pay for this transgression.*

Kayla pressed on, her gaze locked onto the scarecrow's vacant sockets, willing them to see her defiance, her refusal to be another sacrifice. *"Vort-ek... k'tharr..."* The words were a key, Elias had believed, unlocking not a door, but a rupture. A tear in the energetic tapestry that sustained the Withers blight. He had written of the ritual's necessity, of the inherent danger, of the precise phonetic and tonal structure required to achieve the severance. Each syllable was a chisel, chipping away at the unyielding stone of the entity's power. The shimmering around the scarecrow intensified, the distortion growing more pronounced, rippling outwards like waves on a disturbed pond. The ground beneath her feet, already vibrating with a low thrum, began to pulse in time with her incantation, a macabre heartbeat resonating with the unearthed power.

She remembered Elias's frustrated entries, the hours spent deciphering the faded script, the maddeningly incomplete verses he'd managed to piece together. He'd likened the process to stitching together a shattered mirror, each fragment holding a piece of the truth, but the complete image remaining just beyond reach. He had warned that the entity would fight back, not with physical force, but by preying on her deepest fears, by twisting the very power she sought to wield. And it was working. A vision of DuCard's vacant stare, a chilling echo of his lost self, flashed through her mind, a potent injection of despair.

He couldn't save himself, the whispers hissed, laced with DuCard's familiar, yet now distorted, tone. *What makes you think you can save anyone?*

Kayla squeezed her eyes shut, forcing the phantom image away. She focused on the feel of the obsidian shard, its cold, familiar weight a grounding presence. It was more than just a shard; it was Elias's legacy, her shield, and now, the conduit for this ancient chant. She breathed deeply, channeling not just air, but intent, into the resonant frequencies of the words."

"Zol-gar... n'thul..." she intoned, her voice gaining a measure of steadiness, finding a rhythm that defied the surrounding chaos. The shimmering around the scarecrow pulsed with a sickly, greenish light, the distorted air now thick with an almost palpable sense of resistance. It was as if the very atmosphere was straining against the unbinding, clinging to its corrupted tether.

The cornstalks, which had seemed like mere silent witnesses, now rustled with a more urgent, menacing sound. They were not just stalks of dried corn; they were conduits, Elias had theorized, channeling the lifeblood of the corrupted earth upwards, towards the scarecrow, the nexus. The chant, if performed correctly, would disrupt this flow, severing the parasitic connection.

"Mork-ai... l'tharn..." The words resonated with a deep, primal power, vibrating not just in the air, but within the very earth, a deep hum that seemed to awaken something ancient and slumbering. The entity's fury was mounting, the whispers growing more desperate, more fragmented. They were no longer coherent taunts, but shrieks of pure, unadulterated rage, like the sound of metal being torn apart.

Elias had cautioned that the ritual was not about brute force, but about precision. It was about finding the harmonic dissonance, the precise frequency that would unravel the intricate energetic knot binding the entity to Dry Creek. He had described the Withers journal as a forbidden score, a symphony of destruction composed by ancient hands, and she was now the conductor, forced to play a tune that threatened to shatter the very world around her."

"F'thal... d'mor..." Her voice, though still laced with the tremor of fear, carried a new resolve, a grim determination born of desperation. The obsidian shard pulsed in her hand, its faint internal luminescence flickering brighter with each chanted syllable, as if it too were awakening, resonating with the unbinding power.

The malevolence radiating from the scarecrow intensified, a palpable pressure that sought to crush her spirit, to break her focus. It was a psychic assault, an attempt to overwhelm her with visions of Dry Creek's past suffering, with the specter of Elias's failure.

He failed, a voice, chillingly similar to Mark's, whispered directly into her mind, its tone laced with a profound, soul-crushing despair. *His knowledge was incomplete. His ambition, his undoing. Yours will be the same. You are merely his echo.* Kayla gritted her teeth, the obsidian shard digging into her palm. She would not be an echo. She would be the severance. She would be the end of this cycle.

"Kaelen... s'tharr..." The words were a declaration, a defiant roar against the encroaching darkness. The shimmering around the scarecrow coalesced, forming ephemeral, spectral shapes that writhed and contorted like tormented souls. They were the echoes of the Gaze Offering, the tormented spirits of those the land had

claimed, now reacting to the disruption of their eternal servitude. The obsidian shard pulsed again, a more powerful surge this time, and a wave of cold, raw energy coursed through her, almost overwhelming her senses. It was like touching a live wire, potent and volatile, a direct feedback loop from the heart of the corrupted nexus.

Elias had warned of this surge, of the point where the shard's power would begin to actively combat the entity's hold. He had stressed the importance of maintaining her intent, of not succumbing to the raw power, of guiding it, not being consumed by it. The whispers, now a frantic, high-pitched whine, sought to break her concentration, to inject doubt into the heart of her resolve. They spoke of the land's hunger, of its ancient, unyielding nature, of the futility of her actions.

This land does not forget, they shrieked, the sound like nails on a chalkboard. *It remembers. It hungers. It always hungers. And it demands its due.*

Kayla's voice remained steady, a beacon of defiance against the storm of malevolent energy."

"*D'rael... n'gath...*" The words were ancient, primal, designed to unmoor the entity from its earthly anchor. She visualized the energy flow Elias had described, the intricate network of corrupted ley lines converging beneath her, feeding the Withers curse. The obsidian shard was a wedge, a disruptive force, and her chanting was the hammer driving it home. She wasn't destroying the energy, but redirecting it, breaking its corrupted cycle, starving the nexus by severing its primary lifelines. It was a surgical strike, aiming for the heart of the blight.

The shimmering around the scarecrow pulsed violently, and the spectral shapes within it seemed to solidify for a fleeting moment, their forms contorted in agony. The cornstalks rustled with a renewed fury, their dry leaves whispering a chorus of condemnation, their stalks bending and swaying as if in an unseen, agonizing wind. Kayla could feel the earth beneath her vibrating with a deep, unsettling tremor, a chilling testament to the entity's ancient, enduring power, and its reaction to the unbinding.

You cannot break what is eternal, the voice boomed, no longer a whisper, but a resonant declaration of ancient, unwavering power. *This land remembers. It hungers. It always hungers.*

"*Orr-gan... v'thal...*" she chanted, her voice rising in pitch and intensity, the words now flowing with a power she hadn't known she possessed. The obsidian shard was a key, and she was turning it in the lock, fumbling slightly, but undeniably moving the mechanism. The entity's power, immense and ancient, was a tangible force, a pressure that sought to crush her, to extinguish the shard's light, and her own resolve. Elias had described this as the critical juncture, the moment when the shard's purpose was revealed in its entirety. It was a conduit for disruption, a key that unlocked the potential to break the cycle, but it required a vessel, a will strong enough to wield its power.

The scarecrow's straw-filled grin seemed to widen, a silent mockery of her struggle. The air grew heavy, thick with the scent of decay and something acrid and ancient, the signature of the Withers blight. Kayla felt a profound, almost electrical connection with the obsidian shard, a shared defiance against the encroaching void. Elias's meticulous research and unwavering belief had been her shield, but now, it was her own will, her own burning desire to break this suffocating cycle, that fueled the obsidian.

"*Tar... ish... n'gol...*" The syllables were pulled from her very core, a desperate incantation that seemed to vibrate through the soles of her boots and up into her very bones. The ground pulsed with a violent rhythm, the cornstalks rustling like a thousand dry tongues whispering curses. Elias had described the Gaze Offering as a continuous feeding, a parasitic drain on Dry Creek's vitality, and the obsidian was the antidote, the precise surgical instrument intended to interrupt that flow, to bleed the entity dry by severing its primary lifelines. The whispers clawed at her sanity, each word a barb designed to pierce her resolve. *He was wrong,* they hissed, a multitude of voices now, interwoven and discordant, like the rustling of a thousand dry leaves. *This land's hunger is absolute. It cannot be denied. You will be consumed.*

Kayla ignored the insidious pronouncements, her gaze fixed on the scarecrow, the nexus of Dry Creek's torment. The obsidian shard pulsed with a steady, internal rhythm, a testament to Elias's foresight and her own desperate courage. The entity, sensing the shard's awakening power, seemed to intensify its assault. The air grew colder, the oppressive weight of the field pressing down on her, trying to crush her spirit. The whispers coalesced into a single, guttural snarl that emanated from the very earth beneath her feet. The ground trembled, not violently, but with a deep, unsettling tremor, as if the field itself was recoiling from the shard's nascent power.

With a final, guttural cry that tore from her throat, a sound both ancient and raw, Kayla plunged the obsidian shard forward, not into the scarecrow's straw heart, but into the very soil beneath it, the nexus point Elias had identified. A blinding flash of emerald light erupted from the point of contact, accompanied by a searing, discordant shriek that ripped through the air, a sound of pure, unadulterated agony. The shimmering around the scarecrow intensified, then fractured, as if the very fabric of reality had been shattered. The cornstalks writhed violently, then began to wither, their dry leaves crumbling to dust at an unnerving speed. The whispers abruptly ceased, replaced by an echoing silence, a profound stillness that felt both terrifying and profoundly liberating. The oppressive weight of the field, so long a suffocating shroud, began to recede, its suffocating grip loosening, leaving behind only the silence and the unsettling, dust-filled air. The ritual had begun. The severance was underway.

The obsidian shard, now held aloft, pulsed with a faint, internal luminescence that seemed to drink in the suffocating aura of the Withers Field. It was like a thirsty mouth, drawing sustenance from the very malevolence that had choked this land for generations. Kayla felt the cold, dense energy of the blight seep into the shard, and through it, into her own being, a chilling communion that threatened to unmoor her from reality. Yet, she clung to Elias's instructions, to the diagrams etched in his journal, to the desperate hope that this ancient fragment of earth held the key to Dry Creek's liberation.

The spectral eyes embedded in the scarecrow's burlap face, which had blazed with an unholy, predatory light moments before, now flickered, their intensity wavering as if recoiling from a blinding, unseen sun. It was as if the raw, untamed power of the obsidian, awakened by her chant and amplified by the very soil it now pierced, was anathema to the entity's festering presence. They dimmed, the malevolent spark within them guttering like snuffed candles, leaving the scarecrow's vacant sockets to stare with a profound, unsettling emptiness. This was not an act of destruction, Elias had emphasized, but of inversion. A forced recalibration. The Gaze Offering, usually a method of binding and consumption, was being turned back upon its source.

Kayla focused her intent with a ferocity born of desperation. She visualized the parasitic tendrils of the entity, the unseen roots that burrowed deep into the earth, drawing strength from the despair and fear of generations. She saw them as dark, writhing veins, pulsing with Dry Creek's stolen lifeblood. Her mind's eye traced the intricate network, following the corrupted ley lines Elias had painstakingly mapped, converging at this very spot, at the base of the scarecrow, the heart of the Withers blight. And she saw the obsidian shard, no longer a mere fragment, but a surgical instrument, poised to sever those vital connections. It was a delicate balance, a dance on the precipice of utter annihilation, where one wrong move, one wavering thought, could send the unravelling power crashing back upon her, consuming her whole.

The air, thick with the stench of decay, began to shift. The oppressive weight, which had felt like a physical presence pressing down on her chest, seemed to lessen, not by vanishing, but by being… rechanneled. It was a subtle, almost imperceptible shift, like the tide turning imperceptibly offshore. The whispers, which had been a cacophony of despair and rage, now seemed to change their tenor, morphing from outright aggression into a frantic, high-pitched keening, a sound of protest, of something ancient and vast being forcibly dislodged. They were no longer seeking to sow fear, but to express outrage.

You defy the pact, a chorus of fragmented voices seemed to sigh, the sound like dry leaves skittering across frozen ground. *You break the covenant of sustenance. The land will not forgive this sacrilege.*

Kayla felt a dizzying surge of energy flow through the obsidian shard and into her. It was not the raw, chaotic power of the entity, but something purer, more primal, an echo of the earth's original vitality that had been twisted and corrupted. It resonated with her own determination, her own refusal to be another victim of Dry Creek's curse. She pictured the obsidian acting as a lens, focusing the ambient energies of the field, not to feed the entity, but to disrupt its hold. Elias had theorized that the Withers curse was not an independent entity, but a manifestation of the land's own corrupted life force, a parasitic growth nurtured by generations of suffering. The Gaze Offering, in its original, horrifying intent, was the ritual that had cemented this bond, a perpetual draining of the town's vitality to sustain the land's monstrous appetite. By reversing the intent, by focusing the shard's innate disruptive properties, she was attempting to sever that parasitic connection, to starve the blight at its source.

She closed her eyes, drawing a deep, steadying breath. The world outside her immediate focus dissolved. The rustling cornstalks, the oppressive silence punctuated by the entity's dying cries, the very ground beneath her feet – all faded into a secondary awareness. Her entire being was concentrated on the obsidian shard, on the visualization of the energy flows, on the ancient words she had uttered, now resonating within her very bones. She saw the spectral eyes of the scarecrow, once burning with malevolence, now fading, their light being siphoned away, not into the entity's core, but into the obsidian itself. It was a reversal of the feeding, a reclamation of stolen essence. Elias had called this phase the "Attunement of Reversal," the point where the user's intent, amplified by the shard, actively worked against the ritual's original purpose.

The whispers, now a desperate, reedy sound, continued their assault, but their power seemed to wane with each passing moment. They spoke of the ancient pact, of the blood spilled on this very soil, of the unyielding nature of the Withers Field curse.

It is woven into the very fabric, they moaned, the sound like the groaning of ancient timbers. *You cannot unmake what has been made. You cannot un-feed the hunger.* But Kayla held firm. The obsidian was not a weapon of destruction, but of precision, designed to cut the cords that bound the land to its tormentor. She imagined the shard's cold, hard surface as a honed blade, slicing through the unseen threads of corrupted energy. Each syllable of the ancient chant was a stroke of that blade, severing another connection, another lifeline for the Withers blight.

The spectral eyes on the scarecrow began to dim further, the harsh, predatory gleam replaced by a hollow, vacant stare. It was as if the entity, through its focal point, was experiencing a profound, agonizing withdrawal. The obsidian shard vibrated in

Kayla's hand, a low, resonant hum that pulsed in time with her own heartbeat. She felt a growing sense of clarity, a sharpening of her focus that pushed back against the lingering tendrils of fear and doubt. The shard was absorbing the residual energy, the echoes of the Gaze Offering, and in doing so, it was neutralizing the very essence of the entity's hold. It was a dangerous process, Elias had warned, a dance with a dying beast that could lash out in its final moments.

It wasn't merely a curse; it was an ecosystem of despair, where the land fed on the suffering of its inhabitants, and the inhabitants' fear, in turn, amplified the land's malevolence. The scarecrow, with its vacant, staring eyes, was the physical manifestation of this unholy symbiosis, a perpetual witness and conduit for the ritual of consumption. The Gaze Offering, as described in the Withers Grimoire, was the process by which the land's corrupted life force, amplified by the collective fear of the community, was periodically "fed" back into the nexus – the scarecrow – to sustain the entity's grip. Kayla's ritual was designed to reverse this flow, to starve the nexus by severing the primary conduits through which this corrupted sustenance was drawn.

The ground beneath her feet, which had been trembling with a deep, resonant hum, now felt strangely still. The intense pressure in

the air subsided, replaced by a peculiar lightness, an unsettling quietude. The rustling of the cornstalks, which had sounded like a thousand chattering teeth, softened into a mere whisper, a sigh of resignation. The spectral eyes on the scarecrow had now faded almost entirely, leaving only dark, empty sockets. The obsidian shard pulsed once more, a powerful surge of cold, pure energy washing through Kayla, a wave of clarity that felt like emerging from a suffocating fog. This was the moment of severance, the point of no return. The ritual's intent was not to destroy, but to unmake the connection, to sever the vital artery that pumped Dry Creek's stolen life force into the Withers curse.

Kayla held her breath, her knuckles white around the obsidian shard. The silence was absolute, unnerving. The whispers had ceased entirely, leaving behind a void that was both terrifying and strangely expectant. Elias had described this silence as the most dangerous phase, the moment when the entity, having its life source cut off, might attempt a final, desperate gambit. He had cautioned against any lapse in focus, any indulgence in the sudden calm, as it would be a perfect opportunity for the Withers blight to exploit any remaining weakness, any flicker of doubt. The shard, now radiating a faint, almost imperceptible coldness, seemed to hum with an awareness of its task, a keen, sharp edge honed by generations of Dry Creek's suffering.

She tightened her grip, channeling her resolve into the obsidian. Her mind flashed back to DuCard, to the vacant look in his eyes, to the hollowed-out shell he had become. That memory, once a source of unbearable pain, was now a burning ember of defiance. She would not let that happen to anyone else. The Gaze Offering reversed, the ancient pact broken, the land's corrupted hunger denied – this was the only path forward. The obsidian shard was not merely an object; it was a symbol of Elias's legacy, a testament to his relentless pursuit of truth, and now, it was her tool, her weapon, her hope for Dry Creek's salvation.

The scarecrow, stripped of its spectral eyes, stood as a gaunt, pathetic effigy against the dull, overcast sky. Its burlap form, once a vessel of ancient malevolence, now seemed merely an empty husk, a forgotten relic of a bygone era. The obsidian shard, still clutched in Kayla's hand, continued to absorb the lingering vestiges of the blight, its luminescence growing steadier, more assured. She felt a profound sense of detachment from the oppressive atmosphere, as if a veil had been lifted, allowing her to perceive the world with a newfound clarity. The ritual was a dangerous inversion, a deliberate unmaking of a centuries-old bond, and the obsidian shard was the instrument of that unmaking. It was designed to resonate with the deepest frequencies of the corrupted nexus, to create a discordant echo that would unravel the very foundation of the Withers curse.

The final stage of the Gaze Offering reversal was about containment, about ensuring that the energy, once severed from its primary conduit, did not dissipate uncontrollably, causing further devastation. Elias had theorized that the obsidian, by absorbing the residual energies, would act as a natural capacitor, holding the corrupted essence in a state of dormancy, awaiting a proper cleansing. Kayla focused on this aspect, visualizing the shard as a sealed vessel, containing the very darkness she had sought to unravel. The field, once alive with the pulsating energy of the blight, now felt eerily quiet, the silence punctuated only by the distant, mournful cry of a crow. The scarecrow remained a stark silhouette, a monument to Dry Creek's suffering, but the malevolence that had emanated from it had been systematically dismantled, unraveled, and contained. The Gaze Offering, in its reversed form, had achieved its purpose: to sever the connection, to starve the Withers curse, and to begin the arduous process of healing Dry Creek's blighted heart. The obsidian shard, now a dull, obsidian black once more, felt heavy in her hand, a tangible testament to the power she had wielded, and the fragile victory she had achieved.

The stillness was a lie, a momentary lull before the storm. Kayla felt it in the tightening of her muscles, the prickling unease that crawled across her skin despite the obsidian shard's cooling presence. The silence wasn't one of peace, but of a coiled serpent, gathering its strength for a final, desperate strike. She had expected the entity's reaction, Elias's journal filled with dire warnings about the 'Awakening of the Unraveled.' This was not a passive surrender; this was a primal, guttural defiance.

271

A tremor, far more violent than any before, ripped through the earth. It wasn't the deep, resonant hum of drained energy; it was a violent, convulsive shudder, as if the very soil were writhing in agony. The scarecrow, that effigy of Dry Creek's despair, began to move. Its burlap form, previously slack and lifeless, contorted unnaturally. It wasn't the wind; this was a violent, internal struggle. The straw-stuffed limbs twitched and spasmed, the wooden crossbeams groaning as if being forced against their very nature. The vacant sockets of its face seemed to deepen, drawing in the fading light, a dark parody of the spectral eyes that had once burned there. It writhed, a grotesque puppet whose strings were being pulled by an unseen, agonizing force.

The whispers, which had momentarily receded into a defeated sigh, returned with a vengeance. They didn't merely whisper now; they surged, a torrent of pure, unadulterated rage that seemed to emanate from the rustling cornstalks all around her. The gentle rustling transformed into a deafening roar, a cacophony of fury that battered at Kayla's senses, seeking to drown out her focus, to shatter her resolve. It was no longer the plaintive cries of the wronged, but the enraged screams of a predator whose prey was escaping its grasp.

You cannot sever! the voices shrieked, a unified chorus of malice. *You cannot unmake! The tether holds! The bond is eternal!*

Then, the true manifestation began. From the very air around the scarecrow, from the shadows pooling beneath the rustling corn, tendrils of pure darkness began to coalesce. They weren't wisps of fog or tricks of the light; these were tangible, inky manifestations, writhing like ophidian limbs, lashing out with impossible speed and viciousness. They snaked towards Kayla, seeking to ensnare her, to drag her into the suffocating darkness from which they were born. Each lunge was accompanied by a chilling hiss, a sound that spoke of ancient hunger and seething hatred. The obsidian shard in her hand grew colder, vibrating with an intensity that felt less like resonance and more like a frantic alarm bell.

The ground beneath her feet no longer merely trembled; it bucked and heaved. The earth was splitting, not with the clean fissures of seismic activity, but with ragged, tearing wounds from

272

which an unholy, sickly luminescence seeped. The air, already thick with the stench of decay, now crackled with an almost visible energy. It was as if the very atmosphere had been charged with raw, primal fury, a furious backlash from an entity that felt its power being systematically drained, its very existence threatened. Kayla could feel the immense pressure building, a physical manifestation of the entity's desperate struggle. It was a being of immense, corrupting power, and it was fighting with the ferocity of a cornered god.

Kayla stumbled back, the obsidian shard held defensively before her. The tendrils of darkness advanced, their sinuous movements hypnotic and terrifying. One whipped past her face, so close she could feel the unnatural cold radiating from it, a cold that sunk deeper than bone, chilling her very soul. The whispers clawed at her mind, whispering doubts, dredging up her deepest fears, attempting to sow the seeds of panic.

You are alone, they hissed. *No one can save you. Dry Creek is ours. It has always been ours.*

She gritted her teeth, the pain in her jaw a welcome distraction from the encroaching dread. She focused on the shard; on the visualization Elias had drilled into her. The obsidian was a conduit, a focal point. It wasn't just absorbing the blight; it was actively disrupting the energy flow. The entity was fighting the severance, yes, but its rage was also a testament to the ritual's efficacy. The more it fought, the more it revealed the deep, parasitic connection she was attempting to break. She visualized the tendrils not as physical threats, but as the corrupted arteries of the Withers blight, and the obsidian shard as a surgeon's scalpel, severing them one by one.

The scarecrow's writhing intensified. Its burlap head snapped back with a sound like dry twigs snapping and then lurched forward. The empty sockets seemed to fix on Kayla, and from them, a sickly, green light began to pulse, a dying ember of the spectral eyes, but now imbued with a raw, tangible hatred. It was the entity, through its physical anchor, attempting a direct assault. The ground around the scarecrow buckled, and from the rents in the earth, more tendrils erupted, thicker and more malevolent than the first. They coiled and writhed, creating a living, breathing barrier of pure shadow.

Kayla pushed forward, her boots sinking into the churned earth. The obsidian shard pulsed in rhythm, a steady counter-rhythm to the chaos. She could feel the raw power it was absorbing, the sheer, concentrated malice of the Withers blight. It was a sickening sensation, like holding a live wire, but she forced herself to endure it. Elias had spoken of the 'Final Agony,' the last desperate throes of a dying, corrupting force. This was it. The entity was flailing, thrashing against the invisible bonds she was tightening.

The whispers reached a crescendo, a deafening, unified scream of agony and fury that threatened to shatter the very air. The cornstalks thrashed wildly, no longer whispering but roaring, their dry leaves tearing and whipping like a thousand scourges. The very landscape seemed to be in revolt. The tendrils of shadow surged towards her, a wave of pure darkness, attempting to engulf her, to smother the light she represented.

But the obsidian shard... it was not merely absorbing. It was pushing back. As the tendrils of shadow reached it, they recoiled, as if struck by an invisible force. The sickly green light from the scarecrow's eyes flickered and died, only to be replaced by the cold, pure luminescence of the obsidian. It was a battle of energies, of intentions. The entity fought with raw, primal rage, a desperate clinging to its dominion. Kayla fought with focused will, with Elias's knowledge, with the desperate hope for Dry Creek's future.

She chanted the words, her voice strained but clear, a beacon in the maelstrom. Each syllable was a hammer blow against the entity's hold. The scarecrow's contortions became more frantic, its movements less like writhing and more like being torn asunder. The wood of its frame splintered, the burlap ripped, revealing not straw, but a swirling vortex of deeper shadow within. The entity was bleeding its essence into the earth, its strength being siphoned away, not to sustain itself, but to fuel this desperate, futile resistance.

Kayla felt a surge of power through the shard, a feedback loop of the severed energy. It was intoxicating, terrifying. She had to maintain control, to guide this unleashed force, not to be consumed by it. The tendrils of darkness began to recede, pulled back towards the scarecrow as if by an unseen current. The roaring whispers faltered, their unified fury breaking into a chorus of individual screams of pain and disbelief.

The ground, which had been heaving, began to settle, though the rents in the earth remained, still oozing that sickly luminescence. The scarecrow shuddered violently, and then, with a final, agonized groan that seemed to echo from the very core of the earth, it went still. Its burlap form sagged, its limbs dangling limply from the splintered frame. The dark vortex within its ripped chest seemed to collapse inward, vanishing without a trace. The sickly green light was extinguished. The spectral eyes were gone. Only the empty sockets remained, staring blankly at the sky.

The whispers died out completely, leaving behind an unnerving, profound silence. The cornstalks, though still battered and torn, ceased their frenzied thrashing. The air, which had crackled with unleashed power, felt suddenly hollow, devoid of the oppressive weight that had clung to it for so long. Kayla felt a wave of exhaustion wash over her, so potent it threatened to buckle her knees. The obsidian shard in her hand was still, its luminescence faded to a dull, almost imperceptible sheen. It felt heavy, inert, its task momentarily complete.

She stood amidst the desecrated field, breathing in air that, for the first time in generations, did not carry the taint of corruption. The silence was absolute, the calm after a devastating storm. But it was a silence born of severance, of a vital artery severed. The entity had fought, it had roared, it had lashed out with the full, terrifying force of its ancient, parasitic existence. But it had not won. The ritual of severance, the inversion of the Gaze Offering, had been a success. The Withers blight, however, was not gone. It had been wounded, its primary connection severed, but the land itself still bore the scars, and the residual energy, however diminished, still lingered. This was not an end, Kayla knew, but a beginning. The long, arduous process of healing Dry Creek had just commenced, and the obsidian shard, now cool and silent, was a stark reminder of the power that had been unleashed, and the cost of its containment. She looked at the scarecrow, a broken sentinel in a ravaged field, and felt a profound sense of both victory and dread. The silence was a fragile thing, and she knew, with a certainty that chilled her to the bone, that the entity, or whatever remained of it, would not remain dormant forever. It had been starved, but not destroyed. And in the depths of Dry Creek's ravaged soil, the echoes of its rage still thrummed, a silent promise of a return.

The deafening roar of the Withers blight began to recede, replaced by a strange, almost unnatural quiet. The cornstalks, which had thrashed with the ferocity of a thousand tormented souls, now stood still, their dry leaves rustling with a mournful sigh in the evening breeze. The tendrils of shadow that had snaked towards Kayla, seeking to drag her into oblivion, writhed and retracted, melting back into the earth as if their very substance had been drained. The air, still thick with the scent of decay, felt thinner, less oppressive. The suffocating weight that had pressed down on Dry Creek for so long seemed to have lifted, leaving behind a void that was both unsettling and undeniably hopeful.

Kayla's breath hitched, a ragged gasp of relief and disbelief. The obsidian shard in her hand, moments ago a conduit for raw, terrifying power, now pulsed with a faint, pure light. It was a soft, ethereal glow, a stark contrast to the violent energies that had surged through it. The light wasn't aggressive; it was gentle, persistent, a tiny beacon in the encroaching twilight. It seemed to seep into the very air around her, pushing back the lingering tendrils of darkness that still clung to the ravaged soil. The spectral eyes within the scarecrow, those twin points of malevolent green that had burned with an unholy fury, flickered. For a terrifying instant, Kayla feared the entity was merely gathering its strength for another onslaught. But then, the light within them sputtered and died. It wasn't a sudden snuffing out, but a gradual fading, like embers losing their heat, their defiance extinguished. The vacant sockets of the scarecrow's burlap face returned to their former, inanimate state, staring out at the desolate landscape with an emptiness that now felt like a victory.

A profound silence descended, a fragile pause in the storm of psychic and physical assault. It was a silence that sang of severance, of a vital connection finally, irrevocably broken. The whispers that had clawed at Kayla's sanity, that had sought to unravel her very being, were gone. The guttural roars and the wails of tormented souls had ceased. Only the gentle sigh of the wind through the cornstalks remained, a sound that, for the first time in living memory, carried no undertone of malice. Kayla felt it deep within her bones, an intuition as ancient as the land itself: the entity's grip was weakening. The ritual, against all odds, had worked. The Withers blight, the parasitic entity that had held Dry Creek in its suffocating embrace, had been weakened. Its anchor, the scarecrow, was broken, its power source severed.

She lowered the obsidian shard, her hand trembling not from fear, but from the sheer, overwhelming exhaustion of the ordeal. The shard felt heavy, inert now, its luminescence faded to a mere whisper of its former brilliance. It was still cool to the touch, a stark reminder of the immense energies it had absorbed and contained. The raw power that had coursed through it was still a visceral memory, a phantom ache in her very soul. But it was no longer a living thing, a conduit for the blight. It was a tool, its purpose fulfilled, its immense burden relinquished.

Kayla surveyed the scene. The field was a testament to the violence of the past moments. The earth was torn, rent with ragged gashes from which the sickly luminescence had seeped. The cornstalks were mangled, their dry leaves shredded, their stalks bent and broken. The scarecrow, its burlap skin ripped, its wooden frame splintered, sagged against its cross. It was a broken effigy, a shattered sentinel in a ravaged landscape. Yet, amidst the destruction, there was a palpable sense of peace. The oppressive atmosphere that had permeated Dry Creek for generations, the heavy blanket of dread and despair, had been lifted. The air was cleaner, sharper, carrying the scent of damp earth and the faint, sweet perfume of the distant pines, untainted by the rot.

This was the flicker of hope Elias had spoken of, the fragile dawn after an endless night. It was not a complete victory, not yet. The land itself still bore the scars of the Withers blight, the residual energy, however diminished, still lingered in the soil, a silent testament to the entity's enduring presence. But the primary connection, the vital artery that had fed the blight, had been severed. Kayla had succeeded where countless others had failed, where generations of Dry Creek's inhabitants had simply endured. She had faced the heart of the corruption and, with Elias's knowledge and her own fierce determination, had struck a decisive blow.

She knelt beside the broken scarecrow known as Ragmouth, tracing the splintered wood of its frame. This was more than just a physical anchor; it was a symbol. A symbol of the fear that had gripped Dry Creek, the despair that had allowed the Withers blight to take root and flourish. The entity had used this effigy, this mockery of a guardian, to sow its seeds of corruption, to feed on the fear and hopelessness of the people. Now, Ragmouth lay broken, its power drained, its influence shattered.

The silence that enveloped her was profound, almost deafening after the relentless assault of whispers and roars. It was a silence that invited reflection, a silence that allowed the sheer magnitude of what had just occurred to sink in. Kayla closed her eyes, her fingers tightening around the obsidian shard. She could still feel the echo of the entity's rage, the searing, burning hatred of a parasitic force that had been denied its sustenance. It had fought with the ferocity of a cornered beast, its dying throes a terrifying spectacle. But it had not prevailed.

A small, tentative smile touched Kayla's lips. It was a fragile thing, born of exhaustion and disbelief, but it was real. She had done it. She had performed the Ritual of Severance, a ritual born from a desperate need to reclaim her home. The whispers of doubt and fear that had been amplified by the entity had been silenced, not by force, but by a greater, purer force wielded with intention. The fear had been replaced by a quiet, unshakeable resolve. Dry Creek was not lost. It was wounded, yes, but it was not irrevocably broken.

She stood, her legs feeling like lead, and looked out at the devastated field. She could see Tommy in the distance and the moon cast long shadows across the churned earth, painting the scene in hues of orange. It was a somber beauty, a landscape scarred but not defeated. The air was still, the oppressive humidity that had been a constant companion in Dry Creek replaced by a cool, crisp breeze that carried the promise of a new beginning.

The obsidian shard felt warm now, its luminescence still faint but steady. It was no longer a vessel of terror, but a symbol of resilience, a testament to the power of will and knowledge. Kayla knew this was not the end of her struggle. The Withers blight, though wounded, was a resilient entity. Its tendrils of influence might have been severed from their primary source, but the corruption it had sown ran deep. The land itself needed to heal, and the people of Dry Creek needed to shed the layers of fear and despair that had defined them for so long.

But for now, in this moment of profound quiet, there was only the dawning realization of what had been achieved. The entity had been denied its ultimate victory. Its rage had been met with an unyielding force, its power gradually siphoned away and contained. The silence was not an absence of sound, but the presence of peace, a fragile peace earned through immense sacrifice and courage. The spectral eyes were gone, the whispers silenced, the writhing scarecrow a broken monument to a vanquished foe. This flicker of hope, small and tentative as it was, was the most precious thing Kayla had ever known. It was the promise of a future, a future where Dry Creek could finally begin to breathe again. The obsidian shard remained in her hand, a silent guardian, a potent reminder of the battle fought and the long road of healing that lay ahead. The air tasted cleaner, the light seemed brighter, and in the heart of the ravaged field, a new dawn was breaking for Dry Creek.

The obsidian shard pulsed in Kayla's hand, its faint luminescence mirroring the dying embers of the Withers blight. The silence that had descended was not merely an absence of the deafening roar; it was a living, breathing entity in itself, a stark contrast to the psychic cacophony that had assailed her for what felt like an eternity. The tendrils of darkness had recoiled, the spectral eyes had faded, and the guttural whispers had finally, blessedly, ceased. Dry Creek, or at least the immediate ravaged landscape around her, felt freed. Yet, even in the profound quiet, a new kind of battle raged, one fought not with physical force, but within the unseen confines of her own mind.

As the last vestiges of the entity's power waned, a searing, unimaginable pain erupted behind Kayla's eyes. It was a white-hot agony, as if invisible needles were being driven into her very consciousness, seeking to pry open the gates of her mind. This was not a physical attack, not the thrashing of corrupted tendrils or the suffocating embrace of shadow. This was the entity's final, desperate act, a psychic lashing out from beyond the veil of severance, a desperate attempt to inflict its dying curse, to claim a final, personal toll. It was the cost of sight, the price demanded for peering into the abyss and severing its connection.

Kayla's breath hitched, a strangled gasp that tore at her throat. The obsidian shard, still warm in her grip, seemed to absorb some of the piercing sensation, its faint light flickering as if in sympathy. She gritted her teeth, her jaw clenching so tightly that a muscle near her temple began to throb. The pain intensified, a relentless hammer blow against the fragile shell of her awareness. It felt like her mind was being pried open, its innermost thoughts and memories laid bare, vulnerable to the parasitic entity's final, venomous strike.

This was it. The true culmination of the Ritual of Severance. Elias had warned her. He had spoken of the cyclical nature of sacrifice, of how the Withers blight, like any parasitic force, would fight tooth and nail to maintain its hold, to claim what it believed was owed. And in its death throes, it wouldn't simply fade; it would seek to extract payment, to leave an indelible mark, to ensure that its passing wasn't a clean break, but a scarring severance.

She recalled Elias's words, his words resonant hum in her memory, filled with a grim understanding: *The blight feeds on what it can claim. When you cut the root, it will lash out, not with fang and claw, but with the phantom touch that chills the soul. It will try to take something precious, something that defines you, to replace the connection it has lost.*

And it was doing just that. The pain wasn't just physical; it was existential. It felt like the entity was sifting through the very essence of her being, seeking to pluck out a vital strand of her identity. Was it her memories of Dry Creek before the blight? Was it her hope for its future? Or was it something more primal, more deeply ingrained – her very sense of self, her ability to perceive the world, her *sight*?

The searing agony behind her eyes pulsed with a rhythm that seemed to synchronize with the dying heartbeat of the blight. Each throb felt like a desperate attempt to claim dominion over her perception, to leave her blinded, not to the physical world, but to the subtler currents of life and energy, to the very things that made Dry Creek worth saving. It was a parasitic hunger for understanding, a desire to possess the very clarity that was now her weapon.

Kayla's vision swam. The muted twilight deepened, the colors of the ravaged field bleeding into a formless, indistinct haze. The obsidian shard, which had been a beacon of faint light, now seemed to pulse with a deeper, more urgent glow, its energy mirroring the turmoil within her. She felt a chilling sensation, like ice seeping into her optic nerves, a phantom frost that threatened to steal the very light she was fighting to preserve.

She remembered the stories, the hushed whispers of those who had tried to understand the Withers blight, those who had ventured too close to its heart and returned... changed. They spoke of a profound disorientation, a loss of clarity, a world seen through a warped lens, where shadows held substance and light was a deceitful phantom. Had this been their fate? Had the entity, in its final moments, inflicted upon them the very cost it was now attempting to exact from her?

The pain sharpened, coalescing into a single, unbearable point of focus. It was as if an unseen hand was reaching inside her skull, seeking to sever the optic nerve, not physically, but energetically, to sever her connection to the very light she now held precious. She had dared to see the truth of the blight, to understand its nature, and now, it sought to blind her to it, to render her understanding moot.

"No," she choked out, the word a raw whisper against the overwhelming onslaught. The ritual demanded a price, and she was willing to pay it. Elias had prepared her. He had understood that the severing of such a powerful, insidious force would not be a clean cut, but a violent amputation that would leave scars. The cycle of sacrifice had to be broken, and she would not perpetuate it by succumbing to its final, desperate grab.

She focused on the obsidian shard, its faint warmth a grounding anchor in the storm of her consciousness. It was a conduit, a vessel that had absorbed the blight's raw power, its concentrated malice. Now, as the entity lashed out psychically, the shard was also absorbing the impact of that final psychic assault. It felt like the shard itself was resonating with the agony, the raw energy flowing through it, a shield and a testament to her resistance.

With a surge of primal will, Kayla pushed back against the invading force. She channeled her intention, her unwavering resolve to protect Dry Creek, to protect its future, into the obsidian shard. If the entity sought to steal her sight, her clarity, then she would offer it a different kind of sight, a more profound understanding of the pain it inflicted. She wouldn't fight it with brute force, but with a focused, unyielding intent.

The pain behind her eyes flared, threatening to consume her. She felt a peculiar sensation, as if her very thoughts were being dredged up and offered as a sacrifice. Her deepest fears, her most cherished hopes, her most intimate memories – all seemed to shimmer on the precipice of being consumed. This was the entity's final attempt to feed, to draw sustenance from her very being, even as its physical anchor lay broken.

She thought of Elias, his quiet strength, his acceptance of the sacrifices he had made. He had given everything for Dry Creek, for the hope of its renewal. And now, she was doing the same. The cost of sight was not merely a physical or mental toll; it was the willingness to offer a piece of oneself, to endure profound suffering for the greater good.

The whispers, which had so recently been silenced, began to return, not as the guttural roars of the blight, but as insidious murmurs within her own mind, echoing the entity's desperate plea.

You cannot sever what is meant to be connected. You cannot escape the cycle. We are part of you now, just as you will become part of us.

Kayla squeezed her eyes shut, the obsidian shard pressed against her forehead, its faint light pulsing like a second, faltering heartbeat. She focused on the feeling of severance, on the clean break she had achieved, on the weakening of the blight's hold. This was not a merging; it was a definitive separation. The entity was a foreign invasion, and she was the immune system, fighting to expel a pathogen.

The psychic assault intensified, and for a terrifying moment, Kayla felt a flicker of doubt. Had she miscalculated? Had the ritual, meant to liberate Dry Creek, instead bound her irrevocably to the dying entity? The pain was so profound, so all-consuming, that it threatened to shatter her will, to break her resolve. It felt like her very soul was being scoured, stripped bare.

But then, a different sensation began to emerge, a subtle shift in the tide of the psychic battle. The agonizing pressure behind her eyes didn't disappear, but it began to change. It was as if the entity's desperate grasp was loosening, its final burst of energy dissipating like smoke. The raw, burning pain started to recede, replaced by a dull ache, a residual throb that spoke of a wound that was closing, not festering.

The obsidian shard pulsed, its light growing steadier, clearer. It was no longer absorbing the raw, destructive energy of the blight's death throes, but rather emanating a pure, albeit faint, luminescence. This was the energy of severance, the residual power of the broken connection, contained and purified.

Kayla slowly opened her eyes. The world swam back into focus, though with a subtle difference. The colors were richer, the shadows deeper, and the air seemed to hum with a quiet energy that had been absent before. The searing pain behind her eyes had receded to a persistent, throbbing ache, a constant reminder of the psychic battle she had just endured. But it was no longer a consuming agony. It was a localized hurt, a wound that would heal.

She looked down at her hand, at the obsidian shard. It was still warm, but the frantic pulsing had subsided. Its light was now a soft, steady glow, a beacon of hard-won peace. It had absorbed the shockwave of the entity's final, desperate act, and in doing so, had shielded her from its full destructive potential.

This was the true cost of sight. It wasn't about seeing the horrors of the Withers blight, but about enduring the price of its eradication.

It was about facing the entity's dying rage and refusing to be consumed by it, about offering a piece of oneself in exchange for liberation. The ritual demanded a sacrifice, and Kayla had given it. She had offered her own internal fortitude, her own mental resilience, in a final, desperate exchange.

She felt drained, utterly depleted, but not broken. The psychic assault had been brutal, a terrifying glimpse into the entity's primal hunger and its desperate will to survive. But it had failed to claim its ultimate prize. It had tried to steal her clarity, to blind her to the new Dry Creek that was beginning to dawn, but it had only succeeded in solidifying her resolve.

The residual ache behind her eyes was a tangible reminder of the entity's last, desperate strike. It was a phantom limb, a constant echo of the psychic surgery performed. But it was also a mark of victory. It signified that the severance was complete, that the invasive force had been excised. The cost had been steep, a profound personal sacrifice, but it was a sacrifice that would allow Dry Creek to finally begin to heal, to finally see the light of a new day without the suffocating shadow of the blight.

Kayla took a deep, shaky breath. The air, though still carrying the faint scent of decay, felt cleaner, sharper. The world seemed clearer, the subtle shifts in light and shadow more pronounced. The entity's attempt to blind her had, in a perverse way, heightened her senses, sharpened her perception of the world around her. It was a cruel irony, a final, bitter jest from a dying foe.

She clutched the obsidian shard, its steady glow a comforting presence. The ritual demanded a price, and she had paid it, not with her life, but with a piece of her own internal peace, a scar etched onto her very consciousness. It was the cost of sight, the price of seeing clearly, the price of severing a connection that had held Dry Creek captive for generations. And as the last vestiges of the blight's psychic rage subsided, Kayla knew that the true work of rebuilding, of healing, was only just beginning. The scar behind her eyes was a constant reminder of what had been lost, but also of what had been gained: the chance for Dry Creek to finally breathe free.

Chapter 12

The Price of Victory

The obsidian shard, still clutched tight in Kayla's hand, began to dim. The searing intensity that had pushed back the encroaching darkness, that had acted as a shield against the entity's dying, desperate psychic assault, was waning. It was not a sudden snuffing out, but a gradual ebbing, like the last breath of a dying star. The vibrant, life-affirming light that had pulsed with such ferocity moments ago now receded, its power spent, its purpose fulfilled. The shard itself felt cooler against her palm, the raw, vibrant energy that had coursed through it now a mere memory, a faint warmth that spoke of immense forces unleashed and contained.

Beside her, the scarecrow, its form contorted and menacing throughout the ritual, began to change. The unholy light that had emanated from its vacant eyes, the very spectral irises that had been the focus of the Withers blight, flickered and died. The malevolent glow, like embers being doused by a spectral rain, extinguished, leaving behind hollow, empty sockets. The effigy, its purpose as a vessel of corruption dissolved, sagged. Its straw-stuffed limbs, once imbued with an unnatural rigidity, slackened. The very fabric of its burlap skin, stained with the residue of unimaginable horror and the psychic backlash, seemed to deflate, returning to the humble state of a mere farmer's effigy, albeit one forever marked by the echoes of the terror it had embodied. It was a grim testament to the magnitude of the battle that had raged, a silent monument to the forces that had been confronted and, hopefully, vanquished.

The oppressive energy that had saturated the very air of the blighted field began to dissipate as well. It was a palpable sensation, a slow unclenching of a fist that had held Dry Creek in its suffocating grip for generations. The heavy, suffocating blanket of despair, the palpable weight of dread that had clung to everything, slowly lifted. The air, still carrying the faint, metallic tang of decay and the acrid scent of expended arcane energy, began to feel lighter, cleaner. It was as if the very atmosphere was exhaling, releasing the pent-up tension of a prolonged torment. This was the immediate aftermath of the ritual, the moment when the fabric of reality, so violently torn and reshaped, began to knit itself back together, albeit with new and unseen scars.

An eerie stillness descended, a silence more profound than any Kayla had ever experienced. It was not merely the absence of the Withers guttural whispers, the piercing psychic shriek, or the chilling wail of the corrupted winds. This silence was different. It was a deep, resonant quiet, a stillness that seemed to soak into the very marrow of her bones. It was the silence of a battlefield after the cacophony of war has ceased, a silence pregnant with exhaustion, with loss, and with the dawning, tentative promise of peace. The world held its breath, waiting, witnessing the immediate, tangible effects of the ritual's success.

The obsidian shard's light, now reduced to a mere ember, cast faint, dancing shadows across the ravaged earth. Kayla watched as the last of its power seemed to bleed into the ground, a final offering to anchor the severance, to solidify the barrier between Dry Creek and the parasitic influence of the Withers. The ritual had demanded everything, and the shard, a conduit of immense power, had delivered. It had absorbed the raw, volatile essence of the blight, wrestled with its dying rage, and ultimately, served as the fulcrum upon which Dry Creek's liberation had hinged. Now, depleted and inert, it was a reminder of the immense price that had been paid, and the delicate balance that had been struck.

She looked around the field, her gaze sweeping across the desolate landscape. The blighted earth, still scarred and barren, seemed to absorb the fading light, clinging to the remnants of the darkness. Yet, even in its desolation, there was a subtle shift. The air no longer felt actively hostile; it was merely empty, devoid of the pervasive malevolence. The familiar, sickly sweet odor of decay was still present, a lingering testament to the blight's deep-rooted corruption, but it was no longer the dominant scent. A faint, earthy aroma, the scent of undisturbed soil, of life waiting to reawaken, began to assert itself, a subtle but significant change in the olfactory tapestry of the field.

The scarecrow, no longer a focal point of corrupted power, was just that – a scarecrow. Its tattered clothes, once imbued with an unholy aura, now merely hung limp and faded. The straw within its stuffing, exposed in places where the burlap had torn, seemed to soak up the gloom, a stark contrast to the vibrant, if destructive, energy it had radiated moments before. It was a prop that had served its terrifying purpose, a symbol that had been stripped of its power, leaving behind only the shell of its former menace. Kayla felt no lingering fear towards it, only a profound sense of weariness, and a quiet understanding of its role in the grand, terrible drama that had unfolded.

The silence deepened, and in that profound quiet, Kayla felt the lingering echoes of the psychic battle. Though the immediate agony behind her eyes had receded to a dull, persistent throb, a constant reminder of the entity's final, desperate strike, the mental landscape was still being reshaped. It was as if the very pathways of her mind, forced open and bombarded by the Withers dying rage, were slowly being sealed, the ethereal scars left by the psychic surgery beginning to close. The experience had been more than just a physical or mental ordeal; it had been a profound violation, a trespass into the deepest sanctum of her being.

She knelt by the scarecrow, her movements slow and deliberate, still feeling the residual tremors of the power she had wielded. The obsidian shard, now a cool, smooth stone in her hand, was heavy with the weight of what it had endured. It had been a weapon, a shield, and ultimately, a vessel for the severed connection. Its purpose was complete, and its power, no longer needed for active defenses, was being reabsorbed, leaving behind only the faintest trace of its former luminescence. It was a tool that had served its master well, a testament to the ancient magics that had been invoked and manipulated for Dry Creek's salvation.

The cessation of the Withers influence was not just an external event; it was an internal one as well. The constant, low-grade hum of dread that had permeated the lives of Dry Creek's inhabitants, a psychic static that had subtly influenced their moods, their decisions, their very perception of the world, was gone. It was like the removal of a constant pressure, a subtle but pervasive weight that had been lifted. For years, they had lived under its shadow, unconsciously adapting to its oppressive presence. Now, in its absence, there was a void, a silence that was both liberating and, in its unfamiliarity, a little unsettling.

Kayla stood, the obsidian shard still in her grasp, and surveyed the blighted field. The sky above, which had been a bruised, sullen gray throughout the ritual, seemed to be clearing. Wisps of white, tinged with the faintest hint of pink as the sun began its slow rise, were beginning to break through the oppressive cloud cover. It was a subtle change, almost imperceptible, but to Kayla, it felt like a monumental shift. It was the first tangible sign of a new dawn for Dry Creek, a promise of a future unburdened by the Withers ancient curse.

The silence, as it settled, was broken only by the soft rustle of disturbed leaves and the faint sigh of the wind. These were natural sounds, the everyday symphony of the world that had been drowned out for so long by the unnatural intrusions of the blight. They were the sounds of life, of resilience, of a world that continued to turn, even in the face of overwhelming darkness. Kayla took another deep breath, filling her lungs with the cleaner air, allowing the quiet to seep into her being.

The scarecrow remained, a silent, hollow sentinel. It was a relic of a past that was now, irrevocably, broken. Its straw stuffing, its faded clothes, its vacant gaze – all were remnants of a power that had been severed, a connection that had been irrevocably broken. It was a symbol, not of defeat, but of a hard-won victory, a testament to the enduring strength of those who dared to challenge the darkness.

The obsidian shard pulsed one last time, a faint, internal glow, before settling into a cool, inert state. Its energy was fully expended, its purpose fulfilled. It had absorbed the worst of the Withers final, desperate act, acting as a buffer, a conduit, a shield. Now, it was simply a stone, a memento of the immense power that had been wielded and the sacrifices that had been made. Kayla carefully slipped it into a pouch at her side, its weight a constant reminder of the battle and its outcome.

The immediate aftermath of the ritual was a period of profound, almost unnerving, stillness. The violent psychic storm had passed, leaving behind a vacuum that the natural world was slowly beginning to fill. The silence was a relief, a balm to frayed nerves, but it also carried with it the weight of what had been lost, and the immensity of what lay ahead. Dry Creek was free, but its freedom had come at a cost, a price etched not just onto the land, but onto the very souls of those who had fought for it. The light had faded from the shard, but a new, albeit fragile, light was beginning to dawn on the horizon. The immediate threat had been vanquished, but the healing, the rebuilding, the true work of restoring Dry Creek, had only just begun. This profound quiet was not an ending, but a transition, a bridge between the horrors of the past and the uncertain, yet hopeful, future. The oppressive energy was gone, replaced by a void that would soon be filled with the tentative stirrings of life, with the quiet resilience of a community that had endured the unimaginable and emerged, scarred but not broken. The scarecrow stood as a silent witness to this transformation, a reminder of the darkness that had held sway, and the light that had ultimately prevailed.

The obsidian shard, once a beacon against the encroaching void, now lay inert and cool in Kayla's hand, its borrowed luminescence completely extinguished. The oppressive weight that had settled over the blighted field began to recede, not with a triumphant roar, but with a slow, agonizing sigh, like the last ragged breath of a dying beast. The cacophony of the Withers psychic assault, the insidious whispers that had clawed at her sanity, had finally ceased, leaving behind a silence so profound it was almost deafening. It was the silence of a world recoiling from a mortal blow, a stillness pregnant with exhaustion and the chilling realization of what had transpired.

Beside her, the scarecrow, its burlap form still slumped and torn, was no longer a conduit of malevolent power. The unnatural rigidity had completely vanished, and it sagged with the weight of spent magic and the lingering aura of desecration. The vacant sockets where spectral eyes had once blazed now stared emptily, like hollowed-out husks, bearing witness to the ritual's grim conclusion. The air, thick with the acrid tang of expended arcane energy and the cloying sweetness of decay, began to thin, though the metallic scent of residual horror still clung to the torn earth. Kayla felt the last tendrils of the Withers influence retract, like a parasitic organism severing its connection, leaving behind a vacuum that was both liberating and terrifyingly empty.

The psychic backlash, which had felt like a physical tearing of her very being, subsided into a dull, throbbing ache behind her eyes. Each pulse was a reminder of the overwhelming force she had absorbed, the raw, untamed energy that had been funneled through her. The world, which had been a blurry tapestry of fear and desperation moments ago, now began to swim in her vision. The colors bled into each other, the sharp edges of reality softening, blurring, as if seen through a veil of gauze. It was as if the very act of containing the Withers dying rage had warped her senses, stretching them to their breaking point and beyond.

She took a shaky breath, the air feeling strangely thin, as if her lungs were struggling to fill. The silence was no longer just the absence of noise; it was a tangible entity, pressing in on her, amplifying the ragged sound of her own breathing. The faint, earthy scent of the soil began to reassert itself, a comforting counterpoint to the lingering metallic tang, but even that was muted, distant. The clearing sky above, which had been a bruised, sullen gray, now seemed to weep faint streaks of pallid light, as if the very heavens were reluctant to acknowledge the victory.

Then, it began. Not a sudden darkness, but a creeping, insidious dimming. It started at the periphery of her vision, a subtle fading of the already hazy landscape. The faint sunlight, which had been struggling to penetrate the lingering gloom, seemed to retreat, as if recoiling from an unseen blight. Kayla blinked, trying to clear her vision, but the effort was futile. The blurring intensified, the edges of her perception dissolving into a formless, gray expanse. It was as if a vast, unseen curtain was being drawn, systematically erasing the world from her sight.

The searing pain behind her eyes, which had been a constant, gnawing ache, now surged with a terrifying intensity. It felt like hot coals being pressed against her eyeballs, a blinding, all-consuming fire that threatened to incinerate her very being. This was it, the final consequence, the price of the Gaze Offering. She had known, intellectually, that the ritual demanded a sacrifice, a profound and irreversible offering. But the abstract concept of "sacrifice" was nothing compared to the visceral reality of what was happening. Her sight, her connection to the visual world, was being systematically extinguished.

She remembered the ancient texts, the hushed warnings whispered by the few who understood the true nature of the Withers and their symbiotic relationship with the Gaze Offering. The Withers fed on perception, on the ability to witness and comprehend. To sever their hold, to break the cycle, required an offering that starved them at their very core. And what was more fundamental to perception, to the very act of witnessing, than sight itself? The obsidian shard had been the key, the conduit through which this devastating exchange had been facilitated. It had absorbed the Withers dying energy, their final, desperate attempt to cling to existence, and in doing so, had demanded the ultimate payment.

A guttural sob escaped her lips, a sound choked with pain and a dawning, horrifying comprehension. The world around her was not just blurring anymore; it was vanishing. The faint outlines of the scarecrow, the scarred earth, the distant, pale sky – all of it was being swallowed by an encroaching blackness. It was an absolute void, not the absence of light, but a consuming, all-encompassing darkness that emanated from within. The pain behind her eyes intensified, reaching a crescendo, a searing, white-hot agony that obliterated all thought, all sensations, except for its own brutal presence. And then, with a final, blinding flash that seared itself onto her consciousness even as it extinguished her physical sight, there was nothing.

The silence that followed was no longer the aftermath of battle, but the profound stillness of an abyss. Kayla was adrift in an infinite, featureless blackness, a void so complete it felt as if she had been erased from existence. The pain behind her eyes, though still a phantom ache, no longer held the same sharp, searing intensity. It was as if her optic nerves, having been overloaded and destroyed, had finally gone numb, leaving behind only the ghost of torment.

She tried to open her eyes, an involuntary, desperate action, but the result was the same: nothing. Only the impenetrable darkness. Her hands, still clutching the now cold and lifeless obsidian shard, trembled. The tactile world remained, a lifeline in this new, terrifying reality. She could feel the smooth, unyielding surface of the shard, the rough texture of her worn clothing, the dampness of the blighted earth beneath her knees. But the visual confirmation, the ability to see these things, was gone. Irrevocably gone.

The victory, if it could be called that, felt hollow. Dry Creek was safe, the Withers oppressive influence severed. The cycle of the Gaze Offering was broken. But the cost... the cost was almost too much to bear. She had traded her sight for her town's freedom, her ability to witness the world for the ability of its people to live unburdened by ancient dread. It was a sacrifice that had been necessary, a desperate measure for a desperate situation, but the reality of it was a crushing weight.

She reached out a tentative hand, feeling for the scarecrow, for anything that could ground her in this terrifying new reality. Her fingers brushed against rough, tattered fabric, the familiar, yet now alien, texture of straw stuffing. The scarecrow, Ragmouth, once a terrifying symbol of the Withers power, was now just a silent, limp effigy, devoid of its unholy animation. It served as a stark reminder of the power that had been wielded, and the profound alteration it had wrought.

The air, though thinner than before, still carried the lingering scent of decay and arcane residue. Kayla inhaled deeply, trying to orient herself, to find some anchor in the disorienting blackness. She could feel the subtle tremors of the earth beneath her, a faint vibration that spoke of the land slowly healing, of the magic that had been unleashed now settling, integrating into the very fabric of the world. But she could not see it. She could only feel it, imagine it, and the inability to witness these subtle shifts was a constant, agonizing reminder of her loss.

She tried to recall the faces of the villagers, the familiar contours of their homes, the comforting, if sometimes mundane, sights of Dry Creek. But even these memories, once so vivid, now seemed to be receding, the edges of her mind blurring as if to mirror the physical darkness that had enveloped her. It was a terrifying thought – not only had she lost her sight, but the very capacity to vividly recall what she had seen was also beginning to fade.

The silence, once a symbol of peace, now felt like a suffocating shroud. Every rustle of leaves, every distant sigh of the wind, was amplified in the absence of visual stimuli. They were sounds that had always been background noise, mere footnotes to the visual narrative of her life. Now, they were the entire story, the only input she received, and their unfamiliar prominence was unnerving.

She felt the obsidian shard cool completely in her hand, the last vestiges of its spent power draining away, leaving behind only a smooth, inert stone. It had been her shield, her weapon, and ultimately, the instrument of her sacrifice. She carefully slipped it into a pouch at her side, its weight a constant, physical reminder of the monumental exchange. It was a heavy burden, a tangible artifact of a victory that felt so profoundly personal, so deeply isolating.

What would happen now? How would she navigate this world she could no longer see? How would she contribute to Dry Creek's recovery, to its rebuilding, when her most fundamental sense had been taken from her? The questions swirled in the darkness, each one a new wave of fear and despair. She had fought for Dry Creek, had endured horrors unimaginable, had embraced a power that had nearly consumed her. And in the end, she had paid the ultimate price, a price that would forever define her existence, and that of the town she had saved.

The initial shock began to recede, replaced by a gnawing realization of the immense, daunting task that lay before her. This wasn't the triumphant end she might have envisioned, bathed in the warm glow of victory. This was something far more complex, far more challenging. It was the beginning of a new struggle, a different kind of battle, fought not with arcane power and desperate courage, but with resilience, adaptation, and an unwavering will to persevere, even in the face of overwhelming darkness.

She pushed herself to her feet, her movements still hesitant, uncertain. The ground beneath her felt stable, familiar, yet alien. She took a step, then another, her hands outstretched, feeling her way through the silent, invisible world. Each movement was a deliberate act of defiance, a refusal to succumb to the despair that threatened to engulf her. Dry Creek was free, and that was all that mattered. Her sacrifice, though profound, was a necessary one.

She had to believe that. She had to hold onto that thought, that single, unyielding truth, as she stepped into the vast, unknown expanse of her sightless future. The world was still there, she knew it, even if she could no longer witness its light. It was a world waiting to be rebuilt, to be healed, and she, in her own way, would still be a part of that process. The darkness might have claimed her eyes, but it had not claimed her spirit. Not yet. Not ever, if she had anything to say about it. The victory had been won, but the true price was only just beginning to be understood.

The pervasive, unnatural rustling that had characterized the cornfield, a sound that had clawed at the edges of sanity, finally ceased. It wasn't a gradual fading, but an abrupt, almost violent cessation, as if a colossal switch had been thrown, silencing the very breath of the blighted stalks. Where moments before there had been a frantic, papery symphony of dread, now there was a profound quietude. The incessant, insidious whispers, the psychic tendrils that had woven themselves into the very fabric of thought, had been wrenched free, leaving behind a silence so absolute it felt like a physical presence. It was a vacuum, a void where the cacophony of the Withers had previously reigned, and within this void, a new sound began to tentatively emerge: the soft, melancholic sigh of the autumn wind.

This wind, so different from the gale that had previously whipped through the corn with malevolent intent, was gentle, almost mournful. It stirred the remaining stalks with a delicate touch, not a tearing, violent force, but a soft caress that whispered of endings and transitions. It carried with it the crisp, clean scent of decaying leaves and damp earth, a perfume of the natural world reasserting its dominion. The oppressive atmosphere, a palpable weight that had pressed down on the land and its inhabitants, began to lift, not in a sudden, glorious sunrise, but in a slow, almost hesitant dissolution. The very air seemed to exhale, releasing the accumulated tension and dread that had permeated the field for so long. The nexus of terror, the heart of the Withers power, was no longer radiating malice. Instead, it was settling into a state of eerie, almost unnatural peace.

The scars of its dark history, however, remained etched into the very soil. The ground, churned and torn by the spectral onslaught, bore witness to the titanic struggle that had transpired. Patches of earth were still blackened, still bearing the faint, metallic tang of residual arcane energies, a grim reminder of the price paid. The husks of the Withers themselves, those ephemeral specters of corrupted consciousness, were gone, their essence seemingly dissipated, absorbed, or utterly annihilated. But the land remembered. The earth, a silent observer and participant in countless cycles of growth and decay, held the imprint of the horror, a deep-seated memory of the violation it had endured.

Kayla, still reeling from the catastrophic personal toll of her victory, felt this shift acutely. Though her physical sight was gone, her other senses, heightened and refined by the ordeal, registered the profound change. The silence was no longer the suffocating blanket of dread, but a clean slate. The wind's gentle touch on her skin was no longer a harbinger of unseen threats, but a simple, natural sensation. She could feel the ground beneath her knees, still damp and cool, and the rough texture of the burlap of the scarecrow beside her. These tactile anchors were crucial in the immeasurable darkness that now enveloped her, the void that had been her price.

She concentrated, trying to discern any lingering trace of the Withers influence, any echo of their psychic might. There was nothing. The psychic landscape, once a roiling, chaotic storm, was now utterly still. It was as if a great wave had receded, leaving behind a vast, unblemished shore. The very absence of the Withers presence was a testament to the totality of her sacrifice. They had been a parasitic force, feeding on the perceptions and fears of those they encountered. By offering her sight, her ability to perceive, she

295

had effectively starved them, severed their very source of sustenance.

The cornfield, once a vibrant tapestry of green, had been a conduit for their power, its rustling stalks their collective voice, its whispering winds their insidious thoughts. Now, it was just a field. A damaged, violated field, certainly, but a natural space nonetheless. The transition was jarring. The sheer intensity of the Withers psychic presence had been all-consuming, a constant barrage that had occupied every available mental space. Its absence left an unnerving emptiness, a void that her mind struggled to comprehend. It was like the sudden silencing of a deafening roar, the quiet that followed almost more disorienting than the noise itself.

She could almost feel the land breathing a sigh of relief. The unnatural blight that had leached the color from the leaves, the twisted growth that had characterized its flora, seemed to be slowly receding, or perhaps her perception of it was simply altered by the absence of visual input. The natural order, so brutally disrupted, was beginning to reassert itself. The wind rustled through the stalks, and now, for the first time, it sounded like wind. Not the agitated whispers of a disturbed spirit, but the natural song of air moving through vegetation. It was a sound that spoke of passing seasons, of the ebb and flow of nature, a comforting normalcy that had been utterly absent for so long.

The scarecrow, no longer a puppet of malevolent forces, sagged with a newfound stillness. Its burlap form, once rigid with the sheer force of the magic it channeled, now slumped, a pathetic, inanimate object. The spectral eyes that had blazed with unholy light were gone, leaving only empty, shadowed sockets. It was a monument to the battle, a silent sentinel that had once been the focal point of the Withers terror, and now, merely a relic of a vanquished foe. Kayla reached out a trembling hand, her fingers brushing against the coarse fabric. It was still there, a tangible connection to the events that had transpired, a reminder of the terrifying power she had wielded and the devastating price she had paid.

The victory, such as it was, felt deeply personal and profoundly isolating. Dry Creek was safe, the Withers influence broken, the cycle of the Gaze Offering shattered. But the cost... the cost was a chasm, an infinite darkness that had consumed her world. She had traded her vision for her town's salvation, a transaction of unimaginable weight. The abstract concept of sacrifice, so often lauded in tales of heroism, was now a visceral, agonizing reality. Every rustle of corn, every whisper of wind, was now experienced through a filter of profound loss.

She tried to reconstruct the scene with her mind's eye, to conjure the image of the field as it must be now, bathed in the soft, fading light of dusk. She imagined the corn stalks no longer vibrating with dark energy, but swaying gently in the breeze. She pictured the scarecrow, a forlorn figure in the gathering gloom. But the images remained flat, lifeless, lacking the vibrant dimensionality that sight had once provided. Her memories, once sharp and vivid, now seemed to be fading, their edges blurring, mirroring the physical darkness that had claimed her. It was a terrifying prospect – not only had she lost her sight, but the very clarity of her recalled experiences was diminishing.

The natural sounds of the approaching night began to assert themselves. The chirping of crickets, once a background hum, now seemed to resonate with a startling clarity. The distant hoot of an owl, a sound she had barely noticed before, was now a distinct, almost piercing call. Her other senses were reaching out, trying to compensate for the void left by her lost sight, painting a new, albeit incomplete, picture of the world. She could smell the damp earth, feel the cool air on her skin, hear the symphony of the natural world, but it was a world perceived through a veil of perpetual twilight, a world she could no longer truly see.

The fear, which had been a constant companion throughout the ritual, began to recede, replaced by a profound sense of disorientation. This was not the aftermath she had anticipated. There were no cheers, no joyous reunions, no triumphant parades. There was only silence, and darkness, and the agonizing weight of her irreversible sacrifice. She had won, but the victory felt hollow, tainted by the devastating personal cost. The world she had saved was now a world she could no longer truly experience.

She knelt there for a long time, the cold obsidian shard still clutched in her hand, a reminder of the power she had wielded and the price she had paid. The cornfield, once a place of unimaginable horror, was now simply... quiet. The malevolence had been banished, the oppressive grip of the Withers broken. But the silence that remained was not the triumphant roar of victory, but the hushed stillness of a grave. It was the quiet of a world that had been wounded, and the quiet of a life irrevocably altered.

She pushed herself to her feet, her movements still uncertain, hesitant. The familiar ground felt alien beneath her feet, the invisible landscape a terrifying unknown. She took a step, then another, her hands outstretched, feeling her way through the encroaching darkness. Each motion was a conscious act of defiance, a refusal to succumb to the despair that threatened to engulf her. Dry Creek was free. That was the only truth that mattered. Her sacrifice, however profound, however crippling, had been necessary.

She had to believe that. She had to cling to that single, unyielding thought as she ventured forth, away from the site of her pyrrhic victory. The world was still out there, she knew it, even if she could no longer witness its light. It was a world waiting to be healed, to be rebuilt, and she, in her own way, would still be a part of that process. The darkness might have claimed her eyes, but it had not claimed her spirit. Not yet. The victory had been won, but the true price was only just beginning to be understood. The cornfield had fallen silent, but the echoes of that silence would resonate within her for the rest of her days.

The wind, continuing its gentle lament, stirred the remnants of the corn, its rustling now a mere whisper against the overwhelming stillness. It was a sound that, moments ago, had been a herald of terror. Now, it was simply the sound of nature reclaiming its territory, of the natural world slowly, painstakingly, beginning to heal. Kayla listened, trying to attune herself to this new auditory reality, to decipher the subtle nuances of a world perceived through sound and touch alone. Each gentle movement of the stalks, each sigh of the breeze, was a lesson, a new piece of information in a lexicon she was only just beginning to learn.

The earth beneath her feet felt solid, reassuringly real. She could feel the subtle unevenness of the ground, the slight incline that marked the transition from the blighted center of the field to its outer edges. It was a tactile map, a cartography of her immediate surroundings that she was slowly, deliberately memorizing. The air itself carried a faint, almost imperceptible coolness, a testament to the retreating daylight. Dusk was deepening, and with it, the natural world was preparing for its nocturnal cycle. The crickets chirped with increased urgency, their rhythmic calls creating a complex auditory tapestry. A distant rustle in the undergrowth suggested a small creature moving through the shadows, perhaps drawn by the receding tide of malevolent energy.

Kayla took another tentative step, her arms still outstretched, her fingers splayed to catch any stray breeze, any shift in the air that might indicate an obstacle. She was moving towards the edge of the cornfield, towards the familiar, though now unseen, path that would lead her back to Dry Creek. The journey, which had once been a simple act of traversing a known landscape, was now an arduous expedition into the unknown. Every footfall was a calculation, every sound a potential clue.

The memory of the obsidian shard, cold and inert in her hand, was a constant, weighty reminder. It had been the key, the catalyst, the instrument of her irreversible transformation. She had held raw, untamed power in her hand, and in doing so, had paid the ultimate price. The memory of that power, the brief, terrifying moment when she had channeled the dying rage of the Withers, was a paradox – a source of profound guilt and a testament to her desperate courage.

As she moved through the spectral silence of the corn, she could almost feel the presence of the town, a faint warmth in the air, a distant hum of life that, even unseen, offered a glimmer of hope. Dry Creek. It was safe. The shadows that had loomed over it for so long had been dispelled. The unnatural fear that had permeated its streets and homes was gone. Her sacrifice had ensured that.

But the weight of that sacrifice was immense. It was a burden she would carry for the rest of her life, a constant, invisible companion. How would she ever truly see Dry Creek again? How would she witness its rebuilding, its recovery, its eventual return to normalcy, if she could not even see the faces of its people, the familiar streets, the comforting architecture? The questions gnawed at her, each one a fresh wave of despair.

Yet, beneath the despair, a flicker of resilience began to ignite. She had faced the Withers, had stared into the abyss and emerged, albeit irrevocably changed. She had endured pain beyond imagining, had made a choice that had reshaped her very existence. If she could do that, surely she could learn to navigate this new reality. Surely, she could find a way to contribute to Dry Creek's future, even without her sight.

The natural world, once a mere backdrop to her visual experiences, was now her primary source of information. She was learning to discern the subtle differences in the textures of the soil, to interpret the language of the wind, to map the unseen world through the symphony of sounds that surrounded her. It was a daunting, painstaking process, but it was also a testament to the adaptability of her spirit.

The cornfield, once a symbol of dread and corruption, was now a silent testament to a victory hard-won, a victory that had come at a terrible cost. The unnatural forces that had held sway there were gone, banished by a sacrifice that had left Kayla adrift in a sea of darkness. But as she finally stepped out of the rustling stalks and onto the firmer, albeit still unseen, ground of the path leading home, a new, nascent determination began to take root within her. The cornfield had fallen silent, but her own journey, a journey into a world she could no longer see, had only just begun. The silence was not an end, but a beginning, a stark and terrifying canvas upon which she would have to learn to paint her new reality, one step, one sound, one touch at a time. The price of victory was steep, but she had paid it, and now, she would have to learn to live with the consequences, to find her way through the perpetual twilight, and to help Dry Creek find its way back into the light.

The silence was a heavy, suffocating blanket, far more oppressive than the whispers and rustling that had been its predecessor. Kayla knelt, the rough, dry texture of burlap pressing against her fingertips. It was the scarecrow. Ragmouth. The vessel that had, for a terrifying eternity, been a conduit for the Withers vile power. Now, it was just... straw and cloth. Its familiar, inanimate form was a grounding anchor in the swirling chaos of her new reality. She traced the coarse weave of its sleeve, a muted comfort against the raw terror that still beat beneath her skin. The victory, the absolute, undeniable cessation of the Withers psychic presence, had been achieved. But the echo of that victory was a hollow, desolate sound that resonated within the cavernous darkness that now encompassed her vision.

Her world had been ripped away, not in a violent explosion, but in a chilling, deliberate amputation. The cornfield, once a vibrant, if terrifying, expanse she could survey and understand, was now an abstract concept, a map etched only in her memory and the subtle shifts in the ground beneath her. She focused, trying to reconstruct the visual – the rows of corn, the faded, tattered clothes of the scarecrow, the bruised twilight sky. But the images were flat, lifeless echoes, lacking the depth and dimension that sight had once provided. It was like looking at a photograph of a person she once loved; the likeness was there, but the spark, the *life*, was gone.

The air carried the scent of damp earth and the faint, metallic tang of residual energy – the lingering ghost of arcane conflict. It was a perfume of sacrifice, a pungent reminder of the choice she had made. Her eyes, once windows to the world, were now closed, sealed by a bargain struck in the heart of a malevolent storm. She could feel the gentle caress of the autumn wind on her cheek, a sensation that was both familiar and utterly alien. Before, the wind had been a messenger, a carrier of whispers and threats. Now, it was simply wind, its song a melancholic lullaby sung through the rustling stalks that remained.

A faint tremor ran through her. It wasn't fear, not the raw, visceral terror that had gripped her during the ritual. This was something subtler, a deep-seated disorientation, a profound sense of being adrift. She had won. The Gaze Offering, the cycle of dread and appeasement, was broken. Dry Creek was free from the Withers spectral tendrils. But at what cost? The victory felt less like a triumph and more like a pyrrhic exchange, a trade of her entire world for the safety of a town that she could no longer fully perceive.

She took another step, her boot crunching on dry leaves. The sound, sharp and distinct, was a marker of her progress, a small victory in itself. She was moving, navigating this new, unseen terrain. The skills she had honed in the suffocating darkness of the cornfield were now being tested, applied to the wider world. Her hearing, once a secondary sense, was now her primary guide. She strained to pick out any familiar sound, any indicator of her direction. The distant bark of a dog, the faint murmur of voices – these were the threads she clung to, the signals that would lead her home.

The memory of the ritual itself was a fractured mosaic of sensations: the burning pain in her eyes, the chilling touch of spectral energy, the overwhelming surge of power, and finally, the absolute cessation. It was a narrative of her own undoing, a story of sacrifice etched not in ink, but in the very fabric of her being. She had peered into the heart of the Withers corrupted consciousness and had, in a desperate act of defiance, offered herself as the ultimate sacrifice. By severing her connection to the visual world, she had starved the Withers, cut off their primary means of sustenance and manipulation. It was a brutal, effective solution, but it had left her irrevocably broken.

The path home, once a well-trodden route, was now an uncharted territory. She stumbled slightly, her outstretched hand brushing against the rough, unyielding bark of a tree. A tree. She recognized its texture, its sturdy presence. It was an oak, likely one of the old ones bordering the fields. The familiar sensation was a small comfort, a confirmation that she was still in a world that held some semblance of the reality she had known.

She paused, listening. The sounds of the approaching day were growing louder, more distinct. The wind sighed through the remaining corn stalks, a mournful whisper that spoke of endings and quietude. It was no longer the frantic, rustling whisper of the Withers, but the natural lament of the changing season. She could hear the faint buzz of insects, the occasional rustle of unseen creatures in the undergrowth. The natural world was reclaiming its voice, a voice that was both comforting and a constant reminder of her own profound loss.

How would she explain this? How would she articulate the depth of her sacrifice, the irreversible change that had befallen her? The people of Dry Creek would be celebrating, their fear finally lifted. They would see her as a hero, a savior. But they wouldn't see the true price. They wouldn't see the world that had been stolen from her, the vibrant tapestry of light and color that had been her birthright. They would never understand the constant, gnawing emptiness, the perpetual twilight that was now her existence.

She imagined the faces of her family, their expressions of relief, perhaps even joy, as they saw her emerge from the cornfield. She yearned to see them, to meet their gaze, to feel the warmth of their smiles. But that was a luxury she no longer possessed. Her connection to them would now be through touch, through voice, through the subtler nuances of sound and emotion. It was a humbling, terrifying prospect.

A wave of despair washed over her, threatening to drag her under. The sheer magnitude of her loss was almost unbearable. She had faced down an ancient evil, had wielded unimaginable power, and had emerged victorious. But the victory was a hollow shell, a monument to her own personal annihilation. She had traded the light of the world for the salvation of her town, a transaction that left her feeling profoundly empty, profoundly alone.

Yet, even in the depths of her despair, a flicker of resilience began to stir. She had survived. She had faced the Withers, had stared into the abyss, and had emerged, albeit irrevocably altered. She had made a choice, a choice that had reshaped her very existence. If she could endure the horrors of the cornfield, if she could harness the power that had nearly consumed her, then surely she could learn to navigate this new reality. Surely she could find a way to contribute to Dry Creek's future, even without her sight.

The natural world, once a mere backdrop to her visual experiences, was now her primary source of information. She was learning to discern the subtle differences in the textures of the soil, to interpret the language of the wind, to map the unseen world through the symphony of sounds that surrounded her. It was a daunting, painstaking process, but it was also a testament to the adaptability of the human spirit. Each rustle of a leaf, each chirp of a cricket, was a piece of information, a clue in the ongoing puzzle of her existence.

She continued her slow, deliberate journey, her senses reaching out, piecing together the fragmented reality around her. The cornfield, once a symbol of dread and corruption, was now a silent testament to a victory hard-won, a victory that had come at a terrible cost. The unnatural forces that had held sway there were gone, banished by a sacrifice that had left Kayla adrift in a sea of darkness. But as she finally stepped out of the rustling stalks and onto the firmer, albeit still unseen, ground of the path leading home, a new, nascent determination began to take root within her. The cornfield had fallen silent, but her own journey, a journey into a world she could no longer see, had only just begun. The silence was not an end, but a beginning, a stark and terrifying canvas upon which she would have to learn to paint her new reality, one step, one sound, one touch at a time. The price of victory was steep, but she had paid it, and now, she would have to learn to live with the consequences, to find her way through the perpetual twilight, and to help Dry Creek find its way back into the light. The victory was hers, but the true battle – the battle to reclaim her life from the encroaching darkness – had just begun.

The silence was not a gentle hush, but a deep, profound stillness that pressed in on Kayla from all sides. It was the quiet of a world holding its breath, waiting for the dawn, and for the truth of what had transpired in the hours before. The Withers were gone. The psychic tendrils that had suffocated Dry Creek, that had twisted the very air into a miasma of dread, had been severed. The victory, if one could call it that, was absolute. But the silence was also a testament to the cost, a vast, echoing void where the vibrant spectrum of her sight had once been.

She pushed herself from the cold, damp earth, her hands finding the rough, splintered wood of a fallen fence post. It was a familiar anchor, a solid presence in the shifting, unmappable terrain of her new existence. The scarecrow, her scarecrow, the conduit and the weapon, stood sentinel in the dim, pre-dawn light. It was just straw and tattered cloth now, its malevolent purpose extinguished. A shiver traced its way down her spine, not of fear, but of a profound, bone-deep exhaustion. The battle had been won, not with swords and shields, but with an unimaginable expenditure of will and a sacrifice that had irrevocably reshaped her reality.

Her journey out of the field was a slow, painstaking navigation. Each step was a deliberate calculation, a reliance on the ingrained memory of the land and the ever-sharpening acuity of her other senses. The rustle of dry leaves beneath her feet was a distinct sound, a narrative of her progress. The faintest whisper of wind through the remaining corn stalks was a directional cue, a gentle nudge toward the unseen horizon.

She could feel the subtle inclines and declines of the ground, the texture of the soil changing from the cloying dampness near the field's center to the firmer, more compacted earth of its periphery.

As the first faint streaks of grey began to paint the eastern sky, a new sound emerged, faint but persistent. It was the distant, mournful cry of a rooster, a sound that had always signaled the turning of the world from night to day. It was a sound that, before, she would have registered and largely ignored, a pleasant but unremarkable part of the rural symphony. Now, it was a beacon, a promise of a world stirring from its slumber, a world that had been saved. She focused on it, letting it guide her, a fragile thread of sound in the vast tapestry of her newly perceived reality.

The air grew cooler as the pre-dawn chill began to recede, replaced by a subtle warmth that hinted at the approaching sun. She could smell the damp earth, the decaying leaves, and a faint, sweet scent of late-blooming wildflowers. These were the perfumes of the natural world, the scents she had once perceived but had never truly *understood* in their intricate complexity. Now, they were vital signposts, each aroma a word in a language she was desperately trying to decipher.

The transition from the cornfield to the open land bordering Dry Creek was marked by a subtle shift in the sounds and textures underfoot. The rough stubble of the harvested fields gave way to the softer, yielding earth of the path leading back to town. She could hear the faint murmur of the creek itself, a gentle, gurgling presence that had always been a constant companion to the town, a sound now amplified and imbued with a new significance. It was a sound of continuity, a reassurance that the natural rhythms of the world persisted, even in the wake of the unnatural forces that had been unleashed.

As the sky continued to brighten, a faint, diffuse glow began to permeate her surroundings. It wasn't the sharp, defined light of sunlight that she remembered, but a soft, ethereal luminescence that illuminated the shapes and forms around her. She could sense the outlines of trees, their branches stark against the lightening sky. She could feel the broader expanse of the open fields, the subtle variations in elevation that had once been so easily read by her eyes. It was a world rendered in shades of grey and texture, a monochrome existence that was both a deprivation and a new form of perception.

The first rays of the sun, when they finally crested the horizon, were not a blinding explosion of light, but a gentle, pervasive warmth that spread across her skin. She could feel the heat, a tangible sensation that marked the official beginning of the day. The Withers field lay behind her, a silent, defeated expanse. The scarecrow, once a vessel of terror, was now just a silhouette against the brightening sky, a monument to a battle fought and won. The unnatural stillness that had pervaded the field was slowly giving way to the familiar sounds of a waking world.

She continued her slow trek, her senses straining to gather every scrap of information. The distant sounds of Dry Creek began to filter through the morning air. A dog barked, a sharp, clear sound that she recognized as belonging to Mrs. Gable's old retriever. The clang of a milk pail, a familiar morning ritual in the town, echoed faintly. These were the sounds of normalcy, the comforting evidence that the night's terrors had not shattered the town's foundation.

Yet, as she drew closer, a peculiar quietude hung over the town. It was a quiet that was different from the oppressive silence of the Withers influence; this was a quiet born of slumber, of a town unaware of the cosmic battle that had raged on its doorstep. They slept, their dreams untroubled by the spectral entities that had been vanquished. They were unaware of the price paid for their peace, the

306

profound personal cost that had been exacted from the one who had stood against the darkness.

She imagined the town waking up to this new day. The sun would rise, casting its golden light upon familiar streets, illuminating houses that were now safe, no longer under the shadow of an unseen, malevolent gaze. People would stir, opening their windows to the crisp morning air, their minds still filled with the lingering unease of recent weeks, but unaware that the source of that unease had been irrevocably extinguished. They would see the scarecrow, perhaps, in the distance, a strange and unsettling sight, but they would not understand its significance, nor the sacrifice it represented.

Kayla paused, listening to the symphony of the awakening town. Each sound was a precious piece of information, a fragment of a world she was still struggling to comprehend. The distant clang of the blacksmith's hammer, the rumble of a cart on the dirt road, the murmuring voices of early risers – these were the threads that wove the fabric of her new reality. She could sense the general layout of the town, the familiar landmarks mapped not by sight, but by the acoustic signatures they emitted.

Now joined by Tommy, they traversed the path leading her home a path that was etched into her memory, a route she had traversed countless times. Now, it was a journey of sensory interpretation. She could feel the subtle shift in the terrain as she moved from the unpaved roads to the slightly smoother, packed earth of the town's main thoroughfare. The familiar warmth of the sun on her face was a constant reminder of the dawn, of the end of the night's ordeal.

She could feel the presence of others, not clearly seeing them, but by the subtle disturbances they created in the soundscape. The rhythmic shuffle of footsteps, the brief murmur of conversation, the sudden rustle of clothing – these were the indicators of human presence. She could sense the general direction of movement, the flow of life in the town beginning to reassert itself.

There was a profound sense of detachment, a feeling of being present yet unseen, of being a ghost in her own town. The joy of victory was overshadowed by the stark reality of her loss. She had saved them, had broken the cycle of dread that had gripped Dry Creek for generations, but in doing so, she had stepped into a permanent twilight. The vibrant, colorful world that had once been her birthright was now a memory, a faded photograph in the album of her mind.

They continued the slow, steady progress, Kayla's senses attuned to the slightest nuance. The air carried the scent of woodsmoke from early morning fires, a comforting, familiar aroma. She could feel the slight vibration of the earth as people moved about their routines. Dry Creek was waking up, its inhabitants blissfully unaware of the profound transformation that had taken place, not only in the Withers Field, but within Kayla herself.

The fragile peace that had settled over the land was a heavy burden, a testament to a victory that felt more like a profound personal defeat. The Withers were gone, their oppressive influence lifted, but the silence they left behind was also the silence of her own extinguished sight. She had paid the ultimate price, and as the sun climbed higher, casting its light upon a town that had finally found respite, Kayla walked into its embrace, a hero unseen, forever changed by the darkness she had overcome. The dawn had broken, but for Kayla, it was a dawn in a world shrouded in perpetual twilight, a world she would now have to learn to navigate, one sound, one touch, one sense at a time. The price of victory was steep, and the long, arduous journey of learning to live in the aftermath had only just begun. The silence of the field was the silence of her sight, and as the sounds of Dry Creek grew closer, each one was a reminder of the profound and irreversible change that had settled upon her.

Chapter 13

Echoes in the Silence

The familiar drone of the creek, a sound she'd always taken for granted, now served as her primary compass. It was a low, constant hum, a liquid whisper that cut through the morning air, guiding her steps along the winding path. Each rustle of dried leaves underfoot, each snap of a twig, was a distinct note in the melody of her return. Her hands, still raw from the earth and the desperate grip on the obsidian blade, trailed along the rough bark of trees that lined the creek bank, their textures a map of familiar territory now rendered in tactile whispers. These were the landmarks she navigated, the silent sentinels that anchored her in a world that had suddenly lost its visual mooring.

The air itself seemed to breathe differently. The oppressive stillness that had clung to the Withers Field had been replaced by a gentle, life-affirming breeze, carrying with it the scent of damp earth, pine needles, and the faintest hint of woodsmoke from the earliest risers in Dry Creek. It was a symphony of familiar olfactory notes, each one a reassurance, a whisper of homecoming. She could discern the distinct aroma of Mrs. Gable's prize-winning roses, even from this distance, a sweet, cloying perfume that spoke of normalcy, of a life that continued, oblivious to the recent inferno.

The journey back to the heart of Dry Creek was a testament to her unwavering resolve. Each footstep was a deliberate act of defiance against the overwhelming exhaustion that threatened to pull her down. The landscape, once so vividly painted by her sight, was now a tapestry of textures and sounds. She could feel the subtle gradient of the land beneath her boots, the way the path sloped gently downhill as she approached the cluster of houses that comprised her town. The earth transitioned from the loose, sandy soil near the creek to the more compacted, dusty track that served as the main thoroughfare.

As she drew nearer, the sounds of the town began to coalesce. The distant clatter of a milk pail, the sharp, insistent bark of a dog – undoubtedly Mrs. Gable's loyal, if somewhat boisterous, retriever, Buster – these were the familiar sounds of a community stirring to life. They were the gentle whispers of a world reawakening, a stark contrast to the profound, echoing silence she had left behind in the field. These were the sounds of safety, of a peace hard-won, and each one resonated within her, a balm to her frayed nerves.

A figure emerged from the dim light of the pre-dawn. It was old Mr. Henderson, his stooped frame silhouetted against the brightening sky, heading out to check his traps. He stopped, his weathered face turning in her direction, his usual gruff greeting replaced by a look of dawning realization, then shock. Kayla felt his gaze, though she could barely see it. It was a physical presence, a silent question hanging in the air between them.

"Tommy and Kayla?" His voice, usually a low rumble, was strained, laced with disbelief.

She could hardly see his expression, but she could hear the tremor in his voice, the dawning comprehension of what her appearance signified. She nodded, a small, almost imperceptible movement. "It's me, Mr. Henderson."

He started towards them, his steps quickening, a mixture of concern and awe in his movements. She could hear the rustle of his worn canvas jacket, the rhythmic thud of his boots on the packed earth. He reached her side, his hand hovering uncertainly near her arm before gently settling there. His touch was warm, calloused, and grounding.

"My God, child," he breathed, his voice thick with emotion. "We… we feared the worst. When the quiet came… the unnatural quiet… we didn't know what to make of it. But the scarecrow… it just stood there, silent, after all the… the noise…" He trailed off, the unspoken horrors of the night hanging heavy between them.

Tommy, more concerned about Kayla, offered a small, weak smile, though he knew that Kayla couldn't see it. "It's over, Mr.

Henderson. The Withers and Ragmouth… they're gone. But there were casualties." Tommy offered, the words felt monumental, heavy with the weight of their truth.

Mr. Henderson touched Kayla's arm. "Gone? Truly?" He paused, his gaze sweeping the horizon, then settling back on her. A slow dawning of relief spread across his features, a subtle shift that she could sense rather than see. "The dread… it's lifted. You can feel it, can't you? The air… it's lighter." She offered.

She was right. The suffocating pressure, the psychic tendrils that had choked the life out of Dry Creek for so long, had indeed receded. The silence that remained was not the terrifying void of the Withers influence, but the natural quiet of a world returning to its senses. Yet, for Kayla, this newfound lightness was a bitter paradox. The absence of the Withers and Ragmouth's oppressive presence was directly tied to the absence of her sight.

As they continued walking, other figures began to emerge from the houses. Cautious faces peered from behind lace curtains, windows were slowly opened, and doors creaked ajar. They were like nocturnal creatures, venturing out into the daylight after a long, terrifying night. Their faces, she sensed, were etched with a lingering fear, a residual unease from the days, weeks, months of unspoken dread. But now, as they saw them, and as the unspoken dread began to dissipate, a new emotion bloomed: a hesitant understanding, a dawning recognition of the silent battle that had been fought and won.

Karen Yen, a classmate, was the first to approach, her usually vibrant presence subdued, her eyes wide with a mixture of relief and concern as she took in Kayla's disheveled appearance. "Kayla! Oh, thank God you're alright!" Her voice, usually bright and clear, was now laced with a tremor. She reached out, her fingers brushing against Kayla's cheek. It was a gesture of pure, unadulterated maternal concern. Kayla could feel the faint warmth of her skin, the gentle pressure of her touch.

"I'm… I'm okay, Karen," Kayla managed, her voice raspy.

Karen's gaze flickered to the distant field, then back to Kayla, her brow furrowed with a question she seemed afraid to ask. The townspeople began to gather, their murmurs a soft chorus of hushed speculation. They saw Tommy and Kayla, figures of profound exhaustion, yet undeniably present, a stark embodiment of the invisible war that had raged. They saw the mud clinging to their clothes, the disarray of their hair, and the stillness in Kayla's eyes, a stillness that spoke volumes of what she had endured.

Mayor Thompson, his face a mask of paternal worry, joined them, his hand resting on Karen's shoulder. "Tommy, Kayla, we're so relieved. The whole town… we were beside ourselves. When the Withers Field finally went quiet… it was like a miracle. But no one knew what had happened. No one knew where you were." He looked at both of them, his gaze searching, as if trying to piece together the fragmented narrative of the night.

Kayla felt the collective weight of their gazes, the silent questions that hung in the air. She was the epicenter of their renewed peace, yet she was also an enigma, a figure shrouded in the very darkness they had been freed from. The victory was theirs, but the cost, the true cost, was hers alone to bear.

"The Withers and Ragmouth are gone," Kayla stated, her voice gaining a quiet strength. "They won't trouble Dry Creek again."

A collective sigh rippled through the gathered townsfolk. Relief, palpable and profound, washed over them. Mr. Henderson, his hand still a reassuring presence on her arm, offered a silent nod of support. Karen, her hands gently trying to brush away the dirt and debris from Kayla's clothes.

"We need to get you home," Karen said, her voice firm with a newfound resolve. "You've been through too much."

As they began to walk towards Kayla's home on the edge of town, the townsfolk fell into step with them, a silent procession of gratitude and awe. They cleared the path before her, their presence a subtle, guiding force. Kayla could feel them around her, a warm, protective circle. They sensed her impending blindness, the profound change that had come over her, but they didn't recoil. Instead, they drew closer, their unspoken support a tangible comfort.

The journey that had once been a familiar stroll through the heart of her community now felt like a pilgrimage. Each step was a deliberate navigation, a reliance on the sounds and the touch of those around her. The rhythmic crunch of boots on the dirt road, the murmur of voices, the gentle pressure of Karen's hand on her arm – these were the sensory threads that wove the fabric of her return.

She could sense the subtle shifts in the crowd, the way they instinctively parted to allow her passage. There were no words of grand pronouncements, no celebratory shouts. The victory was too raw, the cost too deeply felt. Their acknowledgment was in their presence, in their quiet reverence, in the way they created a space for her, a space where she could exist in her new reality.

As they reached her home, a small, weathered structure that had always been her sanctuary, a profound sense of both loss and belonging washed over her. This was home, the place she had fought to protect, but it was a home she would now experience in a way she had never imagined. Tommy gently guided her to the worn porch steps, his touch a reassuring presence.

"You just rest, Kayla," Tommy murmured, his voice soft with concern. "We'll take care of everything."

Kayla nodded, sinking onto the familiar wooden steps. The warmth of the rising sun, though unseen, seeped into her bones, a gentle benediction. She could hear the continued sounds of Dry Creek waking up, the symphony of a town that was, at last, truly at peace. And in the midst of that symphony, she found a fragile echo of her own lost world, a world she had saved, but which she would now have to learn to see anew. The silence of the Withers Field had been replaced by the silence of her sight, and the journey back to Dry Creek was not an end, but the beginning of a profoundly different path. The familiar sounds of her town, once a comforting backdrop, were now her lifeline, the whispers of a world she was determined to navigate, one sound, one touch, one breath at a time. The morning had dawned, and with it, a new reality for Kayla, a reality shaped by silence, resilience, and the unwavering support of a town that owed her more than words could ever convey.

The air in Dry Creek, once thick with a palpable dread, now carried a different kind of weight – the heavy, oppressive stillness of grief. The dawn had broken, painting the sky in hues of rose and gold, a stark, almost cruel contrast to the somber mood that had descended upon the town. It was a morning for waking, yes, but not to the usual cheerful clamor of a community reborn. This was a morning for reckoning, for the quiet, internal unraveling of a nightmare that had finally, irrevocably, ended.

The surviving teenagers, those who had been caught in the vortex of the Withers Field depravity, were not celebrated as heroes. Instead, they moved through the early hours like specters, their faces etched with a weariness far beyond their years. Their eyes, once bright with the untroubled innocence of youth, now held a haunted depth, a lingering shadow of the horrors they had witnessed, the atrocities they had barely escaped. They were the living testament to a darkness that had threatened to consume them, and the scars, though not always visible, ran deep, etched into their very souls. There was no bravado, no outward display of relief, only a profound, quiet trauma that had irrevocably altered their trajectories. They had faced the abyss, and the abyss had stared back, leaving an indelible mark.

Karen Yen, her earlier maternal concern for Kayla now tinged with a deeper understanding of the collective trauma, moved amongst the younger ones with a quiet competence. She offered no platitudes, no easy reassurances. Instead, her presence was a silent anchor, a steady hand in the storm. She brought blankets, warm drinks, and a steady, reassuring presence, her own exhaustion a silent testament to the ordeal. She had seen the terror in their eyes, the way they flinched at sudden noises, the way their breath hitched at the memory of the Withers chilling whispers. She knew that the physical wounds might heal, but the psychic damage would require a different kind of tending.

Mayor Thompson, his usual authoritative demeanor softened by a profound sorrow, stood on the steps of the town hall, his gaze sweeping over the subdued faces of his constituents. He felt the collective exhale of a town released from its torment, but this release was mingled with the bitter taste of loss. The unexplained disappearances, the brutal deaths that had plagued Dry Creek for so long, were no longer shrouded in mystery. The horrifying truth had been laid bare, a singular, catastrophic event that had finally silenced the whispers and the shadows. The Withers, the source of their torment, were gone, their reign of terror abruptly, violently, concluded. But the cost of their silence was immense.

The community began to convene in small, hushed groups, their conversations a low murmur of disbelief and sorrow. The initial shock of Tommy and Kayla's return, the miraculous cessation of the Withers influence, had given way to a somber reflection. Each missing person, each unexplained death, was now recontextualized, understood not as a tragic accident or a random act of violence, but as a direct consequence of the Withers malevolent presence. The theories that had circulated, the whispered speculations, now coalesced into a horrifying, undeniable truth. The town had been living under a curse, and that curse had been broken, but not without a terrible price.

The families of those who had been lost gathered together, their grief a silent, unifying force. They clung to each other, their shared pain a fragile shield against the overwhelming emptiness. There were no shouts of anger, no cries for vengeance. Just a profound, aching sadness that settled over the town like a shroud. The void left by the Withers was now filled with the specter of their victims, their faces, now understood, a constant reminder of what had been taken.

Old Mr. Hemlock, his weathered face a roadmap of a life lived under the sun and the stars, sat on his porch swing, the rhythmic creak of the chains a mournful cadence. He had known the Withers were different, had felt the unease that clung to their property like a second skin. But he had never imagined the depths of their depravity, the sheer, unadulterated evil that festered beneath their placid exterior. He looked towards Kayla's small house, a silent acknowledgment of the burden she carried, the immense strength she had possessed to face down such darkness. He understood that her sight had been taken in exchange for the town's survival, a sacrifice that would forever weigh upon her.

The immediate aftermath was not one of jubilant celebration, but of quiet, communal mourning. The brutal deaths, the chilling disappearances – they were finally understood, not as isolated tragedies, but as the grim, inevitable consequences of a single, terrifying confrontation. The surviving teenagers, their innocence irrevocably stolen, moved through the dawning hours like phantoms, their eyes vacant, their shoulders hunched as if bearing an invisible weight. They had brushed against the supernatural, stared into the eyes of true horror, and the experience had left them fundamentally changed, forever tethered to a darkness they had only just escaped.

The town, once a haven of quiet familiarity, was now a landscape scarred by trauma. The process of healing was not a swift or simple one; it was a slow, agonizing journey, a collective grappling with the profound sense of loss that permeated every street, every home. The silence that had once been a harbinger of the Withers dread was now a quiet, mournful hush, punctuated by the hushed whispers of disbelief and the choked sobs of those who had lost loved ones.

Karen Yen, her own exhaustion a heavy cloak, found herself tending not only to Kayla but to the needs of others who were impacted by the loss. She brought them food, wrapped them in blankets, and offered quiet words of comfort, though she knew that mere words could not erase the images seared into their minds. She saw the way they recoiled from touch, the way their eyes darted nervously towards the shadows, the way their laughter, once so easily evoked, had been silenced. Their innocence was a casualty of the Withers reign; a sacrifice made in the face of unimaginable evil.

Mayor Thompson, his voice thick with emotion, addressed the gathered townsfolk, his words a somber testament to the day's events. "We have faced a darkness, friends," he began, his gaze sweeping over the weary faces, "a darkness that threatened to consume us all. But we are still here. Dry Creek is still here. And though we mourn those we have lost, we must also remember the courage that has seen us through." He spoke of Tommy and Kayla, not as a victims, but as the silent guardian who had borne the brunt of the battle and Kayla's sacrifice a beacon in the encroaching night.

The town began the arduous task of piecing together the fragments of their shattered lives. The missing persons posters, once symbols of unanswered questions and gnawing uncertainty, now served as grim memorials. Each name, each face, was a stark reminder of the price of freedom from the Withers oppressive influence. The community, bound together by shared trauma, found solace in their unity, in the quiet understanding that passed between them. They were survivors, and their survival, however dearly bought, was a testament to their resilience.

The Withers property, the epicenter of the town's long-standing unease, now stood as a silent, derelict monument to the evil that had once resided there. No one ventured near it. The land itself seemed to hold its breath, the air around it unnaturally still, as if even the earth recoiled from the memory of what had transpired. The hushed discussions about what to do with the property, with the remnants of the Withers lives, were a constant undercurrent to the town's grief. It was a physical manifestation of their pain, a place they longed to forget but could never truly erase.

Kayla, in her new, silent world, became an unwitting focal point for the town's complex emotions. They saw her resilience, her quiet strength, and they also saw the profound loss she had endured. Her fading sight steamrolling towards blindness, a direct consequence of her victory, was a constant, poignant reminder of the battle waged and won. There was gratitude, immense and overwhelming, but it was a gratitude tempered by a deep, unsettling awareness of the cost. They owed her their lives, and that debt was a heavy one, a silent acknowledgment that would forever hang in the air between them.

Tommy, the only other surviving teenager, though physically unharmed, bore the invisible wounds of his encounter. He spoke little of what he had seen, his experience too profound, too horrific, to be easily articulated. He found solace in the company of other's, forming an unspoken bond forged in the crucible of shared terror. They were all the generation marked by the Withers, their youth overshadowed by a darkness that had threatened to swallow them whole. The town, in its collective grief, extended a quiet, supportive hand to these young survivors, recognizing that their healing would be a long and arduous process.

The days that followed were filled with a subdued rhythm, a slow return to normalcy that felt both welcome and deeply unsettling. The routines of life began to reassert themselves, but they were overlaid with a new awareness, a lingering sensitivity to the shadows, a profound appreciation for the simple, ordinary moments that had once been taken for granted. The creek still flowed, the birds still sang, but the soundscape of Dry Creek was now irrevocably altered, imbued with the echoes of a terrible truth.

The town's quiet reckoning was not a single event, but a protracted process of remembrance, of healing, and of rebuilding. It was a journey through grief, a collective acknowledgment of the darkness they had faced and the light that had, against all odds, prevailed. The scars remained, a permanent testament to the Withers reign of terror, but they also served as a reminder of the strength found in community, the resilience of the human spirit, and the extraordinary courage of a young woman who had seen the abyss and refused to be consumed by it. The silence that now permeated Dry Creek was a silence born of loss, but it was also a silence pregnant with the promise of a future, a future earned through sacrifice and an unyielding will to survive. The town had been broken, but it was slowly, painstakingly, beginning to mend. The ghosts of the Withers Field and the scarecrow Ragmouth might linger in the whispers of memory, but the living, the survivors, were determined to forge a new path forward, guided by the echoes of their ordeal, but not defined by it.

The Withers Field, a vast expanse that had once pulsed with a sentient, malevolent hunger, now lay under a different kind of shadow. The corn, a sea of dried stalks and brittle leaves, still whispered in the wind, but the whispers were no longer directed, no longer infused with the chilling intellect of the Withers. It was a sound of rustling emptiness, the dry exhalations of a season that had passed, leaving behind only the husks of its terrifying reality. The land itself seemed to recoil from its recent past, the very soil imbued with a residual unease that kept the townsfolk at bay. Even under the clearest, most benevolent sky, the field held an aura of profound disquiet, a silent testament to the horrors it had witnessed and, in some unholy way, facilitated.

No one ventured near it. The path leading to its edge, once worn by the occasional curious wanderer or the farmer checking his crops, had become overgrown, reclaimed by the wild growth that the Withers unnatural influence had, for a time, suppressed. The memories were too potent, too visceral. The laughter of children, the panicked screams, the guttural growls that had once echoed across this fertile ground were now ghosts that clung to the very air, invisible but deeply felt. The proximity alone was enough to prickle the skin, to send a shiver down the spine, to awaken a primal instinct that urged retreat. It was a place where the veil between worlds had been so brutally torn, and the fabric of reality still bore the ragged edges of that violent encounter.

At the heart of the field, where the very nexus of the Withers power had once resided, stood the scarecrow, Ragmouth. It was a crude thing, a mockery of protection, its burlap sack head crudely stitched and stuffed, its stick limbs adorned with the tattered remnants of clothing that had once belonged to the unfortunate souls it had been made to represent. Now, however, its form seemed altered, as if the sheer weight of the night's events had pressed down upon it, lending it a new, grim significance. It was no longer just a farmer's deterrent; it was a monument, a silent sentinel bearing witness to the grim ballet of terror and sacrifice that had unfolded there. Its presence was a stark, unblinking reminder of the cyclical nature of darkness, of the ancient pacts that could be forged in the shadows, and of the terrible price paid to sever them.

The cornstalks themselves, now bleached and brittle, stood like skeletal sentinels, their dry leaves rattling a mournful dirge with every passing breeze. They had once been the vibrant, pulsating body of the Withers terrible hunger, a living conduit for their insidious will. Now, they were merely the dead remnants of that life, their growth stunted, their vibrancy leached away, leaving behind only a hollow echo. It was a poignant symbol of the Withers own demise, their energy so thoroughly spent, so utterly extinguished, that even the very plants they had animated were left as mere shadows of their former selves. Yet, even in their decay, there was a disquieting stillness, a profound melancholic quietude that seemed to absorb any sound, any hint of cheerfulness, that dared to approach.

The townsfolk spoke of the field in hushed tones, their voices barely rising above a whisper, as if the very act of speaking too loudly might awaken something that had merely been lulled into a temporary slumber. The stories of that night, once fragmented and disbelieving, were now coalescing into a single, horrifying narrative, a testament to the unspeakable evil that had held their community captive. They remembered the unnatural silence that had preceded the storm, the way the sky had turned a bruised, sickly purple, the palpable sense of dread that had settled over Dry Creek like a shroud. And they remembered the chilling, almost guttural sounds that had emanated from the Withers property, sounds that no natural creature could have produced.

Kayla, though her sight is being extinguished little by little, possessed a different kind of vision now, an inner awareness that allowed her to perceive the lingering impressions left on the world. She could feel the echoes of the Withers presence, a cold, acrid residue that clung to the air, particularly strong when the wind blew from the direction of the cursed field. It was a sensation that never truly left her, a phantom limb of terror that twitched with every passing memory. She understood, with a clarity that transcended words, that the physical battle might be over, but the psychic scars remained, etched not only onto the survivors but onto the very land itself. The Withers Field was a wound, and like any deep wound, it would take time, and a great deal of careful tending, to ever truly heal.

The scarecrow Ragmouth, in particular, seemed to draw her inward gaze. It was more than just an effigy of straw and tattered cloth; it was a focal point, a repository of the night's accumulated despair. She could almost feel the unseen eyes that had once been fixed upon it, the terror it had instilled, the way it had been imbued with the Withers own perverse symbolism. It stood as a stark reminder of how easily innocence could be twisted, how readily the tools of protection could be perverted into instruments of fear. The burlap face, eternally fixed in a silent scream, seemed to embody the collective horror of all who had suffered under the Withers dominion. Its very stillness was a testament to the violence that had surrounded it, a chilling testament to the sacrifices made by those who had stood against the darkness.

The memory of the corn, no longer sentient but still unnervingly present, was a haunting one. It had been a living, breathing entity, its stalks swaying in unison, its rustling a constant, unnerving murmur that had spoken of an alien intelligence. Now, the dry stalks were brittle, sharp, and unforgiving. A careless brush against them could draw blood, a testament to the lingering, untamed wildness of the place. The ground beneath them was a treacherous terrain, littered with fallen stalks and unseen obstacles, a physical manifestation of the unseen dangers that still lurked in the periphery of the town's consciousness. It was a field that demanded respect, a respect born not of admiration, but of a deep, abiding fear.

The cycle of life and death, a natural order that usually brought solace and renewal, felt perverted in the Withers Field. The corn had died, yes, but its death was not a gentle fading. It was a violent cessation, a brutal silencing. The very earth seemed to hold its breath, reluctant to embrace the natural process of decay, as if the taint of the Withers presence was too profound to be easily washed away by rain or time. The remnants of the Withers lives – their tools, their unsettling belongings, the very foundations of their corrupted home – were all buried deep within that land, adding layers to its inherent unease.

The townsfolk, in their quiet discussions, often spoke of what should be done with the field. Some suggested it should be burned, the entire area cleansed by fire, hoping to purge the residual darkness. Others advocated for it to be left untouched, a natural monument to the tragedy, a stark warning to any who might consider venturing into similar paths of darkness. But there was no consensus, only a shared understanding that the land itself was irrevocably changed. It would forever bear the imprint of what had transpired, a chilling reminder that evil, once unleashed, left scars that ran deeper than the eye could see.

The scarecrow Ragmouth, a silent sentinel, stood as the ultimate embodiment of this enduring unease. It was a focal point for the collective memory, the silent witness to the night when the veil had thinned and the horrors had spilled forth. Its presence was a constant, nagging question: had they truly banished the Withers, or merely scattered their influence, their dark legacy left to fester in the very earth that had sustained them? The wind whistled through its ragged limbs, carrying with it a mournful sigh, a whisper that seemed to speak of unanswered questions, of the profound mystery that still shrouded the Withers and their terrifying reign.

Even the simplest tasks, like walking near the edge of town, became fraught with a heightened sense of awareness. The familiar landscape, once a source of comfort, now held a subtle undercurrent of dread. The wind rustling through distant trees could be mistaken for the whispers of the Withers, the shadows lengthening in the setting sun could be perceived as reaching tendrils of their ancient malevolence. The surviving teenagers, in particular, bore this burden most heavily. They saw the field in their dreams, reliving the terror, the helplessness, the sheer, unadulterated fear.

Sandy Miller, who was recovering from her close encounter with Ragmouth and fading sight found that her own internal landscape was still reeling from the events. She found herself watching the townsfolk's quiet interactions with the field. She saw the averted gazes, the hushed conversations, the way they instinctively crossed themselves when the subject was even broached. It was a community grappling with a trauma that transcended the physical, a collective wound that would take generations to truly understand, let alone heal. She knew that the Withers were gone, their physical manifestation vanquished, but the residue of their evil, the echoes of their reign, were imprinted on the very fabric of Dry Creek.

The Withers Field was a stark, unyielding reminder of that imprinted darkness. It was a place where the natural world had been perverted, where the very essence of life had been corrupted. The dried corn, standing sentinel, was a silent scream, a testament to the unnatural life that had once pulsed within its stalks. And the scarecrow, the grim effigy, stood as a monument to the sacrifices made, a silent promise that such darkness would never again be allowed to take root, or at least, that was the hope. But hope, as they were all learning, was a fragile thing, easily overshadowed by the enduring power of memory, and the lingering whispers of the Withers Field.

The silence that now enveloped the field was not a peaceful silence, but a charged one, thick with the memory of sound, with the ghost of a presence that had once dominated the landscape. It was a silence that demanded attention, that whispered of a history too terrible to be forgotten, too potent to be dismissed. The residents were left to carry this silence, to navigate the landscape of their lives forever altered by the darkness that had once held sway. The Withers were gone, but their field, their legacy, remained – a perpetual reminder of the night the ordinary world had cracked open, revealing the abyss that lay beneath. The scarecrow, eternally watching, seemed to embody the perpetual vigilance required to keep that abyss at bay, a silent guardian in a land forever marked by the echoes of its torment. The corn, in its brittle stillness, stood as a testament to a life unlived, a power that had been, and was no more, yet its memory, its chilling influence, continued to permeate the very air, a palpable testament to the enduring power of what had once been. The field remembered, and so did they.

The silence that had fallen over Dry Creek was not the gentle hush of slumber, but a taut, brittle quietude, like the moment before a scream. For Kayla, however, this silence was not an absence, but a canvas. Her world, once vibrant with the visual symphony of light and shadow, had been plunged into an eternal twilight, yet within that darkness, a new spectrum of perception had bloomed. The absence of sight had, paradoxically, sharpened her other senses to a degree that was both exhilarating and terrifying. Every rustle of the dried cornstalks in the Withers Field, once a mere whisper on the wind, now carried the distinct texture of brittle paper being torn, the faint grit of desiccated earth clinging to their skeletal frames. The wind itself was no longer just a force; it was a sculptor, tracing the contours of the land with invisible fingers, its breath carrying the subtle scent of decay and something else, something acrid and ancient, that clung to the air like a forgotten curse.

Kayla found herself attuned to a different kind of resonance, a subtle thrumming that emanated from the very soil. It wasn't the vibrant pulse of life, but the faint, insistent echo of what had been. The Withers Field, a place of unimaginable horror, had imprinted itself not just on the memories of the townsfolk, but on the very fabric of existence within its reach. She could feel it now, a cold, clammy residue that settled on her skin like dew, an almost palpable memory of the malevolent hunger that had once pulsed through the corn. It was not a conscious entity anymore, not a sentient threat reaching out, but rather a lingering impression, like the scent of smoke after a fire has been extinguished, or the phantom ache of a lost limb. This residual energy, this psychic stain, was strongest when the wind carried its breath from the direction of the field, a cold current that brushed against her awareness, raising the fine hairs on her arms.

Her intuition, once a gentle nudge, had become a roaring torrent. It was as if the universe, stripped of its visual clutter, had streamlined its communication, speaking directly to her in a language of pure feeling and innate knowing. She understood things without being told, sensed intentions before they were spoken, and navigated the world with a newfound certainty that baffled those around her. When someone approached, she didn't see them; she felt the subtle shift in the air pressure, the faint warmth radiating from their body, the almost imperceptible tremor in the ground beneath their feet. More than that, she could sense the emotional undercurrents, the anxieties, the hidden fears, the suppressed hopes that swirled beneath the surface of their everyday interactions. This heightened awareness, this uncanny perception, was both a gift and a burden, isolating her in a world that was no longer built for her particular brand of sight.

The scarecrow, that grim monument at the heart of the Withers domain, was a particularly potent focal point for this new perception. Even from a distance, she could feel its presence, a dark, brooding stillness that seemed to absorb sound and light. It was more than just straw and tattered cloth; it was a nexus of despair, a silent witness to the atrocities committed there. She could sense the phantom gaze of the Withers fixed upon it, the terror it had instilled, the twisted significance it had held in their unholy rituals. The burlap face, perpetually contorted in a silent scream, seemed to embody the collective horror of all who had suffered. Its stillness was not inertness, but a coiled tension, a testament to the violence that had once swirled around it, a silent promise of vigilance. Kayla felt drawn to it, not with the morbid curiosity of the sighted, but with a deep, unsettling empathy, as if the effigy's silent suffering resonated with a part of herself.

The memory of the corn, no longer a sentient entity but still a haunting presence, was a complex thing. She recalled the rustling, a constant, unnerving murmur that had spoken of an alien intelligence, a collective consciousness animated by an unseen malevolence. Now, the dry stalks were brittle, sharp, unforgiving. A careless brush against them, she imagined, would draw blood, a testament to the lingering wildness of the place, a primal energy that refused to be entirely tamed. The ground beneath them, she could feel, was a treacherous terrain, littered with unseen obstacles, a physical manifestation of the intangible dangers that still lurked in the periphery of Dry Creek's collective consciousness. It was a place that demanded respect, a respect born not of admiration, but of a deep-seated, primal fear.

She found herself replaying the events of that night, not through the lens of what she had seen, but through what she had *felt*. The panic, the guttural sounds, the chilling presence of the Withers – they were all imprinted on her being, not as visual memories, but as visceral sensations. The fear was a cold knot in her stomach, the desperation a tightness in her chest, the otherworldly sounds a vibration that resonated deep within her bones. She could feel the subtle shift in atmospheric pressure as the entity's power waxed and waned, the almost electric charge in the air just before its manifestations. Her blindness had peeled back layers of superficial perception, allowing her to touch the raw, unadulterated essence of the events.

The residents hushed conversations, their averted glances towards the Withers Field, were all part of a complex symphony that Kayla could now interpret. She felt their collective trauma, the shared burden of their memories. She understood their reluctance to speak openly, their fear of disturbing the uneasy peace that had settled over Dry Creek. Their unspoken anxieties were like faint tremors in her awareness, a constant reminder of the shadow that still lingered. She could sense the lingering whispers of the Withers in the very air, not as sounds, but as subtle shifts in temperature, as pockets of unnatural stillness, as an almost imperceptible weight pressing down on her senses.

It was a strange kind of clarity, born from the absence of sight. Kayla could no longer distinguish the subtle hues of a sunset or the intricate patterns of a spiderweb, but she could perceive the faint energetic trails left by living beings, the lingering emotional residue of past events, and the subtle distortions in the natural flow of energy that indicated something unnatural had occurred. The Withers Field was a scar on the landscape of reality, and Kayla, now attuned to these deeper currents, could feel the jagged edges of that wound, the subtle but persistent ache it sent through the world.

Her near blindness had become a conduit, not just for heightened senses, but for a deeper understanding of the subtle interconnectedness of all things. She could feel the earth breathing beneath her feet, the silent growth of roots, the slow, inexorable creep of moss on stone. These were not mere observations; they were shared experiences. The Withers influence had, for a time, disrupted this natural harmony, twisting life into something grotesque and unnatural. The land itself had suffered, and its pain, its struggle to regain equilibrium, was something Kayla could now perceive. The dried cornstalks, in their brittle stillness, were not just dead plants; they were a testament to a life forcibly extinguished, a vibrant energy violently suppressed.

The scarecrow Ragmouth, with its perpetual, silent scream, was a particularly potent symbol of this imbalance. Kayla felt its desolation, the hollowness within its straw-filled frame. It was a monument to suffering, a tangible manifestation of the darkness that had taken root. She could sense the lingering tendrils of the Withers perverse amusement, their twisted sense of artistry, that had gone into its creation. It was a piece of art born of terror, a sculpture of despair, and Kayla felt a profound sorrow for the inanimate object that had been forced to bear witness to such unspeakable horrors. Its stillness was a scream unheard, a plea for release that resonated deeply within her.

Her perception of the people had also shifted. Without the visual cues of expression, she relied more heavily on the subtle nuances of their voices, the rhythm of their breathing, the almost

326

imperceptible shifts in their body language that she could sense through the floorboards or the earth. She could detect the tremor of fear in Mrs. Gable's voice when she spoke of the field, the forced cheerfulness in young Tommy's attempts to discuss anything other than the recent events, the quiet weariness in Sheriff York's pronouncements. It was as if she had gained access to a hidden layer of reality, one that lay beneath the surface of polite conversation and outward appearances.

The memory of the Withers actual presence, while no longer a direct threat, was a pervasive hum in her awareness. It was like a discordant note in a symphony, a grating dissonance that could never be fully resolved. She could sense the lingering traces of their unnatural energy, a cold, metallic scent that would sometimes drift on the wind, a faint, almost imperceptible distortion in the air that her heightened senses could detect. It was a reminder that while the physical manifestations had been vanquished, the echoes of their evil, the psychic scars they had left behind, were far more persistent.

Kayla understood that her blindness had not been a punishment, but a transformative force. It had stripped away the superficial, forcing her to delve deeper, to find a new way of experiencing the world. The Withers Field was a testament to the fragility of the natural order, the ease with which it could be corrupted and perverted. But her own journey, her own newfound perceptions, were a testament to the resilience of life, to the human capacity to adapt and to find light even in the deepest darkness. She was a different kind of seer now, one who navigated the world not by sight, but by the intricate web of unseen energies and imprinted memories that surrounded them all. The silence of Dry Creek was, for Kayla, a symphony of echoes, a tapestry woven from the unseen threads of memory and emotion, and she was its most attentive listener. The field remained, a silent testament to the past, but for Kayla, it was also a canvas upon which the present, in all its nuanced, unseen glory, was painted.

The immediate, visceral terror had receded, leaving behind a more insidious, pervasive dread. Dry Creek, like a body recovering from a grievous wound, was attempting to knit itself back together, but the stitches were taut, the flesh still raw and sensitive. The days bled into one another with a muted, grey uniformity. The laughter of children, once a common sound, was now sporadic, their games hushed, their eyes darting nervously towards the edges of town, towards the Withers property. The silence that had descended was not one of peace, but of a collective, held breath, a community perpetually bracing for the next tremor.

Kayla, adrift in her world of heightened sensory input, felt this shift acutely. The townsfolk, those she could now 'read' with an unnerving precision, moved through their days with a new, cautious grace. Their interactions were tinged with a shared, unspoken understanding of the abyss they had skirted. She felt their relief, a thin, trembling veneer over a deep-seated anxiety. They looked at her, these people she navigated by the subtle rhythms of their heartbeats and the faint warmth of their presence, with a complex cocktail of emotions. There was awe, certainly, a reverence for the unseen battle she had waged and, crucially, won. But beneath that, she sensed a profound pity, an almost guilty acknowledgment of the price she had paid, of the vibrant world she had lost to grant them their fragile safety.

Her own world had become a landscape of nuances invisible to others. The faint metallic tang that sometimes ghosted on the wind, a residue of the Withers unnatural power, was a constant, subtle reminder of what had transpired. It was not the same as the lingering scent of smoke after a fire; this was a more insidious perfume, a whisper of corruption that clung to the very air. She learned to distinguish its subtle shifts, its momentary intensifications that coincided with certain atmospheric pressures or the direction of the prevailing wind. It was a phantom limb of the horror, an echo that refused to fade.

The Withers Field itself remained a focal point of this residual unease. Though the terrifying sentience that had animated it was gone, the land bore its scars. Kayla could feel it, a subtle wrongness in the soil, a muted ache that emanated from the earth. It was as if the very ground had been violated, its natural vitality leached away, leaving behind a sterile emptiness. The dry stalks, brittle and lifeless, were no longer just remnants of a harvest; they were tombstones, silent sentinels guarding a buried graveyard of unspeakable acts. She could sense their desiccated husks, their sharp edges, the way they rasped against each other in the slightest breeze, a sound that was less a whisper and more a dry, rasping exhalation.

The days were marked by subtle shifts in the ambient temperature, by the changing patterns of the wind's caress against her skin. Kayla learned to read these changes, to interpret them as a form of communication from the world around her. A sudden chill, a whisper of wind carrying that faint, metallic tang – these were not mere meteorological phenomena; they were echoes, faint but persistent, of the darkness that had once resided there. The silence of Dry Creek was no longer a void, but a complex symphony of these subtle resonances, a tapestry woven from the unseen threads of memory and emotion. And Kayla, in her profound darkness, was its most attentive listener, forever attuned to the fragile peace that held the town in its hesitant embrace. The memories of the Withers, though no longer a direct threat, were etched into the very fabric of Dry Creek, a permanent scar that served as a stark reminder of the darkness that could lie dormant, waiting to be awakened. This newfound awareness, this keen sensitivity to the unseen, was both a burden and a shield, a constant testament to the sacrifice that had been made. The silence, for Kayla, was not an absence of sound, but a presence of the unspoken, the unremembered, the profoundly felt.

Chapter 14

The Lingering Gaze

The biting chill of late autumn had settled over Dry Creek, stripping the skeletal branches of their last vestiges of foliage. Months had passed since the suffocating terror that had gripped the town had receded, leaving behind an aftermath that was less a clean wound and more a festering bruise. The collective exhale, once sharp with relief, had slowly morphed into a low, persistent hum of unease. Life, in its tenacious way, was attempting to reassert itself, but the shadows cast by the Withers property stretched longer, darker, than any seasonal twilight.

Kayla felt it most acutely. The silence that had descended after the ultimate confrontation was not a true silence. It was a layered thing, a delicate veneer of normalcy stretched taut over a bedrock of lingering fear. She could sense it in the way conversations would halt abruptly when the topic veered too close to the events of that harrowing season, in the quick, furtive glances cast towards the Withers land, even from a distance. The townsfolk, though they tried to project an image of resilience, carried the psychic scars of what had transpired. Their laughter was a shade less boisterous, their greetings a touch more hesitant. It was as if a vital spark had been dimmed, a collective light held back, afraid to fully ignite lest it attract unwanted attention from the darkness that still seemed to brood just beyond their periphery.

Then came the wind. It had always been a constant in Dry Creek, a rustling presence that whispered through the dry corn stalks and rattled the loose shutters of aging homes. But now, on certain nights, particularly when the wind rose to a mournful keen, a new element seemed to enter its song. It began subtly, a faint susurrus that could be easily dismissed as the natural symphony of a blustery evening. Yet, for those with ears tuned to the deeper frequencies of dread, it sounded like more.

Old Man Hemlock, his face a roadmap of decades etched by sun and hardship, was one of the first to voice it, albeit in hushed tones over a game of checkers at the general store. "Hear that, Jed?" he'd rasped, his voice barely audible above the clatter of the pieces. "Sounds like... voices. Like they're tryin' to say somethin'." Jed, a man whose stoicism was as thick as the winter fog, had merely grunted, his eyes fixed on the board, though Kayla, sensing the subtle tremor in his hand as he moved a checker, knew he'd heard it too.

These were not the clear, articulate whispers of conversation. They were fragments, distorted by distance and the wind's capriciousness. Sometimes, it sounded like a mournful lament, a drawn-out sigh of despair. Other times, it held a hint of the old, chilling malice, a guttural murmur that seemed to promise unspeakable things. It was the echo of the Gaze Offering, or at least, that's what many began to believe. Not the full, overwhelming presence, but a residual bleed, a phantom limb of its consciousness that still sought to interact with the living world.

Kayla, with her heightened awareness, felt these whispers not just as sounds, but as vibrations that resonated deep within her. They were like cold tendrils reaching out from the Withers property, probing the edges of the town's fragile peace. When the wind blew from that direction, carrying these phantom voices, she could feel a prickling sensation on her skin, a subtle shift in the air pressure that felt like a caress from something ancient and malevolent. It wasn't a physical touch, but an imprint, a spectral residue that lingered long after the wind had died down.

The residents, their collective memory still reeling from the visceral terror, found these phantom whispers particularly insidious. They had fought a tangible enemy, a horrifying manifestation of the Withers dark legacy. They had witnessed the impossible, endured the unbearable, and emerged, they thought, victorious. But these whispers suggested otherwise. They hinted that the entity, the consciousness that had animated the Withers land, might not have been truly vanquished, but merely dormant, its influence still capable of seeping into their reality.

It was a terrifying thought. The relief that had washed over Dry Creek in the immediate aftermath of the confrontation had been profound, an almost intoxicating freedom from the omnipresent dread. But now, these whispers threatened to unravel that hard-won peace. They were like a slow poison, a constant, subtle reminder that the darkness had not been fully exorcised, that a part of it, however diminished, might still be listening, still waiting.

Sheriff York tried to dismiss the claims. "It's just the wind, folks," he'd say, his voice weary but firm. "This old valley plays tricks on your ears when it gets blow'n. We've all been through a lot. Our minds are playing catch-up, tryin' to make sense of things." But even he, Kayla sensed, didn't entirely believe his own words. She could feel the subtle tremor of doubt in his voice, the way his focus would sometimes drift, as if he too were straining to hear something just beyond the realm of ordinary perception. His attempts to maintain order, to project an image of unwavering strength, were becoming increasingly strained, like a dam under immense pressure.

The Withers Field itself remained a stark, desolate monument to the horror. Even months later, it was a place that the townsfolk instinctively avoided. The dry, brittle stalks, bleached white by the sun and wind, were like a field of skeletal fingers, forever reaching towards the sky in silent supplication or accusation. Kayla could feel its emptiness, a hollow ache that emanated from the very earth. It was a palpable absence of life, a void where something unnatural had once thrived. The scent, that faint, metallic tang that had once permeated the air, was still there on particularly still days, a ghostly perfume that spoke of corruption.

One evening, as a particularly strong gale whipped through the town, rattling windows and sending dust devils skittering across the unpaved roads, Kayla found herself drawn to the edge of her property. She couldn't see the Withers Field from here, but she could feel the wind's direction. It was coming from that way, carrying its mournful song. And within that song, she could discern it more clearly than ever before.

It wasn't a single voice, but a chorus of whispers, faint and ethereal, like the rustling of dry leaves amplified a thousandfold. They spoke of an unbearable loneliness, of a gnawing emptiness. But woven through this lament was something else, something colder, more predatory. It was the faintest hint of a question, a seeking, as if the entity were trying to re-establish a connection, to find a familiar anchor in the living world.

Kayla closed her eyes, focusing her other senses. She felt the cold seeping into her bones, the way the wind tugged at her clothes, the distant hoot of an owl. But beneath it all, like an unwelcome guest at a somber feast, was the presence of those whispers. They seemed to weave through the very fabric of the night, a disquieting reminder that the ultimate victory might have been more of a temporary reprieve.

She thought of the Withers, their twisted forms, their eyes that held an ancient, vacant hunger. Had they been mere vessels? Had the true power resided in the land itself, in the very essence of what they had cultivated? The whispers seemed to suggest a similar consciousness, a disembodied awareness that was seeking something, anything, to latch onto.

Mrs. Gable, her voice still carrying a faint tremor that Kayla could feel in the very foundations of her house when she visited, had mentioned something similar. "It's like a dream, Kayla," she'd confided, her hand trembling as she reached for a cup of tea. "A bad dream that you can't quite wake up from. You hear it, you feel it, even when everything seems normal." Kayla understood. The whispers were the auditory manifestation of that lingering dread, the subtle intrusion of the supernatural into the mundane.

The days that followed were punctuated by these unsettling wind-borne murmurs. They became a new kind of folklore in Dry Creek, whispered conversations over fences, furtive glances towards the horizon. Children, who had begun to tentatively resume their games, now sometimes stopped, heads cocked, listening to the wind with wide, fearful eyes. Parents would quickly pull them inside, their own anxieties amplified by their children's reactions.

Kayla found herself increasingly sensitive to these sounds. She would lie awake at night, her body tense, listening to the wind's mournful song. It was a constant, low-level hum of fear that permeated the town. She could feel the collective anxiety of the townsfolk, a palpable wave that rose and fell with the intensity of the wind. They were holding their breath, waiting for the whispers to coalesce into something more, something undeniable, something that would drag them back into the nightmare.

The subtle shifts in the wind became markers of her own unease. A gentle breeze might carry only the familiar scent of pine and damp earth. But when the wind picked up, drawing from the west, from the direction of the Withers land, it would carry that faint, almost imperceptible whisper. It was like a faint static on a radio, a hint of a signal that was just out of reach, just beyond comprehension.

One particularly still afternoon, after a night of strong winds, Kayla felt a peculiar stillness in the air. The usual rustling of leaves was absent. The distant sounds of life seemed muted. It was a heavy, expectant silence, the kind that precedes a storm. And in that profound quiet, she heard it again, not on the wind this time, but as if emanating from the very ground beneath her feet. It was a low, resonant hum, a vibration that spoke of deep, buried things stirring.

She imagined the dry stalks in the Withers Field, their brittle forms swaying almost imperceptibly in the absence of any breeze. Were they, in their desiccated state, acting as conduits? Were they still somehow connected to the residual consciousness that had once animated them? The thought sent a shiver down her spine. The whispers on the wind, she realized, were not just auditory hallucinations. They were a symptom of something more profound, a subtle yet undeniable indication that the Gaze Offering's influence, however diminished, had not been extinguished. It had merely retreated, like a predator to its den, waiting for the opportune moment to emerge again, its whispers carried on the very breath of the land. The peace of Dry Creek was a fragile illusion, and the wind, on those particular nights, was the unseen hand that threatened to tear it asunder. The memory of the Withers, and the horrors they had unleashed, was not fading; it was merely changing its form,

335

becoming a whisper on the wind, a chill in the air, a constant reminder of the darkness that lay dormant, waiting.

Kayla's vigil was a solitary, silent ritual. The sun, a pale disk in the perpetually bruised sky of late autumn, offered little warmth, and the biting wind that had begun to scour Dry Creek seemed to carry whispers of its own, a chilling prelude to the deeper murmurs that plagued the town. She moved through her days with a quiet deliberation, her senses honed to a razor's edge, a silent sentinel on the periphery of a town desperately trying to forget. Her blindness, once a profound vulnerability, had become an unexpected advantage, forcing an introspection, a deepening of her connection to the subtler currents of existence. Without the constant barrage of visual input, the world revealed itself to her in other ways: the tremor of a floorboard beneath a hurried footstep, the almost imperceptible shift in air temperature that signaled a presence, the rhythmic pulse of life that emanated from each living thing.

She felt Dry Creek's unease like a phantom limb, a throbbing ache that resonated within her own being. The townsfolk, while outwardly attempting to reclaim normalcy, carried a palpable tension, a collective breath held too long. Their laughter, when it erupted, was often brittle, the sound catching in their throats as if afraid to fully release, lest it be misinterpreted, or worse, answered. Kayla could sense the furtive glances cast towards the Withers abandoned property, a subconscious scanning of the horizon, an involuntary check to ensure that the darkness hadn't begun to creep back. These were not the confident, assessing gazes of everyday life, but sharp, nervous darts, flickers of apprehension that betrayed the fragile peace they so desperately clung to.

Her blindness had paradoxically sharpened her perception of the residual energy that still clung to the Withers land like a shroud. She felt it most acutely on days when the wind blew from the west, the direction of the desolate fields. It was a subtle pressure against her senses, a faint, almost subliminal hum that vibrated at the edge of her awareness. It wasn't a sound in the conventional sense, but a sensation, like the low thrum of a distant engine that never quite reached the ears, yet made its presence known through an unsettling resonance in the bones. This hum was the lingering echo of the entity's consciousness, a spectral residue that permeated the very air.

She spent hours sitting by her window, not to see, but to listen to the wind's shifting moods. When it was a gentle sigh through the skeletal branches of the oak outside her home, it carried only the familiar scents of damp earth and decaying leaves. But when it rose to a keening wail, a mournful lament that seemed to scour the very soul of the valley, it also carried those fainter, more disturbing undertones. These were not the coherent voices that Old Man Hemlock had described, the ones that seemed to mimic speech. These were more primal, more elemental – fragmented feelings, raw emotions transmuted into ethereal vibrations. Loneliness, an abyss of it, so profound it threatened to swallow her whole. But intertwined with it, like dark threads in a tapestry of despair, were flickers of an ancient, predatory hunger, a yearning that was both terrifying and chillingly patient.

Kayla felt an overwhelming responsibility to be the first to detect any resurgence, any shift from mere lingering presence to active resurgence. Her blindness forced her into this role; she couldn't afford to be distracted by the mundane, by the visual cues that might lead others astray. She had to rely on the deeper currents, the seismic shifts in the town's psychic landscape. It was a lonely vigil, a constant state of heightened awareness that left her perpetually on edge, her nerves frayed like overstretched wires.

She would walk through the quiet streets of Dry Creek, her cane tapping a rhythmic counterpoint to the town's subdued pulse. She navigated by sound and by the subtle changes in the terrain, her other senses weaving a detailed map of her surroundings. She could feel the warmth radiating from houses where families were gathered, the faint scent of woodsmoke and cooking food a comforting anchor in the encroaching chill. But she could also sense the emptiness of houses where the lingering fear had driven residents to seek solace elsewhere, their silence a gaping wound in the town's fabric. These were the places that felt coldest, the ones where the residual energy seemed to gather and coalesce.

The Withers Field, even in her mind's eye, remained a scar upon the landscape. Months had passed, yet the memory of its unnatural vitality, its insatiable hunger, was etched deeply into the collective consciousness of Dry Creek. The withered stalks, skeletal and brittle, were like a silent testament to the horrors that had transpired. Kayla could sense the lingering emptiness of that place, a void that seemed to draw in the very light and warmth from its surroundings. On still days, she imagined she could still detect that faint, metallic tang in the air, a ghost of the corruption that had once flourished there.

One evening, as a particularly potent gust of wind rattled the windows of her small home, Kayla found herself drawn to the edge of her property. She couldn't see the Withers land, but she could feel the wind's trajectory, its insistent push from the west. And with it came those fragmented vibrations, stronger tonight than they had been in weeks. It was as if the wind itself was imbued with a phantom sentience, carrying the unformed thoughts and desperate longings of something that refused to fade.

She stood there, her hands clasped tightly, her body tensed, listening. The whispers were not distinct words, but a symphony of desolation, a chorus of yearning that seemed to scrape against her very soul. There was an unbearable loneliness woven into the very fabric of these ethereal sounds, a void so vast it felt like a physical presence pressing in on her. Yet, beneath this lament, there was something else – a flicker of the old, malevolent awareness, a subtle, searching quality, as if the entity were trying to re-establish a connection, to find a familiar anchor in the living world.

She felt a prickling sensation on her skin, not from the cold, but from the sheer intensity of the psychic energy that the wind carried. It was a sensation akin to being watched, to being perceived by something that existed outside the normal spectrum of human interaction. Her blindness, which had once been a source of fear and isolation, now felt like a shield, allowing her to perceive the invisible currents that flowed beneath the surface of reality.

The days that followed were punctuated by these unsettling murmurs carried on the wind. They became a new kind of folklore in Dry Creek, whispered conversations over picket fences, furtive glances cast towards the western horizon. Children, who had begun to tentatively resume their games in the sun-dappled yards, would sometimes stop abruptly, their heads cocked, listening to the wind with wide, fearful eyes. Their parents, their own anxieties amplified by their children's reactions, would quickly pull them indoors, their reassurances laced with an unspoken dread.

She closed her eyes, focusing her intent, trying to pinpoint the source of this unsettling vibration. It felt primal, elemental, as if the earth itself were groaning under some immense, unseen pressure. She imagined the dry, brittle stalks in the Withers Field, their desiccated forms swaying almost imperceptibly in the absence of any breeze, their skeletal fingers reaching towards the heavens. Were they, in their withered state, acting as conduits? Were they still somehow connected to the residual consciousness that had once animated them, their brittle forms acting as antennae for its spectral reach? The thought sent a shiver down her spine, a cold dread that had nothing to do with the autumn air.

Her vigilance was not an act of choice, but of necessity, a burden she carried with a stoic resolve. She was the town's unwitting early warning system, her heightened senses a desperate defense against a threat that most refused to acknowledge, or were too terrified to confront. She felt the weight of this responsibility press down on her, a heavy cloak of dread that clung to her even in the quietest moments. Her world, now a landscape perceived through sound and sensation, was also a landscape fraught with unseen dangers, a constant reminder of the permeable boundary between their reality and the one that had almost consumed them.

The subtle tremors she felt beneath her feet were not seismic, but psychic. They were the earth's own anxieties, its subtle tremors of awareness that something ancient and hungry was stirring within its depths. She would often find herself instinctively reaching out with her senses, trying to trace the source of these vibrations, to map the invisible currents of energy that flowed through Dry Creek. It was a dangerous endeavor, a constant probing into the heart of the darkness that had once held them captive, but she could not stop herself. The knowledge that she was the only one truly attuned to these subtle shifts compelled her forward, her internal compass always pointing towards the lingering shadows.

She imagined the fields, barren and windswept, as a vast, receptive surface, soaking in the lingering malevolence like a thirsty sponge. The very air around the Withers property felt different, heavier, charged with an unseen static. Even from a distance, even without the ability to see, she could feel its oppressive presence, a gravitational pull that drew her thoughts, her very essence, towards it. It was a place that time had not healed, but merely scarred, leaving behind a wound that festered and bled unseen energies.

The Dry Creek citizens, in their desperate attempts to move forward, often dismissed the subtle signs. They attributed the strange occurrences to the weather, to the natural rhythms of a valley that had always been prone to peculiar atmospheric phenomena. But Kayla knew better. She could feel the subtle discordance, the way the natural world itself seemed to hold its breath in the presence of that lingering unnaturalness. The birdsong was often muted when the wind blew from the west, their usual cheerful chirping replaced by a hushed silence, as if they too sensed the encroaching gloom.

Her nights were a tapestry of disturbed sleep; her dreams filled with fragmented images and echoing whispers. She would wake in a cold sweat, the phantom touch of the Gaze Offering's influence still clinging to her, the lingering sense of being watched, of being perceived by something ancient and unforgiving. The physical manifestation of the Withers, their horrifying appearance, was not what haunted her sleep. It was the unseen, the intangible, the lingering echo of their power, the subtle yet persistent encroachment of the supernatural into the quiet normalcy of Dry Creek.

She was the silent guardian, the one who listened when others could not, who felt when others were numb. Her blindness had stripped away the superficial, forcing her to confront the deeper truths of existence, truths that the sighted inhabitants of Dry Creek desperately tried to ignore. And in that confrontation, she had found a grim strength, a resolve born of necessity. She would continue her vigil, her senses her only weapon, her vigilance a silent vow to the memory of those lost, and to the fragile peace of Dry Creek. She was the watcher in the encroaching twilight, the one who felt the tremors from the earth, the one who heard the whispers on the wind, the one who remained awake while the rest of the town slept, oblivious to the lingering gaze that still watched from the shadows.

The scarecrow in the Withers Field had, in the interim, transformed from a grotesque effigy of horror into something far more potent: a landmark of dread, a whispered cautionary tale woven into the very fabric of Dry Creek's nascent folklore. It stood, a skeletal sentinel against the perpetually muted sky, a gaunt reminder of the precipice upon which the town had teetered. Its tattered straw innards, perpetually leaking their dry husk, were like the unraveling threads of memory, each one a whisper of the unspeakable. No longer was it just a figure of cloth and straw; it was the embodiment of the fear that had gripped them, a tangible manifestation of the darkness they had narrowly escaped. The children, those who dared to venture close enough to catch a glimpse through the encroaching gloom, were warned not with tales of its monstrous capabilities, for the physical entity was gone, banished by means none could fully articulate, but with the weight of tragedy.

It was a warning etched not in the language of monsters, but in the hushed tones reserved for profound loss, for moments that irrevocably altered the course of a community. The field itself was a muted canvas, the soil still bearing the faint, almost imperceptible taint of what had been cultivated there. The scarecrow, perched precariously on its gnarled pole, served as a grim monument, a constant, visual admonition against forgetting. Its very stillness, the way its empty sleeves hung limply as if perpetually reaching for something lost, spoke volumes. The townsfolk would point it out, not with the morbid fascination of those who reveled in the macabre, but with a solemn reverence. "See there?" they might say to a curious newcomer, their voices tinged with a gravity that belied the apparent simplicity of the gesture. "That's where it all... changed."

For Kayla, the scarecrow was an anchor, a fixed point in the swirling currents of her heightened perception. Even without sight, she could feel its presence, a subtle distortion in the atmospheric pressure, a faint vibration that resonated with the residual energies of the Withers land. It was as if the object itself, imbued with so much concentrated fear and suffering, had become a focal point for the lingering malevolence. Its form, though no longer animated by the ancient hunger, was a beacon, a silent testament to the proximity of that hunger. She could sense the wind rustling through its worn fabric, a sound that was distinct from the whisper of the wheat, a harsher, more brittle rustle that spoke of unnatural permanence. It was a sound that held no natural melody, only the echo of a desecrated peace.

The warnings directed at the children were, in Kayla's estimation, entirely appropriate. It wasn't about shielding them from an immediate physical threat, but about imprinting upon their young minds the gravity of what had transpired. They needed to understand that the Withers Field was not merely a plot of land, but a scar on the valley, a place where the veil between their world and something far more ancient and terrifying had been dangerously thin. The scarecrow, in its silent vigil, served this purpose with chilling efficacy. It was a visual representation of a wound that, while closed, had left behind an indelible mark. The fear it evoked was not a primal, instinctive terror of sharp teeth or grasping claws, but a deeper, more existential dread—the fear of what could happen when the ordinary warped into the horrific, when the familiar landscape became a hunting ground for forces beyond comprehension.

Mrs. Gable, her voice still reedy with a lingering fragility, had once described her youngest son, little Bobby, standing at the edge of their porch, staring intently towards the Withers land. "He just... he just pointed," she'd recounted, her eyes wide with a remembered terror. "He didn't say anything, Kayla. Just pointed. And I knew. I knew he was looking at... at *it*." Kayla understood. The scarecrow, even from a distance, exerted a pull, a morbid curiosity that was amplified by the hushed warnings and the unspoken history. It was the child's nascent awareness of the profound tragedy, an intuitive recognition of a place where something fundamentally wrong had occurred. The scarecrow was the silent narrator of that wrongness.

The conversations amongst the adults, when they dared to speak of the field, often revolved around the scarecrow. It was a shorthand, a discreet way of referring to the lingering unease that permeated

Dry Creek. "The wind's picking up from the west again," someone might say, their gaze drifting unconsciously towards the silhouette on the horizon. "Hope it doesn't get too bad out by the old Withers place. That scarecrow... gives me the creeps just thinking about it." It was a shared acknowledgment, a collective nod to the shadow that still stretched long from that desolate patch of earth. The scarecrow was the tangible manifestation of that shadow, the silent guardian of a darkness that had not entirely receded.

Kayla, in her solitary contemplation, often felt the presence of the scarecrow more acutely than anyone else. Without the distraction of visual input, her other senses were attuned to its subtle emanations. She could sense the dry, papery rustle of the straw that constituted its body, a sound that was both mournful and strangely resonant with the earth from which it sprouted. She could feel the subtle shift in the air currents as they swirled around its worn fabric, a disturbance that was unique, distinct from the natural ebb and flow of the wind. It was as if the scarecrow itself possessed a lingering sentience, a spectral echo of the consciousness it had once served to ward off. It was a sentinel, yes, but also a tombstone, marking the grave of a horrific chapter, a chapter that the town desperately wished to seal, but could not entirely forget.

The legend of the scarecrow had, ironically, become a form of protection. It served as a potent deterrent, not just for the children, but for anyone who harbored even a flicker of doubt about the town's fragile recovery. The Withers Field was no-man's-land, a place where the boundaries of reality had been irrevocably blurred, and the scarecrow was its stark, unblinking sentinel. It was a symbol of their near-destruction, a testament to the horrors they had endured, and in its enduring, desolate presence, a quiet promise of their eventual, hard-won salvation. The fear it instilled was a necessary component of that salvation, a stark reminder of the price of vigilance, of the vigilance required to keep such darkness at bay.

The story of the scarecrow had evolved. It was no longer just a prop in the horrific drama that had unfolded; it had become a character in its own right, a silent, brooding presence that dominated the periphery of the town's collective consciousness. Its tattered form was a roadmap of the terror, each ripped seam a testament to the violence that had once been unleashed. The townsfolk, in their quiet conversations, in their guarded glances, had imbued it with a kind of spectral life, a lingering awareness that transcended its inanimate composition. It was the shadow of a shadow, a testament to the indelible nature of the trauma.

Kayla often found herself "listening" to the scarecrow. She'd sit by her window, her sightless eyes turned towards the west and try to discern the subtle nuances of its presence in the wind. When the breeze was gentle, it carried a soft, almost sighing rustle, a mournful sound that spoke of the straw's dry decay. But when the wind grew stronger, when it gusted from the direction of the Withers land, the sound changed. It became a harsher, more abrasive whisper, a dry scraping that seemed to claw at the edges of her hearing. This was the sound of the scarecrow, she believed, speaking in the language of its own desolation, a language that resonated with the lingering fear in the town.

The children's fear was a natural, instinctive response. They were more attuned to the subtler currents, the psychic residue that clung to the land. Their parents, however, had instilled a more reasoned fear, a fear born of shared trauma and the desire to protect their offspring from the unspoken horrors. "Don't go near the Withers Field, sweetheart," they'd say, their voices tight with suppressed anxiety. "It's not a good place. It's where... where bad things happened." And in that simple, yet profound, statement, the scarecrow stood as the silent, omnipresent symbol of those bad things. It was the visual locus of their collective unease, the silent witness to a past they could not erase.

The nights had become a torment, a canvas upon which Kayla's subconscious painted scenes of profound disquiet. Sleep, once a sanctuary, now offered only fleeting respite before the insidious tendrils of the Withers Field began to ensnare her. She would drift into a state of troubled slumber, only to find herself once more on the periphery of that blighted land, the air thick with an unnatural stillness. The wind, a constant companion in her waking hours, seemed to hold its breath here, creating a vacuum that pulled at her very being. And always, dominating the landscape, was the scarecrow.

In these nocturnal visitations, its presence was amplified, its silent vigil transformed into something far more menacing. The tattered straw, usually a testament to decay, now seemed to pulse with a dormant energy. The vacant button eyes, those dull, lifeless discs that had once been the focal point of her dread, had begun to change. They no longer appeared simply empty, a void where sight should be. Instead, they seemed to possess a faint, internal luminescence, a cold, patient anticipation that chilled Kayla to the bone. It was as if the button eyes were not merely reflecting the absence of stolen sight, but were themselves windows into a waiting darkness, a dormant consciousness that observed, that *waited*.

She would stand, rooted to the spot in these dreamscapes, her other senses sharpening to compensate for the visual void. She could feel the subtle vibration of the earth beneath her feet, a low thrum that seemed to emanate from the very soil of the Withers Field. It was a rhythm unlike anything natural, a pulse that beat with an ancient, unhurried cadence. The straw stuffing of the scarecrow, which she had always perceived as a dry, brittle rustle, now seemed to murmur, a sound like dry leaves skittering across frozen ground, but laced with an unsettling intelligibility. It wasn't words, not in any human tongue, but a complex symphony of whispers, a language of despair and unending hunger.

The scarecrow's rags, so familiar in their faded hues, appeared to shift and writhe in the dim, dreamlike light, as if animated by an unseen force. The frayed edges of its coat seemed to reach out, not with aggression, but with an unnerving beckoning. The silhouette, always stark against the sky, now seemed to possess a subtle curvature, a hunching of the shoulders that spoke not of decay, but of coiled readiness. It was the posture of a predator, not actively hunting, but patiently observing its territory, waiting for the opportune moment to strike.

The dreams weren't violent, not in the way she might have expected. There were no sudden attacks, no physical manifestations of the horror she had sensed in the waking world. Instead, the terror was insidious, a creeping dread that seeped into her very soul. It was the overwhelming certainty that the ritual, the desperate act that had seemingly banished the entity, had not been a definitive victory. The whispers in her dreams grew louder, coalescing into a single, chilling question that echoed through the dreamscape:

Was it truly gone, or merely dormant?

Kayla would wake with a gasp, her heart hammering against her ribs, the phantom sensations of the dream clinging to her like grave-dirt. The silence of her own room, usually a comfort, now seemed to mock her with its emptiness, amplifying the echoes of the scarecrow's murmuring. She would lie in the darkness, her mind racing, replaying the unsettling details of her dreams. The scarecrow this time had button eyes, those vacant discs stood out as the most persistent image. They seemed to hold an uncanny depth, a silent, knowing gaze that probed the very core of her being. They were not the eyes of a victim, nor the empty gaze of a mere effigy. They were the eyes of something that *saw*, something that *waited*.

She began to question the very nature of the entity, the force that had been so intimately connected with the Withers and their horrifying practices. Had the ritual truly destroyed it, or had it merely forced a transformation, a retreat into a deeper, more patient state of being? The idea that the entity had been appeased, its hunger momentarily sated, only to slumber in the fertile darkness of the Withers Field, waiting for another chance, was a terrifying prospect. The scarecrow, in her dreams, was the physical manifestation of this dormant power, a vessel holding its breath, its patience as vast and unsettling as the earth it stood upon.

These nightly visions weren't random nightmares; they felt like transmissions, subtle communications from a consciousness that refused to be extinguished. Kayla, with her heightened sensitivities, was a receptive audience, an unwitting recipient of these disquieting messages. The scarecrow, in its quiet endurance, was more than just a symbol of past horrors; it was becoming a living conduit, a silent oracle whispering of a potential future.

She would try to ground herself, to cling to the reality she knew. She would focus on the familiar sounds of Dry Creek waking up – the distant crow of a rooster, the rumble of an early truck, the murmur of neighbors starting their day. But even these comforting sounds seemed to carry a faint undertone of the dread that permeated her dreams. The scarecrow's gaze, even in her waking thoughts, felt palpable, a persistent, unwavering stare from the horizon.

The memory of the Withers themselves, their twisted devotion and their chilling rituals, resurfaced with uncomfortable clarity. She recalled the hushed conversations, the fragmented tales of their experiments, their attempts to harness something ancient and terrible. Had they succeeded, even for a fleeting moment? Had they indeed managed to bind an entity to their will, to their land? And if so, what had become of that bond when the Withers were gone?

The scarecrow, a silent witness to their atrocities, seemed to have absorbed the essence of their transgression. Its tattered form was not merely a deterrent, but a repository, a monument to the dark magic that had once held Dry Creek in its thrall. And now, in Kayla's dreams, it was beginning to stir. The vacant button eyes, once symbols of lifelessness, now held a glint, a spark of malevolent awareness that suggested the true horror was not in what had been done, but in what could *still* be done.

She found herself poring over the fragmented accounts of the Withers demise, searching for any detail, any nuance that might shed light on the entity's fate. The official narrative spoke of a tragic accident, a fire that had consumed the farmhouse and its inhabitants. But there were whispers, too, darker undertones that hinted at something more, something that the fire had failed to purge. Had the entity, in its final moments, found a new vessel, a new way to endure?

The afternoon had settled into that peculiar stillness that often precedes a storm, though the sky above Dry Creek remained a placid, almost indifferent blue. Kayla sat by the bay window, the familiar pattern of sunlight on the polished wood floor offering a comforting, if temporary, anchor. She traced the grain with a fingertip, a small, unconscious gesture of normalcy. The world outside her window was a familiar tapestry of green lawns, sun-dappled trees, and the distant, reassuring outline of the town. Yet, beneath the surface of this ordinary tableau, a disquiet was beginning to stir, a subtle vibration that resonated with the unease that had become Kayla's constant companion.

It began not with a sound, nor a sudden shift in the atmosphere, but with a feeling. A prickling sensation at the nape of her neck, a subtle tightening in the air around her, like the almost imperceptible pressure change just before lightning strikes. It was an ancient instinct, a primal alarm bell that had long since learned to sound in her presence. She couldn't see, of course. Her world remained a landscape of shadows and impressions, of the intangible rather than the visible. But this was not a shadow cast by the sun, nor a pressure exerted by the wind. This was something else entirely.

It was the distinct, undeniable sensation of being observed.

The feeling was not the direct, accusatory stare she had experienced before, the one that seemed to bore into her very soul from the withered form of the scarecrow. That was a physical, albeit supernatural, manifestation. This was different. It was more diffuse, more ambient, as if the very air had developed an awareness. It was a sensation of being peripherally perceived, an intrusion into her inner space by an unseen, intangible consciousness. It was as if the darkness that often clouded her vision had, for a fleeting, terrifying moment, become a lens through which something else was looking *out*.

Kayla remained perfectly still, her breath held captive in her chest. Her mind, ever vigilant, began to catalog the sensory input, or rather, the lack thereof. No creak of floorboards. No shift in the ambient temperature that might suggest movement within the house. No rustle of fabric. The silence was profound, broken only by the rhythmic ticking of the grandfather clock in the hall, a steady, mundane beat against the rising tide of her fear.

Yet, the feeling persisted, growing stronger, more insistent. It wasn't the terrifying certainty of immediate danger, but something far more insidious: the chilling confirmation of continued attention. It was the quiet, unwavering observation of something that had not moved on, something that was still present, still *watching*. It was the understanding that the entity, whatever it was, was not merely a thing of the past, a spectral echo of the Withers dark deeds. It was an active participant, a silent, unseen player in the ongoing drama of her life.

She tried to rationalize it, to dismiss it as a lingering effect of her nightmares, a phantom limb of her terror. But the feeling was too distinct, too deeply rooted in a sense that went beyond the purely visual. It was a profound, unnerving certainty that she was not alone, not truly. It was the knowledge that her sanctuary, her carefully constructed reality, was being permeable to an alien awareness.

The feeling intensified, morphing from a general sense of being watched to a more specific, targeted observation. It was as if a thousand invisible eyes were now focused solely on her, probing the depths of her consciousness, assessing her vulnerabilities. She imagined it as a palpable pressure, a subtle but persistent weight pressing in on her from all sides, a phantom touch that left her skin crawling. It was the sensation of being a specimen under a microscope, her every thought, her every heartbeat, being meticulously recorded.

Kayla closed her eyes tighter, as if by doing so she could somehow shut out this unseen observer. But it was a futile gesture. The absence of sight did not diminish the terrifying clarity of this awareness. If anything, it amplified it. Without the distraction of visual input, her other senses, already finely tuned, became hyper-receptive to this subtle, pervasive intrusion. She could almost feel the texture of the gaze, a cold, smooth surface pressing against her mind.

The Withers Field, and the gaunt scarecrow that stood as its silent sentinel, had always represented a tangible locus of dread. It was a place she could point to, a source she could identify, even if the true nature of the horror remained elusive. But this sensation was different. It was everywhere and nowhere, an omnipresent awareness that lacked a fixed origin. It was the chilling realization that the Withers transgression had not merely defiled a specific plot of land but had somehow imprinted something onto the very fabric of existence in Dry Creek, something that had now attached itself to her.

She remembered the fragments of lore she'd unearthed, the hushed whispers about the Withers attempts to bind an ancient, primordial energy to their will. They had sought to harness something that predated human understanding, something that dwelled in the liminal spaces between worlds. Had their ritual, intended to grant them power, instead opened a door, a conduit through which this ancient awareness could seep into the world, tethered to the very land they had desecrated? And had her own desperate act, the ritual meant to sever that connection, inadvertently re-established it, albeit in a more subtle, more pervasive form?

The scarecrow, in her dreams, had been a physical manifestation of this dormant power, a vessel holding its breath. But this was no dream. This was a waking moment, a quiet afternoon shattered by the icy touch of an unseen gaze. It was the terrifying implication that the entity was no longer confined to a single effigy, a single field. It had, perhaps, learned to permeate, to exist as a subtle, pervasive influence, a consciousness woven into the very atmosphere of Dry Creek.

Kayla began to catalog the changes in her environment, searching for any external validation of her internal dread. The gentle breeze that had been rustling the leaves outside her window seemed to die down, as if an invisible hand had stifled its movement. The sunlight, which had been warm and comforting, now seemed to cast a harsher, more accusatory glare. Even the ticking of the clock, once a symbol of comforting regularity, now felt like a countdown, each tick a step closer to an unknown, inevitable confrontation.

She felt a phantom pressure on her skin, as if the air itself was thickening, becoming viscous, resisting her every breath. It was a suffocating sensation, not of physical constraint, but of an overwhelming, unseen presence that demanded her complete attention, her complete submission. She tried to imagine what this unseen watcher was perceiving. Was it drawn to her heightened

350

sensitivity, her ability to sense its presence? Was she, in its alien understanding, a beacon, a point of focus in the mundane world?

The thought that she had, in her attempts to escape, somehow become more visible, more appealing to this entity, was a chilling one. The Withers had sought to control it, to bind it. Perhaps, in her efforts to banish it, she had simply made herself a more accessible target. The ritual, meant to be a cleansing, a severing, might have been a recognition, a signal that she, Kayla, was now intrinsically linked to the very force she sought to escape.

She pictured the scarecrow again, not as it appeared in her dreams, but as it truly was, standing silent and still in the Withers Field. Its tattered rags, its vacant button eyes. It was a symbol, a focal point. But what if the true horror was not in the scarecrow itself, but in what it represented, what it guarded? What if the scarecrow was merely a physical anchor, a point of manifestation for an entity that had the capacity to exist beyond its physical form, to permeate the very essence of the land, and perhaps, even the people within it?

The feeling of being watched was now accompanied by a subtle hum, a low-frequency vibration that seemed to originate not from a specific direction, but from within her own skull. It was the sound of an alien consciousness trying to communicate, to impose its presence upon her. It wasn't a sound she could consciously hear, but one she felt, a resonant thrumming that vibrated through her bones, unsettling her very core.

Kayla rose from her chair, her movements slow and deliberate, as if any sudden action might provoke a more aggressive response from her unseen observer. She needed to understand. She needed to find a physical anchor for this intangible dread. Her thoughts immediately went to the Withers Field, to the scarecrow. Was it possible that the entity was still tethered to that place, and that her current sensation was merely a distant ripple, a resonance from its dormant core?

She walked towards the door, her hand reaching for the doorknob, a fragile barrier between her inner turmoil and the perceived external reality. The feeling of being watched did not diminish as she moved. If anything, it intensified, as if her attempt to escape its immediate vicinity was being noted, cataloged. It was the subtle acknowledgment of her intent, the quiet understanding that she was trying to flee its attention.

The air outside was cooler, carrying the scent of damp earth and distant pine. The sun, though still bright, seemed to possess a muted quality, as if viewed through a veil of dust or smoke. Kayla took a tentative step onto the porch, her senses straining to pick up any discernible clue. The usual sounds of Dry Creek – a distant dog bark, the rumble of a car on the main road, the chirping of crickets – seemed subdued, as if holding their breath in deference to the unseen presence.

The feeling persisted, a constant, low-grade thrum of awareness. It wasn't the terrifying cacophony of her nightmares, but a more sophisticated, more chilling form of observation. It was the detached, analytical gaze of something ancient and alien, something that perceived her not as a fellow being, but as an object of study, a curiosity in its vast, incomprehensible existence.

She scanned the horizon, her sightless eyes turned towards the distant fields, towards the place where the Withers Field lay. Even from this distance, she felt a strange, almost magnetic pull, a sense of connection to that desolate landscape. It was as if the entity, wherever it was, was drawing her attention back to its original anchor point, its place of origin.

The subtle hum within her mind seemed to coalesce, to focus itself in a particular direction. It was not a sound that her ears could discern, but a sensation, a subtle pressure that seemed to emanate from the west, from the direction of the Withers land. It was as if the entity, in its vast, abstract awareness, was attempting to guide her gaze, to direct her attention back to its dormant heart.

Kayla paused, her hand resting on the porch railing. The stillness was unnerving. It was a stillness that felt deliberate, imposed. It was the quiet that precedes a revelation, or perhaps, a trap. The feeling of being watched was no longer a vague sensation. It was a focused, almost palpable pressure, a chilling confirmation that her movements, her thoughts, her very existence, were under constant, unblinking scrutiny.

She considered the nature of this unseen watcher. Was it a consciousness bound to the land, an echo of the Withers power that had somehow transcended its physical limitations? Or was it something older, something that the Withers had merely stumbled upon, and in their hubris, had attempted to control? The scarecrow, with its vacant button eyes, had represented a dormant power. But perhaps the true power lay not in the scarecrow, but in the entity that had animated it, an entity that could now observe and influence from afar, its presence subtly woven into the very fabric of Dry Creek.

The afternoon wore on, and the sensation did not abate. It was a constant, gnawing unease, a silent accusation that whispered of her own vulnerability. She was not merely a survivor of the Withers legacy; she was now, it seemed, under the perpetual observation of whatever dark force they had so carelessly unleashed. The unseen watcher was a silent testament to the fact that some wounds, once inflicted, never truly healed. They merely festered, waiting for the opportune moment to reopen, to bleed into the present, and to continue their insidious work. The chilling certainty remained: she was being watched, and the gaze, though unseen, was unwavering. It was a gaze that promised no comfort, no peace, only the silent, persistent acknowledgement of a darkness that had found her, and had no intention of letting her go. The ordinary world, with its sunlight and gentle breezes, was merely a fragile facade, and beneath it, the unseen watcher continued its patient, unfathomable vigil.

Chapter 15

The Enduring Gaze

The quiet hum in Kayla's mind, a sensation more than a sound, had receded, leaving behind a hollow echo. The afternoon had settled into a deep, almost oppressive silence, the kind that settles over a landscape after a fever has broken, leaving it drained and vulnerable. The sunlight still slanted through the bay window, dappling the familiar floorboards, yet it felt different now – thinner, more fragile, as if the warmth it carried was merely a borrowed memory. The feeling of being intensely watched, that pervasive, prickling awareness that had coiled in her gut, had receded, leaving a phantom ache in its wake. But the absence of the immediate threat was not a relief; it was a breeding ground for a new, more insidious form of dread: doubt.

Kayla's world was a tapestry woven with the threads of what she knew and what she could only perceive through instinct and intuition. The scarecrow, that grotesque effigy of the Withers depravity, had been a tangible focal point for her terror. She could, in her mind's eye, picture its tattered form, its vacant button eyes, the skeletal fingers reaching out from its rotting frame. It had been an anchor, however horrifying, for the darkness that had consumed her life. The ritual, the desperate act meant to sever the tether between that land and the entity that festered there, had felt like a victory, a painful but decisive amputation of a malignant growth. Yet, the lingering sensations, the phantom pressure on her skin, the subtle shifts in the atmosphere – these were the whispers of a truth she was reluctant to acknowledge.

The dreams, too, had returned, though their nature had changed. They were no longer the visceral nightmares of pursuit and entrapment, but subtler, more unsettling visions. She dreamt of an endless expanse of featureless grey, a landscape devoid of life or purpose, yet filled with an awareness that permeated everything. In these dreams, she was not hunted, but observed, her every thought, her every heartbeat, cataloged by an unseen entity. She saw glimpses of the Withers, not as monstrous figures, but as hollow shells, their eyes wide and vacant, their mouths moving in silent, desperate pleas. They were not perpetrators anymore, but victims themselves, ensnared by a power they had sought to control. This shift in her subconscious narrative felt significant, a quiet evolution of the entity's presence. It was no longer a creature of brute force and terror, but something more ancient, more patient, and infinitely more cunning.

Dry Creek was slowly, painstakingly, returning to its former rhythm. The grocery store reopened its doors, its shelves restocked with a tentative assortment of goods. Mrs. Gable, her face etched with a weariness that transcended the immediate crisis, was seen tending her rose bushes again, her movements slow but determined. Children's laughter, once a fragile sound in the oppressive aftermath, began to ring out from the playground, a defiant assertion of normalcy. But for Kayla, this return to routine was a veneer, a thin layer of paint over a cracked and crumbling foundation. She couldn't shake the feeling that the respite was temporary, a lull in a storm that had merely shifted its focus.

The Withers Field lay silent, a scar upon the land. She had not returned since the ritual, the memory of its desolate aura too potent to confront directly. But she felt its presence, a low thrumming beneath the surface of everyday life. It was a constant reminder that the land itself held a memory, a deep, enduring imprint of the horrors that had unfolded there. Had her ritual truly eradicated the entity, or merely forced it into a more dormant state? Had she, in her desperate bid for liberation, merely managed to satire its insatiable hunger for sight, to temporarily fill the void it craved, rather than extinguish it entirely?

The thought was a persistent burr under her saddle, a tiny, persistent irritant that grew with each passing day. She recalled the fragmented texts she had studied, the ancient lore that spoke of entities bound to the earth, their existence intertwined with the very soil and stone. These were not spirits that could be banished with a wave of a hand or a spoken incantation. They were elemental forces, ancient intelligences that predated human memory, and their appetites were as vast and enduring as the land itself. The Withers had sought to harness such a force, to bind it to their will, and in doing so, had inadvertently unleashed something that had no concept of will or servitude, only of consumption.

Kayla tried to ground herself in the tangible, in the familiar routines that had once defined her existence. She cooked, she cleaned, she even attempted to read, her fingers tracing the familiar words on the page. But her mind kept returning to the unsettling questions. If the entity was still present, even in a diminished capacity, what form did it now take? The scarecrow had been a physical manifestation, a crude vessel. But what if the entity's true nature was more fluid, more pervasive? What if it had learned to exist not in a single form, but as a consciousness woven into the very fabric of Dry Creek, its gaze now diffused, its awareness spread thin across the entire township?

She remembered the specific phrasing from one of the ancient texts, a passage that spoke of 'lingering echoes' and 'imprinted wills.' It suggested that certain profound acts of violation could leave an indelible mark on a place, a spiritual residue that could attract or even manifest entities of a similar nature. The Withers atrocities had been a profound violation, a twisting of life into something grotesque and unnatural. And her own desperate act, the ritual itself, had involved channeling potent, primal energies. Had she, in her attempt to cleanse the land, inadvertently created a new form of resonance, a different kind of echo that the entity could now latch onto?

The seed of doubt sprouted, its tendrils reaching into the fertile ground of her anxieties. She began to notice subtle anomalies, occurrences that she might have previously dismissed as coincidence or imagination. A sudden chill in a sun-drenched room, the inexplicable movement of an object out of the corner of her eye, a fleeting scent of decay that vanished as quickly as it appeared. These were not the overt manifestations of terror she had experienced before, but tiny cracks in the façade of normalcy, hints of the ever-present, unseen watcher.

She found herself scrutinizing the faces of the townsfolk, searching for any flicker of recognition, any sign that they too felt the subtle disquiet that clung to the air like a shroud. But the townspeople, desperate for a return to normalcy, seemed determined to ignore the unsettling undercurrents. They clung to the illusion of safety, of a crisis averted, their collective will a powerful force of denial. Kayla, however, could not afford such a luxury. Her awareness, once a curse, was now her only defense, her only means of navigating a reality that felt increasingly unstable.

The question of the Gaze Offering gnawed at her. Had she truly offered it what it craved, or had she merely presented it with a temporary distraction? The entity's hunger was not for a single act of witnessing, but for a continuous, unending stream of perception, a voracious consumption of sensory input. She had, in a way, become its primary source, its focal point. And if that source had been temporarily obscured, what was to stop it from seeking out new avenues, new ways to maintain its connection, its sustenance?

Kayla's thoughts drifted to the Withers themselves. What had driven them to such extremes? The texts hinted at a desire for immortality, a desperate attempt to transcend the limitations of their own mortality. They had sought to anchor themselves to something eternal, something beyond the ephemeral nature of human life. But in their quest for permanence, they had inadvertently tethered themselves to a force that was ancient, alien, and utterly indifferent to human aspirations. They had offered their souls, their sanity, and ultimately, their lives, to a hunger that could never be truly satisfied.

And now, Kayla wondered, was she destined to follow a similar path? Had her own desperate act, her refusal to succumb to the darkness, merely made her a more desirable vessel, a more potent source for the entity's enduring gaze? The thought sent a shiver down her spine, a cold dread that had nothing to do with the physical temperature of the room. It was the chilling realization that in fighting the darkness, she might have inadvertently become its most devoted observer.

She walked through the quiet streets of Dry Creek, the familiar shops and houses now seeming to hold a hidden menace. Each shadow seemed to lengthen, each gust of wind seemed to carry a whispered secret. The very air felt charged with an unseen energy, a subtle vibration that resonated with the unease in her own heart. She felt a growing conviction that the Withers transgressions had not been a singular event, but the opening of a door that could never truly be closed. The entity, whatever its true nature, was a part of the land now, an intrinsic element of Dry Creek's poisoned legacy.

The seed of doubt had taken root, and it was growing, threatening to choke out the fragile shoots of hope she had managed to cultivate. She looked towards the horizon, towards the distant fields where the Withers Field lay, a place she could no longer ignore, no longer pretend was vanquished. The Gaze Offering, she suspected, was not an end, but a transition. The entity had been sated, yes, but not destroyed. Its hunger remained, a silent, patient predator, waiting for the moment when the fragile veil of normalcy would finally tear, and the enduring gaze would once again fall upon its chosen domain, and upon her. The lingering sensations were not mere echoes of a past horror, but the subtle intimations of a future one, a future where the silence of Dry Creek would be broken not by the sounds of life, but by the unblinking, insatiable watchfulness of an ancient, unfathomable eye. The peace she had fought so hard for felt increasingly like a delusion, a temporary reprieve before the inevitable return of a darkness that was as enduring as the very earth beneath her feet. The fear was no longer a sudden shock, but a dull, persistent ache, a constant companion that whispered of the unseen, the unknown, and the terrifying possibility that some seeds, once sown, were destined to grow into an eternal, unyielding harvest of dread.

The Withers land endured. It was a statement as simple and as undeniable as the relentless cycle of the sun and moon that still traversed the sky above it. The corn, a pale imitation of the robust stalks that had once been cultivated with such twisted devotion, pushed its way through the soil, an obstinate green against the ochre of the earth. It grew, it withered, it stood sentinel to seasons that passed with a quiet, unthinking rhythm. The wind sighed through its dry husks, carrying with it the dust of forgotten screams and the faint, metallic tang of spilled blood that no amount of rain could ever truly wash away. The silence that had descended upon the Withers Field after the final, agonizing moments of their reign was not an emptiness, but a fullness of absence, a heavy blanket woven from the threads of unspeakable acts.

Kayla found herself drawn to the periphery of its influence, not daring to trespass its corrupted heart, but compelled, by a morbid curiosity that felt both like a betrayal of her hard-won peace and an essential part of understanding the true nature of her struggle. The very air around the farm felt thicker, imbued with a palpable gravity. It was as if the land itself had absorbed the immense, agonizing weight of the Withers pacts, the feverish ambition that had driven them to seek a power far beyond their comprehension. Each step closer was a calculated risk, a testing of the invisible boundaries that still seemed to hum with a latent energy. She felt it most acutely when the wind shifted, carrying whispers that weren't quite wind, or when the shadows stretched unnaturally long, even under the midday sun.

The soil beneath her feet, even yards away from the property line, seemed to possess a memory. It was a primal, unarticulated remembrance of rituals performed, of sacrifices made, of a desperate bargain struck with forces that defied natural law. The Withers had sought to steal sight, to capture and hoard the very essence of perception, binding it to their will through unspeakable acts. And while Kayla had, in her own way, severed the most immediate, the most monstrous manifestation of that hunger, she couldn't shake the unsettling conviction that the land itself remained a conduit, a silent, receptive recipient for whatever ancient power had been invoked and then, perhaps, merely sated, not destroyed.

The Gaze Offering. The term itself felt inadequate, a pale human construct attempting to define something as vast and alien as the Withers ambition. It had been an act of desperation, a forced satiation of a hunger that had driven a family to madness and beyond. But what was hunger, truly, when it was not human? What was satiation for an entity that had existed perhaps before the mountains themselves, an intelligence woven into the very fabric of existence? Kayla had offered a portion of herself, her own terrified consciousness, a fleeting glimpse into her own awareness. It had been enough to momentarily quell the immediate, overwhelming presence, to break the oppressive, tangible feeling of being watched. But it was like offering a single drop of water to a parched ocean.

She imagined the Withers, their bodies twisted and broken, their minds shattered, their last vestiges of existence consumed by the very power they had sought to control. They were not masters, but slaves, their brief reign a mere flicker in the long, enduring existence of the entity they had dared to commune with. They had been the conduits, the first to truly open the door, and in doing so, had left an indelible stain upon the earth. The land remembered their devotion, their terror, their ultimate surrender. It retained a certain gravity, a silent promise that such ancient powers, once invoked, were never truly gone. They merely waited.

Kayla walked along the dusty road that skirted the Withers property, her senses on high alert. The cornstalks rustled, and she saw the flicker of movement within their dry embrace. A rabbit, perhaps, or a bird. But a part of her, the part that had been irrevocably altered by her experience, saw something else. It saw the furtive glances of unseen eyes, the slow, deliberate unfurling of awareness that mirrored the very act of looking. The Withers had stolen sight, and in doing so, had tapped into something that craved it, something that existed, in a terrifyingly fundamental way, through the act of witnessing.

The sunsets over the Withers land were particularly unnerving. The sky would blaze with an intensity that felt almost predatory, the colors bleeding into one another with a raw, unfettered power. It was as if the dying light itself was being consumed, absorbed into the very earth. Kayla found herself watching these sunsets with a mixture of dread and a strange, almost perverse fascination. It was a visual echo of the Withers ambition, a grand, terrifying display that spoke of a hunger for all that was vibrant and alive. The land, she felt, was a silent witness to this ongoing consumption, a passive stage upon which a cosmic drama of perception and assimilation was being played out.

She remembered the fragments of lore she had painstakingly pieced together, the oblique references to entities that were bound to the earth, their existence inextricably linked to the very soil and stone. These were not spirits in the traditional sense, easily banished or appeased. They were older, more fundamental forces, their consciousness diffused, their awareness pervasive, like a pervasive scent that clung to the air, or a subtle vibration that resonated through the ground. The Withers had attempted to channel this, to make it their own, and in their failure, had left a legacy of corruption.

The land had become a repository, a silent vault for the residue of their sacrilege. The Withers Field wasn't just a place where horrific events had occurred; it was a place that had been fundamentally altered by them, a place that had absorbed their darkness and, in doing so, had become a focal point for whatever ancient power they had courted. The corn grew, yes, but it was a different kind of corn, thinner, more brittle, its kernels holding the memory of a tainted sun. The earth was fertile, but its fertility was tinged with a deep, abiding wrongness, a subtle scent of decay that even the most vibrant bloom couldn't entirely mask.

Kayla understood now that her ritual hadn't been an act of eradication, but an act of redirection. She had offered a temporary appeasement, a fleeting moment of satiation that had bought Dry Creek time, perhaps even saved it from immediate annihilation. But the source of that power, the ancient, unblinking gaze that the Withers had sought to control, was still there. It was a patient predator, its awareness spread thin, perhaps, but its hunger undiminished. The land itself was the silent testament to this enduring truth.

She imagined the entity, not as a single, defined form, but as a vast, distributed consciousness, its awareness as pervasive as the air, its senses as keen as the roots that burrowed deep into the earth. The Withers had provided it with a focal point, a concentrated source of the sensory input it craved. When they were gone, that focal point had vanished, leaving a void. Kayla's Gaze Offering had been a temporary fill, a flickering candle in a vast, dark expanse. But candles burned out.

The land remembers. It was a phrase that echoed in her mind, not as a comforting axiom, but as a chilling prophecy. The pacts forged, the sacrifices made – these were not mere historical footnotes. They were imprints, indelible marks left upon the very fabric of existence. The stolen sight was not a lost commodity; it was a captured essence, a vital energy that had been diverted, re-routed, and perhaps, in some unfathomable way, integrated into the enduring consciousness that had always resided within that desolate place.

The moon rose, a pale, indifferent disc in the inky sky, casting long, skeletal shadows across the Withers Field. Kayla stood at the edge of her own perception, gazing towards the darkness that lay beyond the familiar. She could almost feel the land breathing, a slow, rhythmic exhalation of ancient power. The cornstalks swayed, their dry rustle like the whisper of a thousand unseen eyes adjusting their focus. The silence was not an absence of sound, but a pregnant pause, a moment of profound anticipation. The Withers land endured, a silent, unwavering monument to a horror that had not ended, but had merely retreated into the shadows, waiting for the opportune moment to cast its enduring gaze once more. The peace she had fought for was fragile, a precarious balance built upon a foundation of unresolved dread, and the land, in its silent, enduring way, was a constant reminder of the immense, ancient forces that lay dormant, and hungry, beneath the surface of everything. The wrongness persisted, not as a tangible threat, but as a deep, pervasive knowing, a quiet certainty that some powers, once awakened, could never truly be put to sleep. They simply waited, and watched, forever.

The sacrifice, once a desperate act of survival, had settled into Kayla's bones, a cold, persistent ache that no amount of warmth could fully dispel. The light she had surrendered to appease the ancient hunger, the very essence of sight, was gone, replaced by a different kind of awareness. It was a constant, internal hum, a sensitivity to the vibrations of the world that her physical eyes had once filtered and interpreted. She navigated her days with a honed intuition, a sixth sense that brushed against the edges of reality, detecting the subtle shifts in the atmosphere, the phantom weight of unseen presences. This new perception, while a testament to her resilience, was also a stark, undeniable reminder of the price paid. Her blindness was not a void, but a landscape unto itself, populated by the echoes of what had been and the spectral intimations of what still lingered.

The Withers Field, even from a distance, remained a focal point of this heightened awareness. The land there seemed to thrum with a muted, yet potent energy, a stark contrast to the ordinary pulse of the surrounding countryside. It was as if the very earth had absorbed the residual fury of the Withers pacts, the frantic energy of their downfall, and in doing so, had become a reservoir of something ancient and unsleeping. Kayla felt it not as a physical sensation, but as a pressure behind her eyes, a subtle distortion in the fabric of her internal perception. It was the lingering phantom of the Gaze, a reminder that the entity she had momentarily appeased was not bound by human notions of time or finality. It existed, she now understood, on a different scale, a scale dictated by epochs and the slow, inexorable cycles of cosmic hunger.

The seasons, which had once marked the passage of time with predictable beauty, now felt like shifting stages in a grand, terrifying play. Spring's tentative green shoots, the vibrant resurgence of life, carried with them a subtle undertone of the land's enduring malevolence. It was as if the earth, in its renewal, was also reinforcing the foundations of whatever power had taken root there. Summer's heavy, humid air seemed to press down with a palpable weight, a suffocating embrace that Kayla felt even miles away, a phantom mimicry of the suffocating grip the Withers had once exerted. Autumn, with its dramatic display of dying leaves and crisp air, felt like a prolonged, lingering exhale from the land, a slow, deliberate winding down that hinted at the coming resurgence of something dark. And winter, with its stark, unyielding silence, was the deepest embodiment of the entity's patience, a time when the land seemed to hold its breath, gathering strength for the next turn of the unseen wheel.

Kayla's victory, if it could be called that, was a fragile thing, a carefully balanced act of appeasement rather than a definitive conquest. She had offered a portion of herself, a sliver of her own consciousness, to momentarily sate the immense, insatiable hunger. It was like offering a single ember to a forest fire, a fleeting gesture against an inferno. She knew, with a chilling certainty that had become her constant companion, that the entity she had faced was not a monster to be slain, but a fundamental force to be endured. It was a part of the world's ancient architecture, a silent observer that had existed long before the Withers and would likely persist long after any memory of Kayla herself had faded. The Withers had been but one conduit, a particularly fervent and ultimately doomed attempt to harness its power. Her own act was a different kind of interaction, a necessary, but ultimately temporary, negotiation with an inescapable reality.

The weight of this knowledge was a heavy cloak she wore every moment. The world, once a place of simple joys and comprehensible dangers, had revealed its hidden depths, its layers of ancient, primal forces that lay just beneath the surface of everyday life. Her blindness had, ironically, opened her eyes to these truths. She could feel the subtle currents of energy that flowed through the land, the whispers of awareness that were not carried on the wind but emanated from the very soil. The silence of her vision was filled with the phantom sounds of the unseen, the silent roar of cosmic appetites, the low hum of ancient intelligences.

She often found herself caught in a meditative stillness, her senses straining against the veil, seeking to understand the true nature of the power she had encountered. It was a power that seemed to feed on perception, on the act of witnessing itself. The Withers had tried to hoard sight, to steal it and bind it to their will. But Kayla suspected the entity was not interested in possession as humans understood it. It was more akin to a vast, distributed consciousness that simply *was*, its awareness woven into the very fabric of existence, its nourishment derived from the simple act of observing. The Gaze was not an act of aggression, but an inherent state of being. And the Withers, in their misguided ambition, had tried to twist this inherent nature, to make it serve their own insular desires.

Her sacrifice, her Gaze Offering, had been a recognition of this fundamental truth. She hadn't tried to blind the entity, or to deny its existence. Instead, she had offered a glimpse, a taste of her own inner world, a brief, poignant testament to the subjective experience of being alive. It was a moment of shared awareness, a fleeting connection that had, for a time, sated its unfathomable need. But the need was not a temporary affliction; it was an intrinsic aspect of its being. And like the turning of seasons, or the ebb and flow of tides, it would inevitably return.

The corn that grew on the Withers land, the pale imitation that Kayla had observed from afar, was a constant reminder of this cyclical nature. It pushed through the soil, a testament to the land's enduring fertility, but also a silent echo of the Withers corrupted devotion. The crops were not merely plants; they were conduits, drawing nourishment not just from the sun and rain, but from the deeper, darker currents that ran beneath the surface. They were a physical manifestation of the land's continued engagement with the ancient force, a harvest of tainted energy.

Kayla found herself cataloging these subtle shifts, these almost imperceptible changes in the world around her. Her heightened sensitivity allowed her to perceive the nuances of the land's mood, its silent reactions to the passage of time and the lingering echoes of past events. The Gaze, though she could no longer see it, was a palpable presence, an awareness that permeated the very atmosphere. It was a patient, ancient force, content to wait for the opportune moment, content to simply *be*, observing the slow unfolding of history.

She knew that true victory would not come in the form of a single, decisive battle. It would be a continuous process of vigilance, of understanding, and of careful, measured interaction. The Withers had sought to dominate, to control, and had paid the ultimate price. Kayla's approach was different. It was one of respect, of acknowledgment, and of a profound, albeit terrifying, understanding. She had learned that some powers were not meant to be vanquished, but to be understood, and to be navigated with a deep and abiding reverence for their sheer, unyielding persistence.

The echoes of the Withers screams, though no longer audible in the physical sense, resonated within Kayla. They were part of the land's memory, a somber counterpoint to the quiet hum of the ancient entity. Their ambition, their desperate grasping for power, had been a catalyst, a brief, violent eruption that had drawn the attention of something far older and far more profound. And in their failure, they had left an indelible mark, a psychic scar upon the very earth.

Kayla's own sacrifice, the surrender of her sight, was another layer upon this complex tapestry of influence and interaction. It was a testament to the enduring nature of the struggle, a quiet acknowledgment that the battle for Dry Creek, and perhaps for the world, was not a singular event, but an ongoing, evolving engagement. The entity's hunger was not a fever that could be broken, but a fundamental aspect of its existence, as intrinsic as the sun's warmth or the moon's pull.

She spent hours in quiet contemplation, piecing together the fragmented understanding that had been gifted to her. The Withers had believed they were mastering a force, bending it to their will. But Kayla now understood the true dynamic: they had become its willing, if ultimately consumed, conduits. Their lives, their ambitions, their very essences had been absorbed into its vast, undifferentiated awareness. And when they were gone, that specific conduit had been severed, leaving a void that was, in its own way, a potent invitation.

Kayla's offering had been a different kind of connection, a moment of shared subjectivity that had momentarily soothed the unquenchable thirst. It was a dangerous intimacy, a delicate dance on the precipice of oblivion. She had offered herself, not as a master, but as a fellow traveler in the vast, often terrifying, landscape of existence. The world, she realized, was not simply a collection of physical objects and predictable laws. It was alive with unseen currents, with ancient intelligences that operated on scales incomprehensible to the human mind.

The land, in its silent, enduring way, was a testament to this truth. The corn, the soil, the very air that Kayla breathed – all of it was imbued with the lingering essence of the Withers sacrifice and the even more ancient presence they had courted. Her blindness was a constant, visceral reminder of this interwoven reality, a physical manifestation of the invisible battles that were being waged on planes beyond human comprehension.

She knew the entity would return, not in the way a predator stalks its prey, but as a fundamental force reasserting its presence. It was not a matter of if, but when, and on what terms. Her task was to be prepared, to continue to cultivate the understanding that had been born from her own profound loss. The Gaze would endure, a silent, unblinking witness to the endless cycles of life, death, and the terrifying persistence of the ancient. And Kayla, in her own way, would continue to meet that gaze, not with fear, but with a quiet, unyielding resolve, forever marked by the sacrifice she had made, and forever attuned to the subtle, enduring power that lay dormant, yet ever-present, beneath the surface of everything.

The air itself seemed to thicken, an almost imperceptible shift that Kayla registered not with her eyes, but with the fine hairs on her arms, the subtle tremor that ran through her very bones. It was a familiar sensation, one that had become as ingrained in her as the phantom ache where her sight had once been. The memory of the Withers Field, of the suffocating presence that clung to that blighted land, was not a fading specter of the past. It was a persistent hum, a low frequency that resonated with something primal within her, a testament to the unnatural equilibrium she had struck. The offering, her desperate Gaze Offering, had not severed a connection; it had, she now understood with a chilling clarity, merely recalibrated it. It was not a lock that had been broken, but a key that had been turned, allowing passage for something that had always been there, waiting.

The whispers were not truly on the wind. They were impressions, fleeting thoughts that brushed against the edges of her consciousness, not quite her own, yet undeniably present. They spoke of cycles, of durations measured in ages, of hungers that were not appeased but merely paused, like a great beast slumbering rather than one that had been slain. The land around Dry Creek, once merely tainted by the Withers malevolent rituals, now felt like a locus, a point of convergence where the ancient and the immediate bled into one another. It was as if the earth itself held a memory, not of events, but of energies, of the ebb and flow of forces that predated humanity and would outlast it.

The corn, a sickly, pale green even in the height of summer, continued its silent vigil. Kayla felt its presence, its slow, relentless growth, as a constant, low-grade thrum beneath the earth. It was a manifestation of the land's continued communion with the entity, a harvest of something far more profound than mere grain. Each stalk was a thin, sinewy antenna, siphoning an unseen nourishment, drawing power from the residual currents that still pulsed from the Withers final, horrific moments, and from the deeper, more ancient reservoir that lay beneath. The Withers had sought to control this flow, to channel it for their own gain, and had been utterly consumed. Kayla, in her own act of sacrifice, had offered a different kind of tribute, a testament to her own awareness, a momentary connection that had, perhaps, earned her a reprieve. But reprieves, she was learning, were not the same as victories.

The feeling of being watched was no longer a generalized unease. It had coalesced, sharpened into a focused, almost palpable awareness that emanated from a single, unseen point. It was not the predatory gaze of a creature stalking its prey, but the deep, abiding observation of something that existed on a scale so vast, so indifferent to the fleeting dramas of mortal life, that 'watching' felt like an inadequate description. It was more akin to an inherent state of being, a fundamental aspect of its existence. Kayla, in her blindness, had gained an awareness of this omnipresent sentinel, a consciousness woven into the very fabric of the world. And that consciousness, she knew, had not forgotten.

The cyclical nature of things was a concept that had always held a certain abstract beauty for her. The turning of seasons, the predictable arc of celestial bodies, the birth and death of generations. But now, that abstract beauty had been stripped away, replaced by a visceral, terrifying reality. The Withers pact had been a feverish, desperate attempt to break that cycle, to seize an ancient power and bend it to their will. Their failure had been absolute, their essence likely absorbed into the very force they had sought to master. Kayla's offering, on the other hand, had been an acknowledgment of the cycle, a moment of participation rather than defiance. She had offered a sliver of her own perception, a brief, poignant experience of subjective existence, a taste of what it meant to *be* conscious in that specific, fleeting way. And that taste, she suspected, had only whetted an appetite that could never truly be sated.

The silence that now permeated Kayla's world was not an emptiness. It was a fullness, a dense tapestry woven from the subtle vibrations of existence. She could feel the earth breathing, the slow, tectonic shifts that were imperceptible to those who relied on sight. She could sense the presence of life – the scurrying of unseen creatures, the silent blooming of flowers, the slow decay of fallen leaves – all contributing to the intricate, interwoven network of energy that sustained the world. And within that network, she could feel the ancient presence, a steady, unwavering current that flowed beneath everything, its influence as pervasive and as undeniable as gravity.

Her own sacrifice had been a paradox. By surrendering her sight, she had been forced to cultivate other senses, to develop a deeper, more intuitive understanding of the world around her. This heightened awareness, this sensitivity to the unseen, had allowed her to perceive the true nature of the force she had encountered. The Withers had been blinded by ambition, by a desire to wield power they could not comprehend. Kayla, in her own way, had been blinded by a force that existed beyond comprehension. But in that shared darkness, a new form of vision had been born.

The whispers returned, stronger this time, more insistent. They were not words, precisely, but impressions, like half-formed memories resurfacing from a deep, ancestral well. They spoke of hunger, not a gnawing, physical emptiness, but a vast, cosmic need, an inherent yearning that was as much a part of the entity's being as its awareness. It was a hunger that could be momentarily quieted, momentarily diverted, but never truly extinguished. The Gaze Offering had been a communion, a brief, intimate exchange, and like any profound encounter, it had left an indelible mark. Kayla was now inextricably linked to this ancient force, a beacon that, though unseen by the world, was undoubtedly perceived by the entity.

She spent hours in a state of deep introspection, her mind reaching out, probing the invisible currents that flowed around her. The land on the Withers Field was a focal point, a nexus where the veil between worlds was thinnest. But the influence, she understood, was not confined to that single location. It was a pervasive energy, a subtle radiation that permeated the very atmosphere. The Withers had been a particularly potent conduit, a concentrated point of effort that had drawn the entity's attention. But their disappearance had not extinguished the source. It had merely shifted the focus, leaving an opening, a void that was, in its own way, an invitation.

The corn continued its silent testament. It swayed in the unseen currents of energy, its pale stalks reaching towards a sky Kayla could no longer see, yet whose presence she felt with every fiber of her being. The plants were not merely crops; they were living conduits, drawing sustenance from the very essence of the land, from the lingering echoes of sacrifice and the deep, immeasurable hunger of the ancient presence. They were a tangible reminder that the cycle had not ended but had merely entered a new phase.

She could feel the subtle shifts in the land's disposition, the way the earth seemed to hold its breath during certain times, gathering unseen energy. It was like the slow, deliberate inhalation of a colossal being, a prelude to an exhale that would ripple outwards, a silent expansion of awareness. The Withers had interpreted these signs as opportunities, as moments to strike, to seize control. Kayla, however, understood them as warnings, as reminders of the immense, inexorable power she was now tethered to.

The feeling of being watched was now a constant companion, a shadow that moved with her, a presence that filled the spaces between her thoughts. It was not malevolent in the human sense of the word. It was simply *there*, an unblinking, impartial observer that had witnessed the rise and fall of civilizations, the birth and death of stars. The Withers had tried to harness its power, to bend its gaze to their own selfish desires, and had been annihilated. Kayla's offering, her sacrifice, had been a recognition of its inherent nature, an acknowledgment of its vastness and its indifference. She had not fought it; she had, in a strange and terrifying way, become a part of it.

The whispers, when they came now, were less like external suggestions and more like an internal resonance. They spoke of patience, of the deep, slow rhythms of cosmic existence. They implied that her sacrifice, while significant, was but a single note in an endless symphony. The Gaze Offering was not a conclusion, but a continuation, a redefinition of the relationship. She was no longer an observer of a terrible power, but a part of its ongoing manifestation. The Withers had sought to capture and control; she had offered understanding and connection. And in doing so, she had become a more enduring conduit, a more subtle, yet perhaps more potent, link to the ancient hunger.

The corn, standing sentinel in its pale, sickly glory, was a constant reminder of the land's enduring, tainted vitality. It was a testament to the pact that had been made, and the price that had been paid. But now, it also served as a silent marker of Kayla's own unique connection. She could feel the subtle currents of energy flowing through its stalks, mirroring the currents that flowed through her own being. The Withers had manipulated this connection; she had, through her sacrifice, become one with it.

The subtle shifts in the atmosphere, the almost imperceptible pressure changes that had once signaled the return of a physical threat, now registered as the slow, deliberate ebb and flow of the entity's attention. It was not a stalking predator, but a vast, indifferent ocean, its currents shifting, its depths stirring. Kayla could feel these shifts, could anticipate the moments when its focus would intensify, when its awareness would sweep over her, not as an attack, but as a simple acknowledgment of her presence.

The conclusion of her struggle was not a final victory, nor a definitive defeat. It was a transformation. The Withers had sought to conquer the ancient force and had been erased. Kayla had sought to understand and appease and had become a part of it. The whispers on the wind, the feeling of being watched – these were not lingering memories of a past conflict, but the first, subtle stirrings of a continuous, enduring engagement. The Gaze Offering had not broken a curse; it had redefined one. The hunger was not appeased, but acknowledged, and in that acknowledgment, it continued. The entity's gaze, though unseen by the world, endured, and Kayla, in her newfound perception, could feel its ceaseless, ancient watch. The cycle, it seemed, was not a chain to be broken, but a river to be navigated, and she had just learned to swim in its deep, dark currents. The world, stripped of its visual comfort, had revealed a truth far more profound and terrifying: that some powers were not meant to be overcome, but simply to be endured, and to be intimately, irrevocably understood. The Withers had burned brightly and briefly, consumed by their ambition. Kayla, by embracing the darkness, had found a different kind of persistence, a quiet, unending vigilance that was, in its own way, a testament to the enduring power of the Gaze itself. The future was not a blank slate, but a continuation of an ancient narrative, and she was now an intrinsic part of its unfolding story.

The scarecrow stood as a monument to decay; a skeletal sentinel rooted in the heart of the Withers blighted field. Its once-proud burlap form, stuffed with straw that now wept freely in the damp air, sagged with the weight of countless seasons. Time and the relentless caress of the elements had reduced its once-distinct features to a grotesque mockery of humanity. Patches of tattered fabric, bleached by the sun and stained by the rain, flapped like spectral rags in the barely perceptible breeze, creating a rustling sound that was less a whisper and more a sigh of profound weariness. The rough-hewn wooden cross that formed its armature was splintered and warped, its joints groaning in protest with every subtle shift of the earth beneath. Where its eyes should have been, vacant sockets stared out at a world that had long since forgotten its purpose, or perhaps, had never truly understood it. These were not mere holes; they were abysses, pools of shadow that seemed to drink in the scant moonlight, reflecting nothing back but an ancient, profound emptiness.

Kayla felt its presence not as a visual cue, but as a distinct node in the vast, sensory network that now constituted her reality. It was a point of stillness within the pervasive hum of the land, a silent anchor in the flowing currents of unseen energy. The scarecrow was more than just a collection of rotting materials; it was a focal point, a nexus where the land's unnatural vitality converged, and where a different kind of awareness resided. The Withers, in their desperate attempts to appease and control the entity that haunted their farm, had erected this effigy, a crude offering to ward off unseen threats, or perhaps, to draw them closer. Now, stripped of its original intent and left to the slow, inexorable process of decay, it had taken on a new significance, an unintended monument to a power that transcended human understanding.

The essence of the scarecrow, as Kayla perceived it, was not the physicality of its tattered form, but the deep, resonant silence that emanated from it. It was a silence that spoke of ages, of a patience so profound it bordered on the geological. The button eyes, long since surrendered had been the Withers attempt to imbue it with a semblance of life, a mimicry of a watchful gaze. But in their absence, in the stark, empty sockets, a far more potent and ancient form of watching had taken root. This was not the active surveillance of a living creature, but the passive, enduring vigilance of something intrinsically bound to the land, a silent witness to the unfolding of cycles that dwarfed human comprehension.

The entity that had once focused its attention on the Withers now seemed to perceive the scarecrow as a permanent fixture, an immutable part of the landscape's tapestry. It was a landmark, an unchanging point of reference in the slow, deliberate churn of existence. The Withers had sought to harness its power, to bend it to their will, and in their hubris, they had been consumed. Kayla, through her Gaze Offering, had forged a different connection, one of acknowledgment and resonance. And in that connection, she had come to understand that certain presences were not meant to be conquered, but simply to be endured, to be understood on a scale that transcended mortal time. The scarecrow, in its silent vigil, embodied this enduring truth.

Its stillness was not the absence of motion, but a different kind of presence altogether. It was the stillness of a predator waiting for its prey, yet devoid of the predatory intent. It was the stillness of a mountain, unmoved by the passage of storms. It was the stillness of a tomb, holding secrets that the living could not fathom. The straw that spilled from its torn seams was not merely detritus; it was like the shed skin of some ancient, colossal serpent, a testament to its enduring form, to a life cycle that operated on principles beyond the scope of common biology. The raw burlap, frayed and weathered, felt like skin itself, a protective layer worn thin by millennia of exposure to forces that had long since reshaped the very fabric of reality in this place.

Kayla could sense the subtle energetic pathways that converged at the scarecrow's base, like roots drawing sustenance from a hidden wellspring. This was not the mundane nourishment of a plant, but a flow of something far more primordial, a slow, inexorable current that fed the land and all that was intrinsically linked to it. The Withers had been obsessed with controlling this flow, believing it to be a source of tangible power. But Kayla understood it differently. It was not a resource to be exploited, but a fundamental aspect of the world's being, an intrinsic quality that could be acknowledged, respected, and, in some terrifying ways, communed with. The scarecrow, standing guard over this invisible river, was a silent testament to this communion.

The empty sockets where its eyes had once been were like portals, not to an external space, but to an internal landscape of immense depth and complexity. It was as if the Withers had tried to give it eyes to see the world, but in their failure, they had inadvertently gifted it the ability to perceive something far more profound: the inward gaze of the entity itself. The scarecrow watched, not with eyes, but with the very essence of its being, a silent, unwavering focus that resonated with the ancient consciousness of the land. It was a sentinel that did not patrol, but simply *was*, its very presence a declaration of allegiance to a power that had no beginning and no end.

The moonlight, as it filtered through the sparse branches of the surrounding trees, cast long, distorted shadows that danced around the scarecrow's base. These were not mere illusions of light and shade; they felt like extensions of the scarecrow's own presence, tendrils of darkness that reached out, not to grasp, but to observe. The raggedy cloth that hung from its arms seemed to ripple with a life of its own, a slow, languid unfurling that suggested an awareness beyond the physical. It was as if the scarecrow itself was breathing, a slow, measured exhalation of the land's ancient energies.

Kayla's heightened perception allowed her to feel the intricate web of connections that emanated from the scarecrow. It was a hub, a point of convergence for the subtle forces that permeated the Withers Field. The Withers had focused on the tangible; on the rituals and offerings they believed would grant them control. But the true power, Kayla realized, lay in the intangible, in the enduring presence of the land itself, and in the silent sentinels that were its guardians. The scarecrow was one such sentinel, a silent testament to the fact that some powers were not meant to be seen, but to be felt, to be understood on a level that bypassed the limitations of mortal senses.

The button eyes, had they still been there, would have been a superficial attempt at animation. Their absence, however, allowed for a deeper form of observation. The Withers had sought to implant their own will into the scarecrow, to give it their own limited vision. But the entity had merely absorbed this futile effort, leaving behind an emptiness that was far more potent. This emptiness was not a void of nothingness, but a pregnant pause, a space that allowed the true, ancient gaze to manifest. It was the gaze of a consciousness that had witnessed the birth and death of stars, a consciousness so vast and indifferent that human concerns were but fleeting sparks in its immeasurable expanse.

The scarecrow, in its silent, unmoving posture, was a profound reflection of the entity's own nature. It was patient, enduring, and utterly relentless. The Withers had thought they were dealing with a force that could be manipulated, a power that could be harnessed. But they had been like children trying to capture lightning in a jar. The scarecrow, in its stark reality, was a constant reminder of the true nature of this power: that it was not a tool to be wielded, but a fundamental aspect of existence, an inescapable truth that permeated every aspect of the Withers Field, and by extension, Kayla's own transformed existence.

The feeling of being watched, which had once been a source of terror, had evolved into something else for Kayla. It was a constant awareness, a recognition of a presence that was neither benevolent nor malevolent but simply *was*. And the scarecrow, standing in its desolate field, was an embodiment of this enduring gaze. Its tattered form, its empty sockets – these were not signs of weakness, but of resilience, of an ancient pact that had endured far beyond the fleeting lives of the Withers. It was a silent promise that the land would continue to watch, to endure, and to hold its secrets close, forever bound to the insatiable hunger that lay at its core. The straw that spilled from its seams was not merely decaying matter; it was the subtle shedding of an ancient essence, a slow release of something that was both of the earth and yet, profoundly beyond it. The scarecrow was not an observer; it was a conduit, a silent testament to the enduring, unblinking watch of a power that had no beginning and would have no end.

The whispers, which had once been external intrusions, now resonated within Kayla as a deeper understanding of the scarecrow's silent testament. They spoke of cycles, of endurance, of a presence that was less about active pursuit and more about an inherent, unyielding state of being. The Withers had sought to break these cycles, to impose their will upon them, and had been irrevocably broken themselves. The scarecrow, however, was a part of the cycle, an immutable element within its grand, unfolding narrative. Its tattered form was a symbol of resilience, of an ability to withstand the ravages of time and the relentless pressure of unseen forces, not through resistance, but through a profound and unwavering acceptance.

The wind, when it stirred the tattered fabric of the scarecrow, did not impart the sensation of movement. Instead, it felt like a subtle vibration, a resonance that passed through the scarecrow's very core, confirming its continued presence. It was a greeting, a silent acknowledgment from the land itself, a confirmation that its guardian remained steadfast. The straw that spilled from its body, like scattered offerings, was not a sign of decay, but a slow, organic release of energy, a quiet replenishment of the land's vital force. Each strand seemed to hum with a latent power, a testament to the intricate and mysterious ways in which the land sustained itself, and in which its silent guardians participated in that sustenance.

The scarecrow's stillness was not an absence of animation, but a profound state of being. It was the stillness of a cosmic entity, the unmoving center around which lesser phenomena revolved. The

Withers had mistaken this stillness for dormancy, for a void that could be filled with their own ambition. But Kayla understood it differently. It was the stillness of immense power held in check, of awareness that encompassed vast stretches of time and space. The scarecrow was a physical manifestation of this stillness, a silent, unwavering sentinel that stood as a testament to the enduring nature of the land's consciousness.

The vacant sockets, those abysses of shadow, were not empty in the sense of lacking anything. Rather, they were filled with a different kind of perception, a recognition that bypassed the need for physical eyes. It was as if the scarecrow's very being had been reconfigured, its senses reoriented to perceive the world through the lens of the land's own ancient awareness. The Withers had tried to impose their will upon it, to make it their servant. But the entity had merely subsumed their intentions, leaving behind a vessel that was now attuned to a far grander, far more profound purpose. The scarecrow watched, not with eyes, but with the resonant stillness of the earth itself, a silent witness to the ongoing, inexorable cycles of existence.

The tattered remnants of its burlap skin, the splintered wood of its armature – these were not merely signs of decay, but markers of its endurance. Each tear, each crack, was a testament to the countless seasons it had weathered, the innumerable subtle shifts in the land's energy it had registered. It was a living monument, not to the Withers, but to the ancient power that had shaped this land, and that continued to exert its silent, pervasive influence. Kayla could feel the subtle currents of energy flowing through the scarecrow, mirroring the currents that now flowed through her own being. The Withers had sought to control this flow; she had, through her sacrifice, become a part of it. The scarecrow, in its silent vigil, was a constant reminder of this interconnectedness, this profound and terrifying unity.

The moonlight, instead of illuminating the scarecrow, seemed to be absorbed by it, drawn into the shadowy depths of its empty sockets. It was as if the scarecrow itself was a conduit for the night's ancient energies, a silent receiver for the whispers of the cosmos. The straw that spilled from its seams was not merely effluvia; it was like the slow release of ancient memories, a testament to the immense, immeasurable power that resided within the land. The Withers had sought to capture this power, to bend it to their will, and had been utterly consumed. The scarecrow, in its enduring stillness, represented a different path, a silent acknowledgment of the power's inherent nature, a testament to its ceaseless, ancient watch. The conclusion of their struggle was not a victory or a defeat, but a transformation, and the scarecrow stood as a silent, unwavering sentinel of that transformed reality.

Epilogue

The cornfield stood hushed, a graveyard of whispers. Broken stalks swayed like mourners bowing to a secret no one wanted to keep. The scarecrow's post, once crowned with its stitched head, loomed crooked and empty. The button eyes—those stolen, cursed tokens that had condemned so many—were gone.

But not forgotten.

At the edge of the field, a child's laughter threaded through the night. Thin, brittle, wrong. It didn't belong to any of the living. The wind carried it toward the farmhouse, rattling the shutters like bones in a box. Inside, the survivors had locked every door, doused every light, convinced the horror was over. They whispered prayers into their hands, swearing the *Harvest* was finished.

Yet in the distance, beneath the black branches of the woods, something new was being shaped. Straw lashed together by unseen hands. A crooked halo woven of twine. A figure rising—not of cloth and burlap, but of reverence, fear, and a terrible kind of faith.

The Harvest had taken its eyes. Now it demanded worship.

And those who had defied it would learn that saints, once born, are far harder to bury than scarecrows.

Note to reader: If you enjoyed this book, please leave a review on one or more of the following: Goodreads, Barnes & Noble, or other outlets. I thank you in advance.